The Legacy of t

N Cooper

First published in 2025 by Blossom Spring Publishing
The Legacy of the Lost Witch Copyright © 2025 N Cooper
ISBN 978-1-917938-05-1
E: admin@blossomspringpublishing.com
W: www.blossomspringpublishing.com

Chapter 1: The Cracks Beneath the Surface

Clara sat cross-legged on her bed, a well-worn textbook open on her lap. The faint glow of her desk lamp cast soft shadows across the room, illuminating the scattered notes and highlighters around her. The ticking of the clock on the wall marked the slow crawl towards eleven o'clock. The start of Year 10 and her GCSEs were just around the corner, and with her dreams of becoming a vet looming large, Clara knew there was no time to waste.

Her dad's faint humming drifted up the stairs, mingling with the distant clinking of dishes in the sink as he tended to them, his usual nightly routine. It was comforting, grounding her in the mundane normality of her life, an antidote to the storm of anxiety raging in her chest.

"Just one more chapter," she muttered, flipping the page of her biology book. But the words on the page swam before her eyes, merging into an unreadable blur. She pressed her fingers to her temples, her head beginning to ache from hours of staring at diagrams of circulatory systems.

As she leaned back against the pillows, her gaze fell on the necklace resting against her collarbone, a delicate silver chain with a starburst pendant. The pink gem at its centre shimmered like a distant star. Clara's fingers brushed against it instinctively. She'd worn it every day since her mam had given it to her, just before she died. It was more than jewellery; it was a tether to a part of her life that often felt like a dream.

She sighed and set her pen down, closing her textbook. Her eyes flicked to the window, where the night stretched out in peaceful quiet. But just as she reached for her phone to check the time, a strange pressure began to build behind her eyes, a dull, insistent ache, as if something were pushing its way into her mind.

"Ugh, not now," she murmured, squeezing her temples. The ache deepened, radiating through her skull and down into her chest. Then, without warning, a sharp electric jolt surged through her, freezing her in place. Her breath hitched as an intense, foreign sensation swept over her, a strange mix of heat and cold, light and dark, all at once.

Her hand flew to the pendant as a cracking sound echoed in her ears. She looked down in horror as the pink gem began to fracture, tiny lines splintering across its surface. The light within the gem pulsed erratically, flickering like a failing bulb.

"No, no, no!" Clara gasped, clutching the necklace. Her heart pounded as she watched the cracks spread, until, with a faint pop, the gem shattered. Tiny shards fell into her lap, glinting like pieces of starlight before dimming into lifeless fragments.

The sensation vanished as quickly as it had come, leaving Clara breathless, her chest heaving. The room seemed to hold its breath, and the air felt thick. Her fingers trembled as she touched the broken shards, cool and sharp against her skin.

"What ... just happened?" she whispered, her voice breaking the oppressive silence.

The necklace lay lifeless in her palm, its warmth gone. Clara stared at the pieces, her chest tightening. It felt as though something more than the necklace had shattered, as if the fragile connection to her mother had been severed in that instant.

Her mam had fastened the necklace around her neck with a gentle smile. *No matter what happens, Clara, this will keep you safe.* And now it was gone. Clara had never been entirely sure if the necklace truly kept her safe, but it had always brought her comfort. It was a tether to her mam, a reminder of the love they'd shared. Deep down, she couldn't help but wonder. Maybe it had kept her safe, in its own way. Or perhaps it was what the necklace represented that gave her the strength she needed.

Clara tried to steady her breathing, but her hands refused to stop trembling. She glanced at the clock: 11:05. The night stretched on, heavy with questions she didn't know how to answer. Why had the gem broken? And what was that feeling, that surge of something other that had coursed through her?

For a fleeting moment, Clara felt as though something had been unlocked within her, a faint hum beneath her skin, like an engine quietly coming to life. It was gone as quickly as it began, leaving her unsure if it had been real or just her imagination.

She stood and crossed to her dresser, placing the shards carefully into a small jewellery box. Her reflection in the mirror caught her attention. She looked pale, her brown eyes wide with uncertainty.

As she stared at herself, she couldn't shake the feeling that the breaking of the necklace wasn't just a coincidence. It felt deliberate, like something had been waiting, watching, for the right moment to break free.

She climbed back into bed, wrapping her blanket tightly around her shoulders, but sleep felt impossible. The shattered necklace lay heavy on her mind, and though the room was quiet, her thoughts swirled with unease.

Deep down, she couldn't help but feel it: something had changed. And whatever it was, there was no going back.

*

The following morning, Clara was awake early. Sleep eluded her. She sat on the edge of her bed, staring at the shattered remains of the pink gem in her palm. She reached out with shaking hands as the jagged pieces caught the morning light.

The necklace had been more than just jewellery. It was the last thing her mam had given her, clasping it around her neck with a soft smile and whispered words Clara could still faintly hear: *Always keep this with you, Clara. It's special, just like you.*

She'd worn it every day since her mam's death, clutching it during anxious moments, holding it close when grief felt overwhelming. Now it lay broken, its protective warmth gone, leaving Clara feeling raw and exposed.

Her breath hitched, and tears blurred her vision. "Why now?" she whispered into the silence, the ache in her chest almost unbearable.

The shattered gem felt like losing her mam all over again, as if the fragile tether to her memory had been severed.

Clara ran her thumb over the empty starburst charm, its edges sharper, its centre hollow. For the first time in years, she slipped the chain from her neck, setting it beside the shards. The sight of it, so fragile and incomplete, made her chest tighten further.

She pressed the pieces into her palm, her voice trembling. "I tried to take care of it, Mam. I didn't know it could break." The words hung in the air, unanswered, her tears slipping silently onto the broken gem.

Setting the fragments on her dressing table, Clara stared at them, grief and guilt swirling in her chest. Yet beneath the burden of loss, a flicker of resolve stirred. Her mam had given her the necklace for a reason, and it had broken for a reason. Whatever had changed, Clara needed to understand it.

She climbed under her covers, knowing she must get ready for school soon, her gaze lingering on the shards as she was lost in thought about that it all meant.

*

A few days had passed, and the kitchen was quiet, except for the faint drone of the fridge. Clara stood at the counter, sifting through the usual pile of post: takeaway menus, bills, and a leaflet advertising window cleaning. It was all so boring, until she saw the envelope.

It sat at the bottom of the pile, cream-coloured with a wax seal pressed into its centre. Two serpents intertwined to form a perfect circle, their emerald eyes catching the morning light. Her name, *Clara Collins*, was written across the front in looping gold script.

Her breath caught as she noticed the envelope: no stamp, no address. Its smooth, heavy parchment felt strange under her fingers. She broke the seal, unfolding the leaflet inside. Her eyes widened as she read:

The Annual Hull Festival of Magic
Step into a world of magical wonder!

Date: Saturday 15th June
Time: Midday
Location: Warehouse 13, Dockside Row, Hull

Discover music, dancing, and dazzling performances alongside the finest magical wares and enchantments.

Clara blinked, the leaflet trembling slightly in her hands. "Festival of Magic?" she murmured, her voice barely audible in the stillness of the room.

It had to be a joke. Someone had gone to an extraordinary amount of effort to make it look convincing: elegant script, thick parchment, embossed lettering, but the claims were absurd. Magical wares? Elemental shows? Ridiculous. No one believes in magic because magic isn't real, right? And yet ...

Her eyes flicked to the nightstand, where her mam's broken necklace lay in its box. As she neared the broken shards, the pink gem reflected a hint of light, its once vibrant glow forever extinguished. A feeling of sadness overwhelmed her, sharp and familiar, as her fingers instinctively brushed against the leaflet, tracing the embossed gold crest at the bottom.

"This can't be real," she said aloud, her voice shaking slightly. But even as the words left her mouth, she didn't believe them. Something about the leaflet felt ... different. Not just the weight of the parchment, but the way her chest tightened as she read the words, as if they were meant for her alone.

Clara googled *Festival of Magic,* which came up with nothing.

Clara sat on the edge of her bed, the invitation resting in her lap. The air felt heavier, as though the words on the parchment had shifted something in her world that she couldn't undo. She ran her fingers over the gold lettering, her mind racing.

Why her? Why now? Could magic be real?

Her gaze drifted back to the jewellery box. She wanted to hold onto the necklace, even in its shattered state, unable to part with the last real connection to her mam. Now, as she stared at it, a strange unease crept through her. What if the necklace breaking wasn't just a coincidence?

She pressed a hand to her chest, trying to steady the rising tide of emotions. That pull she'd felt when she first read the invitation lingered in her bones, a quiet, undeniable insistence that she couldn't explain. It wasn't loud or forceful, but it was steady, like a thread tugging her towards something she didn't yet understand.

Clara closed her eyes, letting the memory of that night wash over her, the rush of emotions, the strange sensations that had coursed through her when the gem shattered. It all felt connected to this moment, this parchment.

The thought sent her mind spinning. Fear warred with curiosity, and beneath it all, a nagging sense of inevitability. This wasn't just an invitation to a festival; it was something bigger. She could feel it deep in her core, like a truth she wasn't ready to face.

She carefully folded the leaflet and tucked it under her pillow. Her chest was tight with apprehension, but beneath the fear was a flicker of something else.

Hope.

Whatever this was, whatever it meant, Clara knew one thing for certain: she couldn't turn away from it. She didn't have all the answers, but maybe, just maybe, this was the first step towards finding them.

*

Clara couldn't help but keep looking at the leaflet. Was it real? What would it mean if it were real? The possibilities. Questions swirled around Clara's mind like a tornado. She was used to sharing practically everything with her dad. But this felt different. It wasn't just the absurdity of a magical festival that made her pause; it was the strange pull she felt, as though the leaflet was hers and hers alone. Whatever it was, she wasn't ready to share it yet.

In the kitchen, her dad was humming softly, his familiar tune weaving through the clink of a mug being stirred. Clara hovered in the doorway, watching him finish making his tea, his movements steady and certain.

"Hey, baby girl," he said, catching sight of her. "You okay? You look like you've got something on your mind."

Clara hesitated, the words forming and dissolving in her mind. She wanted to tell her dad about the invitation and to ask him if it was all just a joke. But something stopped her. The leaflet didn't feel like something she could explain, not yet.

"Nothing," she said finally, offering him a small smile. "Just … school stuff."

He smiled back, warm and reassuring. "Don't overdo it, alright? You've got plenty of time to figure things out. There's no rush."

Clara nodded, though her thoughts were far from settled. "Yeah, I know. Thanks, Dad."

After getting a glass of water, she went back to her room and retrieved the leaflet from under her pillow one more time. It wasn't that she didn't want to share it with her dad; it was that it felt too fragile, too unreal. Until she could make sense of it herself, it felt right to keep it close, a secret for her alone.

As she sat up in her bed reading, the leaflet sat next to her, almost calling out to her.

Her gaze flicked to her phone on the bedside table. There was someone else she could tell.

She hesitated only a moment before tapping on Chloe's name. Her best friend picked up immediately, her was voice bright and teasing.

"Hey you! What's up? Did you finally finish that biology assignment, or are you calling for my help?"

Clara laughed, though it sounded thin even to her ears. "I have finished it, and if anyone would need help, it would be you." She gave a soft laugh. "Look, I need to tell you something. It's ... weird."

"Go on," Chloe said, curiosity sharpening her tone. "You know I love weird."

Clara glanced at the leaflet again, the looping gold script catching her eye. "I got this leaflet. It's an invitation to a festival, a magical one."

"Magical? Like fireworks and costumes?" Chloe said, confused.

"No. Real magic," Clara whispered.

"You do realise magic isn't real, right?" Chloe's voice held doubt.

But Clara couldn't shake the feeling of the leaflet in her hands. "I even googled it and came up with nothing. I'm telling you, Chloe, this feels ... different. It feels real. And also, it came in an envelope that was sealed with wax. How weird is that?"

Chloe let out a soft sigh, the kind she always did when she was thinking. "Wax seal? Whoever sent it went all out for authenticity." She sighed, then spoke again. "Alright," she said slowly, "I'm up for it. But if this turns out to be some weird cosplay convention with nerds chasing us around in wizard robes, you're buying me a pizza."

Clara laughed, a bubble of relief breaking through her nerves. "Chloe, we're nerds too. And deal. But what if it's real?"

"Yeah, but we're cool nerds. And if it is somehow

real, then you're buying me a pizza and we will need to reevaluate our entire existence," Chloe replied.

As the call ended, Clara stared at the leaflet in her hand, her thoughts jumbled in a whirlwind of curiosity and fear. The elegant script glowed faintly, almost like it was enchanted. It didn't feel like a joke, not entirely. But if it was real, what did it mean?

Excitement bubbled under her skin, knotted with a creeping terror of the unknown. For the first time in her life, Clara felt as though she was standing at the edge of something vast and uncharted, unsure whether to step forward or turn away.

*

The days leading up to the 15th dragged on. Clara had always loved school, but now each day was marked by the dullness of school, homework, and dinner with her dad. A genuine excitement and wonder lingered around the festival, tugging at her like a string tied to her heart. Every now and then, she would glance at the leaflet, which seemed to fade more with each passing day, its colours dimming as if counting down to the moment she would find out the truth.

Chapter 2: Festival of Magic

The morning of the 15th dawned crisp with grey clouds, the kind of day that held its breath. Clara rose early, excitement and nerves buzzing through her as she tucked the leaflet into her coat pocket.

Clara reached for her bedroom door when her phone buzzed.

Chloe: *Feeling awful. Really sorry I can't come today.*

Disappointment sank in Clara's chest. Chloe was her anchor, the one who made daunting things less scary. For a moment, she considered not going. Who went to a festival alone? Especially a magical one.

Her fingers brushed the leaflet in her pocket, the parchment strangely warm, as though it were alive. She felt the faint pull again, that same whisper she'd been hearing since it arrived, urging her forward.

"Guess it's just me, then," she murmured, slipping her phone back into her pocket.

Clara had already booked a taxi, and as the time neared, she stood by the window, staring out at the world beyond the glass. The anticipation was still there, but now it was mixed with nerves, her mind spinning with questions. What if it wasn't real? What if it was?

The sound of the taxi engine snapped her out of her thoughts. She grabbed her bag and headed out, the leaflet pressing against her side as she climbed into the car.

The taxi wound through Hull's streets, the familiar rows of houses giving way to graffiti-covered shop fronts and cracked pavements.

"You meeting friends there, love?" the driver asked.

"Uh … not exactly," Clara said, her voice hesitant.

The journey grew quieter as they turned into an industrial

area, the warehouses standing tall and grim against the grey sky. Finally, the taxi rolled to a stop in front of a row of abandoned buildings.

Clara leaned forward, her stomach twisting. This couldn't be right. She double-checked the leaflet, the address matching perfectly with the Google Maps location.

"Is this it?" she asked, her voice faltering.

The driver gave her a sceptical look. "Looks abandoned," he said. "Want me to wait?"

Clara hesitated too. The chill of sank into her chest. It didn't resemble a festival; it was the kind of place her dad would tell her to avoid. But then her fingers brushed the leaflet again, the faint warmth still pulsing against her skin.

"No, I'm fine. Thanks," she said, paying the driver before stepping out.

The summer air was surprisingly cold, even for a June morning in England, and the scene felt eerily surreal. As the taxi pulled away, leaving Clara standing alone in front of the warehouses, she scanned the area, shoving her hands into her coat pockets to stop them from trembling.

This was stupid. Foolish. She was chasing an impossible idea, all because some weird leaflet had shown up out of nowhere. But just as she was about to turn back, she noticed something, a narrow alleyway tucked between two of the buildings, almost invisible unless you were looking for it.

She squinted at a floating sign above the alley:

Magic Festival Open to All Witches and Wizards.

Clara froze, her breath catching. She stood outside wondering if all this was real or it was just an elaborate joke. Then, driven by the pull in her chest, she stepped forward. Whatever waited beyond, she had to see it.

Clara walked cautiously down the alley, where huge doors loomed ahead. The doors creaked open, revealing a swirling mist inside that had an orange glow. Her breath hitched, and she stepped forwards without realising she had made the decision.

The mist engulfed her, cool and strangely light. Clara walked cautiously, her pulse hammering in her ears. Then, just as suddenly as it had swallowed her, the fog parted, and she stepped into another world.

Cobblestone streets stretched before her. Stalls glowing, lit by floating lanterns. Laughter and music filled the air, ribbons of colour dancing across the sky. At the square's centre, a fountain's sparkling water twisted weightlessly above its basin.

It was beautiful and impossible.

The festival's beauty was overwhelming, but so was the sheer unfamiliarity of it all. Every stall, every sound, every flash of magic seemed designed to dazzle, yet Clara couldn't shake the gnawing doubt in her chest. Was she really meant to be here? Did she belong in a world so far removed from her own?

Clara wandered forward, her eyes darting from one wonder to the next. At one stall, a man in a cloak sold quills that wrote in mid-air, leaving trails of glowing ink that hung like constellations. At another, a woman poured shimmering liquids into vials that pulsed with light, each labelled with promises like Joyful Dream, or Unbreakable Courage.

Nearby, a tiny dragon-like creature the size of a house cat perched on a vendor's shoulder, its colourful scales shifting as it snapped at a piece of meat dangling from his hand. Clara watched in awe as the vendor grinned and scratched the creature behind its spiky ears.

At a jewellery stall, a hovering necklace caught her eye, its gemstone shifting like a restless flame. "A Ruby of Kildareea. Each one offers protection as strong as dragon scales," the well-dressed vendor said with a wink. "If you can afford it."

Drawn by the sound of music, Clara moved towards the centre of the square, where a crowd had gathered. A woman stood on a small platform, her crimson robes billowing as if caught by an unseen breeze. She sang, her voice rich and haunting, carrying words Clara didn't understand but felt deep inside.

The crowd fell silent, entranced. The song seemed to weave through the air, curling like smoke and settling around them.

Come gather around, the night is alive,
With spells that take flight and wands that revive.
From valleys enchanted to mountains so high,
The Moondancers take wing and the firebirds fly!

Where merfolk sing low in the shimmering deep,
And shadowy hounds through the wild forests creep.
There's power in laughter, there's strength
in the cheer,
For magic grows brighter when hearts have no fear!

With spirits that guard and Starfeathers bold,
In tales of the brave and legends of old.
Through battles they've fought with courage
and might,
They conquered the dark and reclaimed the light!

So raise up your voices, let joy fill the sky,

For magic endures where the bold never die.
Together we stand with wand, song, and cheer,
In a world full of wonders and magic held dear!

The crowd clapped in time, cheering and dancing as the song reached its final verse. Clara felt her heart lift, her feet tapping along with the beat. She'd never experienced anything like this, a celebration of magic, of bravery, and of creatures beyond imagination. In that second, surrounded by joy and enchantment, Clara felt as though she were exactly where she was meant to be.

The woman's voice became gentler, the final note hanging in the air like a breath before it vanished. The crowd erupted into applause, and Clara breathed out, realising she had been holding her own breath.

As Clara wandered further into the festival, the magic seemed endless. Clara passed stalls selling potions that bubbled and shimmered, with the smell of roasted chestnuts and something sweetly floral, like honey mixed with lavender.

But for every wonder that made her gasp, there was an odd sense of unease beneath it all. Whispers rippled through the crowd. Clara heard two witches standing close to a stall of magical sweets, their faces pale and voices low.

"... escaped from Blackspire," one murmured, clutching her cloak.

The other nodded grimly. "The Dark Wizard is free. They say the wards weren't just broken, they were shattered."

The other nodded grimly. "If the Dark Wizard is free, no one is safe, especially not the Nightfalls."

Clara froze. The words sent a chill through her chest,

though she didn't know why. The witches' whispers fell lower, their urgency swallowed by the busy crowd. Clara stepped back, her heart racing. Whoever they were talking about, he was obviously dangerous, someone people feared. Clara found it terrifying.

Clara moved deeper into the festival, her steps hesitant but her curiosity pushing her forward. The sights and sounds wrapped around her, bright and impossible, like a dream she couldn't wake from. Everywhere she turned, there was something more extraordinary: a stall selling golden, glowing apples, a string quartet playing music independently, a flock of paper birds soaring into the air, morphing themselves into stars mid-flight. The pure wonder engulfed her. It was awe-inspiring yet also incredibly overwhelming; magic was real, and an entire other world existed. How could this be?

She stopped at a quieter stall, drawn to rows of tiny bottles that shimmered like liquid rainbows. A hand-painted sign above them read: *Dream Elixirs: Guaranteed the Best Dreams of Your Life.*

"First time at a festival, love? You look a little out of place," a voice said.

Clara turned to see an old woman smiling at her from behind her stall. Her hair was a frizzy cloud of silver, her eyes glinting with age and wisdom. The woman looked at Clara like she knew something she didn't.

Clara hesitated, then nodded. "Is this all … real?"

The old woman's expression changed to utter surprise. "By the Moon and Stars. Surely you've seen magic before?"

Clara's heart quickened as she pulled out the leaflet to show the woman. "No, it's my first time seeing actual magic. I received this leaflet, but … I don't know if I belong here."

The woman's face softened, her gaze turning thoughtful. "Oh, but you do. If you're here, it means you've got magic in your blood. You wouldn't even be able to perceive the festival otherwise, let alone receive a leaflet."

Clara felt a strange chill run through her. "But I can't be magic. I'm normal, and so is my dad."

The woman tilted her head. "And your mum?"

Clara swallowed hard, the familiar ache tightening in her chest. "She died when I was four. But I'm pretty sure there would've been a sign she was magical."

"Not unless she wanted you to see, love. So, what about mum's family? What are they like?" the woman asked, intrigued by the situation.

Clara paused, with a sadness in her eyes as she thought of her mother. "I never met her side of the family."

The woman's eyes gleamed knowingly. "Your mum must've been a witch, then. Seems you've gone your whole life not knowing who you truly are and where you belong."

Clara stood there feeling slightly faint and unsteady. A million questions raced through mind before one landed. "But how could I belong to a magical world and never know it?"

The old woman leaned in, her eyes sharp. "Tell me, child, did your mum ever give you a piece of jewellery? A bracelet, perhaps? Or a necklace with a beautiful stone?"

Clara hesitated, startled by the woman's question. "She did," Clara replied slowly. "It was a necklace. I wore it every day until recently. The gem … it just broke on its own."

The woman straightened slightly, her expression unreadable. "Ah, then that explains it," she murmured, more to herself than to Clara.

"Explains what?" Clara asked, her chest tightening.

The woman's gaze was kind, though her voice carried an edge of gravity. "It wasn't just a necklace, dear. It was a charm, a protective one, from the sound of it. Such things aren't mere jewellery. Charms like that can be woven with powerful magic, meant to enhance or curb one's abilities. Some can be used to shield their bearer."

"Shield?" Clara repeated, her fingers brushing her collarbone instinctively. "Shield me from what?"

"From many things," the woman said cryptically. "Protection from harm, yes, but also from being seen. Some charms are designed to cloak a person, to hide them even from those who might seek them. They keep you safe, but they also keep you … apart."

Clara's breath caught. "Apart from what? From who?"

The woman's expression grew sombre. "Perhaps your mother thought it best. Such charms don't break without reason, you know. The magic within them is strong, but it's not endless. Whatever caused it to break … well, child, that's something you'll need to discover for yourself. Tell me, love," she said, her voice both gentle and probing, "have you ever made something happen just by thinking about it? Something more than coincidence?"

Clara hesitated. Memories flickered at the edges of her mind, things she'd never thought much of before: the way she always knew when her dad was upset, even when he tried to hide it, how she could find lost items with uncanny accuracy, the strange feeling she sometimes got, as though she was connected to things around her.

"I guess," she said slowly. "I can … sense things about people, things they don't necessarily want to share. I can't control it, though. My dad says I'm very intuitive."

The woman's eyes gleamed with curiosity as she leaned closer, her voice soft yet commanding. "Tell me, dear, what do you sense about me?"

Clara frowned, uncertain how to answer. She focused on the woman: her sharp emerald eyes, the faint lines on her face, the way her hands rested lightly on the table. Nothing stood out. Nothing unusual.

"I … I don't sense anything," Clara admitted, feeling embarrassed. "You just seem … normal."

The woman chuckled, a warm, knowing sound. "Ah, but sensing isn't seeing, child. Close your eyes. Don't think. Feel."

Clara hesitated, then did as she was told, closing her eyes and trying to push past the doubt swirling in her mind. For a moment, there was only stillness. Then, like a wave hitting the shore, it hit her. A swell of emotions that weren't her own, calm and steady, with a deep undercurrent of something she couldn't quite name.

Clara gasped softly, her eyes flying open. "I … you feel calm," she said, her voice trembling slightly. "But underneath, there's … something else. Like … sadness, maybe? No, not sadness. Loss."

The woman's smile softened, and for a moment, her expression betrayed something deeper, an unspoken truth. "Very good, dear," she said quietly. "You felt me, didn't you? That's not something just anyone can do."

"What does that mean?" Clara asked, her heart racing.

"It means," the woman said, her voice warm but firm, "that you're not just any witch. You're an empath witch, child. You feel the world differently than others do, and that is a rare and powerful gift."

Clara's stomach fluttered, a small thrill mixed with disbelief. "Empath ... witch?"

The woman chuckled. "And a lost one, at that. You're quite good at finding what's hidden, just not yourself, eh."

Clara stared, her thoughts swirling too fast to make sense of.

The woman's expression was gentle, but her eyes were sharp and full of intent. "Listen to me, love," she said, her voice dropping to a low murmur. "Being an empath is a rare and precious gift, but it comes with a price."

Clara blinked, startled. "A price?"

The woman nodded. "Not everyone will take kindly to the idea of you knowing what they feel. It unsettles people, makes them wary. No one likes the thought of someone peering into the parts of themselves they'd rather keep hidden."

Clara's stomach felt knotted. But I didn't even know I could do it."

"I know," the woman interrupted gently. "You will learn to control it in time. Use it wisely, and only when you must. The world doesn't need to know what you can do. Not yet."

The weight of her words settled over Clara like a heavy cloak. She was a witch but also a witch with a rare ability. A flood of feeling hit her all at once, then the woman snapped her out of her daze.

"Don't worry though, love," the woman said, pulling a blank piece of parchment under her stall and a wand from beneath her cloak. "Here. This'll help."

Clara watched as the woman waved her wand over the

parchment, murmuring words that sounded like whispers on the wind, words Clara didn't understand.

She waved the wand. "Talamora Leanadh … Magical Services." For a moment, nothing happened. Then, like ink bleeding through water, lines began to appear on the paper. A map unfurled itself, alive with movement.

Clara leaned closer, her breath catching. Tiny dots bustled about the paths, stalls rearranged themselves, and glowing markers pulsed on the page. One mark stood out, labelled, "Magical Services."

"It's … it's like a magical version of Google Maps," Clara whispered.

The woman squinted at her. "I don't know what that is, but it's a Land's Guide spell. It'll show you where you need to go. And they should be able to help you find your way."

Clara traced the glowing path with her finger, her heart racing. "Magical Services … will they be able to tell me about my mam? About my family?"

The woman's expression grew thoughtful. "Maybe. They'll certainly have some answers, if you're ready for them."

Clara hesitated, the weight of her father's silence pressing against her. "Why wouldn't my dad ever tell me?"

The woman sighed softly. "Those without magic often don't see what's right in front of them. Maybe he didn't know. Or perhaps he was trying to shield you from a world he didn't understand."

Clara swallowed hard. The thought of her dad keeping something so monumental from her felt impossible. She looked back down at the map, the glowing path seeming to pulse in rhythm with her heartbeat.

The woman stepped closer, her expression softening but her voice lowering to an urgent whisper. "A word of advice: be wary of those who seek power they do not deserve. Dark forces stir once more now that the Dark Wizard walks free again."

Clara blinked, her unease deepening. "Who is that?" she asked, her voice faltering slightly.

The woman hesitated, her eyes glinting with a shadow of fear. "He was once a promising young wizard, but the stories say he stumbled upon magic too ancient, too dangerous: power that was forbidden for good reason. It began to consume him, twisting him from the inside. Whatever light he once had was extinguished, leaving only darkness."

A chill ran down Clara's spine as the woman's words settled over her. She had heard of evil people and cruelty in stories, but this was something else, evil bound to unimaginable magic.

"Will anyone be able to stop him?" Clara asked, clutching the map tighter in her hands.

The woman gave a thin, almost wistful smile, her gaze distant. "They did catch him years ago, but not before he destroyed towns and massacred countless people. Perhaps they will catch him soon enough. But the powerful ones have a way of eluding justice, until those brave enough rise up and defeat them."

The words hung in the air like an unspoken challenge. The woman straightened, her expression softening again. "Good luck, young witch," she said warmly.

Clara nodded, swallowing the lump in her throat as she clutched the map to her chest. "Thank you."

The woman gave her a knowing smile before Clara went on her way to Magical Services, alone with her thoughts and a gnawing sense that her life had just irrevocably changed. So far, Clara wasn't sure if belonging to another world was a blessing or a curse.

*

As Clara navigated her way through the busy festival, feeling shaky but determined, the map glowed faintly in her hands, guiding her through the twisting paths of the festival. She passed stalls selling enchanted trinkets, glowing flowers, and rare Ashstone amulets said to ward off fire. She paused briefly at a booth where a man juggled fireballs that twisted into shapes: a lion, a dragon, a phoenix. For a moment, the flames seemed to form a man's face, and Clara's breath caught. Clara blinked, then it vanished, leaving her hollow and unsettled with her heart thudding.

As she moved on, the festival's noise began to fade. The stalls grew sparser and the air cooler. The cobblestone path narrowed, lined with ivy-covered walls that seemed to move when she wasn't looking. Her grip tightened on the map as she went around a corner. This wasn't any part of Hull she had seen before, and in that moment, she knew that her life would never be the same.

As she continued to follow the map, she came across an old building. There it was: a small wooden door, plain and unassuming, with *Magical Services* carved above it.

Clara stood still for a seconds, her heart hammering. This was it, the moment she stepped into something entirely unknown.

She reached out, her fingers brushing the handle. It felt warm beneath her touch, almost alive. With a deep breath, Clara pushed the door open and stepped inside.

The door creaked open, and Clara stepped into a dimly lit room. Floating candles cast flickering light over stacks of papers and a box of trinkets humming with magic. A man in shimmering robes sat behind a large oak desk, his glasses perched on his nose as he scribbled in a glowing ledger. Clara sensed he was kind and would help her.

A quill hovered in mid-air, dipping itself into an inkpot before scratching letters onto a sheet. As each letter was completed, it folded itself neatly, popped into an envelope, and was sealed with wax that poured and stamped itself without a single touch. The envelope gave a little quiver, then shot into a large, enchanted sack that seemed to breathe with life. Letters kept darting into the sack, one after another. When it was finally full, the sack let out a faint hum, then whooshed up through the air and vanished from the room in the blink of an eye.

"Ah, hello there! Welcome to Magical Services," the man greeted with a warm smile, his eyes twinkling with a touch of mischief. "Name's Rupert. How might I assist you on this fine, enchanted day?"

Clara's eyes widened, and she couldn't help but whisper, "That's amazing. Where did it go?" as she stared at the empty space it had left.

The man glanced up, his eyebrows lifting slightly. "Gone to deliver the letters, of course. And it's only a simple enchantment spell. Something you should've learned at school."

Clara blinked, taken aback. "We didn't learn anything like that at my school. I only realised magic was real like … an hour ago."

Rupert raised his eyebrows, his grin wide and playful. "By the Moon and Stars! Hidden in the shadows of stardust, were you?" he laughed, the twinkle in his eyes brightening. "Not to worry, young witch. We shall get you to where you're meant to be. "So, what's your name?"

"Clara," she said. "Clara Collins."

Rupert paused, his quill freezing mid-air. "Collins, you say? And your parents?"

"My dad is Jeff Collins," Clara explained, shifting uncomfortably. "My mam ... she was Helena Nightfall. But she died when I was four."

The room seemed to grow quieter at the mention of her mother's name. Rupert straightened in his chair, his eyes narrowing slightly as he studied her. "Nightfall, you say?" His tone had shifted, the cheerful tone replaced with something more serious.

Clara nodded, feeling her pulse quicken. "Have you heard of them?"

"Oh, my dear," Rupert murmured, leaning back in his chair. "I haven't just heard of them. The Nightfalls are one of the most prominent magical families in Britain. Old magic, wealth, power, you name it. And you, it seems, are one of them."

Clara blinked, her mind reeling. "Really?"

He reached into his robe, pulling out a wand. "Let me just check something."

Rupert gently took her hand, a small pin extending from the tip of his wand to prick her finger. Clara flinched, watching as a single drop of her blood floated into the air, glowing softly. Rupert muttered, "Crann Anam," and the blood twisted, stretching into a shimmering family tree.

Clara gasped as the tree expanded before her, branches reaching upward. Her father's side stopped abruptly, but her mother's side grew endlessly, a sprawling network of names that filled the room with soft golden light. At the very top, the name *Nightfall* glowed brighter than the rest.

Rupert nodded, his expression thoughtful. "You are indeed a Nightfall," he said, his voice quiet. "No question about it."

Clara stared at the glowing branches, her mind spinning. "So ... my mam's family ... they're really magical?"

He nodded. "You're a half-breed witch. But you still belong to one of the most prestigious families in Britain." He looked at her, curiosity evident in his gaze. "That could explain why no one's heard of you." He leaned in slightly, his voice dropping to a whisper. "Powerful magical families such as yours tend to keep their bloodlines ... exclusive. Yours mixing with the non-magical world? Quite the scandal, I imagine. Or, if it hasn't stirred the cauldron yet, it certainly will now."

Clara bristled at his words. "A scandal? And am I seriously related to a prestigious magical family? Surely there's some sort of a mistake!"

Rupert raised his hands defensively. "No mistake. The spell confirmed your heritage, and you're definitely related to them. And yes, magical families like the Nightfalls tend to keep to themselves. If your mother married a non-magical person, well ... let's just say it explains a few things."

"The Nightfalls are more than just a family," Rupert said, his voice dropping. "They're tied to some of the oldest, most powerful magic in Britain. And with that power comes ... complications."

Rupert turned back to his desk, pulling out a blank piece of parchment. "Best inform them of your presence, don't you think? They'll certainly want to know about you."

"Wait," Clara said quickly, her heart pounding.

"You're telling them now?"

"Of course," Rupert replied, already scribbling furiously. "The Nightfall name carries weight. They'll want to meet you immediately."

Clara opened her mouth to protest but stopped herself. Part of her wanted to know more, wanted answers about her mother, her heritage, and the life she'd never known. But another part of her wasn't ready. Meeting them sounded terrifying, like stepping into another world where she didn't belong.

Rupert paused, his quill hovering in midair as he glanced at Clara. His eyes softened ever so slightly. "I know this must be overwhelming," he said, his tone quieter now. "Dealing with such things takes strength. It isn't about being ready for everything; it's about stepping forward, even when you're not sure you can. From what I can see, you've already taken the hardest step by walking through that door. That's something, isn't it?" He smiled faintly, returning to his writing. "Your family might be powerful, yes, but I have a feeling you are too. You just haven't realised it yet."

Clara wasn't so sure.

With a flick of his wand, Rupert murmured, "Scriptus Volare," and the parchment folded itself into a scroll. Melted wax poured itself onto the scroll, and a stamp pressed down, sealing it with a golden crest. The scroll shot upward in a flash of light, vanishing through the ceiling.

Clara stared at the empty space where it had disappeared, her stomach twisting with nerves. "What happens now?"

"Now," Rupert said, settling back into his chair with a satisfied smile, "we wait for their response. And trust me, they won't take long."

Clara sat down, her hands folded tightly in her lap. There were slight remnants of the family tree still glowing in the air above her, the name Nightfall shimmering ever so faintly, like a beacon. She couldn't stop staring at it, her thoughts tangled.

All her life, she'd wondered about her mam, who she'd been, where she'd come from. Now the answers were closer than ever, but still, they felt impossibly far away.

The air in the room seemed heavier now, the candles giving off a weak flicker. Clara felt a strange mix of excitement and dread, as though she were standing at the edge of something vast and uncharted. She took a deep breath, her heart racing as she whispered to herself, "I hope I'm ready for this."

Chapter 3: A Whole New Family

Clara sat in the small waiting room at Magical Services, her fingers curling tightly around the edge of her chair. The smell of lavender and parchment was lingering, but it didn't calm her nerves. She shifted in her seat, sneaking another glance out the window.

Her breath caught the moment a shadow swept past the glass, swift and otherworldly. A winged creature descended, pulling a cart, its silver coat shimmering as though it had been spun from moonlight. It moved with an impossible elegance, its wings folding seamlessly as if it had done this a thousand times before.

"That's ... incredible," Clara whispered, leaning closer to the window.

Rupert, seated behind the oak desk, barely glanced up. "That? Oh, just a Moondancer," he said with a dismissive wave of his hand. "Fancy mode of transport for the magical elite. Your family likes to travel in style."

Clara's stomach twisted. "My family are here?"

"Indeed," Rupert said, straightening his glasses. "Nightfalls through and through. Looks like they've come to collect you."

The words landed like a weight in Clara's chest. She turned her attention back to the window, her heart pounding as three figures stepped out of the cart. Their robes, a mix of emerald and silver, moved like water, catching the light with every step. Clara glanced down at her own clothes, suddenly aware of every crease, a stubborn stain near her cuff, she looked like someone who'd wandered into a dream meant for someone else.

The older man at the front carried himself with a commanding presence. His silver-streaked hair was swept back, and his sharp, calculating gaze seemed to take in everything around him in an instant. Behind him walked a woman – poised and graceful, her emerald cloak glinting faintly in the sunlight. Her expression was serene, but her eyes scanned the surroundings with quiet precision. The third figure, a younger man, hung back slightly. His hands were behind his back, and though his features mirrored the older man's sharpness, his expression carried a hint of scepticism.

Clara's grip on the chair tightened, fingers digging in as if anchoring herself to something real, as the three entered the office. The room seemed to grow smaller as their presence filled it. Rupert cleared his throat and stood, gesturing towards Clara.

"Good day to you, my lords and my lady," he said with a flourish. "May I present Clara … Nightfall," he said, nodding with reassurance. "She belongs to your family; I performed a soul tree spell, and there's no doubt she's one of you."

The family barely acknowledged him, their attention fixed on Clara as if they were studying a puzzle. Clara stood there, scared to say a word.

The young man finally broke the silence, his voice edged with disdain but his eyes betraying something more: uncertainty. "But, Mother, are we truly to trust the word of strangers?" His sharp tone couldn't hide the flicker of resentment that crossed his face.

Clara noticed how his gaze lingered on her, assessing and wary. It wasn't just doubt; it was a challenge. She couldn't tell if he wanted her gone or was afraid she might actually belong.

"And did you see this place as we flew in? Its ghastly."

Clara felt a strange twinge ripple through her as she

listened to his words. His smile was carefully measured, hiding something restless underneath, like a storm locked behind glass. A flash of disdain bubbled in the corners of her mind, fleeting but potent, and she wasn't sure if it came from him or from her own instinctive reaction to his arrogance. She stood up, trying to steady her voice. "I'm not claiming to be anyone," she replied, her tone wavering slightly. "Today has been … a lot to deal with," she said, her tone sharper now. "I didn't even know magic existed until just over an hour ago, which is already something astronomical to process. Then I find out I belong to a prestigious family, your family. So, please excuse my bluntness, but I didn't ask for this, any of it. I just want answers. My mam was Helena Nightfall. That part I know to be true. That's all I know. And just to add, Hull is not *ghastly*. It has been my home my entire life and I love living here. It's not a wealthy city like where you probably live, but its people are amazing and look out for one another and really care about our community. Also, we don't think we're better than other people."

The young man grinned at Clara, clearly unfazed by her words. "So, you didn't know magic existed until today," said the young man, his tone curt. "And yet we're meant to believe you're one of us? Forgive me if I remain unconvinced." He pulled out his wand, his eyes narrowing as he fixed her with an unwavering stare.

Clara held back a sigh, her patience thinning. She looked back at him with barely concealed annoyance. "Do you honestly think I'd lie about who I am?"

The young man's expression remained unmoved, his gaze cold and assessing. Clara glanced briefly at the older man and woman, hoping for a sign of reassurance, some sense that they believed her. But they only stood there, silent and watchful, their expressions unreadable. It was as if this test had been their plan all along.

Frustration tightened in Clara's chest. She had imagined her mam's family might be welcoming or at least be curious. Instead, she felt as if she were being examined, every part of her scrutinised for a flaw.

Rupert stood off to the side, clearly uneasy, his hands twisting together as he watched. He looked as though he wanted to speak, to remind them of his confirmation, but something about the young man's presence silenced him. It was clear that questioning the Nightfalls was not something he dared to do.

"Now, then," the young man commanded, his voice low and steady as he raised his wand, "we'll perform this spell once more, shall we? Just to be certain." He took a breath, eyes fixed on her with that same unyielding look, before muttering the incantation, "Crann Anam."

A faint glow appeared at the tip of his wand, and Clara felt a prickle in her fingertip as a drop of her blood rose into the air. The tiny droplet pulsed, hovering before her, and then it began to spell out the names in shimmering letters again, one by one, each name branching out and connecting to another. Her mother's name appeared instantly after Clara's.

Clara's gaze flickered to the younger man, catching a brief hint of surprise in his eyes, a flicker that quickly vanished as he forced his expression back into an indifferent mask.

"You don't belong here," he said, his voice low enough that only Clara could hear. "Your mother left this world behind for a reason. Don't think you can just waltz in and take your place among us."

A heavy silence filled the room, the import of his words settling over them all. Clara felt a sense of vindication, even if their acceptance felt grudging at best. This was her family, like it or not. She had always felt like some part of her was missing … could her family be it? Only time would tell.

She felt the weight of the older man's presence before he even spoke, a quiet authority that filled the room like a shadow. Beneath his composed exterior, there was a cold edge, sharp and unyielding, that brushed against her senses like a chill wind.

The older man exchanged a glance with the woman as he began to speak. "I am Eldric Nightfall," he said, his tone deliberate, each word carefully measured. "As head of the Nightfall family, it seems I have the honour of calling myself your grandfather, though the circumstances are … unexpected. And this is Selene, your grandmother," he said, his voice heavy with authority. "We are one of the oldest families in England. And it seems our lineage continues with you." He paused, his gaze fixed on her as if trying to see something beyond her outward appearance. "Your mother decided to give up on magic … and our family … many years ago. I hope you do not offer the same disappointment."

Her grandmother's face softened, and she placed a gentle hand on her husband's arm. "Let's give her a chance to make her own path." She turned to Clara. "You're Helena's daughter," her grandmother said, her gaze softening. "That makes you one of us, whether you're ready to believe it or not. You've been kept from this world for so long … it's time you stepped into the place that has always been waiting for you."

Her grandmother stepped forward, her expression

thoughtful. "We haven't seen or heard from your mother in over fifteen years," she said. "And we certainly didn't know you existed." Her gaze mellowed just a bit as she studied Clara. "She does look like Helena, doesn't she?"

Her grandmother's warmth was subtle, like the lingering heat of embers rather than a roaring flame. Clara sensed a careful precision in every word and gesture, as though she measured everything she said. Yet beneath the polished exterior, Clara caught glimpses of something else, a quiet sadness, a loss that hadn't entirely healed.

Her grandfather studied her closely, his face etched with thought. "Your mother chose a different path, one that kept her … and you … far from our world," he said, his voice steady but distant. "We gave up searching years ago and hoped one day she would return home."

Clara's voice came out softer than she intended. "I don't know why she left … or why I never knew about any of you. As far as I know, she never spoke of her family. And since she died, it's just been me and my dad."

Her grandmother's expression shifted, a trace of sadness creeping in. "Helena was … strong-willed. She chose to leave, but none of us imagined she'd never return, nor keep you hidden as well." She paused, her gaze lingering on Clara. "You have a look of your mother, you know."

The younger man, who had been standing a step behind, crossed his arms, his gaze still cold and wary. "I'm Cassius Nightfall, by the way, heir to the family legacy. And just to be clear, it's a very big legacy indeed."

Clara felt her cheeks flush. "I'm not here to claim

anything," she said, her voice firmer now. "I just wanted to understand … why I got the invitation and what it meant. I never imagined there was a whole other world out there. And a whole other family."

Her grandfather straightened, his tone becoming brisk. "We shall make arrangements for you to stay with us at Nightfall Manor," he said. "There is much for you to learn, and it is best done under our guidance." His tone darkened slightly. "The Nightfall name is more than a name, Clara; it is a legacy, a mantle forged through centuries of power and sacrifice. But with that legacy comes responsibility … and danger. You may not understand it now, but you will. In time, you will learn that being a Nightfall is a privilege but can also be a burden."

Clara blinked, her brow furrowing as the word settled heavily in her chest. "Danger?" she asked, her voice wavering. "What kind of danger?"

Before Eldric could answer, Cassius leaned casually against the mantelpiece, a sly smile tugging at his lips. "Well," he said, drawing out the word, "there is the small matter of a dark wizard on the loose again. Let's just say he's not exactly a fan of the Nightfalls."

Clara's heart skipped, her eyes darting between Cassius and her grandparents. Before she had a chance to respond, her grandmother spoke.

"Not now, Cassius," she said sharply, her tone clipped. She shot him a warning look before turning to Clara with a reassuring smile. "You'll frighten the poor girl."

Cassius held up his hands in mock surrender, but his grin didn't falter. "Just stating facts, Mother."

Clara's grandmother ignored him, her attention fixed on Clara. "Worry not, dear. All is safe at Nightfall

Manor. Our home is one of the most secure places in the magical world. No harm will come to you under our roof."

Clara nodded, though her pulse still thrummed in her ears. The mention of the Dark Wizard again, no matter how casually Cassius had brought it up, was not something she could easily brush aside.

"Who is he?" she asked hesitantly, her voice barely above a whisper.

Her grandmother hesitated, her eyes flicking to Eldric. "Perhaps it's best we discuss such matters another time."

Clara was ready to pursue the matter but thought against it. The Nightfall name might carry great weight, but Clara was beginning to realise it also carried shadows. Shadows that, sooner or later, she may have to face.

Clara stood stiffly, her mind drifting back to the words 'Nightfall Manor'. They felt grand and alien, so far from the small, cosy home she shared with her dad in Hull. The thought of leaving him behind tugged at her heart.

Her fingers fidgeted with her sleeve as doubts swirled. What if she didn't belong? What if she wasn't enough? This world of magic and polished smiles wasn't hers. She barely understood magic, let alone the expectations of a family she'd never known.

Her breathing quickened, anxiety bubbling beneath the surface. But somewhere in the chaos of her thoughts, a flicker of curiosity stirred. What if she did belong? What if this was her chance to uncover the pieces of her mam's life that had always been out of reach?

It wasn't enough to quiet her nerves, but it was enough to stop her from running. For now.

"I ... I'd need to talk to my dad first, before I make

any decision and agree to stay at Nightfall Manor," she said quickly, trying to steady her voice.

Her grandmother stepped forward, her expression softening. "Of course," she said gently. "Family is important, and we would never take you away without his blessing."

Her grandfather nodded, though his tone carried less flexibility. "We will speak to him together. The sooner he understands the importance of this, the better."

Clara nodded, though her stomach churned. The thought of these strangers entering her home, speaking to her dad, and pulling her into their world felt overwhelming. She glanced at Rupert, who was already scribbling something onto a parchment.

"We shall leave for your father's at once," her grandfather stated. "You'll return home, and we'll make our introductions. Then we shall leave for Nightfall Manor."

*

As the Nightfalls moved to leave, Rupert handed Clara a small scroll. "A record of your magical registration," he explained. "Don't fret, young lady," he added, his voice warm but distant. "Your family has a way of … taking charge. Whether that's a comfort or a headache, well, you'll find out soon enough."

Clara nodded, tucking the scroll into her bag.

Before stepping outside with her family, Clara turned back to Rupert, offering him a warm smile, her gratitude genuine.

"Thank you, Rupert," she said softly. "I know I probably haven't been the easiest to deal with today. It's a lot to take in, but you've helped me find the family I never knew existed."

Rupert's face softened, and he gave a slight bow, clearly touched. "It was my pleasure, Miss Nightfall. Kindness costs nothing but unfortunately doesn't come easy to all." He looked at Cassius before quickly looking away.

Clara smiled, feeling a surge of warmth and appreciation for the man who had, in a way, become her first ally in this strange new world. With a final nod, she followed her family outside, bracing herself for what lay ahead.

She followed the Nightfalls out of the office, her heart pounding with every step. The Moondancer stood waiting, its silver coat gleaming under the sunlight. Clara hesitated, glancing back at the office door, as though Rupert might call her back and offer an escape.

But he didn't.

Her grandfather turned to her, his sharp gaze softening for a moment. "Come, Clara," he said, his voice quieter now. "There is much for you to discover."

Clara took a deep breath, her feet moving forwards despite the heaviness in her chest. She climbed into the cart, her stomach twisting as the door closed behind her.

As the Moondancer lifted into the sky, Clara stared out of the window, watching the buildings below shrink below her. Her fingers brushed the scroll in her bag, her thoughts tangled.

The world she had known was falling away like a crumbling bridge and being replaced by a new one, brighter, stranger, and far more dangerous than she could have imagined.

Chapter 4: Permission for Self-Discovery

As they settled into the carriage, her grandfather turned to Clara, his gaze sharp. "What is your address, Clara?"

Clara hesitated for a second, still unaccustomed to their brisk manner. "Twenty-four Elmbridge Avenue, in Hull." she replied, feeling a mix of pride and defensiveness over her modest home.

Her grandfather gave a curt nod and leaned forwards towards the front of the carriage. "Twenty-four Elmbridge Avenue, Kingston-Upon-Hull," he commanded, his voice low and authoritative. The Moondancer gave a quiet, almost respectful growl, as if acknowledging his words.

Clara nodded, sinking into the plush seat and gripping its edge as the Moondancer let out a low, rumbling call. With a powerful beat of its wings, it lifted off the ground, and Clara's stomach flipped as the ground fell away beneath them.

She looked out of the window as the rooftops of Hull shrank below. She gripped the seat tightly as her face paled, and she clung to her seat, her face paling. "Can … can anyone see us?" she asked, her voice tight.

Cassius let out a sharp laugh. "What a ridiculous question! Hollowers can't perceive magic. If they could, you'd have heard of us by now. They can't see anything beyond their little world." He leaned back, a smirk playing on his lips. "Honestly, it's amazing they've made it this far."

"Hollowers?" Clara repeated, glancing at him in confusion.

Cassius smirked, his tone dripping with condescension. "Non-magical people, of course. As in they are hollow inside … blind to everything around them."

Clara stared out of the carriage window, her stomach

churning. Hull's rooftops stretched below her, familiar yet distant. She was leaving behind her safe, ordinary world for something dazzling and alien. Part of her yearned to cling to what she knew, but another part, a braver part, pulled her forward.

Her grandfather's sharp eyes flicked towards the window, his lips curling faintly. "Hull," he said, his voice cool. "A city past its prime."

Clara stiffened, her fingers tightening around the edge of her seat. "Hull is my home, and I love it. It's shaped me into the person I am: kind, caring, and someone who tries to do the right thing. That's what matters." She lifted her chin, her voice clear and steady despite her grandfather's stern gaze. "Wealth, power, prestige … all of it means nothing if you're not a good person."

Her words hung in the air, sounding far older than her fourteen years, with a quiet defiance that made the carriage feel smaller. For a moment, neither grandparent replied, their expressions unreadable as the steady rumble of the carriage filled the silence.

Her grandmother gave her grandfather a look of caution before turning to Clara. "What your grandfather means, darling, is that Hull is … humble. A place of practicality. And practicality has its merits." She smiled, though there was something patronising in her warmth. "But our world will open doors for you that the people of Hull could never dream of."

Clara frowned, her fingers curling into the folds of her coat. "You make it sound like it's not good enough."

Her grandmother's gaze softened, and her voice carried a placating note. "Not at all, Clara. Every place has its purpose. But you are a Nightfall. You were meant for greater things."

Clara turned her face towards the carriage window, biting back a response. Rain smeared the grey streets as they rattled onward through a world far from the gleaming mansions and hidden magic of her mother's family. Her home was enough. She wasn't sure why they couldn't see that.

Clara gazed out of the carriage window as it glided above Hull, the familiar city sprawling beneath her like a patchwork quilt of streets, rooftops, and lights. Clara's heart steadied with the rhythm, though the view made her world feel suddenly smaller. It was breathtaking in a way that made her forget, just for a second, the whirlwind of magic and mystery that had swept her life into new territory.

Beside her, her grandmother watched her with a gentle smile, noticing the tension in Clara's shoulders. "You'll get used to it, darling. I remember my first time when I was a small child. I thought my heart would leap right out of my chest." She chuckled softly. "You belong here, in a world of magic and wonder. Magic has always been in your blood; you just needed to discover it. You will get used to it in time."

Clara managed a small smile, her grip on the seat loosening as she looked back out of the window. "It's … it's beautiful. Terrifying, but beautiful."

Her grandfather leaned forward, his gaze sharp. "Magic is beautiful, yet it holds the raw untamed force of pure power. Magic is only as strong as the will that wields it. Those who waver or hesitate risk being consumed by it." He held her gaze, his tone cold yet commanding. "To be a true Nightfall, you must understand that control is everything. Magic will bend to your will, or it will break you."

Clara felt a chill settle over her at her grandfather's

words. His warning was clear, almost like a challenge, as if he were daring her to falter. She held his gaze, refusing to look away, though her pulse quickened. This wasn't just about learning spells or fitting into a new world; she was expected to master it, to bend it to her will. The thought unsettled her, and yet deep down, she felt a flicker of determination.

As her grandfather's gaze drilled into her, she straightened her posture, lifting her chin slightly. She might not understand the full impact of magic yet, nor how to belong amongst the elite, but she knew one thing: she would not be intimidated.

They drifted in silence for about 30 seconds, which to Clara felt like a lifetime. Just as she had begun to relax, Cassius cleared his throat, looking at her with a cool, almost calculating gaze. "Since you are to be part of the family now, you should understand what that entails," he said, his tone firm. "Being a Nightfall isn't just a name. It's a duty." His tone was sharp. "Your mother forgot that. Let's hope you don't make the same mistake."

Clara met his gaze, her nerves tightening again. "I understand," she said, trying to keep her voice steady. But as the words left her mouth, she wondered if she truly did understand what was expected of her.

Her grandmother placed a comforting hand on her arm. "There's no need to rush. Learning our ways will take time. We shall provide you with tutors to learn our ways … family and magic."

Clara nodded, her mind buzzing with questions she wasn't yet ready to ask. For now, she focused on the journey ahead, feeling a strange mix of anticipation and dread. Soon enough, they would land, and she would have to face her dad, explain everything she'd discovered, and the changes that were coming. She wondered if he'd understand, if he'd let her go so easily into this world he'd never been part of.

*

As they began to descend, the Hull streets drawing closer once again, Clara's mind swirled with thoughts of the family she was knew and the one she was just beginning to know. In both, she felt a kind of belonging and a kind of loss.

The Moondancer landed smoothly outside her home, the carriage settling softly on the pavement. People bustled about their day, oblivious to its arrival. Clara hesitated, glancing back at her grandmother, who nodded with an encouraging smile.

Clara took a deep breath and stepped out of the carriage, her heart pounding with the realisation that she was about to leave behind everything she'd ever known for a world she could only begin to understand.

Cassius wrinkled his nose as he eyed Clara's small brick house. "This is your home?" he said, his tone dripping with disdain.

Her grandfather placed a hand on his arm, though a faint smirk crossed his lips. "Now, now, Cassius. We mustn't pass judgment."

Cassius uttered in an almost disbelieving manner, "Sorry, Father, but imagine just having to live like … well, like a peasant."

Clara's gaze sharpened as she met Cassius's eyes. "We're not peasants," Clara said, her voice steady. "We're working-class, and we value decency over arrogance. Wealth doesn't make you better than anyone."

Cassius scoffed, waving a hand dismissively.

Clara shook her head, disappointment welling up in

her. Her new family, especially Cassius, felt worlds apart from everything she knew and valued. She knew she would never fully belong among them, especially with their snobbish ways. But she had to learn about the magical world and her mother's family. It was part of understanding who she truly was.

With a last steadying breath, Clara opened the door and led them inside. The familiar smell of home, burning coffee in the pot and her dad's aftershave, hit her at once, calming her nerves.

Her dad, Jeff, was standing by the doorway, his expression shifting from confusion to something darker as his eyes landed on the Nightfalls. "Hello, love, who are these people?" he asked, his voice cautious, though there was a hint of protectiveness in his tone.

Clara took a breath, glancing at her grandmother before answering. "Dad, this is ... my family. Mam's family. This is my grandmother, Lady Selene, my grandfather, Lord Eldric ... And that's my uncle ... Cassius. And that's my dad, Jeff. Dad, they're from ... the magical world." Clara scanned his face, looking for any sign that he knew what she was talking about.

Her dad's jaw clenched, his gaze shifting uncomfortably to the side, as though old memories had suddenly resurfaced. "Your mother wanted to keep you far from that world until you were old enough to decide for yourself," he said slowly, a sadness that Clara hadn't heard before layering his voice. "She ... said that world was dangerous."

He paused, glancing briefly at the Nightfalls, his expression darkening. "She didn't talk much about her family. There were things she didn't want in her life, things she wanted to leave behind ... except for her grandfather. She spoke fondly of him. But he was killed just before we met."

Cassius let out a huff, crossing his arms. "Helena always did think she was better than us, didn't she?" He said smugly. "And yet she chose to waste her life in a place like this." His eyes swept the room with a pointed sneer, his judgement lingering in the air like a shadow.

Her dad's expression hardened. "You have no right to speak about her that way. She was the kindest, most caring person I've ever known." His gaze softened as he looked at Clara. "Her life wasn't wasted. We were given the greatest gift in the world, and that was you, Clara."

He paused, as if gathering his thoughts, then continued, his voice lower but edged with a quiet anger. "After her grandfather was killed, she felt that world had nothing good or safe left in it. She believed that the one who took his life might come for her too. He was searching for something, something she never explained. But she warned that if he found it, both her world and ours would be in danger. That's why she cast a powerful shielding spell around us, so no one from that world could ever find us." He sighed, his eyes filled with both sadness and resolve. "And that's why she gave you that necklace, Clara, to shield you from that world and hide your abilities. Your mam said it would protect you for as long as you needed it to, until you were ready to face that world."

Clara's heart ached as she saw her dad struggling to balance his desire to keep her safe with the need to let her choose her own path.

Clara's grandmother observed Jeff with a pointed gaze, her expression a mix of curiosity and resentment. "Tell me," she said softly, though there was an edge in her voice, "how did Helena die?"

Clara's dad looked at her for a few seconds, his face sombre, before glancing at Clara, who waited, just as eager to hear the truth. "She suddenly became sick, covered with a brownish rash over her entire body. For weeks, the doctors tried to figure it out, running every test they could think of, but they could not figure out what was wrong with her. Whatever it was, it defied all their knowledge." He paused, his voice breaking slightly. "They did their best … but she just kept getting sicker until … she was gone."

Selene's lips tightened. "She died of Shadowmere," she murmured, the name dropping like a stone in the room. "It's a sickness known in the magical world, rare and extremely difficult to cure, but we would've found a way to save her. Helena was foolish to abandon her world. She could have been saved." There was a sadness in her eyes, the loss of her daughter hitting hard.

When Clara's grandmother finished talking, her grandfather leaned forward, clasping his hands together with deliberate precision. His sharp gaze locked onto Clara. "Helena was a Nightfall by blood," he began, his voice low but carrying the weight of an unspoken accusation. "But she chose to turn her back on her family, on everything that could have protected her and even saved her life. And in the end, she paid the price for that choice."

He let the words hang in the air, heavy with quiet reproach, before continuing. "Now you stand at the same crossroads, Clara." His tone sharpened, cold and resolute. "You can choose to remain here in the non-magical world and forget the Nightfall name, the magical world, and cast away all that you were born to inherit. Or you can rise to the occasion and embrace who you are meant to be."

Clara felt the impact of her grandfather's words. Her pulse quickened as the room seemed to grow smaller. She glanced at her dad, whose jaw tightened, his hands gripping his mug as though anchoring himself.

Finally, Clara spoke, her voice quiet but firm. "I'm not walking away from anything," Clara said firmly. "But I won't abandon the life I've built here, either. I may belong to this family, but I also belong to myself."

Her grandfather raised an eyebrow, his silence almost daring her to continue.

"I get that the Nightfall name carries weight," Clara pressed on, her voice gaining strength. "And I'm trying to understand what that means, what it means for me. But I can't just forget where I come from, who I've been my whole life. My dad … my life outside this … it's not something I can just leave behind."

Her grandfather's expression didn't shift, but Clara noticed a flicker of something — respect, perhaps? — in his eyes.

Her grandmother reached over, placing a gentle hand on Clara's shoulder. "Darling, no one expects you to have all the answers right away."

Clara nodded, her hands clasped tightly in her lap. She didn't have the answers yet, but for now, she needed them to know she wouldn't be pushed into a decision she didn't fully understand.

Clara's dad nodded his head. "Helena and I discussed reaching out to you, you know. I begged her to return to your world if it meant she might live. But she refused." He sighed, looking down as if reliving those painful conversations. "She made me promise to keep her past hidden from Clara until she turned eighteen. The necklace should've held until your eighteenth birthday,

Clara, but it seems to have worn off sooner." He turned to Clara, his eyes filled with regret. "I'm so sorry, love. I was only doing what your mam wanted, to keep you safe from all this. I never wanted you to get hurt."

Clara stepped forward, placing a hand on her dad's arm, her voice steady despite the emotions swirling within her. "It's okay, Dad. I know you only did what Mam wanted. I just wish I'd known sooner ... so I could have been a little more prepared." She stepped closer. "I love you, Dad."

Her dad pulled her into a tight hug, his voice thick with emotion. "I love you too, baby girl."

Clara, seated beside her father, gripped his hand tightly, feeling her heart twist. She had never known the full extent of her mother's choice to stay away from her family, and hearing these accusations felt like hearing her mother judged unfairly. She glanced at each of the Nightfalls, trying to gauge their feelings and loyalties, sensing an unspoken tension that seemed to ripple through them.

Clara's grandmother broke the silence. Now, I know I don't know you at all, Jeff," she began, her voice carrying a blend of authority and a faint warmth. "But you did marry my daughter and father my granddaughter. So that, in a way, makes us family."

Her dad nodded, clearly uncomfortable but trying to hold his ground. He looked at Clara, his gaze filled with a mix of worry and pride.

"Jeff, I know this is difficult," Selene said, her tone measured, "but Clara is part of a legacy that stretches back generations. She deserves to understand it, to see the world her mother came from. We only want to guide her."

Clara's dad looked at her, then back at her grandmother,

swallowing hard. "All I want is for Clara to be safe and happy," he said quietly.

"We want that too," Selene assured him. "And I believe, in the right environment, she will flourish. She has much to learn, and we can provide everything she needs. We understand your apprehension," she said, her voice gentle but firm. "Helena made her choices, but Clara's path is her own. We only want to give her the tools to succeed in a world she was born to be part of."

Clara looked between her father and grandmother, sensing the unspoken tension between them but also feeling a new pull, a call to discover this part of herself. She took a deep breath, realising that perhaps she was standing on the edge of a journey only she could undertake. She hesitated. "But I have school next week," she said, feeling a tug of worry about missing her friends and her familiar routine.

Her grandmother waved her hand dismissively, as if the very thought was insignificant. "Nonsense. We'll find a more suitable school for someone of your abilities, Clara."

Clara felt a knot of anxiety form in her stomach, unsure how to respond to the disdain in her grandmother's tone. School was her one steady link to normality, and the thought of leaving it behind felt daunting.

Her grandmother spoke. "We can arrange for Clara to stay until the end of summer. Tell her current school, which as I understand is almost finished for the academic year, that Clara will be staying with her family, who shall take care of her academic studies."

Her dad looked thoughtful, his brow furrowed with worry. "That's a big ask. Clara would miss a month of school."

"Clara can finally learn who she truly is," Clara's grandmother said sternly.

Clara stepped back, nodding towards the kitchen. "Dad, can I speak with you alone for a second?"

He nodded, leading her into the kitchen. He turned to her, sadness filling his eyes. "Clara … I know you're curious about that world, but your mother wanted you kept out of their world for a reason, at least until you were eighteen. She wanted you safe. And now you're all I've got left of her," her dad said, his voice breaking. "I just … I don't want to lose you to the same world that took her from me."

Clara swallowed, feeling her own eyes well with tears. "I know you don't want me to go. To be honest, I'm in two minds myself. If I don't go with them, I may lose my only chance to learn about that world and about where Mam came from. And where a part of me belongs too."

Her dad's voice trembled as he placed a hand on her shoulder. "I don't want you to go, love. But I know this is your choice. This will always be your home. And promise me you'll stay safe."

She hugged him tightly, feeling the strength and warmth she'd always relied on. "I will, Dad. I promise."

After a long pause, he released her, his hand lingering on her shoulder. "Okay then. Go and find out who you are."

With one last squeeze, she stepped away, her heart torn between the safety of her familiar world and the mysteries waiting in the other. She returned to the living room, where her family waited, her expression determined.

Clara took a steadying breath, glancing at her family. "I'll need a few minutes to pack a bag," she said, her voice resolute. "There are things I'll need: clothes, books, those sorts of things." She looked at the Nightfalls, trying to gauge their reactions. "I'm not exactly sure what I'll need going into the magical world, but I won't leave behind everything familiar." She caught her dad's eye and gave him a small, reassuring smile before turning back to the Nightfalls. "I'll be quick." She hesitated, pulling her phone from her pocket. "Will I still be able to use this … over there?" she asked, glancing between her grandparents and Cassius.

"Technology won't work reliably there," her grandmother said with a faint smile.

Clara nodded, slipping it back into her pocket. She wasn't sure how she felt about her lifeline to the familiar world being so unreliable.

Clara made her way upstairs, her mind racing as she looked around her room one last time. She grabbed a small bag, filling it with essentials, clothes, a few favourite books, and a photograph of her mam that always seemed to bring her comfort. She paused, letting her eyes linger on her familiar space, unsure of when she'd be back but knowing in her heart that she was making the right choice. Taking a steadying breath, she hefted her bag onto her shoulder and made her way downstairs, a swell of emotions rising within her. She forced herself to stay composed, even as the reality of leaving her home began to sink in.

In the living room, she gave her dad a tight, lingering hug, the kind that made it clear how much she'd miss him. "I'll FaceTime you every day, if it works" she whispered, hoping to reassure him and herself. The familiar warmth of his embrace grounded her in the second. "I love you, Dad," she whispered, her voice thick with emotion as she tried to keep the tears at bay. She could feel his hand gently patting her back, a silent reassurance that everything would be all right, even as he held on a little longer, as if reluctant to let go. She felt his emotions as clearly as her own, a swirling mix of pride, fear, and heartbreak. His love for her was like an anchor, steady and grounding, but it was laced with an unspoken ache that made her chest tighten. "I'll come back," she whispered, her voice trembling under the weight of his silent plea for her to stay.

Finally, she pulled back, offering him a small, shaky smile before wiping her eyes. Taking a deep breath, she turned to face the Nightfalls, her new family, who stood waiting with unreadable expressions.

Clara's hand tightened around her bag as she glanced back at her father. *I'll come back*, she thought fiercely. *This won't be forever.*

"I'm ready," she said, her voice steady, even if her heart was anything but.

As Clara stepped into the carriage, the weight of two worlds pressed against her. Fear gnawed at her resolve, but deep within, a spark of courage ignited. Whatever lay ahead, she would face it on her terms.

Chapter 5: A Place of Wonder

As the carriage glided through the summer sky, Clara peered out of the window, watching the trees grow denser, their branches twisted and ancient as if hiding secrets of their own. She glanced at her grandmother, curiosity getting the better of her. "Where exactly is Nightfall Manor?" she asked, feeling mystery in every flap of the Moondancer's wings.

"Nightfall Manor is in Thornmire Glade," her grandmother replied. "It's hidden by powerful enchantments, invisible to Hollowers. They only see an endless forest of brambles and shadows. Only magical blood can find the way."

Cassius, sitting across from Clara, let out a small, disdainful chuckle. "It's rather fitting, really," he drawled, his eyes flashing with an edge of superiority. "Hollowers see only what they're allowed to see. Our world remains safe from their ignorance."

Clara shifted in her seat, unsure how to respond. Cassius's disdain was clear, but her mind was too busy reeling at the idea of an enchanted glade hidden from all but those who belonged. Her heart raced with both excitement and apprehension as Thornmire Glade, and her unknown family legacy, drew closer with each second.

As the carriage descended, Clara leaned towards the window, her breath catching at the sight of the sprawling estate. It was grander than anything she had imagined. Yet beneath the awe, unease stirred. How could a place so vast and otherworldly ever feel like home? Her small, imperfect house in Hull had been home. This manor, with its shifting iron gates and shimmering ivy, belonged to strangers. Strangers who, somehow, were her family

Nightfall Manor rose like a dark castle, its spiralling towers and silver-veined walls shimmering as though alive. Summer ivy cloaked the stone in a soft silvery glow, each leaf glinting in the summer light.

Clara's eyes traced the grounds below, catching sight of sprawling gardens filled with strange plants that seemed to sway in steady motion, even without a breeze. At the edge of the gardens was a shining lake, its surface mirror-like, reflecting the manor in perfect detail. Occasionally, ripples spread across the water, hinting at something magical or monstrous hidden just beneath its surface.

The carriage swooped lower, giving Clara a clearer view of the vast courtyard in front of the manor. Cobblestone pathways spiralled out from a large fountain at the centre, where a statue of a magnificent winged creature, part lion, part dragon, stood guard, water spilling from its mouth into a glistening pool below.

As Clara looked out of the window in amazement, she turned to look at her grandmother. "I can't believe you live here! It's enormous!"

Her grandmother smiled, a touch of pride in her eyes as she reached over to pat Clara's hand. "You do too now, darling. Welcome to Nightfall Manor."

As the carriage came to a graceful landing in front of the entrance of Nightfall Manor, Clara took a deep breath, steadying herself. Her eyes travelled up the towering face of the mansion, a mix of amazement and nerves twisting in her stomach. Stepping down from the carriage, she followed her grandparents and uncle towards the imposing front doors, which seemed to give a gentle pulse, as if aware of their arrival.

The heavy oak doors swung open smoothly, revealing Hazel Thornfield, a middle-aged witch with sharp, discerning eyes and a calm presence. Her gaze settled on Clara, softening with a warmth that surprised her.

"Welcome back, Lady Selene," Hazel said, her voice steady but respectful, before her eyes turned back to Clara. "And you must be Miss Clara."

"Indeed," Lady Selene replied, a hint of pride in her voice. "Hazel, this is my granddaughter, Helena's daughter. She'll be staying with us, and I'd like you to show her around and help get her settled in."

"Of course," Hazel replied, dipping her head. She gave Clara a small, reassuring smile. "If you'll follow me, Miss Clara, I'll show you all that Nightfall Manor has to offer."

"Let me take that for you," Hazel said, gesturing at Clara's bag. Before Clara could protest, a gentle flick of Hazel's wand sent it floating upward, disappearing smoothly up the grand staircase.

Clara blinked, her awe momentarily overtaking her nerves. "Does … everything here just happen like that?" she asked, glancing back at Hazel.

"Most things," Hazel replied warmly, her tone calm and reassuring. "You'll get used to it. Now, let's begin the tour."

They moved into the first corridor, the soft glow of floating lanterns lighting their way. The walls hummed faintly, the energy of the manor brushing against Clara's skin like a low current. "This is the Endless Passage," Hazel said, her hand trailing along the wall. "It connects every wing of the estate. If you're in a room, simply turn the door's knob clockwise to return here. To exit near your room, turn it anti-clockwise."

Clara frowned slightly, staring down the corridor's seemingly endless stretch. "Does it... ever actually end?"

Hazel smiled knowingly. "It's not meant to. The Endless Passage adapts to your needs, not the other way around."

They passed several doors etched with glowing symbols. One flickered as Hazel paused, her fingers grazing the frame. "Each room has its purpose," she explained, her tone taking on a hint of reverence. "This one, for instance, is the Moonshadow Grove."

Hazel pushed the door open, and Clara gasped. Inside was a sprawling, enchanted garden that seemed to exist beneath a constant twilight sky. The air carried the faint scent of lavender and honey, while soft light filtered through invisible canopies above, creating shimmering reflections across a shallow pool at the garden's centre.

Clara crouched by the pool, her fingers brushing the water's surface. It rippled, forming the faint outline of a star. "It's beautiful," she whispered.

Hazel stood back, letting Clara take it in. "The Moonshadow Grove has been here for centuries. It's a place of reflection and renewal for those who need it." She tilted her head, studying Clara. "We all find ourselves here eventually."

Clara nodded, feeling the tranquillity of the space settle over her like a warm blanket. But Hazel's gentle touch on her shoulder reminded her there was more to see.

The next stop was the Starbound Library, a cavernous space lined with bookshelves that stretched impossibly high. Floating staircases wound between the shelves, while enchanted orbs of light drifted lazily overhead.

"This," Hazel began, "is the heart of the family's

knowledge. Every text, every relic of our history, is preserved here."

Clara reached for a nearby book, its spine glowing faintly under her touch. "Do all the books ... do that?"

"Only the ones that know you're meant to read them," Hazel replied cryptically. "And beyond those doors," she gestured to a heavily secured iron door, "is the Vault of Whispers. It holds the most powerful relics of the Nightfall family. It hasn't been opened since your great-grandfather's death."

The shadows around the Vault seemed to shift, and Clara shivered. "Why hasn't it been opened?"

Hazel hesitated, her warm smile faltering for just a moment. "Some things are safer left undisturbed."

*

Next was the Dreamcatcher Hallway, its glowing orbs drawing Clara's gaze at once. Hazel led her slowly, giving her time to absorb the significance of the space. "Each orb contains the dreams, hopes, or fears of a Nightfall," she explained. "But only the dreamer can retrieve their orb."

Clara hesitated, standing before one particularly vibrant orb. "What happens if an ancestor's orb ... chooses you?"

"Sometimes," Hazel said, her voice lowering, "your ancestors may guide you. But the dreams don't dictate your path; they only offer possibilities. The choice is always yours."

Clara nodded slowly, her fingers brushing against the doorframe as they moved on.

*

The final stops of the tour were quicker, Hazel's explanations growing brisk as she sensed Clara's energy waning.

The Shifting Staircase moved beneath their feet, the steps rearranging themselves with a soft murmur as Hazel led the way. "It takes you where you need to go," Hazel said simply, watching as Clara tried to predict its movements and failed.

In the Enchanted Kitchen, pots stirred themselves, and knives worked with clockwork precision. "Every recipe honours the Nightfall legacy," Hazel said with pride. "Though I suspect you'll find Bran and me sneaking in a few modern twists."

The Barn brought Clara face to face with the Moondancers, their silver coats shimmering in the low light. One tilted its head towards her, its gaze strangely human, as if assessing her worth. Clara reached out hesitantly but stopped short when the creature snorted softly, its wings rustling.

"They see more than we ever could," Hazel said, watching Clara. "They've been with the Nightfalls for generations."

*

Finally, Hazel led Clara to her bedroom. The moment the door opened, Clara felt the weight of the day lift slightly. The room was elegant but understated compared to the rest of the manor. A four-poster bed stood at its centre, its canopy of enchanted stars twinkling softly. The polished desk and wardrobe gleamed faintly, hints of magic woven into their surfaces.

"This is your space now," Hazel said, her voice kind. "Nightfall Manor will challenge you, but it will also guide you."

Clara stepped inside, her hand brushing the edge of the bedpost. The room felt warm, welcoming, but also distant, like it belonged to someone she wasn't yet ready to be. "Thank you, Hazel," she murmured.

"Goodnight, Miss Clara," Hazel replied, closing the door quietly behind her.

Clara sank onto the bed, staring up at the enchanted stars above. For the first time, the dust of the day's revelations began to settle. This was her family's home, her family's world. But as the stars twinkled softly overhead, Clara couldn't shake the feeling that she had yet to earn her place among them.

*

A soft knock on the door brought her out of her thoughts. "Come in," Clara called, sitting up as the door opened.

Her grandmother stepped in, her presence both regal and warm. She looked around the room, taking in the scene as if checking that everything was exactly as it should be. "I imagine you've had an overwhelming day," she said, her voice carrying a hint of amusement. "Learning about magic, your mother's family, and a world you never knew existed would be a lot for anyone."

Clara managed a small smile. "Yeah, it's … a lot to take in."

Her grandmother nodded, her gaze understanding yet focused. She settled gracefully onto the edge of the chair by the window, folding her hands neatly in her lap. "I'm sure you must have questions. There's no rush, of course, but some things are important to know." Her tone turned slightly serious. "For instance, regarding your Hollower friends."

Clara's eyebrows rose at the term. "What about them?"

"Our world must remain hidden," Selene said firmly. "If a Hollower witnesses magic, their memories are altered, and those responsible are punished. For Nightfalls, some rules bend, but the law is clear: secrecy protects us all."

Clara felt a shiver at the thought of someone tampering with her friends' memories. She bit her lip, processing what her grandmother had said.

Selene seemed to sense her thoughts and softened her tone. "Are you hungry, darling? I could have Hazel send up some food."

Clara shook her head, pulling herself from her thoughts. "No, thank you, Grandmother ... I think I'll just head to bed."

Her grandmother nodded approvingly, standing to leave. "Very well. Tomorrow will be a new day, and there's much more to learn. Sleep well, Clara."

As her grandmother left, Clara pulled the covers up around her, the weight of her new reality settling over her like the warmth of the enchanted blankets. The world she thought she knew had changed, but she was beginning to realise that this was only the beginning.

As she drifted into sleep, she whispered a quiet promise to herself: she would uncover the secrets of her mother's past, of this house, and of her own powers. For now, though, she let herself rest, cocooned in the magic of Nightfall Manor, the place full of wonder.

Chapter 6: Manor in the Morning

The next morning, Clara stirred awake, blinking as the memories of the previous day returned. Nightfall Manor, her mother's family, the sprawling enchanted halls. She grabbed her phone from the bedside table, smiling softly at her dad's message.

Dad: *Good morning, baby girl. How was your first night? I'm missing you already. Love you xx*

Clara typed back quickly. *Good morning, Dad. I fell asleep early, I was exhausted. Love you more xx.*

But as she hit send, her screen flickered, the message distorting slightly, as though it was struggling to cross an invisible barrier. A reply arrived moments later, glitchy but warm.

Dad: *Never forget, I'm always here if you need me. And I loved you first xx*

Clara's chest tightened, a small tear escaping. Even with magic tugging at her reality, her dad's words felt like home.

Despite the strange interference, it felt like a piece of home was still there with her, as if the warmth of her dad's words had somehow crossed the distance, magic or not.

Deciding to try anyway, Clara tapped on FaceTime and called Chloe.

After a few rings, her friend picked up, her image flickering in and out as the call struggled to connect. "Clara?" Chloe's voice came through in fragments. "How was the festival? Where … are you?"

Clara hesitated, her thoughts scrambling for something believable that didn't involve revealing magic. She hated lying to her best friend, but she had no choice. "There was a festival, but it was just … a lot of strange people playing dress-up," she said, her voice faltering slightly. She adjusted the phone, angling it to show a glimpse of her new room despite the glitchy connection. "Long story, but I met my mam's side of the family yesterday. Turns out they're … really wealthy and live in this huge old manor."

Chloe's eyes widened as she caught glimpses of the opulent surroundings. "Wait, what? How did you meet them? And are you in some kind of castle?" Her voice crackled, but the disbelief was clear.

"Yeah, it kind of feels like a castle," Clara said, forcing a laugh. "They didn't know I existed until recently. When they found out, they came looking for me and invited me to stay for the summer. It's all a bit overwhelming." She glanced out the window, trying to ground herself in the misty view beyond. "Anyway, how are you feeling today?"

"Better, thanks," Chloe said, her brow furrowing with curiosity. "But Clara, this is insane. How do you feel about it all? It's so … sudden."

Clara hesitated, the knot in her chest tightening. "I'm still trying to wrap my head around it. It's just … a lot. But I think I'll be okay." She stared at Chloe's face glitching. "Look, the connection here is terrible. I'll text you later, okay? It'll be easier to keep in touch that way."

Chloe nodded, though her concern was obvious. "Okay, just don't disappear on me. Text me when you can."

"I promise," Clara said softly, offering a small, genuine smile before ending the call. She stared at her phone for a moment, a wave of guilt washing over her. Lying to Chloe felt wrong, but the truth wasn't something she could share, not without consequence and her best friend's memory being wiped.

Just as she ended the call, there was a gentle knock on her door, and Hazel entered. "Good morning, Miss Clara. I hope you slept well." With a quick wave of her wand, Hazel sent Clara's bedding into motion, the sheets and blankets smoothing themselves out while the curtains snapped fully open, flooding the room with soft morning light.

"Breakfast is ready in the Grand Dining Hall, so make your way down once you're ready," Hazel announced, glancing at Clara with a satisfied nod.

"I need to shower first," Clara replied.

"I shall see you downstairs, Miss Clara," Hazel stated as she left the room.

She entered her bathroom and turned the taps that came out of the wall. With a hiss, a shower head emerged from the ceiling, soaking yesterday's clothes. "Great," she muttered. "Can't anything be simple here?"

After a slightly damp beginning, Clara managed to shower properly and change into fresh clothes. She made her way through the endless corridors of Nightfall Manor, nearly getting lost before finding the Grand Dining Hall. She stepped inside, taking in the scene before her: her grandmother sitting elegantly at one end of a dark wooden table, a delicate teacup in her hand. At the other end, her grandfather was engrossed in a newspaper that had a holographic story which hovered above the table, showing the news with a voice reading aloud.

"Come and sit down, darling," her grandmother said as she gestured towards a chair.

"Dark Wizard Escapes Blackspire Tower: Magical Assembly Issues Warning," the voice announced, the words ringing with authority.

Her grandmother sat with a deliberate calmness as a spoon stirred her tea, though Clara noticed the faint tension in her shoulders.

Clara hesitated before sitting near the middle of the table, her eyes flicking to the glowing hologram. A blurred figure cloaked in shadow loomed at the centre of the projection. The voice continued:

"The Assembly has tasked the Order of the Elders with finding the fugitive. Should you encounter the Dark Wizard, do not engage under any circumstances. Report at once."

Clara swallowed hard, her pulse quickening. The Dark Wizard being mentioned again. "Who is he?" she asked, her voice trembling slightly. "It sounds like people are really scared of him."

Her grandfather folded the newspaper, dissolving the hologram into thin air. He leaned back in his chair, his sharp gaze settling on Clara. "They should be scared," he said, his tone cold and deliberate. "But fear won't protect them."

Her grandmother sighed softly, her expression turning thoughtful. "What you must understand, Clara, is that the Dark Wizard is no ordinary wizard gone bad. He was a wizard who once stood among the brightest minds of his time, only to fall into ruin. His ambition consumed him, twisting him into something dangerous and unrecognisable."

Clara's brow furrowed as she leaned forwards slightly. "What does he want?"

Her grandfather exchanged a glance with her grandmother, his face unreadable. "Power," he said simply. "And revenge."

Clara's stomach knotted. "But why would he want revenge?"

Her grandmother hesitated, her spoon clinking softly against her cup as she set it down. "That is a long story, one you needn't trouble yourself with now," she said gently. "All you need to know is that he harbours a deep hatred for anyone who opposes his vision. Our family, naturally, falls into that category."

"Why us?" Clara pressed, her voice barely above a whisper.

Her grandfather's gaze darkened, his tone growing colder. "Because we have stood in his way before. And because we possess knowledge and resources he would very much like to claim for himself. That is all you need to know, Clara."

Her grandmother's expression was soft, though her eyes remained guarded. "What matters most is that you understand the danger he represents. He is not someone to take lightly, nor is he someone you should ever cross paths with. Do you understand?"

Clara nodded slowly, but the unease in her chest only deepened. "If he's so dangerous ... can the Order of the Elders stop him?"

Her grandmother placed a reassuring hand on Clara's. "The Order are the best trained witches and wizards in the world."

Her grandfather's tone remained stern. "But he is cunning, Clara. Never forget that. He thrives in the shadows, striking when least expected. If you ever sense his presence, if you hear so much as a whisper of him, you are to come straight to us. Do not hesitate."

The weight of his words pressed heavily on Clara's chest. "I promise," she said quietly, though the knot of unease remained.

Her grandmother's hand lingered on hers for a

moment longer. "The world is not always kind, Clara. But you are safe here. Nightfall Manor is protected in ways few places are. No harm will come to you under this roof."

Clara nodded, but as she glanced at the spot where the hologram had been, the shadowy figure remained etched in her mind. The people at the festival, her family's cryptic warnings, it all painted a picture of someone far more terrifying than she could have imagined.

"You must eat now, darling," her grandmother said, looking at all the food.

The table was laden with dishes that looked almost too exquisite to eat. Every pastry you could think of, juicy sausages and bacon, thickly sliced toast, muffins and bagels. Clara's stomach growled as she eyed the spread.

"Hazel wasn't sure what you'd prefer, so she prepared a bit of everything," her grandmother said, a hint of amusement in her tone.

Clara selected a few pastries and sat down, her eyes darting around as she tried to look composed, though the sheer abundance of food was a little overwhelming.

"A drink, darling?" Selene asked.

"Orange juice, please," Clara said. The glass filled itself, and despite her effort to appear unfazed, a small smile broke through as she sipped.

"Eat plenty; you'll need your strength," her grandmother remarked. "Today you'll start learning how to use magic. But first, there's a special task. You must craft your own wand."

Clara paused, blinking in surprise. "Craft my own wand?"

"Witches and wizards craft their wands from a magical elder tree," Selene explained. "You'll choose your wand, bind it with runes, and seal it with a drop of your blood. That makes it uniquely yours." She sipped her tea. "Although some wands are passed down through families, growing stronger with each generation."

Clara began to eat her pastry, her fingers brushing the warm, flaky edges. She tore off a piece and popped it into her mouth, licking a crumb from her thumb.

"Clara, dear," Selene said gently, though her tone carried a hint of steel. "At the table, we use cutlery, not our hands."

Clara froze mid-chew, her eyes darting to her grandmother, then to the delicate forks and knives set beside her plate. Heat crept up her neck. "Oh, right," she mumbled, quickly wiping her hands on a napkin and fumbling with the fork.

Her grandfather observed her over his tea, his face impassive, though Clara could have sworn his eyebrow twitched. "A Nightfall carries themself with grace, Clara," he said, his voice even but firm. "Our name commands respect. It is not merely about how others see you; it is about how you see yourself. You will do well to learn the ways of magic but also the ways of being a Nightfall. You'll find the latter part the most important."

Clara straightened her back instinctively, suddenly hyper-aware of how she'd been slouching in her chair. "Sorry," she muttered, stabbing at her pastry with the fork and trying not to feel like an idiot.

Her grandmother looked at her with softened eyes. "It will take time, darling. You'll learn. Every gesture matters. A Nightfall always carries the weight of our legacy, even in the smallest of actions."

Clara nodded, her stomach churning with the weight of expectations. She glanced at her knife and fork as though they were foreign objects, wondering how she was supposed to carry the weight of her name when she could barely cut into a pastry without feeling scrutinised.

Clara finished her breakfast, barely saying another word, setting her empty plate aside as she tried to process everything that had just been said. The idea of crafting her own wand was both thrilling and daunting. Adjusting to a standard of behaviour that was now expected of her was just daunting.

"Well, then," Selene said with a slight smile. "Finish up, darling. Your introduction into magic is about to begin."

Clara looked around at the untouched dishes piled high on the long dining table. Pastries glistened under the chandelier's glow, untouched and pristine. Bowls of perfectly ripe fruit remained undisturbed, as though they were more decoration than food. "Is there always this much left over?" she asked hesitantly, glancing at her grandmother.

Selene raised an eyebrow, exchanging a quick glance with Eldric, who said nothing. "Of course," she replied, folding her napkin neatly. "The staff enjoy whatever remains, and the rest … vanishes, I suppose. Magic is quite practical in that regard. It's called cleansing magic; it removes that what is no longer needed."

Clara nodded, though her chest tightened at the thought of such casual excess. Back home, nothing ever went to waste. The stark difference made her feel, for the first time, just how far she was from the life she knew.

Chapter 7: Magical Discovery

Clara's grandmother rose gracefully from her seat and gestured for Clara to follow, giving a slight nod towards the doorway that led to another hallway, and beyond it, the manor's vast grounds. "It's time for your training," she announced, her voice calm yet carrying a quiet pride. Clara's pulse quickened as she rose to follow, the echo of their footsteps resounding through the grand halls of Nightfall Manor. Each step seemed heavy with the magnitude of what lay ahead.

At the end of the corridor, the heavy oak doors creaked open, revealing an expansive courtyard. It stretched wide, bordered by shimmering hedges and statues of witches and wizards, their expressions watchful in the gentle morning breeze.

Her grandmother paused at the centre of the courtyard and turned to face Clara, her expression calm. "Once you have crafted your wand, you shall begin with the basics," she said, her tone steady and inviting. "You are quiet, Clara. Are you ready for this?"

"Yes, Grandmother," Clara replied, though a flicker of doubt whispered in the back of her mind. She wasn't entirely sure if she was ready, but she was determined to try. She glanced around the courtyard again, feeling the statues' silent approval, as though the very air was imbued with her family's history.

"Clara, magic is not just power. It is understanding, control, and purpose. Generations of Nightfalls have trained here, beneath this very sky. Now, it's your turn to claim your place among them." Her grandmother's voice pulled her back to the present.

Clara nodded, her chest tightening with a mixture of

amazement and the burden of expectation. Her eyes wandered to the statues that lined the courtyard, their carved faces etched with wisdom and strength. She imagined the lives they'd witnessed, the triumphs and sacrifices, and wondered if she could ever live up to their legacy.

After a moment, Clara glanced at her grandmother, a question forming on her lips. "Grandmother … how long have you lived here?"

Selene's stern expression softened, a glint of nostalgia in her eyes. "I came to Nightfall Manor when I was nineteen, after marrying your grandfather. It was an arranged match, meant to strengthen our family's heritage. Though it hasn't always been perfect, we've been a good team," she said, her voice gentler now as her gaze swept across the courtyard. "That was nearly seventy years ago."

Clara's eyes widened. "Seventy years?" She blinked, processing the number. "That would make you nearly ninety! You look incredible, Grandmother."

Selene chuckled softly, her eyes alight with warmth. "Magic has its perks, my darling. Witches and wizards often live to see two centuries if they take care of themselves."

"Two hundred years?" Clara whispered, her mind spinning with the possibilities. "That's … incredible. Imagine the things I could do, the places I could see."

Her grandmother's smile turned wistful, her gaze settling on Clara with quiet affection. "Magic may extend our years, but it also deepens the responsibilities we carry. Time shapes us, as does the magic we wield. It will test you, Clara, as it has tested me. But it will also guide you."

She rested a hand on Clara's shoulder, her voice mellowing to a gentle encouragement. "And now it's your time to begin that journey."

Clara met her grandmother's gaze, the importance of her words settling deep within her. She nodded, drawing strength from the moment, even as a flicker of doubt lingered in the back of her mind. If magic was to shape her, she could only hope it would shape her into someone worthy of the Nightfall name.

*

"Perfect timing, Clara," her grandmother said with a hint of pride, gesturing to the tall, distinguished figure beside her. "This is Master Fenwick, a wizard who has guided many of our family members in the magical arts. He will teach you the basics and help you craft your wand."

Clara's eyes swept over Fenwick, taking in his tall, slender frame and the refined cut of his dark robes. He had white hair and an aged face that carried lines of wisdom and experience rather than exhaustion. Despite his years, his sharp eyes sparkled with a youthful energy, giving him an air of composed strength. There was something in his confident posture and calm demeanour that made Clara both curious and slightly intimidated.

"Good morning, Lady Selene," Fenwick said, bowing slightly before turning to Clara. "An honour to meet you, Miss Clara." His voice was deep and steady.

"Thank you … you too," Clara stammered, feeling the nerves bubble under her skin. There was something about the way his eyes seemed to see right through her that made her feel very small.

"I shall leave you to it. Good luck, Clara," her grandmother said as she left.

Fenwick smiled faintly, his tone firm yet gentle.

"Come, Miss Clara," he said, motioning towards a path that led out to the garden. "Today we begin the bond that will tie your magic to your wand."

Clara hesitated as they walked. She glanced sideways at Fenwick, curiosity overtaking her nervousness. "Do we have to keep up with all these formal names?" she asked tentatively. "You don't have to call me Miss Clara. Clara is fine. And wouldn't you prefer to go by just Fenwick instead of Master Fenwick?"

Fenwick's lips twitched in amusement as he adjusted his robes. "Ah, with your family's station, such formalities are not just tradition; they are an expectation. But if it makes you more comfortable, you may call me Fenwick."

Clara nodded, a small smile creeping onto her face. "So, is Fenwick your first or your last name?"

"Technically, it's my last name," he replied with a dry chuckle. "My full name is Glassius Grendus Fenwick, though very few use the whole thing. Most simply call me Fenwick, which I prefer. My mother, however, had a fondness for calling me Glassy." He raised an eyebrow, a touch of humour in his tone. "I was never particularly fond of that, I assure you."

Clara grinned, suppressing a laugh. "I'll stick with Fenwick," she said, glad for this brief moment of lightness in a world that felt so wrapped in tradition.

"Each witch or wizard crafts their own wand. It's more than a tool; it's a reflection of their essence. Most stick to their wands for life. As you grow stronger, so does your wand, holding echoes of the magic you channel through it. That's why older wands, especially those passed down through generations, often grow incredibly powerful.

"Some, when they reach the peak of their power, choose to wield a staff instead. A staff allows for greater focus and control in complex spells, but it isn't necessary. A wand, even a small one, can hold as much power as the witch or wizard who wields it. It's not the size of the wand; it's the skill behind it."

As they walked down the winding path, the scent of damp earth and fresh greenery surrounded them, mingling with the faint frisson of magic which Clara could feel more than see. The path opened into a wide clearing where an ancient tree stood tall and majestic. Its silvery bark shimmered slightly, and its sprawling branches seemed to reach skyward, as though cradling the heavens.

"The Elder Tree," Fenwick murmured, his tone respectful. "Every Nightfall wand begins here. Its branches carry the essence of those who have wielded its wood before you."

Clara gazed at the tree in amazement. At its base lay scattered twigs and branches, each faintly glowing with an inner light. The air felt alive, vibrating with a quiet energy that made the hairs on the back of her neck stand on end. She stepped closer, drawn to the gentle pulsing of magic in the air.

"Your task," Fenwick said softly, "is to find the one that feels … right."

Clara swallowed, her heart thudding in her chest as she stepped towards the scattered branches. She hovered her hand over them, feeling for something she couldn't quite name. A cool tingle danced across her fingers as she passed over one twig; another gave off a faint warmth. Just as doubt began to creep in, her fingers hovered over a branch that pulsed with a steady, comforting heat. It felt welcoming, familiar, like the first touch of an old friend.

"This one," she whispered, picking it up. The moment her fingers closed around the wood, a sense of belonging washed over her. It was as though it had been waiting for her all along.

Fenwick nodded approvingly, his expression softening. "Good. The wood has chosen you, as you have chosen it."

They made their way to a table near the training grounds, covered in deep indigo cloth and adorned with an array of radiant crystals. Each crystal shimmered as if stolen from the heart of a midnight sky.

"These crystals will amplify and balance the wand's energy," Fenwick explained. "Choose the ones that feel right for your wand. Trust your instincts."

Clara carefully examined the crystals, her fingers brushing over their cool, smooth surfaces. She selected three: a pale blue one that glowed softly, a deep green with veins of gold, and a translucent white crystal that sparkled like frost. As she pressed them gently into the wood, the branch seemed to absorb them willingly, its surface shifting to reveal spiralling symbols that glowed like veins of magic.

Fenwick's gaze remained intent as he drew his wand, its dark, polished surface spiralling with delicate glowing vines. Clara watched, captivated by its quiet elegance.

"Now for the final binding," he said, his voice steady and reverent. With a precise flick, he muttered an incantation, and a small, sharp pin appeared from his wand's tip. "Hold still," he instructed, guiding the pin to Clara's fingertip. He pricked her finger, drawing a single drop of blood. The drop hovered in the air before drifting into the wood. The wand absorbed it with a faint glow.

"Now, the spell," Fenwick said, stepping back. His voice carried the weight of ritual. "To bind the wand to you, speak these words aloud: 'Ceangal Fánaíra'."

Clara's voice was steady as she repeated, "Ceangal Fánaíra."

The wand pulsed warmly in her hand, and symbols appeared, flaring briefly before fading into the wood. A deep sense of connection settled over her, as though the wand had become an extension of herself.

"The words mean 'the bond of the eternal path'," Fenwick said softly. "And now the wand is yours, Miss Clara Nightfall."

Clara held the wand, feeling its warmth spread through her fingers, like holding a fragment of sunlight. The feel of magic was exhilarating but unfamiliar, and for a moment, doubt flickered in her mind. Was this truly where she belonged? She glanced at Fenwick, who gave her a reassuring nod, and the doubt began to fade.

Fenwick broke the silence. "It's not the wand that shapes the magic; it's the witch who wields it."

As Fenwick's words sank in, Clara felt a flicker of confidence stir within her. She was beginning to believe that, just perhaps, she was ready to step into this extraordinary new world.

*

"All right, Miss Clara, let's begin. One of the first things you need to know," Fenwick began, his voice steady and touched with gravity, "is that magic is not without consequence. When harnessed with skill and control, it can be as sharp as a phoenix-feather quill. But push it too far, demand too much, and you risk magical drawback."

Clara tilted her head, intrigued. "Drawback?"

Fenwick leaned forward, his expression both serious

and animated, clearly eager to impart this essential lesson. "Every spell you cast draws on your energy. Magic has a way of reminding us not to overreach. We call it the 'Magical Drawback System'. A formal name, yes, but it's how we describe magic's way of pushing back when we push it too far."

He lifted a finger, launching into his explanation. "Let's start with spell rebound," he said, his tone measured. "When you push a spell beyond your skill, it doesn't always behave. Cast a concealment spell too often or without precision, and you might start flickering, appearing and vanishing uncontrollably."

Clara raised an eyebrow, both intrigued and slightly unsettled. "That ... sounds inconvenient."

Fenwick nodded knowingly. "Inconvenient is putting it mildly. But it's all part of learning your limits. Then there's magical fatigue," he continued. "Too many spells in a short time can leave you drained, weak, unfocused, sometimes even unable to stand. I've seen students push themselves so hard they end up with blurred vision or a splitting headache for hours afterward."

Clara frowned at the thought, but Fenwick pressed on, his voice calm but firm. "Transformation spells come with their own risks. Repeated glamour spells, for instance, can lead to 'Transformation Recoil'. Blotchy skin, uncontrollable hair changes ... even temporary baldness, but there are remedies to combat this."

Clara cringed as a shiver ran through her. Fenwick chuckled softly but kept his tone instructive. "And then we have 'Elemental Backlash'," he said. "Overuse of elemental spells: fire, water, earth, air, can lead to rather ... uncomfortable side effects. Cast too many fire spells, and you might feel your hands burning. Overuse water spells, and you could find yourself sweating profusely, even in the coldest weather."

His smile softened as he added, "Lastly, there's 'Physical Manifestation'. High-powered spells can take a toll on your body: bruises, headaches, nausea. A powerful shield spell might leave you sore, as though you've been holding up a physical barrier. Energy-boosting spells, while effective, can leave you with trembling hands or a pounding heart."

Clara absorbed every word, her mind whirring. The power of magic came with far more complexity and risk than she'd imagined.

"These drawbacks can be managed," Fenwick said, his tone encouraging. "Experienced witches and wizards often use enchanted amulets or potions to mitigate magic's toll. But even with those safeguards, you must respect magic's limits. It is both a gift and a responsibility."

Clara nodded, her grip on her wand tightening. "So … smaller spells? Are those safe?"

"Ah, yes," Fenwick said, his expression brightening. "Smaller spells, or even powerful spells used sparingly, carry no risk. They're the building blocks of magic: useful, reliable, and safe, as long as you don't overdo them."

He raised his wand, his tone soft and steady. "Let me show you. For instance, there's *Solas Ceo*, a gentle light spell. It creates a glowing orb that follows your wand, perfect for seeing in the dark." He spoke the incantation, and a warm golden orb bloomed at the tip of his wand, floating gracefully in the air before fading into a faint shimmer.

With a flick of his wrist, he demonstrated another spell. "*Scáth Díon*, a light shield. Quick, easy to learn, and excellent for defending yourself against most spells. Though, naturally, stronger magic might penetrate it."

Fenwick gestured to a nearby leaf on the ground. "And here's *Éirigh*, a levitation charm." With a low murmur of the spell, the leaf floated upward, spinning lazily in the air before settling gently back on the ground. "It's simple, perfect for moving small objects. But try it on something too large, and you'll start to feel the strain."

Clara watched each spell with wide eyes, her mind alive with possibilities. "There are practical charms, too," Fenwick added. "*Tobar Uisce* for conjuring fresh water, for example. You'll use them often, and with practice, they'll feel as natural as breathing."

Fenwick's gaze softened as he looked at Clara. "Learn these foundational spells, and you'll build the discipline to handle more advanced magic. Respect magic's balance, and you'll rarely feel the cost."

Clara shivered, not from fear, but from the weight of understanding. Magic wasn't just a gift; it was a delicate dance of intention and consequence.

"Now," Fenwick said, stepping back to create space, "let's see how you fare. We'll begin with Solas Ceo."

"Now," Fenwick said, stepping back, and fixing Clara with a sharp look. "All right, Miss Clara. Magic begins with focus and intention. Let's see how you do with Solas Ceo. It's not about force; clarity of mind creates clarity of magic."

Clara adjusted her grip on her wand, her palms slightly damp with nerves. She repeated the words silently: Solas Ceo. Solas Ceo. The sound of them filled her thoughts. Closing her eyes briefly, she imagined a golden thread pulling her forward, soft and steady in the dark. She lifted her wand and whispered, "Solas Ceo."

Nothing happened.

Her shoulders sagged as a wave of doubt crept in. "I didn't feel anything," she admitted, her voice edged with frustration.

"Again," Fenwick said, his tone calm but firm. "Magic responds to belief, Miss Clara. Picture the light clearly, its warmth, its purpose. Let it flow through you."

Clara closed her eyes again, this time steadying her breathing. She envisioned the light more vividly, its glow radiating from within her. Opening her eyes, she lifted her wand and said with quiet determination, "Solas Ceo."

A faint flicker appeared at the wand's tip, like a hesitant star in a cloudy sky. It wasn't much, but it was there.

Fenwick's lips curved into a small, approving smile. "A promising start. Now, hold it steady. Magic is like a flame. It needs gentle tending, not force."

Clara adjusted her grip on her wand, her brow furrowed as she whispered, "Solas Ceo." A faint flicker sparked, then fizzled out. She sighed, her shoulders sagging.

"Take a breath, Miss Clara," Fenwick said gently. "Magic isn't forced; it's invited. Picture the light, not just its shape, but its warmth. Feel it, and let it flow."

Clara closed her eyes, steadying her breath. She whispered the words again, her voice soft but certain. This time, a faint orb glowed at the wand's tip. Her heart leapt as it steadied, the warmth spreading through her fingers.

Fenwick smiled, his eyes alight with pride. "Well done, Miss Clara. Your first spell is always the hardest."

Encouraged by her success, and after completing the spell a few more times, they moved on. Fenwick stood beside her, showing the movement with his wand. "Now, Scáth Díon is a protective spell. It's like weaving an invisible cloak around you, shielding you from harm. Think of it as an extension of yourself."

Clara mimicked his motion, raising her wand. She whispered, "Scáth Díon," but nothing happened. The air around her remained still.

"Take your time," Fenwick said, his voice patient. "Magic, especially defensive spells, requires a clear purpose. Picture the shield forming around you. Feel its strength as if it's already there."

Clara closed her eyes, imagining the shield, a glowing barrier encasing her like armour. She could almost feel its warmth, soft yet unyielding. Opening her eyes, she lifted her wand again and said, "Scáth Díon."

This time, a faint shimmer flickered in the air around her. It was barely visible, but it was there.

Fenwick's face lit up with pride. "Well done, Miss Clara! It's small now, but it will grow stronger with practice. Let's refine it."

Clara repeated the spell several more times, each attempt making the shield more visible and solid. By the final try, the barrier shimmered like a bubble of light, encasing her fully. She grinned, her confidence growing.

Next, Fenwick guided Clara to a small leaf resting on a table. "Levitation is one of the oldest spells in existence," he explained. "Éirigh. Simple yet precise. Ask the object to rise, don't command it."

He demonstrated, his wand moving in a graceful arc as the leaf floated effortlessly into the air. Clara watched in amazement as it drifted in a lazy circle before settling back down.

Her turn. She raised her wand, repeating the incantation

softly. "Éirigh." The leaf twitched but didn't lift.

"Control, not force," Fenwick reminded her. "Magic is a partnership, not a demand."

Clara adjusted her stance, taking a steadying breath. She imagined the leaf rising gently, as light as a breeze lifting a leaf. "Éirigh," she said again, her voice calm yet determined.

The leaf rose, wobbling slightly but staying up. Clara's face lit up with excitement. "I did it!"

"Excellent," Fenwick said, his tone proud. "Now guide it. Small movements. Let the magic flow naturally."

Clara guided the leaf in a small circle before letting it settle back on the table. The satisfaction in her chest felt electric.

"Let's end with something refreshing," Fenwick said, gesturing to an empty cup. "Tobar Uisce. A water-conjuring spell. This one is about flow. Imagine water pouring from a hidden spring. Precision is key."

Clara lifted her wand, her excitement bubbling over. "Tobar Uisce!" she exclaimed, but the spell burst forth too eagerly. A jet of water shot past the cup, soaking Fenwick.

Clara froze, mortified. "I'm so sorry!" she blurted.

Fenwick blinked, then burst into hearty laughter, soaked by the water. "No harm done, Miss Clara. Though perhaps a touch of finesse next time."

He uttered, "Tirimardra," drying himself as he motioned with his wand. "Now, try again. Picture the water filling the cup, not flooding it. A gentle touch, Miss Clara."

Clara took a calming breath, steadying her focus. "Tobar Uisce," she whispered. This time, a steady trickle of water poured from her wand, filling the cup perfectly. She beamed at the sight.

"Well done," Fenwick said, his voice warm. "Magic responds best to balance. Let excitement drive your curiosity but temper it with control."

*

By the time they wrapped up for the day, Clara's arms ached, and her focus felt stretched thin, but the pride swelling in her chest was undeniable. Fenwick's approving nods and patient guidance had carried her through each spell, leaving her both exhausted and exhilarated.

As they walked back to the manor, Fenwick placed a hand on her shoulder. "Magic is not just about wielding power. It's about understanding yourself, your intentions, and the world around you. Today you've taken your first steps on that journey."

Clara looked at her wand, the wood warm against her palm. She was starting to feel like she belonged. She smiled, her heart light with the thrill of possibility.

Magic wasn't just within her; it was her. And she was excited to see where it would take her next.

*

As they walked back towards the manor, with a hesitant look at Fenwick, she cleared her throat.

"Fenwick, is there … like, a spell to charge my phone? I mean, magic can do almost anything else, so I thought maybe …" Her voice trailed off, feeling slightly ridiculous for even asking.

Fenwick raised an eyebrow, a bemused smile tugging at his lips. "A spell to charge a phone? You modern witches are quite inventive with your requests." He held his hand out for her phone, turning it over as if inspecting a relic. "Fortunately for you, there is a spell for such things, although I don't think it's intended purpose was to boost phone batteries, but it should still work."

He handed the phone back to Clara, drawing his wand with a flourish. "Repeat after me: 'Luas Solas Imbue'. It roughly means 'swift light to fill'. A fitting phrase for charging your strange non-magical contraptions."

Clara took a deep breath and raised her wand, pointing it at the phone. "Luas Solas Imbue," she said, her voice steady. A faint golden light glowed from her wand and flowed into the phone. The battery indicator immediately shot to full.

"It worked!" Clara said, grinning. "That's amazing! Thanks, Fenwick."

"You're welcome," he said with a proud smile.

"What about a spell for boosting signal?" Clara said optimistically.

"Charging a phone is one thing, but boosting your signal? That's another matter entirely."

Clara's face fell. "So, no spell for that?"

Fenwick shook his head. "Unfortunately not. The wards protecting us from the non-magical world are ancient and powerful. They repel all outside interference, including your beloved technology. I'm afraid your signal will always struggle here."

Clara sighed, tucking her phone into her pocket. "Well, it was worth a try."

Fenwick chuckled, giving her a reassuring nod. "Consider it a blessing in disguise. Perhaps this is an opportunity to embrace the magical world more fully. After all, you can't learn about magic by using that thing."

Clara smiled faintly. "I guess you've got a point." But as she followed Fenwick out of the training grounds, she still wished she could FaceTime her dad and Chloe without the signal being poor.

As Clara walked silently, she thought about how her new world would make it difficult to remain a part of her old one.

*

The next day, Clara was wandering the halls, her thoughts spinning like autumn leaves caught in a breeze. As she passed by the Starbound Library, voices drifted through the cracked door. She slowed, recognising Cassius's sharp tone.

"... and now she's here, and everything's suddenly about her," Cassius said bitterly. "As if she's the future of the family. What has she done to deserve that? She didn't even know we existed until recently."

A quieter, unfamiliar voice responded, though Clara couldn't make out the words. Cassius didn't seem to care.

"Don't make excuses," he snapped. "Do you know how hard I've worked to keep the Nightfall name respected? I've done everything expected of me, studied every tradition, learned every bloody rule. And now they're acting like she's the saviour of the family."

Clara's stomach twisted, her fingers tightening on the edge of the doorframe. She hadn't wanted to listen, but she couldn't tear herself away. Cassius's voice carried a frustration she hadn't heard before, his bitterness sharp enough to cut through the air.

"She doesn't even understand what it means to be a Nightfall," Cassius continued, his voice dropping to a harsh whisper. "But she gets to stroll in and take centre stage, just because she has the name. It's not fair."

Clara stepped back, her pulse quickening. The resentment in his voice wasn't just anger; it was hurt, a raw wound hidden beneath his arrogant exterior. She backed away from the library door, her heart heavy with a mix of guilt and frustration.

As she retreated down the hall, Clara tried to shake off his words. She hadn't asked to be part of this world, let alone the centre of attention. But now that she was, could she ever convince someone like Cassius that she belonged, or would she always be an outsider in his eyes?

Chapter 8: Family Gathering

The days passed in a blur of lessons, introductions, and uneasy silences. Then, without warning… a young man with short dark hair and a mischievous smirk strolled into the entrance hall. His long, stylish cloak matched his confident air, blending charm with a hint of rebellion.

"Clara, this is your cousin, Rowan Nightfall," Hazel said warmly. Rowan's casual confidence immediately put Clara at ease.

"So, you're the famous 'Lost Witch of Nightfall'," Rowan said with a laugh, leaning in conspiratorially. "The magical press is having a field day. The family's doing its best to hush it up, but let's just say you've made quite the entrance."

Clara's cheeks warmed as a mix of embarrassment and curiosity bubbled up. "I had no idea I'd be that … interesting," she replied, half-joking.

Rowan chuckled, giving her shoulder a friendly squeeze. "Don't worry, Cousin. Welcome to the family. And trust me, around here, scandal is practically a family tradition." He winked, giving Clara a bit of comfort, a connection to someone her own age who seemed to understand the whirlwind she was caught up in.

Clara looked at Rowan, absorbing the news. Only moments earlier, Rowen had told her the newspapers were calling her, *The Lost Witch of Nightfall*, as they were apparently calling her. Her mind whirled with questions, but she barely had a moment to process them before her grandmother entered, as graceful and composed as ever.

"Hello, Rowan," their grandmother greeted, a hint of surprise in her voice. "You're early."

Rowan grinned, mischief twinkling in his eyes. "I wanted to meet my cousin before the rest of the guests arrived."

"Guests?" Clara asked, feeling a fresh wave of nervousness.

Her grandmother smiled. "It was meant to be a surprise, darling, but I suppose it no longer matters." She gestured to a beautifully wrapped box in her hands. "I've chosen a dress for you, something truly special. Tonight, the entire family will be gathering to officially welcome you. We want to introduce you properly."

Clara's heart skipped a beat as she glanced from Rowan to her grandmother. Her stomach fluttered with a mix of excitement and apprehension. Meeting her extended family sounded daunting, especially with how posh and imposing some of them already seemed. She tried to return her grandmother's smile, grateful but still anxious.

"A gathering ... for me?" Clara managed, her voice laced with anxiety.

"Of course, dear. It's not every day we welcome someone into the fold, a member of the family we never knew existed." her grandmother said, her tone affectionate. "They're all coming just to meet you."

Clara took a deep breath, trying to quiet the nervous energy buzzing inside her. Meeting her new family felt daunting enough, but the idea of so many unfamiliar faces all at once made her heart race.

With that, her uncle strode into the room, his tone sharp as he spoke. "I trust you're prepared for the gathering this evening. Some of the family are eager to meet the newest Nightfall, though I suspect many will be disappointed; she is just like the Hollowers she grew up with. She knows nothing about our ways."

"That's enough, Cassius!" Clara's grandmother interjected, her voice sharp and commanding. "Clara *is* a member of this family, and you will just have to accept it."

Her tone softened as she turned to Clara, her gaze filled with warmth. "Clara, darling, know that you're not a disappointment to us. You'll find your place here, and you'll do so on your own terms."

Her attention returned to Cassius, her expression hardening. "I'm not sure why you expect Clara to know everything overnight. After all, the magical world wasn't built in a day."

Clara shifted, unsure whether to speak up or stay quiet. Her uncle's words fed into the self-doubt about belonging to their world, but her grandmother's reassurance gave her just enough courage to respond.

"I might not have grown up in this world, but that doesn't mean I don't belong here," Clara said, her voice steady despite the nerves fluttering in her chest.

"Yes, Uncle, she may not have grown up in our world, but that doesn't make her any less of a Nightfall," Rowan said with a faint smirk. "Afraid you'll have to share your inheritance with another member of the family?"

Clara glanced at her grandmother, drawing strength from her warm expression, then met Cassius's gaze directly. "I'm still learning, but I'm not going to let anyone tell me I don't deserve to be part of this family."

Cassius tutted and walked off.

But Clara wasn't so sure. The weight of expectation pressed heavily on her.

*

Later that day, Clara found Hazel in the kitchen, where dough was kneading itself for the evening's bread, bowls were being whisked furiously, vegetables chopped with precision, and sauce bubbled in a cauldron-like pot. It was a hive of activity, all humming with magic. The warmth of the kitchen wrapped around Clara like a comforting blanket, soothing her nerves. For a moment, she stood quietly, watching Hazel guide the chaos with her wand, every flick deliberate and assured.

"Miss Clara," Hazel said without looking up, a knowing smile on her face. "What's on your mind?"

Clara hesitated, fidgeting with her hands. "It's … tonight. The gathering. What if I embarrass myself? Or the family? Cassius made it sound like I'll be under a microscope."

Hazel turned to Clara, her expression kind but resolute. Forgive my bluntness … Ignore him," she said, her tone tolerating no argument. "He likes to act as though he's the only Nightfall who matters. Be yourself, and you'll do just fine. I can give you a few pointers, though, if it'll ease your nerves."

Clara nodded quickly, her shoulders relaxing a little. "Please."

Hazel gestured for her to sit at the kitchen table. "First," she began, "remember to keep your posture straight and your chin up. Confidence speaks volumes, even if you don't feel it."

Clara straightened in her chair, trying to look composed.

Hazel chuckled. "That's a start. Now, when you're introduced to someone, offer a firm handshake. Not too strong; no one likes to feel like they're wrestling, but no limp hands either. It shows you respect yourself and the other person."

Clara nodded, mentally filing that away.

"And when you're at the table," Hazel continued,

"start from the outside of the cutlery and work your way in with each course. Use the forks and knives closest to your plate for the main course."

Clara groaned softly. "I do find it a little confusing, all the cutlery."

Hazel laughed. "It's not as complicated as it sounds, dear. Just follow your grandmother's lead if you're unsure. And if you're asked a question, take your time to answer. Speak clearly, but don't feel like you need to fill every silence. Sometimes, it's better to let others do the talking."

She paused, then leaned in slightly, her voice lowering. "And one more thing about the magical side of things. If anyone mentions an old tradition or custom you don't understand, don't try to pretend you know. Just ask politely. Most of them will appreciate your interest far more than false confidence."

Clara exhaled slowly, feeling a little more at ease. "Anything else?"

Hazel tilted her head thoughtfully. "Just one more thing. You're a Nightfall now. This isn't about being perfect; it's about being yourself, with a touch of refinement. Let them see who you are. The rest will come in time."

Clara smiled, feeling a spark of confidence. "Thanks, Hazel. I needed that."

"Anytime, dear," Hazel said, patting her hand. "Now, off with you. I've got lots of food to make, and you've got a family to charm."

As Clara left the kitchen, she felt a little lighter. She might not have all the answers, but with Hazel's advice and a little practice, she knew she could face the evening ahead.

Throughout the morning, Hazel and Bran filled the manor with enchanted bouquets, their vibrant blooms shimmering with magic and filling the air with the scent of sweet honey, sugared berries and whispers of spice so that it was warm and comforting.

Hazel, ever efficient, directed the arrangements with a practised eye, placing bouquets in vases that floated beside her as she inspected every detail. Bran, the groundskeeper, worked quietly alongside her, his touch coaxing the flowers into perfect bloom and adding subtle charms that made the petals shimmer.

Clara watched from the side, taking in the grandeur and beauty of it all. Yet a part of her couldn't shake the feeling of being slightly out of place in the midst of such finery.

Her grandmother rested a reassuring hand on Clara's arm. "You'll do wonderfully, darling. Just be yourself."

Clara managed a small smile, nodding as she looked around. She was beginning to understand that being a part of this family meant living up to expectations, but also, perhaps, discovering parts of herself she hadn't yet known.

*

Clara stood in front of the mirror, smoothing down the silken fabric of her dress. The deep emerald green shimmered as it moved. It was elegant, perfectly fitted, and undeniably formal. She bit her lip, fidgeting with the neckline, her reflection staring back uncertainly.

A soft knock at the door broke into her thoughts, and her grandmother stepped inside. Her presence was as poised as ever, her robes elegant and regal. Selene's gaze softened as she took in Clara's appearance, a kind smile touching her lips. "You look beautiful, my darling," she said, stepping closer. With a flick of her wand, she swept Clara's hair into an elegant style, securing it with a delicate gold clip. "There. Now you're ready."

"It feels strange. I've never worn anything like this," Clara admitted, her voice faltering. "What if I embarrass myself?"

Her grandmother placed a gentle hand on Clara's shoulder, her tone calm and steady. "You won't. You carry the Nightfall name, and tonight is simply the beginning of your journey into it. Grace isn't about perfection. It is about confidence. Walk tall, and no one will notice your nerves. I bet you're stronger than you realise."

Clara nodded, taking a deep breath to steady herself. "Thank you, Grandmother," she said quietly. As her grandmother turned to leave, Clara hesitated before adding, "Grandmother … you look beautiful too."

Her grandmother paused, her expression softening further. "Thank you, darling," she said warmly. "Come along now. Our guests are waiting, and I've no doubt they will be just as proud of you as I am."

*

The evening began, and Nightfall Manor was transformed into a vision of old-world grandeur. Laughter and conversation wove through the halls, mingling with the soft clink of crystal glasses and the quiet hum of enchantments quivering through the chandeliers. Clara stood at her grandmother's side, nerves coiled tightly in her stomach as she watched guests trickle in.

Each one looked like they belonged in some ancient portrait: elegant robes, tailored suits, and polished expressions that masked whatever secrets they carried.

Confidence seemed to radiate off them in waves. Was that something they were born with, or had it been taught to them, like an art form?

She could feel it, the undercurrent of emotions threading through the room. Excitement flickered in quick, bright bursts, while colder, heavier branches of suspicion and curiosity lingered on the edges. And then there was pride, warm and steady, emanating from her grandparents, subtle but constant, like a pulse of magic in the air.

Clara took a slow breath, trying to focus, but the stress of it all pressed in, too much, too fast. For a brief moment, she wondered if they could feel her nerves just as keenly as she felt theirs.

As Clara's grandmother excused herself to greet another guest, Clara found herself momentarily untethered, hovering by the grand marble staircase. She caught snippets of hushed conversations as people moved past, their voices a mix of amusement, calculation, and something else, concern.

"… haven't heard his name in years, but apparently, he's escaped. They think he had help from his followers."

"If the Dark Wizard is free again, the Assembly need to act quickly before it's too late. It was dark times before he was finally caught."

Clara's breath caught.

She turned slightly, pretending to adjust her bracelet, her ears straining. Two older men stood near the golden chandeliers, their expressions unreadable beneath the faint shimmer.

"The Assembly must act quickly," one of them murmured, glancing over his shoulder as if fearing unseen ears. "If they wait, he'll have time to gather his strength. He won't stay in the shadows forever."

A woman scoffed softly, though there was no humour in it. "You think this was chance? His followers helped him. The prison was impenetrable, yet somehow, he's gone. That kind of coordination doesn't happen overnight."

The air in the room suddenly felt thinner, the warmth of the golden chandeliers failing to chase away the creeping chill curling at the edges of Clara's thoughts.

Another man let out a quiet breath, shaking his head. "We need to face the truth: if we don't stop him now, he will become unstoppable. He almost destroyed the magical and non-magical worlds last time"

Clara's stomach twisted.

She didn't even know she had stepped back until her shoulder bumped the wall. A sudden wave of nausea rolled through her, not fear, not exactly, but something deeper, something unnameable. It spread through her chest like a phantom touch, pressing, clawing at the edges of her thoughts.

She sucked in a slow breath, trying to steady herself.

The guests continued their quiet conversation, unaware of the way Clara's pulse roared in her ears, drowning out the laughter and clinking glasses around her.

She had no reason to feel this unsettled.

And yet … somewhere, in the pit of her stomach, she felt it.

She decided to step away, the grand hall suddenly feeling too crowded, the warmth of the light too bright against the rising unease curling inside her. It wasn't fear, not exactly, but something deeper, something she couldn't name.

Before she could steady herself, Cassius's sharp voice

cut through the murmur of conversations as he approached, his polished smile doing little to mask the edge in his tone.

"Ah, the prodigal Nightfall," he said, his words dripping with sarcasm. "You must be enjoying all this attention. Quite the leap from … wherever it is you've come from."

Clara stiffened, the sting of his words landing harder than she'd expected. She should be used to this by now, but tonight, it felt like a thousand eyes were watching.

But this time, she refused to shrink back. Instead, she squared her shoulders and met his gaze, her voice calm. "Actually, I'm still getting used to it, but I'll manage. Thanks for your concern, Cassius."

His smirk remained, but his eyes gleamed with something sharper. "I suppose it's a lot to take in. After all, not everyone is prepared for the responsibilities that come with the Nightfall name."

Clara tilted her head slightly, her grip tightening on the glass in her hand. "You're right. It is a lot to take in. But what's funny is that everyone here seems to think they know who I am or what I'm capable of without even bothering to get to know me. It's almost as if they're more interested in judging me rather than helping me."

Cassius's smirk faltered, just for a fraction of a second.

"I'm simply being honest," he recovered quickly. "Not everyone belongs with the magical elite."

Clara's voice sharpened. "Maybe you should worry less about where I came from and more about proving why you belong."

For a moment, the air between them crackled like static. Cassius opened his mouth, but no words came out.

Clara didn't wait for a response. She turned and walked away, her heart pounding. Her hands trembled slightly, but she held her head high.

Just as Clara was beginning to feel like a spectacle on display, a warm hand touched her arm. She turned to see a woman with a gentle smile and kind eyes, her long red hair and simple elegance making her stand out in a room filled with excess.

"It's lovely to meet you, Clara," Evelyn Nightfall said softly. "This must all feel overwhelming, but you'll find your place."

Clara relaxed instantly. "Thank you. Honestly, it feels like a dream I can't wake from."

Evelyn chuckled, a knowing look in her eyes. "I felt much the same when I married into the family. They're lovely in their own ways, but a bit … much, if you know what I mean." She winked, and Clara laughed, feeling like she'd finally found someone she could confide in.

*

The night stretched on, guests filtering in and out of conversation. She met Lord Edmund Ashbourne, whose presence was as severe as his silver-streaked hair, his gaze appraising her as one might inspect an ancient artefact.

"A late bloomer, I hear," he mused. "Quite the adjustment for you, I imagine."

"Yes, it's all new, but I'm learning quickly," Clara replied, refusing to let his quiet scrutiny unnerve her.

"Good," he said simply, before moving on, leaving an unsettling sensation in his absence.

As the evening began to wind down, Clara found herself standing by one of the tall windows, Evelyn by her side.

"You know, Clara," Evelyn said, a thoughtful look in her eyes, "people are drawn to you, even if they don't know why. You bring something this family needs."

Clara frowned slightly. "What do you mean?"

Evelyn smiled gently. "You're fresh eyes, an open heart. This family … sometimes they forget how to see things as they are. You remind them, just by being here."

Clara let the words settle over her. Not because of her family name but because of who she was.

As the final guests lingered in smaller clusters, sipping the last of their enchanted wines and exchanging pleasantries that felt more like calculated manoeuvres, Clara slipped away towards the grand staircase. The room felt stifling, as though the responsibility of the Nightfall name had settled on her shoulders like an unseen cloak, growing heavier with every passing interaction.

She took a slow breath, trying to shake the lingering unease from overhearing the conversation about the Dark Wizard. The words looped in her mind like a whisper carried by an unseen wind. It wasn't fear, not exactly; it was something deeper. Something she couldn't name.

Just as she steadied herself, her grandmother appeared at her side, her expression unreadable but her presence grounding.

"You handled yourself well tonight," her grandmother said, her voice softer than Clara had expected.

Clara hesitated. "I don't think Cassius would agree."

Her grandmother's lips curled in the faintest trace of amusement. "Cassius is used to being unchallenged. That is no fault of yours."

Clara glanced back at the dwindling crowd, where Cassius stood speaking in hushed tones with Lord Ashbourne. "I still don't understand why he hates me so much."

Her grandmother exhaled slowly, as though weighing her words. "It is not hate, Clara. It is fear. He fears what your presence means. Change is an unsettling force for those who have built their lives upon certainty."

Clara thought about that, about Cassius's sharp remarks and how they barely masked the tension behind his eyes. Fear? It felt strange to think of him that way, but maybe, just maybe, her grandmother was right.

*

As the last guests finally left, Clara let out a quiet breath, relishing the rare moment of silence as the huge doors shut behind the final departure. The manor felt different now, less like a spectacle, more like a labyrinth of secrets settling back into place.

She wandered towards the nearest window, gazing out at the moonlit grounds. The sky was an endless stretch of ink, the stars scattered like dust across the heavens. But something about the night felt ... wrong.

The wind had stilled.

The torches along the courtyard flickered as if struggling against an unseen force.

For a brief moment, the shadows beneath the great iron gates seemed to lengthen, stretching unnaturally, curling like grasping fingers towards the house.

Clara's breath hitched. Just a trick of the light. That's all.

A cool hand touched her shoulder, and she nearly jumped, only to find her grandmother standing beside her once more.

"Go and rest, Clara," she said, her voice kind. "Tonight was only the beginning."

Clara swallowed the urge to ask what she meant.

Instead, she gave a small nod and stepped away from the window, but the feeling of something unseen watching her did not fade.

*

Back in her room, she peeled off the elegant dress, slipping into more comfortable robes. She should have felt relief, but her mind was tangled with too many thoughts: the whispers of the Dark Wizard, the tension with Cassius, Evelyn's kindness, the way the torches outside had struggled against the windless night.

She climbed into bed, pulling the blankets around her. As sleep began to take her, her last thought was not of her newfound family, nor of her place within it.

It was of shadows creeping beneath the gates. And of the lingering sense that something, someone, was waiting.

Chapter 9: Magical Invitation

Clara awoke to her phone vibrating: a text from her dad. It was now part of their routine to text daily, since FaceTime rarely worked.

Dad: *Morning my beautiful girl. I hope you're not pushing yourself too hard. Remember to be kind to yourself. I love you xx*

Clara smiled as she read the text. Her dad knew her well. She had a tendency to push herself too hard at times, determined to be successful at whatever she did.

Clara: *Good morning dad. Yeah, I know I work myself too hard at times, I am working on being kind to myself. It's not always easy when I'm trying to navigate this new world. Remember to eat plenty of salad and vegetables, just like the doctor said. And I love you more xx*

Dad: *I loved you first. Have a great day darling xx*

Clara: *xx*

As Clara sat up in bed, she noticed a warm amber glow spilling across her bed. Blinking, she noticed it came from her windowsill, where a strange, glowing leaf rested. Rising cautiously, her heart quickened as she stepped closer.

The slender leaf pulsed with a magical glow, its veins alive, like fire trapped within its delicate frame. Entranced, Clara brushed her fingers against it.

As Clara touched the leaf, it unravelled like a thread of light, transforming into a warm, glowing parchment that tingled against her fingers. Curiosity burning, Clara began to unfold it, but before she could make out a single word, the letters lifted off the page. They shimmered in the air, arranging themselves into glowing, golden shapes. Her breath hitched as a deep, resonant voice filled the room. It was neither loud nor overpowering, but calm and steady, carrying an authority that seemed to seep into her very bones.

"Welcome, Clara Nightfall," the voice intoned, rich and steady. "By ancient magical law, I invite you to Crowstone Academy of Magic, a haven for the gifted to grow, challenge themselves, and realise their potential."

The voice continued, each word steeped in significance.

"You will enter as an Ascendant Year Eight student. This year marks a critical point in the journey of mastery, where young witches and wizards learn not only to harness their gifts but to wield them with purpose and skill. Though your journey begins later than most, your lineage and potential shall guide you. Support will be provided to ensure you rise to meet the standards expected of you."

The voice continued to explain the structure of Crowstone Academy.

"At Crowstone, you will tread paths both ancient and rare, mastering the secrets of enchantments, wielding the forces of nature, and preserving the sacred balance of our world. Magic is not merely a gift; it is a bond between you and the magical world. Your courage, focus, and determination will be tested, and if you prevail, you will carve your name into our history."

The letters shimmered and began to drift back towards the parchment, their glow fading as they settled back onto the page. The voice lingered for a moment, the final words echoing softly.

"Crowstone welcomes you, Clara Nightfall. May you honour yourself and our academy. Your magical development awaits you."

The room fell silent, the parchment now still and unassuming in her hands, as though it had never come alive. But Clara could still feel the magic in the air, lingering like a whispered secret just out of reach, and in her heart, she knew everything was about to change.

This was only the beginning of her magical journey.

Clara stood in silence, her mind reeling. She had been invited to Crowstone Academy, not just as a student, but as a Nightfall. She was expected to excel, to live up to a standard she hadn't yet comprehended. This wasn't just school; it was the beginning of something greater, a place in a world she hadn't even known she belonged to until recently.

Clutching the parchment, Clara felt both excitement and hesitation building within her. Crowstone was no ordinary academy, and she would have to step into a world that would demand everything of her: her curiosity, her courage, her very heart. Clara was unsure if she was ready for that.

*

Once ready for her busy day, Clara made her way to the Grand Dining Hall. She sat at the dining table, the letter from Crowstone Academy of Magic resting in front of her like a beacon of possibility. Her grandmother sat to her right, sipping tea from a delicate porcelain cup, her posture as composed as ever. Clara ran her fingers over the embossed crest of the letter, her emotions swirling.

"I see you've received your invitation," her grandmother said with a proud smile. "Crowstone is no ordinary school. It's a beacon of excellence, shaping the leaders and innovators of our magical world."

She paused, then added, "And it's not just limited to this country. Some of the most prominent families from around the world make the journey to send their children there. It's reputation speaks for itself. Its name carries weight far beyond these borders, a testament to its legacy and education."

"There are other fine magical schools," her grandfather interjected, the shimmering headlines of his newspaper paused mid-flow, as if attuned to his every thought.

"But Crowstone," he continued, "is among the best. A school steeped in history, tradition, and excellence. The education there rivals, if not surpasses, any magical institution you'll find abroad." He flicked his gaze towards Clara, his sharp eyes studying her for a moment. "You should consider yourself fortunate."

Before Clara could muster a response, the articles resumed as if they had never paused. Moving images of a magical event played briefly above the page, accompanied by a quiet narration.

Her grandfather's words, while brief, lingered in her mind. The weight of the school's reputation, her family's expectations, and the sheer enormity of what lay ahead pressed down on her. Even the magical newspaper, with its seamless ability to adapt and respond to its reader, seemed like yet another reminder of how extraordinary her new world was and how far she had yet to go.

Clara felt a knot form in her stomach, half from nerves and half from the enormity of what her grandparents were saying. "So, it's like the magical version of a really posh private school?" she ventured, trying to wrap her head around it.

Clara's grandmother chuckled softly at what Clara had said, but her grandfather looked up sharply from his newspaper, which promptly paused mid-headline. "Posh," he repeated, his tone carrying a faint air of disdain, as though the word itself were beneath him.

Clara glanced at him curiously, not expecting a lecture.

"The term 'posh', my dear Clara," he began, sitting back in his chair, "is a rather simplistic way for Hollowers to describe refinement, wealth, and taste. It's an abbreviation, in fact, though I suspect most who use it don't know that. It originally stood for 'Port out, starboard home', a reference to the most desirable accommodations on ships, away from the sun's heat during long voyages. Over time, it was used to describe those of privilege."

Clara blinked, surprised by the explanation. "I didn't know that," she admitted.

"Few do," he said briskly, with a wave of his hand. "In magical society, however, refinement isn't about superficial appearances or wealth; it's about legacy, contribution, and power. The word 'posh' feels insignificant compared to the traditions we uphold."

Clara tilted her head, a slight smile tugging at her lips. "So, does that mean we're not posh?"

Her grandfather gave a rare, indulgent smile. "We are Nightfalls, my dear Clara. Nightfalls are beyond 'posh'."

With that, the enchanted text on the newspaper resumed its flow, leaving Clara trying to decide if she was impressed or slightly amused.

Selene's eyes lingered on Clara, her expression measured. "Darling, Crowstone Academy will teach you how to become the best *you* that you can be."

Clara glanced at the letter, her fingers brushing against its shimmering surface. "It sounds incredible," she said honestly, "but … I can't help wondering if I even have a choice in this."

Her grandmother's teacup paused mid-air, her sharp

eyes narrowing slightly. "Of course you have a choice," she replied smoothly, though her tone carried a hint of surprise. "You are a Nightfall, Clara; no one will force you to walk a path you do not wish to take. That being said, the opportunity before you is exceptional."

Clara bit her lip, her voice soft. "It's just … it's a big decision. Starting over at a new school, leaving my dad, my friends … my whole life behind. I need to think about it."

Her grandmother set her teacup down gently, folding her hands in front of her. "Of course, my dear. I understand the importance of such a decision." Her voice softened, but there was still an edge of expectation. "But let me tell you this: Crowstone is not just a school. It is a gateway. It will teach you not only to master your magic but to understand yourself and your place in this world. The magical world is vast and full of potential, Clara. You may feel tied to your old life, but this new one is waiting for you to claim it."

Clara's fingers tightened around the edge of the letter. "It's not just about school," she murmured, her gaze flicking around the Grand Dining Hall. "It's about everything: this world, this family, this … legacy. It feels like so much all at once."

Selene studied her for a moment, her expression softening. "You are right, my darling. Being a Nightfall is more than just a name; it is a responsibility and a privilege. But it is also what you make of it. You have the chance to write your own story within this legacy."

Clara nodded slowly, though her mind raced. "I'll speak to my dad about it. I owe him that much. This decision affects him too."

Her grandmother inclined her head, a flicker of respect crossing her features. "A wise choice. Speak with him, take the time you need to decide. Clara, the world of magic is not something you can ignore forever. Sooner or later, it will call to you."

Clara glanced at the letter one last time before meeting her Selene's gaze. "Thank you, Grandmother. I'll think about it carefully."

As the meal ended and Clara rose from the table, she caught her grandmother's eye again, sensing both the pride and the expectation lingering in her gaze. Clara didn't know what her decision would be yet, but one thing was certain: she wasn't going to rush into it. She would approach it on her own terms.

Chapter 10: The Cloak, Crest and a Magical Opportunity

A few days later, Clara sat silently at the breakfast table, her thoughts circling the decision about Crowstone Academy. It felt like a betrayal of the life she'd always known. Yet denying herself the chance to learn magic and become the witch she was meant to be might be the greater betrayal. Whatever she decided, she wasn't going to let anyone else choose for her.

Across the table, her grandfather lowered his newspaper and fixed her with a piercing gaze. "A Nightfall must maintain a sense of independence, even at your age," he said firmly. "No witch or wizard walks the world without coin in their purse. Today, we'll open your account at Elderstone Bank."

Clara nodded, unsure whether to feel nervous or excited.

*

The carriage landed and rattled down Hidden Row, a magical thoroughfare alive with glowing storefronts and magical wares. Clara's gaze darted between displays of potions, iridescent robes, and enchanted quills, but her thoughts lingered on what lay ahead.

Elderstone Bank loomed before them, its towering marble front gleaming under the morning sun, guarded by watchful stone gargoyles. Clara's breath hitched as they approached.

"It's … impressive," she murmured, glancing at her grandmother.

Her grandmother smiled. "Elderstone is more than a bank … it is a vault of wealth, magic, and legacy. For centuries, it has safeguarded the fortunes of the most powerful magical families. Including ours."

As they entered through the silver-etched doors, Clara felt the weight of history settle over her. The vaulted ceilings shimmered with shifting murals of ancient magical triumphs, and enchanted quills darted beside staff who moved with absolute precision. It was overwhelming and oddly exhilarating.

An elderly banker approached, bowing. "Lord Eldric, Lady Selene. And this must be Miss Clara?"

"Yes," her grandmother said with a nod. "We're here to open her account."

They made their way to a private room draped in velvet, where a crystal vial sat waiting, glowing faintly. The banker explained its purpose; a drop of blood was needed to ensure the highest level of security, binding the account to its user to prevent unauthorised access. "When you want to access your account, you press on this gold tablet, which will verify who you are."

Clara hesitated before holding out her hand. As the wand pricked her finger, she watched a single drop of blood float into the vial and vanish.

"Your account is now bound to you alone, Miss Clara," the banker said. "And the initial deposit?" he asked, looking to her grandparents.

"100,000 gold crests," her grandfather said without hesitation.

Clara blinked, stunned by the number. "Is that … a normal amount? It seems a lot!" she whispered to her grandmother.

Selene's smile carried a trace of amusement. "For a Nightfall, yes. This ensures your independence."

The banker handed her a midnight-blue pouch embroidered with vivid runes. "How much would you like to carry on your person?"

"One thousand gold crests should suffice," her grandmother instructed.

Clara watched as the banker performed a series of precise wand movements, coins materialising in neat stacks before vanishing into the pouch. "This enchanted pouch is yours. It will always return to you if lost and is impervious to theft. Simply state the amount you require, and it will provide the exact sum."

Clara held the pouch, amazed at how light it was. She reached in and took out a coin, its intricate design catching the light. One side bore a phoenix, its wings defiant, the other, an elder tree, its roots sprawling and branches stretching towards the heavens.

"What do the designs mean?" Clara asked, curiosity piqued.

"The phoenix represents resilience and renewal," the banker explained. "And the elder tree symbolises strength and legacy. Both are central to our magical heritage."

Clara nodded, slipping the coin back into the pouch. As they left the bank, her grandmother placed a hand on her shoulder. "This is just the beginning, Clara. The Nightfall legacy is vast and demanding, but I believe you will grow into it."

Clara looked at the pouch in her hand, then back at the towering gates of Elderstone Bank. For the first time, she felt a spark of determination. She didn't fully understand this world yet, but she knew she would carve out her place in it, guided by her family, but ultimately on her own terms.

*

As they stepped out onto the busy cobbles of Hidden Row, Selene gave Clara a thoughtful look. "While we're here, dear, it seems only fitting to update your wardrobe," she said, her gaze flicking to Clara's plain coat. "Something more suitable for your station, and of course, enchanted for your protection."

Clara hesitated, glancing down at her coat. She hadn't given much thought to her clothing since arriving, but now, surrounded by witches and wizards in elegant cloaks, she felt distinctly out of place. Her grandparents blended seamlessly, their robes exuding quiet power and prestige, while Clara stood out in her simplicity.

They entered a shop with a sign that read, *Glimmer & Shade – Fine Magical Garments.* Inside, the air smelled like fresh linen drying under a warm summer breeze, mingling with faint notes of roses and a whisper of cedar from the polished floor. It had enchanted racks that floated with robes in every shade imaginable.

A shop assistant approached, her smile warm and practised. "Lady Selene, Lord Eldric, a pleasure as always. And who is this delightful young witch?

"This is my granddaughter, Clara" her grandmother said with a proud nod. "She'll need a cloak, something protective."

The assistant's eyes lit up. "Ah, I have just the thing." She led them to a display of luxurious cloaks, their fabrics shimmering with embedded enchantments. One caught Clara's eye immediately: a black cloak threaded with silver, its surface sparkling like a clear night sky.

The assistant lifted it carefully. "This cloak offers formidable protection: it wards off harmful spells, shields against magical influence, and guards against the elements. It's also lightweight and comfortable for daily wear."

Clara ran her fingers over the fabric, which felt

impossibly soft yet sturdy. The assistant fastened it around her neck with a clasp shaped like an ancient tree, its branches curving protectively.

Her grandmother guided her to a mirror. "There, darling. You look every bit the Nightfall witch."

Clara stared at her reflection. The cloak settled over her shoulders as if it had always belonged there, its magic humming softly against her. She felt a strange connection, as though she belonged to this world and was not just as an outsider.

Her grandfather stepped forward, his sharp eyes appraising. "A fitting choice," he said. "This cloak is not just for show. Take care of it, and it will take care of you."

The assistant smiled politely. "Could I interest you in anything else today?"

"That will be all," her grandmother replied.

"Five hundred gold crests," the assistant said, her tone neutral.

Clara's eyes widened. "Five hundred?" she whispered, turning to her grandmother. "That's … a lot."

Her grandmother smiled indulgently. "Only the best for our family, dear." She patted Clara's arm lightly, as if such expenses were routine.

Clara glanced back at the till as her grandfather waved his wand, sending a neat stack of coins onto the counter. The ease with which they handled such wealth left her both amazed and uneasy.

As they stepped back into the street, Clara adjusted the cloak around her shoulders. Its magic felt like a quiet reassurance, grounding her in this strange, dazzling world. "Thank you," she said softly, glancing up at her grandparents. The words felt inadequate, but her grandmother's warm smile told her they were enough.

Her grandmother placed a hand on her shoulder. "You are a Nightfall, and this world is yours to explore. Remember that."

*

The Moondancer's steady wingbeats filled the quiet as the carriage glided smoothly through the air, Nightfall Manor far behind. Clara sat in silence, the enchanted pouch resting in her lap. Her fingers absently traced the embroidered runes, her thoughts swirling like the clouds outside the window.

Her grandparents, who had returned to Nightfall Manor, had agreed for Clara to visit her dad. She had wanted this, needed this, to talk to him. But it wasn't just to seek his permission for Crowstone; it was about sorting through her own thoughts too.

Clara shifted uncomfortably on the plush seat, her gaze fixed on the horizon. *Do I even want this?* she thought. Attending Crowstone felt like stepping into a world she didn't fully understand, a world so far removed from the life she had known. Yet, there was a pull deep inside her, a connection she couldn't ignore.

Her thoughts drifted to the broken necklace, the one her mam had given her. She had worn it every day for years, and even now, its absence felt like a missing piece of herself.

Maybe that's what this is about, she thought. A piece of me that's been missing all along. A part of her longed for it, like a whisper carried on the wind, urging her forward.

But then there was her dad, her anchor. He had always been her constant, her safe place. How could she leave him behind to attend a school she would have to sleep at?

The carriage began to descend, and Clara straightened, brushing a strand of hair from her face. Her stomach fluttered with nerves as the familiar streets of Hull came into view. The Moondancer landed gracefully in front of her house, its silver coat glinting in the afternoon light.

Clara stepped out of the carriage. The house looked the same as always, small and cosy, with the faint scent of coffee lingering in the air as she pushed the door open.

Her dad was in the kitchen, humming to himself as he stirred a pot on the stove. The sight of him filled her with a wave of warmth and a feeling of guilt.

"Hey, love," her dad said, turning to her with a warm smile. "Didn't expect you back so soon. Everything alright?"

Clara nodded, slipping off her coat and hanging it on the peg. "Yeah, I just … wanted to see you."

Her dad raised an eyebrow, wiping his hands on a tea towel. "Wanted to see me, or needed to talk about something?"

Clara smiled faintly, sitting down at the kitchen table. "Both," she admitted. She hesitated, then added, "I wanted to talk about … Crowstone."

His smile faltered slightly, and he pulled out a chair, sitting across from her. "What's that, love?" he asked, his tone gentle but cautious.

Clara glanced down at the enchanted pouch on the table, fiddling with the clasp. "It's a magical academy that my grandmother enrolled me in. But before you get annoyed, she's left the decision up to me. I would also need your permission to go," she began, her voice soft. "But I'm still trying to figure out if it's what I really want. I feel … torn."

Her dad leaned forward, resting his elbows on the

table. "Torn how?"

She took a deep breath. "I feel connected to the magical world, to my mam. Like it's a part of me I've never known but always needed. But at the same time, I don't want to lose this, us, my friends, my school, everything I've always known. Going to stay with my family for the summer is one thing, but changing schools? At Crowstone, I'd only be home for two weeks at Christmas … and three months in summer. That's a big difference."

Her dad's expression softened, and he reached across the table, covering her hand with his. "Clara, I know this is a big decision. And I won't pretend it's easy for me to even think about letting you go. But I also know you've always been strong, even when you didn't feel it. If this is something you feel you need to do, I'll support you. You just have to be sure it's what *you* want."

Clara looked up, her eyes meeting his. "That's the thing, Dad. I'm not sure. But a part of me … a deep part of me … feels like it's calling me. Like I'm meant to go. I just don't want you to think I'm abandoning you."

Her dad gave her a sad but reassuring smile. "You're not abandoning me, love. You're growing up. Part of being a parent is knowing the time will come when I'll need to let you go. And that's what your mam would've wanted for you, to be happy, to make your own choices, and to grow into the amazing person you're meant to be. Your mam wanted you to wait until you were eighteen before finding out about magic, but that changed when the necklace broke. Even though you're younger than she planned for, she'd still want this to be your decision."

Tears gathered behind her eyes, but she blinked them back. "Thanks, Dad. I'm still not ready to decide yet, but

… I'm glad we talked."

He squeezed her hand gently. "Take your time, Clara. Whatever you choose, I'll always be here."

As they sat there, the warmth of the kitchen grounding her, Clara felt a flicker of clarity amidst the chaos. The decision was hers to make, and she would make it when she was ready.

Chapter 11: Foundations of Magic

Two days later, Clara stood just outside a small door in Nightfall Manor. She had been summoned by Fenwick, who had arranged for her first lesson to take place inside. Her fingers brushed the handle as she hesitated, unsure what to expect. Before she could open the door, Fenwick appeared at the end of the corridor. "This is where we'll be learning?" she asked, her voice curious.

"Indeed, Miss Clara," Fenwick replied, his expression calm and watchful. "This isn't just any room. It's the Adaptive Chamber, a space unlike any other."

Clara frowned at the unremarkable door. "What exactly does it do?"

Fenwick smirked faintly, gesturing for her to go ahead. "It adapts. Step inside, and you'll see for yourself."

Still sceptical, Clara gripped the handle. A faint vibration shivered through her palm as she eased the door open. At first, the room seemed ordinary: bare stone walls, an empty floor, but with a ceiling that seemed to bear down oppressively. But as Clara stepped further inside, the air shifted, rippling like heat waves.

The walls stretched outward, dissolving into polished wood panelling that extended far beyond where the room's boundaries had once been. Bookshelves rose from the floor, laden with books and scrolls that pulsed with magic. A marble table materialised, strewn with potion ingredients and peculiar artefacts. The air had a quiet energy, alive with the possibilities of the moment.

Clara turned slowly, her wand clutched tightly. "It's like the room's … alive," she murmured.

"In a sense, it is," Fenwick said, stepping inside and letting the door close behind him. "The Adaptive

Chamber doesn't just respond to your needs: it challenges you. It pushes you to grow, often in ways you won't expect."

Clara stopped, her gaze falling on a stack of blank parchment "What kind of challenges?"

Fenwick's expression grew serious. "Growth often comes from discomfort, Miss Clara. This room will reveal both your strengths and weaknesses. But within its boundaries, you'll find the tools to rise above them."

Clara swallowed hard, but her curiosity burned brighter than her nerves. "So, what are we learning today?"

Fenwick gestured to a large chalkboard that shimmered as words etched themselves across it: *Foundations of Magical Society.*

"Today, we begin at the beginning," Fenwick said. "To wield magic responsibly, you must understand the world it has shaped and continues to shape."

Clara sat down, her quill poised above a blank sheet of parchment. Fenwick paced the room, his voice commanding.

"Over two thousand years ago, the first magical families united to form the Magical Assembly, the foundation of our magical society," Fenwick began, his voice steady with authority. "These witches and wizards understood that magic, if left unchecked, could spiral into chaos. The Assembly was not created to rule, but to protect, both magical and non-magical beings alike."

With a flick of his wand, he conjured the crest of the Magical Assembly: a circular emblem with a phoenix rising at its centre, encircled by stars representing the major magical families and guilds.

"Today, the Assembly ensures order and justice in our world. Its members include representatives from powerful families, guilds, and even magical beings such as Starbinders and Mysticforgers."

Clara tilted her head, curiosity sparking in her eyes. "Magical creatures have a say too?"

"Indeed," Fenwick said, his tone approving. "Magic belongs to all who wield it. The Starbinders, for instance, draw their power from the stars and offer insights into the flow of time and destiny, though their visions are rarely clear. Mysticforgers, on the other hand" — he conjured an image of a glowing figure crafting an ornate staff — "are master craftsmen, creating enchanted relics that shape our history."

Clara leaned forward. "Have you ever worked with them?"

Fenwick's faint smile betrayed a touch of nostalgia. "Once, a Starbinder guided me during a crossroads in my life. Their vision was murky, but it revealed enough to steer me towards the path I walk today."

The image in the air shifted, morphing into a dark, shadowy figure. Fenwick's tone grew grave. "But not all wield magic with wisdom. Wizards such as the Dark Wizard, for one."

Clara's pulse quickened. "Who is the Dark Wizard?" she asked, her voice trembling slightly. "People at the festival were talking about him, and Grandfather was reading about his escape in the newspaper."

Fenwick's expression darkened, and the glowing magical crest faded into nothing. "He is a figure of fear, a name whispered with caution across the magical world. He was once a promising young wizard, one of the brightest of his generation. But ambition and greed consumed him. He pursued ancient magic, magic forbidden for centuries because of its destructive power."

"What happened to him?" Clara asked cautiously.

Fenwick hesitated, as if weighing how much to reveal.

"He fell deeper into the darkness he sought to control. Over time, he gathered followers, waging war against the Assembly and magical families who opposed him. His reign of terror lasted two years."

Clara's chest tightened.

Fenwick's gaze softened, though the weight of his words remained heavy. "The Dark Wizard, corrupted by his obsession with ancient magic, sought power and destroyed all those that stood in his way."

"Where is he now?" Clara asked, her voice barely above a whisper.

"He was captured and imprisoned in Blackspire, a fortress built to contain the most dangerous magical criminals. For years, the wards held him, but …" Fenwick's voice grew heavier. "He escaped. His powers have grown, and his ambitions remain unchanged. The Assembly fears dark times are ahead."

Clara shivered. "They'll stop him again, won't they?"

Fenwick regarded her carefully, his voice sombre. "The Dark Wizard doesn't fight alone," Fenwick said, his voice dropping to a whisper. "Years ago, he broke the wards of Elderran Hall, a fortress said to be impenetrable. It wasn't just the destruction; it was the precision. Every enchanted shield, every protective spell … unravelled as though he'd woven them himself. Those inside never stood a chance."

Clara shivered. "What happened to them?"

Fenwick hesitated before answering. "No one knows. Not a trace of them was ever found. Not even a drop of blood."

Fenwick paused, "The Dark Wizard thrives on fear and doubt. He does seem to have a particular hatred towards Nightfalls."

Clara leaned back, her mind swirling with questions. "Why … why does he hate my family so much?"

Fenwick straightened, his expression unreadable. "The Nightfalls have always stood for balance and order, Clara. Your family were leaders in the fight against him before. Perhaps, to him, your family represents everything he seeks to destroy. But that's enough for now. You've much to learn, and too much knowledge too soon can weigh heavily."

Clara swallowed hard, Fenwick's words settling in her chest. The Dark Wizard's connection to her family was undeniable, but the full truth felt just out of reach, shrouded in shadow. She would find out more, one way or another.

Fenwick's words about the Dark Wizard echoed in her mind. She had listened carefully, trying to piece together the fragments of the story, but the more she thought about it, the more unsettled she became.

The idea of someone wielding so much power was terrifying. The way Fenwick had spoken of him, as someone brilliant yet consumed by ambition, made him feel more real, more human, and somehow even more dangerous.

*

Fenwick's lesson continued. "Miss Clara," he said, breaking her thoughts, "the Adaptive Chamber is ready for your first challenge."

The room shifted, the marble floor morphing into a forest clearing. A shimmering scroll appeared on a platform surrounded by glowing runes. "Your task is to retrieve the scroll without triggering the wards. Use the skills you've learned so far."

Clara stepped forward, her heart pounding. The runes

pulsed, their patterns complex and unfamiliar. She closed her eyes, drawing on the patience and focus Fenwick had emphasised.

Step by step, she approached the scroll, weaving around the glowing symbols. The air crackled with hidden magic, and sweat beaded on her forehead. Finally, she reached the platform and extended her hand. The scroll vanished, replaced by a soft, golden light that wrapped around her fingers.

"Well done," Fenwick said, his voice warm with approval. "You've taken your first step towards understanding magic, not just as a tool, but as a responsibility."

There was a calmness that radiated from Fenwick, a steady presence that felt like a deep well of sincerity. His intentions seemed clear, without any hidden layers or veiled motives. With him, there was no guesswork. You always knew exactly where you stood.

*

As Clara left the Adaptive Chamber, her thoughts swirled with everything she had learned. The weight of her family's history, the threat of the Dark Wizard, and the mysteries of ancient magic loomed large. But within her, a quiet determination burned. She wasn't just a student or a Nightfall. She was Clara, a witch who would forge her own path.

Chapter 12: Whispers from the past

A week had passed since Clara had learned of the Dark Wizard's deep hatred for her family, and the knowledge weighed heavily on her, an inexplicable ache rooted deep in her core. It was something she couldn't name.

She had tried broaching the topic with her grandmother, trying to learn more about it, but each attempt was met with vague answers or a swift change of subject. It felt like a forbidden family secret buried under layers of silence. Or perhaps it was simply too painful to speak of.

The unanswered questions gnawed at her, and so Clara decided to occupy herself the only way she knew how: by seeking solace in the Starbound Library. Clara sat there, surrounded by ancient books and portraits of her ancestors, yet she couldn't shake the hollow feeling in her chest. These were her people, her history, but it felt as though she were peering through a glass pane. She missed her dad's steady presence, the sound of Chloe's laughter, and even the familiar hum of their quiet street. Here, magic swirled endlessly, yet she wondered if she truly belonged in its flow.

Unable to find comfort among the shelves and shadows of the library, Clara rose and wandered through Nightfall Manor, feeling its magic with each step. The corridors pulsed with quiet energy, the eyes of ancient ancestors following her as she passed. Turning a corner, she faced the Shifting Staircase, its steps gleaming like a challenge waiting to be met.

The staircase twisted, its steps shifting as though inviting her to climb. Clara stepped on, gripping the banister as it carried her upwards, past floors that appeared and vanished like fleeting thoughts.

The staircase stopped at a corridor she didn't recognise. Shadows danced across the walls, and silvery light seeped under a door at the far end. Clara hesitated briefly, her pulse quickening, before curiosity drew her forward. Each step felt hushed, as though the air itself was waiting.

The door creaked open at her touch, revealing a room bathed in a gentle, eerie glow.

It was the Hall of Mirrors, which Hazel had briefly shown her, saying, "Each one holds glimpses of memories and of your ancestors, and if your intentions are true, they may reveal secrets from their lives."

Clara looked at the ancient mirrors framed in ornate silver and gold. Her footsteps barely echoed on the polished stone as she entered, drawn to the largest mirror at the far end, its pull almost magnetic. Before she realised, she was standing before it.

She stared at her own reflection, her eyes wide, taking in the sombre expression that the mirror cast back at her. Just as she reached out to trace her fingers along its cool surface, a faint glow began to spread across the glass. Words in orange began to appear, twisting and moving in elegant, swirling letters. She stepped back, watching as the words solidified, her heart pounding as a riddle began to reveal itself.

The letters formed slowly, glowing bright against the mirror's surface, casting a warm, otherworldly light across the shadowy room. Clara held her breath, feeling a mix of excitement and apprehension as the words settled into place.

Those who seek the past must prove their heart,
For Nightfall memories are set apart.
To glimpse a life that once was dear,
Answer this truth, known only here.
A tune she sang to calm your fears,
Soft as starlight and close as tears.
What song from her voice would drift you to sleep,
A promise to hold, and a memory to keep?

Clara's pulse quickened, the riddle stirring something fragile yet powerful within her, a memory she had long buried. Closing her eyes, she let the words guide her, reaching into the distant corners of her mind, where warmth, safety, and her mother's voice lingered.

It was barely there, a whisper from years ago, from when she was so young that all she could recall were faint traces of warmth and security, a comforting scent, the softness of being held.

As she concentrated, a distant melody seemed to surface, soft and soothing. It was her mother's voice, gently singing to her, a tune that floated through her mind like a charm created from warmth and safety. She smelled the faint scent of lavender drifting by, and she held onto the memory with all her might as the tune formed in her mind.

Close your eyes and drift away,
To where silver waters sway.
Where the moon watches night and day,
Dreams will guide and fears will stray.
Stars above and stars below,
Safe from shadows, you will go.

Clara opened her eyes, the soft remnants of the song echoing in her heart. Her mother's voice, though faint, seemed to linger, as if it had been waiting all this time for her to remember. She took a steadying breath, feeling the warmth and sadness of the memory, then looked back at the mirror.

"That's it … 'The Silver River Song'," she whispered, feeling the words hang in the air.

As Clara whispered the name of the lullaby, the mirror's silvery glow deepened, casting a strange, warm light across the room. Her reflection faded, the glass rippling as if pulling her into a memory that wasn't her own. She took a small, unsteady step forward, mesmerised as the shapes within the mirror took form.

The mirror shimmered to life, the reflective surfaces rippling like water. Clara held her breath as the first image appeared in the mirror before her. It was her mam, Helena, younger and glowing with life. Standing beside her was a man Clara had never seen before. His dark hair framed a face that was sharp and magnetic, his intense eyes fixed on her mam with unmistakable affection.

The images shifted, pulling Clara into their story.

Her mam stood together with the man in a moonlit garden, their hands brushing as she laughed softly, her golden hair catching the light. The man leaned closer, whispering something that made her blush, their connection radiating through the scene.

Another image. The two sat side by side in a library, surrounded by ancient books and scrolls. Clara's mam traced runes on a scroll, her expression focused, while the man leaned over her shoulder, pointing something out. Their heads were close, their ease unmistakable.

The scene dissolved, replaced by another moment of

intimacy. Her mother and the man danced in a grand hall, her white gown shimmering as the man spun her effortlessly. Their smiles were genuine, their movements graceful.

The warmth of the images began to cool.

*

Clara found her grandmother seated in the drawing room, surrounded by the soft flicker of the fireplace. She looked up as Clara entered, her sharp gaze softening slightly before creasing with concern at the uncertainty in Clara's eyes. Setting down her book, she folded her hands neatly in her lap and studied Clara with quiet intensity.

"Clara, darling, is something the matter?" Selene asked, her voice calm but laced with a hint of unease.

Clara hesitated, her fingers knotting together. "Grandmother ... who was Therin?"

At the sound of the name, her grandmother's expression shifted instantly. The warmth in her eyes vanished, replaced by a cold, guarded look. Her entire posture stiffened, as though Clara had opened a door that was meant to remain locked. "Where did you hear that name?" she asked, her tone low and steely.

Clara swallowed, her voice small but resolute. "I saw him in a memory," she said carefully. "In the Hall of Mirrors. He was with my mother ... they looked close, like they cared for each other."

Her grandmother's jaw tightened, and for a moment, silence stretched between them. Clara wondered if she had pushed too far. Then, with a voice heavy with barely restrained emotion, her grandmother spoke. "That name is not spoken in this house," she said, her words clipped, though a faint tremor betrayed something deeper beneath. "He is a stain on our family's past, one we do not revisit."

Clara felt a pang of frustration, but she pressed on. "But my mother seemed happy with him at first. Then … then they fought … until she managed to escape."

Her grandmother's gaze grew colder, and her voice sharpened. "Clara, you don't understand. Therin is not someone to be romanticised. Whatever your mother saw in him ended when he betrayed this family."

"But why?" Clara asked softly, her voice trembling with a mix of curiosity and defiance. "I want to understand. He was clearly important to my mam at one point, and the fact that the image showed itself to me makes me feel like it's important. You want me to learn about this family and magic. Well, those images seem connected to both."

"Enough," Selene said sharply, her tone like a blade cutting through Clara's questions. Her hands trembled slightly as she rose, her voice dropping into something colder, more distant. "That name carries nothing but ruin. Whatever you saw in that mirror is in the past, and it must stay there. Promise me, Clara, you will not seek answers to questions that can only lead to pain."

Clara hesitated, her chest tightening under the weight of her grandmother's words. "I … promise," she murmured reluctantly.

But as Clara left the room, her mind churned with unresolved questions. If her grandmother wouldn't tell her the truth, she'd have to find it herself. The images from the mirror, her mother's radiant smile, Therin's intense gaze, the sudden shift from warmth to conflict, haunted her. There was more to this story, and Clara couldn't shake the feeling that its echoes still reached across time, entangling her fate with theirs.

As she closed the door to her room, Clara leaned

against it, her mind replaying the memory again and again. What had Therin done to shatter her mother's trust so completely? And why did her grandmother seem more afraid of the truth than of the past itself? Whatever the answers were, Clara knew one thing for certain: this was a story she couldn't leave buried.

*

Clara pushed open the heavy oak doors of the Starbound Library, her breath catching as the towering shelves seemed to rise endlessly before her. The dim glow of floating orbs illuminated the spines of ancient books, their titles shimmering faintly with magical energy. The faint hum of the room enveloped her, a low, comforting murmur of untold knowledge waiting to be discovered.

Her footsteps echoed softly as she approached a central table, its surface cluttered with scrolls and open volumes. Her mind was still spinning with the memory of the Hall of Mirrors, her mother's anguished cry, Therin's cold gaze, and the swirling portal that marked his departure. Her grandmother wasn't going to give her answers, but she could find her own.

"I need to know what it means," she muttered under her breath, running her fingers along the edges of a worn book. The weight of what she had seen pressed down on her, and she didn't know where to begin.

As if sensing her urgency, a nearby shelf creaked softly, its books rearranging themselves with a faint rustle. One volume floated forward, landing on the table in front of her with a quiet thud. The leather cover bore no title, only an engraved bronze crescent. Clara hesitated, then opened it, her heart pounding.

The first page glowed faintly, lines of text unfurling as though written in real time:

The Hall of Mirrors reveals only what it must. It answers only to those whose emotions call to it, and it shows not what we seek, but what we need to see.

Clara stared at the words, her breath shallow. It wasn't just a memory; it was something deeper, tied to her mother, to Therin, to a part of her she didn't yet understand.

Her hands were shaking as she turned the page, but the remaining text was faded, the ink too faint to decipher. Frustration bubbled up in her chest, but she forced herself to stay calm. This was a start, at least.

The library's orbs flickered briefly, causing shadows across the walls. Clara closed the book carefully, her mind alight with questions. The Hall of Mirrors hadn't just shown her a memory; it had chosen to, and that meant there was more to uncover.

As she stepped back into the Endless Passage, clutching the volume tightly, one thought echoed in her mind: *It's not done with me yet, and I'm not done with it.*

*

The next evening, Clara sat in the study, the warm glow of the fire casting shadows across the room. Her grandmother entered gracefully, her emerald robes rustling softly as she crossed the floor. She smiled warmly as she looked at Clara.

"Have you had a chance to think more about Crowstone, darling?" Selene asked, settling into the armchair opposite her. Her tone was gentle, without pressure, but Clara could feel the significance of the question.

Clara hesitated, her hands clasping tightly in her lap. "I have," she said slowly, lifting her gaze to meet her grandmother's. "But before I decide, I want to understand something. What's so important about being a Nightfall and the family legacy? Why is there so much pressure to be … perfect?"

Her grandmother's expression shifted, a flicker of surprise crossing her features before she leaned back, her eyes thoughtful. For a moment, the room was silent except for the faint crackle of the fire. Then she spoke, her voice measured but carrying an honesty Clara hadn't expected.

"It's tradition," her grandmother began. "The Nightfall family has long been seen as a pillar of the magical world. For generations, other magical families have looked to us for counsel, for guidance, and yes, as an example of how to live. The expectations don't come from within, my dear, but from without. It's them who expect us to be perfect."

She paused, leaning forwards slightly, her expression softening. "But can I tell you a secret, Clara?" she said, her voice dropping to a whisper. "No one's bloody perfect. Not us, not the Magical Assembly, nor the other so-called magical elite. Beneath the fine clothes and sprawling manors, we're all just witches and wizards trying to navigate this world the best we can. But for some reason, we allow ourselves to forget that."

Clara blinked, caught off-guard by her grandmother's candour. She sat up straighter, her curiosity piqued.

Selene continued, a faint smile tugging at her lips. "You, Clara, have a gift. You see the world differently. You remind people what's real, what matters. Since the moment I learned I had a granddaughter, I've felt … lighter. Happier. It's the happiest I've been in years, having you here."

Clara's heart leapt at her grandmother's words,

warmth spreading through her as she listened. She'd always felt like an outsider, unsure of her place in this magical world, but her grandmother's words planted a small seed of belonging.

"That's not to say I was unhappy before," her grandmother added with a soft laugh. "But life, traditions, all these expectations, they can make you forget what's important. And what's important, Clara, is to live. To find joy in the moments that matter with the people you care about. That's what I hope you'll come to see, whether you choose Crowstone or another path entirely."

Clara looked down at her hands, her mind racing with everything her grandmother had said. "Thank you," she said quietly, her voice steady despite the whirlwind of emotions inside her. "That means … a lot."

Her grandmother reached out, gently squeezing Clara's hand. "Whatever you decide, my dear, know that you are already more than enough. Perfect or not, you are a Nightfall. And that's all that matters."

Clara exhaled deeply, with a breath she hadn't realised she'd been holding. It felt as though the act of letting go might somehow unlock the tension coiled tightly within her chest. "Okay, Grandmother," Clara began, her voice steady despite the swirl of emotions inside her. "I'll tell you about my decision to attend Crowstone Academy."

Her grandmother's eyes lit up. "Go on, darling," she said, her tone calm but laced with a hopeful eagerness.

Clara shifted in her seat, her fingers brushing over the arms of the chair. "What you said about what it means to be a Nightfall. I know this is what the family wants for me, and my dad told me it's my choice to make. But it's been hard trying to figure out what *I* want."

Her grandmother nodded, her gaze steady and warm.

"It's a big decision, Clara. I don't envy you. But it's clear you've given it the thought it deserves."

Clara hesitated, her voice softening. "I've been thinking about my mam too. I don't know what she'd say if she were here. She hid me from magic until now, so part of me wonders if she'd want me to stay away. But ... she's not here, and this choice is mine. No one else's."

A flicker of sadness crossed Selene's face. "Your mother loved you more than anything, Clara. Of that, I am sure. Whatever her reasons, she wanted you to have a choice when the time came. And now that it has, I'm proud of you for making it with such care."

Clara nodded, her throat tightening as she tried to put her feelings into words. "I feel like something's been missing my whole life. I used to think it was just her, but ... it's more than that. It's magic. It's this world. It's ... who I am. I feel like I've been walking around with only half of myself, and now I have the chance to find the rest."

Her grandmother leaned forwards slightly, her eyes shining with pride. "That's beautifully put, Clara. You've always been a Nightfall, even before you knew it."

Clara exhaled as she looked up at her grandmother. "I'm going to go to Crowstone. But I want to do it on my terms. I want to figure out who I am, not just as a Nightfall, but as me."

Her grandmother smiled, her eyes full of emotion. "You are extraordinary, Clara. I knew it the moment I first saw you. This family, this world, is lucky to have you. And don't worry, darling," she added, her tone warm, "you'll find your way, and I'll be here to guide you every step of the way."

Clara felt a swell of emotion in her chest. "Thank you,

Grandmother. I'm still nervous, but … this feels right."

Selene reached across the small table between them, placing a reassuring hand over Clara's. "Nerves are a sign that you're about to do something important. Trust in yourself, and trust in the magic that's always been within you. Crowstone isn't merely an academy, Clara. It is a place where greatness is forged. Some of the most legendary witches and wizards in magical history once walked its halls. Kidric Firebane, who tamed the Phoenix of Ashmar; Esther Starfall, whose spells shaped the very foundations of the Assembly; even Arlyn Songrace, the only witch to ever seal a rift between realms, all Crowstone graduates."

Clara's eyes widened. "I had no idea …"

"Few do until they step through its gates. But make no mistake, every student carries the weight of that legacy. You will find that the name 'Crowstone' is not just a mark of prestige, but a standard, a promise to the magical world that its students will rise to greatness, as those before them have."

Her grandmother paused, a distant look rippling in her emerald eyes. "And there's something more," she said, her voice lowering. "Few families can claim a deeper connection to Crowstone than ours. Did you know that one of your ancestors, Callidora Nightfall, was among the academy's founders?"

Clara blinked in surprise, leaning forward. "One of the founders? Really?"

Selene nodded, a faint smile playing on her lips. "Yes, Callidora, alongside the Assembly's greatest minds, helped shape Crowstone into the sanctuary of knowledge and discipline it is today. Her vision was to create a place where witches and wizards could not only hone their magic but understand their responsibility to the world. She believed that magic without purpose was little more than stupidity."

Clara sat back, her mind spinning with her grandmother's revelation. She had felt like an outsider in this magical world, but now she couldn't help but wonder if it had always been waiting for her to step into it.

As they sat together, the glow of the fireplace sending rippling light across the room, Clara felt a quiet sense of determination settle over her. The weight of her decision felt lighter, as though she was stepping towards something that was truly hers.

Chapter 13: Bridges Between Worlds

Clara sat across from her dad in their cosy living room, the faint sound of traffic drifting through the open window. The warmth of home enveloped her, grounding her. She fidgeted slightly with her fingers.

"Everything okay, love?" her dad said, looking up from his mug of tea with a warm smile. "Didn't expect you back so soon. Not that it isn't a delight to see you."

Clara nodded. "Yeah, I just … wanted to tell you. I've made my decision about Crowstone Academy."

Her dad's smile faltered slightly as he set his mug down. "Ah." He leaned forward. "What have you decided?"

Clara nodded, her voice steady but tinged with uncertainty. "I'm going. I think … it's where I'm meant to be. It feels like there's a part of me I can only discover there." She looked up, searching his face for any sign of disappointment.

Her dad studied her intently, his expression a mix of pride and sadness. "So, you'll be away most of the year, then?"

"Yeah," Clara admitted, her voice softer now. "But I'll come home for Christmas and summer. And we have this." She gestured to the silver box between them. "We can write whenever we want. It's called an Silverdusk-chest. It's like a magical letterbox, but without the wait for postmen." She smiled faintly. "Grandmother got us them to make it easier being apart."

Her dad's eyes flicked to the chest, curiosity mingling with emotion. "And how does it work?"

Clara opened the lid, revealing its red velvet-lined interior. "You write a letter, put it inside, and close the lid. It sends the letter straight to my matching chest at the manor. I'll do the same when writing to you. It's … surprisingly simple but kind of amazing."

Her dad chuckled, the sound bittersweet. "That's something else. And it's nice of your grandmother to think of it. She's, uh, not what I expected from a magical aristocrat. She seems a little more down-to-earth."

"She's different from the others," Clara said, laughing softly. "Still posh, of course, but … grounded. She's been the easiest to talk to about all this. Most of the rest of the Nightfalls are a bit … much at times."

"A bit much?" her dad teased, raising an eyebrow. "Let me guess, they're not too thrilled about you not being a *proper lady*."

Clara laughed, shaking her head. "Not even close. I think I baffle them half the time. They're used to perfection, and I'm just … me."

Her dad's smile softened, his eyes lingering on hers. "And that's exactly who you should be, Clara. Don't let them, or magic, for that matter, change the best parts of you."

Clara blinked back tears, her hand tightening around his. "Thanks, Dad. I promise I won't forget where I come from or who I am."

He nodded, his voice soft but firm. "Good. Because the kindness and strength you carry, that's what makes you special, not the magic. That's just a part of you, not the whole."

Clara exhaled deeply, the weight of her decision easing as his words settled into her heart. "I'll write to you all the time," she promised, glancing at the glowing Silverdusk-chest. "You'll still be a part of this with me, even if I'm far away."

Her dad chuckled, though his eyes betrayed the sadness he was trying to hide. "You've always had a way of saying exactly what I need to hear, love." He paused, taking a deep breath before smiling. "I'll be fine. You're strong, Clara, stronger than you think. And I know you're going to be amazing there."

Clara's chest swelled with emotion as she leaned forward, hugging him tightly. The familiar scent of his aftershave grounded her, even as her world grew bigger and more complicated.

"I love you, Dad," she whispered, her voice thick with emotion.

"I love you too, baby girl," he said, his voice brimming with pride.

"You know, Dad, you'll have to stop calling me 'baby girl' at some point," Clara said with a small smile. "I am fourteen now."

Her dad chuckled, his eyes warm with affection. "You'll always be my baby girl, Clara. Even when you're forty and I'm an old man. You're the most precious thing in the world to me."

As Clara pulled back, she glanced at the Silverdusk-chest once more, its soft glow a comforting reminder. The world she was stepping into felt vast and unknown, but she knew that no matter how far she went, home and her dad would always be just a letter away.

*

Clara woke up to the familiar scent of coffee drifting from the kitchen and the soft clatter of her dad moving around. She stretched, feeling the warmth of her old room wrapping around her like a cozy blanket. It was a quiet contrast to the vast halls and constant magic of Nightfall Manor, and as she got out of bed, she realised how much she had missed this simplicity.

Her old room hadn't changed. The peeling poster of her favourite band still hung above her bed, and the soft duvet still smelled faintly of lavender. She traced her finger along the desk where she'd spent countless hours studying for exams. Now it would be replaced by lessons in potion-making and spellcraft. The contrast felt strange, jarring and comforting all at once.

*

That evening, they cooked dinner together, laughing as they chopped vegetables and stirred pots, the kitchen filling with warmth and the scent of Clara's favourite meal, shepherd's pie with a twist. Clara's dad would add cheese to the potato and smoked paprika to the mince. As well as being Clara's favourite, it was unfortunately one of the only good meals her dad could cook. When they sat down to eat, they clinked their glasses in a quiet toast, her dad's smile reassuring her that no matter how far her journey took her, she would always have a home waiting for her here.

As they finished the meal, Clara felt a heart-tugging ache settle in her heart. She was ready to go back to Nightfall Manor, to dive back into the mysteries and magic of her new life, but there was a part of her that would always be here, with her dad, in this little house that held so many memories. And as they cleaned up and settled into the evening, she knew that she would carry these moments with her wherever she went.

Later that evening, Clara made her way to Chloe's house. As soon as her best friend opened the door, Clara barely had time to say hello before Chloe threw her arms around her, pulling her into a tight hug.

"Clara! You're finally back! I feel like it's been ages," Chloe said, her voice full of excitement and relief.

Clara laughed, hugging her back just as fiercely. "I missed you so much, Chloe. I have so much to tell you, you won't even believe it."

hey headed up to Chloe's room, where they'd spent countless afternoons talking and laughing, and Clara settled in, feeling a wave of nostalgia wash over her. As she began to recount the incredible events of the past few weeks, Chloe's eyes grew wide.

"So, get this," Clara started, leaning in. "My mam's family … they're like really posh and rich. They live in this massive manor that honestly feels like something out of a fairytale. Huge rooms, massive garden, the works. It's honestly hard to wrap my head around sometimes."

Chloe's mouth dropped open. "No way. You're telling me you're part of some ancient, rich family that lives in a mansion? And they didn't even know you existed?"

Clara nodded. "Yeah, it's … it's weird. They're practically strangers, and yet they're family. They were shocked to find out about me too." She looked down, fiddling with the hem of her sleeve. "Honestly, they were just as shocked when they found out. Although I am sure they were hoping I'd be a little more … refined. Not some girl from a working-class family from Hull."

Chloe grabbed her hand, giving it a reassuring squeeze. "Clara, you're amazing. They're lucky to have you, whether they realise that yet or not."

Clara smiled, feeling her spirits lift. "Thanks, Chloe. And there's more. I'm going to this private school. It's like the best school out there. It's an incredible opportunity and probably the best education I could get, even though it means I'll be away most of the year."

Clara's smile wavered as she looked at her best friend. "But I'm going to miss you so much, Chloe. None of this feels right without you. It's like there's this whole part of me that's out of place."

Chloe's voice wobbled as she spoke. "I'll miss you too, Clara. I don't know what I'll do without you. We've done everything together since … forever."

The two girls hugged each other tightly, both of them fighting back tears, clinging to the comfort of each other's presence. They stayed like that for a while, not needing words, just the silent understanding that their friendship could withstand anything, no matter where life took them.

When they finally pulled back, Clara looked at Chloe, trying to blink away her own tears. "I'll write to you all the time," she promised. "And when I come home, I'll come and see you."

Chloe raised an eyebrow. "Write as in letters? What, are they allergic to texts or email or something?"

Clara shrugged, feigning a laugh. "Yeah. Apparently, they don't allow phones or anything like that at the school. It's super strict. So, letters are the only way to communicate."

Chloe groaned dramatically. "Letters! What's next? Candlelight instead of electricity? I'm going to need some epic updates, Clara. None of that boring *Dear Chloe, school is fine* rubbish."

Clara chuckled, but her smile didn't quite reach her eyes. The knot of guilt in her chest tightened. She hated lying to Chloe, hated how much she had to hide. The truth that magic existed, and she was actually a witch: that's what she really wanted to tell her best friend, but Hollowers weren't allowed to know about magic. Clara could not tell Chloe that the letters would be enchanted to bypass Royal Mail entirely; it was the only way for them to correspond.

Clara had already discussed it with her grandmother, who promised to teach her the necessary enchantment. She would pre-write an address that appeared to be a private school for Chloe's benefit. Once posted, the letters would vanish from the mailbox and magically fly to Crowstone Academy. Similarly, her enchanted letters to Chloe would deliver themselves straight to her best friend's home, bypassing Hollower systems entirely.

"I'll make them good, I promise," Clara said softly.

Chloe smiled, her carefree energy a sharp contrast to the heaviness Clara felt. "Good. I expect gossip, updates, everything."

Clara nodded, forcing a grin, but the weight of her secrets pressed down on her. Letters could bridge the distance, but they couldn't erase the growing chasm between the magical world and the one she'd left behind. She hated how much she had to hide, especially from Chloe.

Clara and Chloe said their goodbyes, which, unsurprisingly, came with more tears and tight hugs that neither wanted to end.

As Clara made her way home, a longing ache settled over her. She was grateful to have seen her best friend, but a quiet sadness lingered. Things between them could never be the same. How could they? Clara was a witch, now part of a world entirely separate from Chloe's.

Clara clung to the hope that she could straddle both worlds, holding onto the life she'd built with her dad and Chloe. But deep down, an undeniable pull towards magic whispered to her, urging her forwards into a world where she felt more like herself than ever before. The thought thrilled and terrified her in equal measure.

*

When Clara got home, she greeted her dad with a tight hug, holding on a moment longer than usual.

"You okay, love?" her dad asked gently, his brow creasing with concern.

Clara stepped back, managing a small smile. "Yeah, everything's fine. It's just a lot to deal with. I'll be seeing you and Chloe so much less, and you're the two most important people in my life. Now I have to build a whole new life away from you both." She hesitated, her voice softening. "I mean, I can't even talk to Chloe about magic … At least I can talk to you about it, though. I'm just going to miss you both so much … and I'll miss home too."

Her dad reached for her hand. "I miss your mam, love. But I see so much of her in you: her curiosity, her strength, her kindness. I think she'd be so proud of the person you're becoming." He placed a reassuring hand on her shoulder. "I know it's hard, Clara. But try to be kinder to yourself. Your whole world has been turned upside down, and it would be a lot for anyone to process. It's okay to not be okay sometimes, love," he said softly, his voice steady and warm. "Life's a rollercoaster, Clara, sometimes calm and steady and other times thrilling and terrifying, where you feel it's too much to handle. But you just have to have the strength to hang on, even through the scariest parts."

He paused, gently squeezing her shoulder. "The trick isn't avoiding those feelings, Clara. It's learning how to sit with them, how to face them without letting them take over. You've already been through so much, losing your mam, adjusting to this new world, and you've come out stronger every time. But it's also okay to let yourself feel sad or scared sometimes. That doesn't make you weak. It makes you human, a magical human, obviously, but still human."

Clara blinked back tears as his words sank in.

He smiled gently, brushing a strand of hair from her face. "No matter how overwhelming things get, you've got people who love you, who'll be there to help you find your way. You're not in this alone, Clara. Not ever."

The knot in her chest eased slightly as she leaned into his embrace. She felt the faintest glimmer of hope, knowing she had someone who believed in her even when she struggled to believe in herself. Having her dad believe in her was so important; it made the load feel a little lighter.

They laughed, wiping away the last of their tears. For the rest of the night, they sat close, talking, laughing, and sharing stories, cherishing the precious time they had together. In those quiet moments, Clara felt a sense of peace, knowing that no matter how different her world had become, some things would always stay the same.

Clara cherished every quiet moment with her dad, but the pull of magic stirred within her, a reminder that her journey was only just beginning. As they said their goodbyes, she saw the love and pride in his eyes and knew she would carry it with her no matter where her path led.

*

The days passed by too quickly for Clara and her dad, but she felt she had to get back to the magical world and continue her journey to becoming a witch.

As Clara stood at the door, her dad pulled her into a

tight hug, his voice low and steady. "You're going to do amazing things, Clara. Just promise me one thing: don't lose sight of who you are."

Clara nodded, her throat tight. "I won't, Dad. I promise."

She glanced at the Silverdusk-chest glowing softly on the table, a tangible connection to the home she was leaving behind. Taking a deep breath, she stepped outside, her heart straddling two worlds as the pull of magic drew her forward.

As she climbed into the carriage, her dad's words echoed in her mind: "Don't lose sight of who you are." She wanted to believe she could hold onto the girl she'd always been, the one who loved quiet mornings with her dad, messy laughter with Chloe, and the simplicity of their little home. But how could she balance that with this new life of magic and grandeur without losing herself? She feared that piece by piece, she might slip away into a world that felt both exhilarating and alien.

Chapter 14: Threads of the Magical World

Clara sat on the edge of her bed at Nightfall Manor, her gaze lingering on the Silverdusk-chest sitting neatly on her desk. Its silver-etched surface shone in the faint light of her room, a quiet reminder of her dad's words when she'd told him her decision to attend Crowstone Academy.

Taking a deep breath, she retrieved a blank piece of parchment. Her handwriting was slow and deliberate as she wrote.

Hi Dad,
I miss you already. I'll keep my promise to write every day if I can, and I hope you're doing okay. Crowstone is going to be a big change, but I am a little excited. Love you always. Clara.

She placed the folded note into the Silverdusk-chest and watched as the lid closed with a soft click. A faint hum filled the air, and when she reopened it moments later, her note had vanished. A few minutes later, the chest clicked open again, and a fresh note appeared inside.

Miss you too, love. Proud of you. Always here if you need me. Love, Dad.

A small smile tugged at Clara's lips as she read the words. Folding the note, she tucked it carefully into her journal, a piece of home to carry with her.

*

The next morning, Clara stepped onto the cobbled streets

of Hidden Row alongside her grandmother. The magical streets bustled with energy, their storefronts shimmering with enchantments. Witches and wizards hurried past, their robes sweeping behind them as floating parcels bobbed in the air like obedient messengers. The air smelled of warm bread, aged parchment, and the faint essence of magic at work.

Clara's grandmother walked briskly, handing Clara a parchment list of school supplies. "We'll need to be efficient today," she said, her tone firm. "You will need the very best for Crowstone, and we have much to gather."

Their first stop was Moonrise Trunks, a shop filled with shelves of ornate suitcases and travelling bags. Clara frowned as her grandmother handed her a small, unassuming suitcase. "It doesn't look like it could hold everything," Clara murmured.

Her grandmother smiled knowingly. "Try opening it."

Clara hesitated, then lifted the latch. Inside, the space stretched impossibly deep, far larger than the case's exterior. She peered inside, half expecting to hear an echo.

"It's enchanted with expansion spells," her grandmother explained. "Light as air, no matter how much you pack."

Next was Evermore Tomes, a towering bookshop that smelled of ink and ancient paper. The shelves stretched so high they vanished into shadow, and ladders moved along the rows of their own accord. The shopkeeper, a sharp-eyed witch with a quill behind her ear, summoned the books from Clara's list with a flick of her wand. Titles like *Theoretical Spellcasting Year 8* and *Practical Applications of Rune Symbology* piled up on the counter.
Clara glanced at the growing stack.

Her grandmother simply tapped the suitcase with her wand. The books vanished into its depths, and Clara felt the weight of it grow no heavier. Clara gave off a smile her grandmother caught, pure amazement at the magic.

At Runewright's Repository, Clara traced her fingers over glowing runestones. Each one pulsed with magic. "You'll need these for practical rune magic," her grandmother explained, selecting a small set. The stones felt warm beneath Clara's touch, as though they carried secrets waiting to be unlocked.

They moved on to Elemental Accessories, where shelves sparkled with vials of moonlit rain, shards of elemental fire, and enchanted earth.

Her grandmother handed her a leather-bound journal. "For tracking your progress in elemental spells," she said. The day continued in a whirlwind of stops: Starbound Apparatus for star charts and an Aether Compass to align with magical tides, and Whisper's Whisk for potion supplies. Clara marvelled at the cauldrons that adjusted their size with a tap and the stirring rods made from rare woods. Each item felt like a piece of a puzzle coming together, a glimpse into the world she was about to step into.

*

After hours of shopping, her grandmother led her to The Enchanted Table, a café tucked into the corner of Hidden Row. Its marble floors gleamed beneath floating chandeliers, and the air was filled with the exciting aroma of pastries and spiced tea.

Clara ordered a pastry that sparkled faintly and a cup of Liquid Gold tea. The tea was warm and soothing, easing the knot of nerves in her stomach. As they ate, her grandmother looked at her with a thoughtful expression.

"How are you feeling about Crowstone, darling?" she asked.

Clara hesitated, her fingers tracing the rim of her teacup. "Excited, I think. Nervous too. It still feels … overwhelming, like being in a dark cave with a tiny light. But every day, that light grows brighter, and I catch glimpses of something magical, something new."

Selene's smile was gentle. "Adjusting to this world will take time, darling, and you've learned so much already. As to Crowstone, it will challenge you, but it will also shape you. You have your family, and you have a strength within you that will see you through."

Clara nodded, feeling a mix of nerves and determination. She wasn't sure she believed in her own strength just yet, but she was willing to try.

*

Their final stop was Starlace Tailors. The shop's interior shimmered with magical embroidery; mannequins that moved as though alive, dressed in Crowstone Academy uniforms in black and silver. As the shop assistant measured her for robes, Clara couldn't help but feel the weight of what they represented. These weren't just clothes; they were a symbol of the life she was stepping into.

As she tried on the uniform, she noticed a girl watching her from across the shop. The girl approached, her sharp blue eyes assessing. "Are you Clara Nightfall?"
Clara hesitated. "Yes."

The girl's lips curved into a cold smile. "I thought so. 'The Lost Witch of Nightfall', wasn't it? Quite the scandal. Half-blood, aren't you?"

Clara's chest tightened as the words hit her like stones dropped in deep water. Before she could respond, her grandmother appeared at her side, her presence commanding.

"Lucinda Vale," Selene said coolly, addressing the girl. "Your family's tiresome obsession with bloodlines hasn't aged well Lucinda. I suggest you mind your manners."

Lucinda's smug expression faltered, and she turned away with a flick of her hair. Clara's grandmother placed a reassuring hand on her shoulder. "Pay her no mind, darling. She's as much a product of her family's insecurities as you are of your strength. Don't forget that."

As they left the shop, Clara glanced down at her neatly packed suitcase, feeling the events of the day settle over her. Hidden Row had been a whirlwind of wonder and challenge, but as she walked beside her grandmother, she felt a spark of determination.

This new world was daunting, but it was also hers to explore. And she would face it, one step at a time.

Chapter 15: School Approaches

As the days passed and the start of school neared, Clara found herself settling into a rhythm. Each morning began with early training sessions in the courtyard under Fenwick's watchful eye. Each day, magic became less foreign, its presence merging with her in ways she hadn't imagined.

Clara spent her evenings at formal dinners with her grandparents, where Cassius's judgmental stares often put her on edge. Yet her grandparents eagerly shared tales of the Nightfall family's history, hoping to help her connect with her roots.

One evening, over a rich dessert that Hazel had prepared, her grandfather leaned back in his chair, a nostalgic glint in his eye. "Did you know, Clara, that one of your ancestors, Idris Nightfall, was once called the Guardian of Shadows?" he began, his voice drawing her in immediately. "Idris lived centuries ago, during a time of great magical upheaval. Some called him mad; others admired him. But everyone agreed he had a gift for binding shadows, using them to shield our lands from those who would use dark magic for harm."

Clara leaned forward, intrigued. "What do you mean by binding shadows?"

Eldric smiled faintly. "Idris could summon shadows to form impenetrable barriers, disorienting enemies and shielding the Nightfall lands from harm. His magic protected the family for decades."

Her grandmother added with a soft laugh, "It's said that even the bravest of intruders would turn back before they reached the heart of the estate. Idris was an expert in his art. Perhaps a bit of his shadowy magic runs through you as well, Clara."

Another evening, as the fire crackled beside them, Selene shared a different tale, her voice soft with devotion. "One of my favourite stories is that of Lyra the Everbright, a distant cousin who lived around the time of the first magical societies. Lyra wasn't as powerful as some of the other Nightfalls, but her magic had a rare quality. She was a healer, Clara, with a heart so pure that her magic responded to the simplest of intentions."

Clara's eyebrows raised. "A healer? Like … fixing injuries?"

Her grandmother nodded, her eyes twinkling. "Indeed. But it was more than that. Lyra had a talent for not only physical wounds but also for restoring the heart and spirit. During a particularly dark time, when fear of magical wars loomed, Lyra dedicated herself to helping both magical and non-magical folk alike. She would travel across the country, bringing comfort and healing to villages, mending rifts between communities. People claimed that she could bring light to any room she entered, that her presence alone was like a comfort to the soul. The Nightfall family always remembers her as a beacon in dark times."

"Did she ever come back here?" Clara asked, touched by the story.

Selene smiled gently. "Not for long. Lyra was a wanderer, and her heart belonged to those she helped. In the end, she chose to remain with the people she had sworn to protect, leaving her mark on them rather than seeking a legacy of wealth or power."

Each story revealed a new dimension of her heritage, filling her with a sense of wonder but also responsibility. This family, her family, had not only wielded power but had shaped lives, protecting and healing in ways Clara had never considered before.

Simple things like her dad's texts — *Good morning, baby girl* — grounded her in the midst of her new magical life.

*

Clara sat in the small study, her hands nervously twisting the edge of her sleeve as Fenwick flipped through a thick book at his desk. The shelves around them were packed with books and magical artefacts. Clara's heart felt heavy in her chest as she tried to focus, but the thought of starting at Crowstone in just a few days loomed over her like a storm cloud.

"You look troubled, Miss Clara," Fenwick said, setting the book aside.

She hesitated, her voice faltering as her worries spilled out. "What if I'm not ready? What if I embarrass myself? I feel like I'm barely keeping up with magic."

Fenwick leaned back in his chair, his hands clasped together. "You've come much further than you realise. When you arrived, you knew nothing about magic. Now you've mastered multiple spells, from simple charms to more advanced enchantments. That's no small feat."

Clara frowned, still unconvinced. "But I still mess up all the time. It feels like I'll never be as good as, well, everyone else."

"Miss Clara," Fenwick said, his voice gentle, "magic isn't the same for everyone. Some witches and wizards struggle to cast even the simplest spells, while others seem to have a natural ability for it. You are one of the latter. You have a gift for magic, a spark that's rare and precious. Yes, you still have much to learn, but that's true of every student, no matter how talented they are."

Clara looked at him, her nerves settling slightly. "You really think I can do this?"

"I don't think it; I know it," Fenwick said with a faint smile. "You've proven it to me time and time again. You just need to keep practising and trust in your abilities. Even the most skilled witches and wizards were once beginners. You started much later than most, and before long, you will surpass many of your peers. Of that, I am sure."

Clara paused, a new thought forming. She fiddled with the edge of her sleeve, then looked up at Fenwick. "Can I ask you something else?"

"Of course, Miss Clara," Fenwick replied, tilting his head curiously.

"Who is Therin?" she asked hesitantly, watching as Fenwick's expression shifted. His easy composure faltered, and for a moment, his face darkened with an unreadable emotion.

"Where did you hear that name?" Fenwick asked carefully, his voice quieter now.

Clara hesitated, feeling the weight of her question. "I saw him in a memory. In the Hall of Mirrors. My grandmother refuses to talk about him, but I know he was important to my mother. It seemed like they were close … but then something changed."

Fenwick leaned back in his chair, his hands steepled in front of him. For a long moment, he didn't speak. Then, reluctantly, he sighed. "Clara, I shouldn't say anything. It's not my place. But … perhaps you deserve to know at least part of the truth."

Clara straightened, her heart pounding.

Fenwick's voice was steady, but there was a heaviness to it as he began. "Therin Shadowthorn was once a young wizard full of promise. He was almost part of your family. Your great-grandfather, Alaric Nightfall, was his mentor."

Clara's breath caught. "So, what happened?"

Fenwick's jaw tightened. "Therin became obsessed with ancient magic, and he believed Alaric knew where to find the relics and scrolls that could grant him unimaginable power. When your great-grandfather refused to help him … Therin killed him for it."

Clara gasped, the air leaving her lungs in a rush. "He killed him?"

Fenwick nodded grimly. "No one knows if Alaric truly had the knowledge Therin sought, but it didn't matter. Therin was blinded by power. And that, Clara, is why your family does not speak of him. He betrayed them in the worst way imaginable. I believe your mother left the magical world after that."

Clara's hands trembled as she absorbed the revelation. "But … he was in love with my mam, wasn't he?"

Fenwick's expression softened slightly. "Yes, he and Helena were close, very close. But whatever feelings they shared were extinguished once he was corrupted by the power of ancient magic."

Clara stared down at her hands, her mind racing. "Why wouldn't my grandmother just tell me this?"

Fenwick sighed. "Because it's painful. Because it's a wound that never truly healed. And because, perhaps, she fears what it might mean for you to know. The Nightfalls have always held themselves to impossibly high standards, and Therin's betrayal was a stain on their legacy. It also led to your mother abandoning the family."

Clara looked up at him, her voice trembling. "No wonder my mam wanted to leave it all behind."

Fenwick's expression darkened. "Indeed, Miss Clara. Some wounds are beyond healing. Or more accurately, one has to go to great lengths in order to heal. And it seems it worked for your mother, meeting your father and having you."

He leaned forward, his tone softening. "Please don't mention this to your grandmother. This part of the story is yours to carry now. But if you ever need guidance, you can always come to me."

Clara nodded slowly, her thoughts heavy. She didn't have all the answers yet, but she knew one thing: she wouldn't let Therin's betrayal define her.

*

Clara sat cross-legged on her bed, the warm glow of the enchanted lantern creating soft shadows on the walls of her room. Her fingers absently traced the edge of the Silverdusk-chest, but her mind was far from the room. Fenwick's words from earlier in the day lingered in her thoughts, like whispers she couldn't quite shake.

Therin. The name carried a weight she didn't fully understand, but she felt it pressed heavily on her family. He wasn't just a shadowy figure in her mother's past; he was tied to her family's deepest wounds. A man who had loved her mother. A man who had betrayed her grandfather, betrayed them both. The layers of it were dizzying. How could someone who was once so close to her family turn on them in such a devastating way? And why did her grandmother avoid speaking about him at all?

Clara exhaled, her gaze drifting to the window, to where the moon hung low over the grounds of Nightfall Manor. She understood, at least in part, why her grandmother found it so hard to speak about her mother's past. Losing her daughter had to have been an unbearable pain, and now Clara was asking her to relive those memories. Perhaps her grandmother's silence wasn't just about shielding Clara; perhaps it was about shielding herself too.

Still, Clara felt a restless pull to know more. She wanted to understand who her mother was, what she had lived through, and what choices had shaped her life. Her mother's love for magic, her decision to leave it behind, her connection to Therin, all of it felt like puzzle pieces that, when put together, might help Clara understand the woman she had only known as 'Mam'.

But how could she ask her grandmother to reopen wounds that had never fully healed? Clara bit her lip, torn between her need for answers and her empathy for the woman who had already lost so much. Maybe, she thought, there was a way to learn without prying directly. The Hall of Mirrors? The Dreamcatcher Hallway? Or perhaps even the Starbound Library? The manor itself seemed to be brimming with secrets, and Clara was determined to uncover them.

For now, though, she would be patient. Her grandmother had given her so much already: her history, her magic, her family name. Maybe, in time, her grandmother would trust Clara enough to share more. Until then, Clara resolved to tread carefully. Her mother's story was woven into the fabric of the Nightfall family, and Clara knew she'd need to unravel it one thread at a time.

*

Later that afternoon, Clara wandered into the kitchen, drawn by the delicious aroma of roasted herbs and warm bread. Hazel's wand moved like a conductor's baton, guiding a knife to chop vegetables and stirring a simmering pot with a wooden spoon. Herbs floated into the mixture, adding bursts of colour and aroma to the air.

Clara hesitated in the doorway before stepping inside. "Hazel, can I help with anything?"

Hazel turned, her kind eyes crinkling as she smiled. "Thank you for the offer, Miss Clara, but it isn't necessary."

After a few moments of silence, Clara glanced at Hazel. "I'm sorry I haven't talked to you much. It's just … a lot to get used to. All of this. Thank you for all you do around here, cleaning up and taking care of everyone. I try to keep my room tidy, but you always make it look immaculate, so thank you for that and for all the delicious food you make every day. I've never eaten so well. My dad … I love him to bits, but he isn't exactly the best cook."

Hazel paused her chopping and turned to face Clara. "You've been nothing but kind, Miss Clara. You don't need to apologise nor thank me for doing my job. But I do appreciate your kind words."

Clara hesitated, then said quietly, "Not all Nightfalls are kind, though, are they?"

Hazel's smiled softly. "I would never speak ill of the Nightfall family," she said carefully, "but I'll admit some are … kinder than others."

Curiosity got the better of Clara. "How do you like it here, working for the Nightfalls?"

Hazel gestured to the kitchen around her. "Some people think the work I do is meaningless, but I love it. I take pride in it. And I adore the Nightfall family, even with their quirks. They've always treated me well, and I'm happy to serve them."

As Hazel continued waving her wand, and bread dough was being magically kneaded, Clara perched on a stool nearby. "Hazel, did you ever go to Crowstone?"

Hazel smiled warmly, shaking her head. "No, my dear. I didn't. I went to a much smaller, less well-known magical school. It rarely produces amazing witches or wizards, but I enjoyed it all the same. My parents and I discussed it but felt my simpler aspirations were not aligned with Crowstone's expectations. My strengths are in service, care and fostering community rather than scholarly. My magic is small and useful for the work I do. But I always admired those who went. I think there's something special about a place that teaches you not just how to use magic but how to become the person you're meant to be. You'll find your way there, Clara, and it'll be something to treasure for the rest of your life."

Clara smiled warmly. "Thanks, Hazel. That means a lot." She leaned her elbows on the counter, her gaze thoughtful. "I think it's amazing that you're happy with where you are, Hazel. You make a difference here every day. I hope I am happy in whatever career I choose."

Hazel's cheeks turned a little pink as she waved her hand dismissively. "Oh, you'll make me blush, my dear. But thank you. Your journey is yours alone. Don't compare it to anyone else's. You're already making your family proud."

Clara smiled. "You're a big part of what makes this place feel like home, you know."

Hazel's cheeks reddened a little more as she waved Clara off. "Go on, now. You'll make me blush."

*

That evening, Clara sat at the grand dining table with her grandmother and grandfather. The food was as exquisite as always, but Clara barely touched her plate, her mind still swirling with worry.

Her grandmother noticed. "You're quiet tonight, Clara. Is something on your mind?"

Clara hesitated, then sighed. "I'm nervous about school. Questions keeping whirling round my mind. What if I don't fit in? What if I don't do well? Am I strong enough to handle it all?"

Selene reached across the table, placing a hand gently over Clara's. "My darling, nervousness is natural. It means you care about it, about finding your place. Just be the best *you* that you can be."

Her grandfather, who had been silently observing, leaned forward, his expression thoughtful. "Courage isn't the absence of fear, Clara. It's recognising fear, facing it, and pressing on despite it. If you were never afraid, there would be no need for courage at all. Nerves and doubts are simply part of the journey. Even the greatest witches and wizards were once uncertain of their own abilities. Confidence doesn't come from always getting it right; it comes from embracing the challenge, learning from mistakes, and standing back up when you stumble."

Clara looked between them, feeling a small flicker of hope. "I guess I just fear … that I won't belong. I never grew up around magic or went to a magical prep school."

"Those are perfectly normal feelings," Eldric said. "But you'll find your place, Clara. And if you stumble along the way, remember, you have us, and you have your own strength. Trust in both."

Clara smiled at him, her curiosity piqued. "Grandfather, what was it like when you went to Crowstone?"

Her grandfather chuckled, leaning back in his chair.

"Oh, it was a different world back then. No fancy enchanted maps to guide you around. We had to learn the hard way. My first week, I got lost in the North Tower and ended up missing an entire afternoon's worth of classes. Professor Barnyard was livid. In fact, he was always furious with me. I was, shall we say, a little mischievous. It took me a while to settle in and truly find what made Crowstone special. But what I remember most were the friendships and the lessons that stayed with me long after I left. You'll learn magic, yes, but you'll also learn about yourself. It's not always easy, but it's worth every moment."

Clara chuckled at her grandfather's story. "You were mischievous? That doesn't sound very … Nightfall of you, Grandfather."

Eldric laughed heartily. "Even Nightfalls have to start somewhere, my darling. It's the mistakes and the unexpected moments that make the journey memorable."

Clara nodded. "I suppose it's comforting to know even you struggled to find your way. Maybe I'll make my own unforgettable memories, hopefully not in the North Tower, though."

"It is your time to carve out your own path," her grandmother said gently. "Crowstone will help shape you into the bright young witch you're already becoming."

Clara nodded, something soft and steady blooming in her chest. The journey ahead still felt daunting, but with the support of those around her, she began to believe she might just be ready to take the first step.

*

Later that evening, as Clara sat by her window, the glow of moonlight spilling into her room, she replayed the conversations in her mind. Fenwick's encouragement reminded her that she didn't need to be perfect, her grandfather's story showed her that even the great Nightfalls had their missteps, and Hazel's quiet wisdom reassured her that the path she was on didn't have to match anyone else's.

Moonlight spilled over the sprawling grounds of Nightfall Manor as Clara gazed out of her window. Hope stirred faintly in her chest. Maybe she could find her own way at Crowstone, a path of mistakes, memories, and magic.

Chapter 16: Where Paths Begin

The Nightfall carriage glided through the sky, pulled by the shimmering Moondancer. Clara sat rigidly, excitement and nerves twisting in her stomach as the air currents whispered beneath them.

"Not long now," Clara's grandmother said, her voice calm but touched with anticipation. She glanced out of the window and then at Clara. "Look ahead, darling. You'll want to see this."

Clara turned, pressing her face close to the glass, and gasped. Rising in the distance was Crowstone Academy, its splendour unlike anything she could have imagined.

Crowstone loomed like a timeless fortress, its towers crowned with gold that caught the sunlight. The castle, alive with centuries of magic, stood as both a school and a guardian of its history.

The vast grounds held sprawling courtyards, glowing greenhouses, and gardens alive with pulsing magical plants whose colours shifted unnaturally.

Encircling the entire property stood a towering iron fence, its intricate design etched with ancient runes that fortified the school. The fence guarded a massive iron gate that marked the entrance to the academy. From the gate, a long, narrow path wound its way to the castle, which bustled with students, professors, and carriages arriving from the path, with a queue stretching all the way to the gate.

Beyond the fence, the dense forest stretched for miles, its dark trees swaying unnaturally, as though stirred by an unseen force. Clara blinked, certain she saw one of the trees shift its roots, gliding a few feet before settling back into place. She shivered, her imagination racing. "It's enormous," she murmured, pressing a hand to the glass. "Bigger than I ever imagined."

Her grandfather gave a small grunt of approval. "As it should be. Crowstone was designed not only to educate but to protect. This is a fortress as much as it is a school, a safe haven for magical knowledge and its guardians."

The carriage descended gracefully towards the gates, where a robed professor stood waiting, parchment hovering mid-air beside him.

"Lord Eldric and Lady Selene," he said, inclining his head respectfully. "Welcome to Crowstone. And this," he added, his eyes settling on Clara with a knowing smile, "must be Clara Nightfall."

Clara managed a timid nod, her heart thudding as the quill beside the professor scrawled furiously across the floating parchment.

"Please proceed," the professor said, gesturing for the carriage to move forward. The gates groaned open with an almost sentient slowness, their runes flickering faintly as they shifted.

The carriage rolled through, following the path that seemed to stretch endlessly towards the castle. As they passed the gardens, Clara caught glimpses of magical plants shifting their petals and glowing softly as if reacting to her presence. A gentle hum of magic seemed to emanate from the very ground beneath them.

When they reached the front of the castle, another professor stepped forwards to greet them. He was younger than the first, his robes immaculate and his demeanour brisk. He looked at Clara expectantly.

"Name, please?"

Clara hesitated, unsure if he was serious. "Er … Clara. Clara Nightfall."

The professor raised an eyebrow, clearly unfamiliar with the name or perhaps just not caring, before glancing at his hovering parchment. "Ah, a new student starting in Year Eight. Welcome to Crowstone."

With a flick of his wand, Clara's suitcase floated gently out of her hands and into the air. "Your bags will be waiting in your room when you get there," he said, his tone professional but slightly distracted. "Now, please go ahead to the headmistress's office, in Eldra's Tower. If in doubt, follow the light." He flicked his wand and small ball of bright light appeared, leading the way.

Clara barely had time to nod before her grandparents began ascending the wide stone steps leading to the castle's entrance, following the small ball of light. The towering wooden doors swung open as they approached, revealing a grand hallway lined with glowing lanterns and shifting wall-hangings.

Inside, the air was cooler, mixed with the faint scent of aged wood and parchment. The stone corridors seemed endless, twisting and turning in ways that made Clara feel disoriented. Her grandparents moved with purpose, clearly familiar with the layout, although the ball of light was still leading in case they misremembered the way. Clara struggled to keep up, her head swivelling to take in every detail.

Portraits lined the walls, their eyes following Clara with faint curiosity. Suits of armour stood at attention in alcoves, some of them shifting slightly as if alive. The sound of distant chatter and footsteps echoed, adding to the overwhelming sense of the scale and magic of the school.

Finally, they stopped in front of a massive wooden door, its surface carved with intricate designs of magical creatures. The door radiated an air of authority and importance, its presence both intimidating and awe-inspiring. On both sides of the door were stone gargoyles that seemed to guard it.

"This is it," her grandmother said. "Eldra's Tower, the headmistress's office."

Clara tilted her head back to take in the towering structure before her. The entire tower was made of silverstone, its surface rippling like water under the soft glow of light shining through the windows.

Her grandparents stood beside her, their poise unshaken. Her grandmother adjusted her gloves with the same grace she always carried, while her grandfather glanced at the door, his sharp eyes scanning it as though reading its secrets.

Clara clutched the strap of her bag, her palms damp. She opened her mouth to speak but froze as the heavy doors creaked open, revealing a tall, imposing woman. Her silver hair was tied back neatly, and her robes were black as the night itself, embroidered with shimmering threads that gave the impression of a starry sky. Her presence was commanding, her piercing gaze enough to make Clara straighten her posture.

"Lord Eldric, Lady Selene," the woman greeted, nodding respectfully to her grandparents before turning to Clara. "And you must be Clara Nightfall."

"Yes," Clara said, her voice barely above a whisper.

The woman's lips curved into a faint smile. "I am Professor Mornvale, the headmistress of Crowstone Academy. It's a pleasure to meet you, Clara."

Clara nodded nervously, unsure of how to respond. She sensed the professor was guarded, as though she was used to giving nothing away.

"Now," Professor Mornvale continued, addressing her grandparents, "if you don't mind, I'd like to have a brief word with you before I speak to Clara."

Her grandparents stepped forward, leaving Clara standing alone at the base of the tower. She watched them disappear behind the doors, her heart pounding as she waited in the silence.

Across the corridor, Clara noticed a boy about her age sitting in a wooden chair near the wall. He was tapping his fingers rhythmically on the armrest, his dark hair neatly combed and his uniform pristine. He looked up when he noticed her staring, giving her a polite nod.

"Hi," Clara said sheepishly, walking over and sitting on a bench near him. "I'm Clara. It's my first day here today. I'm starting in Year Eight."

The boy straightened in his seat, his posture formal. "Leo Rutherford," he said, offering a faint smile. "Same here. Transferring from Wernwood Academy in Switzerland."

"Wernwood?" Clara asked. "Is that another magical school?"

Leo nodded. "Smaller than Crowstone but decent enough. My father has business here, so it made sense to transfer."

"This is my first magical school. I only found out I was a witch recently, so I've got a lot to catch up on."

"How did you not know you were a witch? I've never heard of that happening before," Leo said, his brow furrowing in genuine confusion.

"It's a long story," Clara replied, shifting slightly in her seat. "But I grew up in the non-magical world. My mam was a witch, but she died when I was four. She put some kind of protective charm on me to hide me from the

166

magical world. It only stopped working recently. That's when I got this invitation to a festival; it's only sent to witches and wizards."

Leo leaned forwards slightly. "Why would she want to hide you?"

Clara nodded. "Turns out my mam belonged to a really powerful magical family, and something happened that made her walk away from them. I didn't even know they existed until a few months ago. They've been helping me learn about this world and getting me ready for Crowstone. Honestly, I'd be completely lost without them. My grandparents are with the headmistress now, sorting out some last details, I guess."

Leo tilted his head, studying her for a moment. "So, you've just been thrown into all of this: magic, powerful family, new school … that would be a lot for anyone to handle."

"I'm handling it the best I can," Clara said with a small, nervous laugh. "Some days, it feels like I'm drowning in it all. But I've been practising spells, and I think I'm starting to get the hang of things. Kind of."

Leo smiled, a bit of admiration glinting in his eyes. "Well, for what it's worth, I think you'll do just great."

Clara's cheeks warmed at his words. "Thanks," she said softly, surprised by how much his encouragement eased her nerves.

"You're not alone, you know," Leo added. "It's my first day here too, and while I'm not new to magic, I'm definitely new to Crowstone Academy. If we stick together, perhaps it will be easier to settle in."

Clara smiled at him, feeling the faintest flicker of hope. "Yeah," she said. "That sounds like a good idea."

Leo's expression softened. "We're going to be great

friends, I can just tell."

As Clara looked at Leo, something beneath the surface tugged at Clara's awareness.

It wasn't his words exactly; he was charming and confident enough, perhaps a little too much for her liking. Yet there was a subtle edge to his voice, an undertone of something unsaid. His smile was bright, but it didn't quite reach his eyes. There was a heaviness there, a flicker of discomfort she couldn't place. For a brief moment, a wave of emotions brushed against her: uncertainty, a hint of fear, and something else she couldn't quite name. It was like he was bracing himself against being seen too clearly, as though afraid someone might look too closely and uncover something he wanted to hide.

He's just nervous, Clara told herself, brushing the feeling away. *New school, new people. Anyone would feel out of place.* She thought about her own anxieties since arriving and how overwhelming it had been to step into a world she didn't yet fully understand. Maybe Leo was just struggling with the same thing: his identity, his place in all of this, like so many of them.

Still, the feeling lingered, faint but persistent, like the echo of a song she couldn't quite remember. Clara shook it off, determined not to read too much into it. After all, first impressions weren't always accurate.

Suddenly, the doors to the tower opened again, and her grandparents appeared, their expressions unreadable. Her grandmother stepped forwards and cupped Clara's face gently in her hands.

"This is where your journey begins, Clara," she said softly. "Trust yourself and let the school guide you towards greatness."

Her grandfather placed a hand on her shoulder. "We'll see you again soon. Do us proud."

Clara swallowed hard and nodded, hugging them both before they turned and disappeared down the corridor.

The headmistress reappeared in the doorway, her gaze sweeping over both Clara and Leo. "Come with me, you two," she said, her tone leaving no room for hesitation.

Clara and Leo exchanged a glance before following her into the tower. Inside, the walls shimmered with the same silverstone as the exterior. The air was cool and carried the faint scent of roses and aged wood.

Before the door could close, a boy appeared, his uniform slightly rumpled, his tie undone. He grinned as he saw them approach.

"Finn Adu," Professor Mornvale introduced, her tone annoyed but fond. "One of our more … experienced students. Finn will be your guide today. Finn, this is Clara Nightfall and Leo Rutherford."

Finn was a Ghanaian-British student with tightly curled hair and a rich, dark complexion that caught the light warmly. His easy grin seemed ever-present, and his deep brown eyes sparkled with mischief and intelligence. Finn carried himself with a confident ease, brightening the room with his infectious energy and charm.

Finn gave a slight nod, his grin widening. "Ah, fresh faces. Don't worry, Professor, I'll make sure they survive their first week. Mostly."

Professor Mornvale narrowed her eyes. "Finn, best behaviour, please. I'll check in with you all later, once you have had a chance to settle in." Professor Mornvale's sharp gaze softened as she looked at Clara, Leo, and Finn standing before her. She straightened her robes, her voice calm yet carrying an authority that commanded their attention.

"Crowstone is a place of learning," she began, her eyes moving from one student to the next, "but learning here is not just about magic. Yes, you will study spells, potions, and ancient texts, and I expect each of you to strive for academic excellence. But true greatness lies not just in the magic you wield but in the person you choose to become."

She paused, her tone deepening. "Magic doesn't make you good or wise; that's your choice, one you'll face every day. Treat each other with respect and learn from one another."

Her gaze lingered on Finn, her mouth curving into the faintest smile. "You don't need magic to be kind to one another. And in the moments when your magic falters or you doubt your abilities, remember this: your character will always define you more than your spells. Be the best witches and wizards you can be, yes, but above all, be the best people you can be."

With that, she folded her hands in front of her and nodded at the three of them. "Off you go. Your journey here begins now."

With that, she turned and disappeared back into her office, leaving Clara and Leo standing with their newfound guide.

Her words hung in the air like a quiet spell, and Clara felt her nerves ease just a little. She couldn't help but think that perhaps the hardest magic to master wasn't about wands or incantations but the choices they made about the kind of people they wanted to be.

Finn laughed, throwing a wink at Clara and Leo. "Come on, noobs. Let's get you sorted."

Clara felt a mix of nervousness and excitement bubbling in her chest. She didn't know what the day would bring, but she was ready to find out.

Finn shoved his hands into his pockets and nodded towards the hallway. "Right, then. Let's get this tour started before Professor Mornvale changes her mind. I'll show you the important places … and maybe one or two of the fun ones."

Finn led Clara and Leo through several corridors and down a few flights of stairs before going through a wide stone archway that opened into the school's sprawling grounds. The sunlight cast a warm glow over the fields.

"So," Finn said, hands still in his pockets as he strolled ahead, "a quick tour of the essentials, followed by a crash course in survival skills. You'll need both to make it through your first week here." He gave them a mischievous grin.

Clara and Leo followed Finn through the towering stone archway that led into the heart of Crowstone Academy. The sprawling courtyard stretched out before them, a hive of activity as students rushed between buildings, chatting in animated voices or practising spells with casual confidence. Clara's nerves felt like a coiled spring as she took in the sights. Every corner of the academy was alive with magic.

Finn turned back to look at them, his lopsided grin firmly in place. "Welcome to Crowstone, you two," he said, rubbing his hands together. "The place where you'll either become a legendary witch or wizard … or perhaps you'll set yourself on fire trying. It's all part of the charm."

The school loomed above them, its jagged towers of frosted quartz and shadowstone twisting skyward like frozen storms. The walls glimmered as if draped in a curtain of starlight, their surfaces shifting like liquid metal. The air vibrated softly, carrying an ancient power that brushed against Clara's skin, leaving her both amazed and unnerved.

"Let's start with the Sanctum of Spells, the heart of the academy." Finn gestured towards the central structure, its spires spiralling together like enchanted vines frozen mid-twist. "It's reserved for Year Tens and Elevens, where advanced magical learning takes place. Here, students are introduced to complex and delicate arts such as spellweaving, enchantment creation, and ancient incantations. Under strict supervision, they practise higher-level magic that demands precision and focus, often through one-on-one guidance from professors."

"The Hall of Echoes is right through those doors," Finn said, nodding towards the arched entrance. "It's for the school dances and any other school activities that require such a large space for all the students in the school at once. The only other place big enough is the Great Solstice Hall, but that's where we eat and have assemblies. We'll save that for the last stop on this amazing tour, as it should be about time to meet, greet and eat. Back to the Hall of Echoes, the ceiling shows moving murals of magical battles, rituals, and the academy's history. Oh, and the floor? Looks like starlight but feels like stone. Pretty trippy."

"Inside, you've also got the Everflame Torch," Finn continued. "It's a big fire that never goes out, symbol of the academy's magical heart and all that. Professors get really sentimental about it during speeches. You'll see."

Clara hesitated at the entrance, her gaze fixed on the towering doors. Even from here, she thought she could hear faint whispers, a strange echo that made her both curious and uneasy. She glanced at Leo, who raised an eyebrow, clearly unimpressed, before Finn waved them forward.

*

He led them towards a shimmering bridge that seemed to float.

"This is the Library of Evergrow," Finn said. "The shelves go on forever, and the Hall of Mirrors lets you see moving visions of the books you're reading. It's magical."

Clara's eyes widened. "That sounds incredible."

*

They descended a cobblestone path that led to the academy's famous gardens. Finn swept an arm towards the expanse of greenery. "Behold, the Living Grove. It's enchanted, obviously. Those giant trees? Everroot trees. Their bark changes colour with the seasons, and they'll guide you back if you get lost. Pretty handy."

Clara spotted one of the trees swaying its branches, almost as if waving at them.

"The Wisdomwood willows," Finn continued, pointing to a cluster of smaller trees, "are great if you need cheering up. They hum gently in the moonlight and have been known to drop a wish leaf. Carry it, and you'll get good fortune. Or so they say."

Leo nodded, looking genuinely impressed. "What about those glowing trees?"

"Goldenleaf maples," Finn replied. "Their sap's used in healing potions. Just don't try to tap them yourself. Professor Hawthorne guards those trees like they're her children."

As they moved deeper into the gardens, they passed

the Fairy Garden, where pixie lanterns glowed softly among the flower beds, attracting tiny, winged creatures. Willowlights floated lazily above the plants, their soft light creating ethereal shadows.

"Welcome to the land of magical bugs," Finn said. "The lora fireflies change colour depending on the flowers they visit. Then you've got the bumblesprites, chubby little bees that make honey with healing properties. And those webs you see? Gossamer spinners. Their webs keep pests away and help plants grow. Nature's weird but cool, right?"

Clara smiled, enchanted by the delicate ecosystem surrounding her. "This place feels alive."

"That's because it is," Finn said with a smile.

They moved further into the courtyard, passing students lounging by a fountain where the water shimmered in vibrant, ever-changing colours. Finn pointed towards a glass-domed structure glowing faintly at the far end of the gardens.

"And over there," he said, "is the Botanical Conservatory, where you'll meet the one and only Professor Myra Hawthorne. She's lovely, kind, patient, and smells like freshly brewed tea. She's obsessed with plants that will either heal you or try to eat you, so keep your fingers tucked in during lessons. Last year, a student tried to *befriend* a fanged violet, and well, let's just say he was in for a heck of a week growing back three fingers."

Leo chuckled, while Clara raised an eyebrow. "Noted. No befriending fanged violets."

Clara glanced towards the conservatory, where she could see faint shapes of magical plants shifting within the glass. "What other kind of plants do we work with?"

"Oh, all sorts," Finn said. "Healing herbs, protective

vines, flowers that explode if you sneeze near them, you name it. It can be fascinating … if you like tending to things that grow."

Leo smirked. "Doesn't sound like your kind of lesson."

Finn shrugged. "Professor Hawthorne is great … but the plants? Not so much. Some can be unpredictable and dangerous if you're not careful. Others are harmless enough, but there is something about magical plants that freaks me out."

*

As Finn led Clara and Leo through the sprawling campus of Crowstone, his enthusiasm seemed to grow with every step. The towering spires of the House Towers soon came into view, each one distinct in its architecture and exuding its own magical aura. Clara and Leo couldn't help but slow down, their eyes drawn to the impressive structures ahead.

"Ah, here we are, the House Towers," Finn announced with a flourish, gesturing to the five grand towers rising above the rest of the grounds. "Your future homes away from home. Each house has its own tower, complete with common rooms, dormitories, and study areas. Boys on one side, girls on the other, and each year group gets its own floor. They keep the first-years, sorry, Year Sevens, on the bottom floor. We have to wait until Year Eleven until we get the best rooms in the house … well, school … academy. You know what I mean."

"Aurora's for the scholars and strategists," Finn said. "Brilliant with Magical Histories and Charms. They're a bit bookish, sure, but when brains and wands combine? Unstoppable."

Next, Finn turned to the tower with fiery orange

beams spiralling up its stonework. "Flarewood," he said, smirking. "House of fire and passion, literally. These folks excel in Elemental Manipulation, especially the flashier kinds. Hot-headed, competitive, and occasionally prone to explosions, but they'll always back you up in a fight. If you like big personalities and bigger egos, you'll fit right in."

Clara raised an eyebrow. "Do they really cause explosions?"

Finn chuckled. "Oh, definitely. The professors have a whole section of the training grounds just for Flarewood practice. Safer for everyone that way."

He led them further along, stopping in front of a tower with walls that seemed to blend seamlessly into the surrounding gardens. The air around it smelled faintly of moss and fresh rain. "Evergrove," Finn explained. "House of connection and growth. They're amazing at Botanical Arts and anything involving magical creatures. Very grounded, very patient, but don't underestimate them. Those peaceful types can be sneaky when they want to be."

Leo nodded thoughtfully. "They sound … balanced."

"They are," Finn agreed. "Until they get competitive. Then it's all vines and thorns."

They moved on to a sleek, dark tower. Finn's grin turned mischievous. "And that's Nightspire, the house of cunning, secrecy, and all things shadowy. Masters of Illusions and Binding Magic. They're sharp, resourceful, and usually plotting something. If you hear whispers in the hallways, odds are it's an Nightspire group hatching a plan. Fun to hang out with, but don't let your guard down."

Finally, Finn stopped before a tower with soaring golden spires and banners depicting quills and parchment.

"And last but definitely not least, my house," Finn pointed to the first tower on the left, its walls glowing faintly as if reflecting moonlight. "That's Luminaris," he said. "The house for those with a natural talent for spellcrafting and enchantments. We're known for being meticulous, creative, and sometimes a little too obsessed with detail. We're great people to have on your team if you need a tricky spell woven. I'm biased, obviously, but it is the best house."

Clara glanced at the banners, already feeling a sense of pride. "I like the sound of that," she said, smiling.

Finn clapped her on the back. "You should. Luminaris is where the best people are." He gave Leo a sidelong glance. "No offence if you end up somewhere else, mate."

Leo smirked. "None taken. But I wouldn't count me out just yet."

As they walked on, Finn added, "Each house has its strengths. In the end, it's what you do here that counts. Unless you're in Flarewood, then it's all about being loud and fiery." He winked, and even Leo cracked a smile.

Clara took in the towers, each one unique and pulsing with its own magical energy. She couldn't help but wonder which one she'd end up in and what her journey at Crowstone would bring.

*

Finn led them to the edge of the campus, where a towering coliseum dominated the landscape. Its massive stone walls shimmered faintly with magical wards, while storm-like enchantments swirled above the open roof, crackling with energy. The arena floor shifted and adapted, transforming between jagged rocks, flowing rivers, and open plains as students tested their skills in a controlled environment.

"This is the Tempest Coliseum," Finn said with a dramatic wave of his arm. "It's where the big events happen, tournaments, games, and anything that needs a bit of grandeur. Think of it as the stage for Crowstone's finest magical performances."

Clara stared, mesmerised by the sheer size of the arena and the dynamic magic flowing through its grounds. "So, no practising here?" she asked.

"Not unless you're part of something official," Finn replied, his grin widening. "The Duelling Arena is more your speed for day-to-day spellslinging. That's where you'll, uh, learn to not set yourself on fire, or your classmates."

He led them around the coliseum, pointing out a smaller stone arena tucked away near the edge of the grounds. Its wards shimmered in the sunlight, and several students were engaged in duels, their spellwork lighting up the air between them. "The Duelling Arena," Finn said, gesturing to it with a mock flourish. "Smaller, practical, and definitely less terrifying than the coliseum. Trust me, you'll get plenty of bruises here, but at least the stakes aren't as high."

"Speak for yourself," Leo muttered, watching a dual end with one student flung into a cushioned wall by a burst of wind.

Finn smirked. "Yeah, okay, it can still be rough, but at least there's no audience. Well, unless you count your classmates pointing and laughing."

As they turned a corner, the landscape shifted, revealing the Mystical Lake, its shimmering surface reflecting the sky with an almost unnatural clarity. The water sparkled faintly, as though infused with stardust, and along the banks, students practised manipulating the elements. Spiralling whirlpools formed at their command, while others conjured jets of flame or raised walls of earth with focused precision.

"And this," Finn said grandly, "is the Elemental Training Grounds. Professor Ainsley runs the lessons here. She's an absolute legend, though you might not think so when you're dodging boulders or trying not to drown. This is where you'll learn to control fire, water, earth, and air. And, if you're like me, probably set your own robes on fire in the process."

Clara's eyes widened as a jet of water collided with a wall of fire nearby, sending up a cloud of steam. "It looks intense."

"It is," Finn replied. "But once you figure it out, it's kind of amazing. Just … don't get overconfident. This place has a way of humbling even the best spellcasters."

Clara's eyes widened as she watched a student accidentally send a jet of water straight into another's face. "Is it dangerous?"

Finn grinned. "Only if you're reckless. Ainsley's amazing, though, she's like a force of nature herself. One moment, she's encouraging you to channel your inner calm, and the next, she's hurling a boulder at you to test your reflexes. It's exhilarating."

Leo muttered, "Exhilarating isn't the word I'd use."

They continued past the Elemental Training Grounds and into the shadow of a tall stone structure. Finn gestured towards a dark archway that led underground. "Down there is the Rune Caverns, where you'll meet Professor Darnel. If you like precision, you'll love him. If you don't, well … good luck."

"What's he like?" Clara asked.

"Strict," Finn replied. "He's all about perfection. Once, he made a student redo a protective ward twenty times because the lines weren't symmetrical enough. By the end, the poor kid couldn't draw a straight line to save his life."

Clara laughed nervously. "Sounds … intense."

"Oh, he is," Finn said. "But he's brilliant. His runes are why this place hasn't been overrun by magical beasts or rogue spells."

Finn gestured dramatically to the grand tower on their left, its ancient stonework reaching high into the sky. "Behold, the Tower of Antiquities, home to Professor Valen and the most riveting history lessons you'll ever … endure."

Clara squinted at the tower, its windows glinting in the sunlight. "History? Doesn't sound too bad."

Finn snorted. "That's what everyone thinks. But Valen has a gift for turning ancient wars and magical artefacts into bedtime stories. Just keep a quill moving, nod occasionally, and for the love of magic, don't fall asleep. Rumour is he's been known to spell inattentive students with temporary amnesia, to teach the importance of concentration."

Clara looked genuinely alarmed. "He spells students?"

Finn grinned. "That's what the rumours say anyway, although I doubt he would get away with it with Mornvale. She doesn't miss a trick, that one. Besides, history isn't all bad. You get to learn about epic magical battles, enchanted artefacts, and all the times our professors' ancestors accidentally unleashed catastrophic spells. Makes your own mistakes seem small in comparison."

The tour continued past the Charms Hall, where students were practising enchantments that made objects levitate and dance in midair.

"Charms Hall is home to Professor Winters, master of illusions and glamours," Finn said. "She's got this way of making you believe you're looking at reality when it's just her magic. Brilliant teacher, but don't let her catch you daydreaming. She'll turn your reality into something … terrifying."

Clara couldn't help but laugh. "You've got a story behind that, haven't you?"

"Maybe," Finn said, grinning. "Let's just say watching myself as a troll wearing a dress was a surreal experience."

*

As the tour wound down, Finn led them back towards the main courtyard. The sprawling building loomed behind them, its spires reaching high into the sky as the sun began to dip lower.

"So, what do you think?" Finn asked, turning to face them.

"It's … a lot," Clara admitted. "But it's incredible. I don't think I've ever seen anything like this."

"You'll get used to it," Finn said, his grin softening into something more genuine. "Crowstone can be overwhelming at first, but you'll find your place. Trust me, by the end of your first week, you'll feel at home. The food here is amazing. We eat like kings and queens."

Leo smirked. "And what about you? Tell us something about you."

Finn spread his arms theatrically. "Me? I'm your tour guide, your occasional bad influence, and the guy who'll save your life when the thistleback ferns come for you."

Clara laughed, feeling her nerves ease slightly. As they followed Finn back towards the main building, she couldn't help but think that maybe, just maybe, she was starting to feel a little less like an outsider, like she belonged to this magical place.

After the official tour, Finn led Clara and Leo away from the main paths, his grin widening with each step. "Now that we've covered the basics, let me show you the real Crowstone. You didn't think I'd let you two stick to the boring stuff, did you?"

Clara glanced nervously at Leo, who shrugged but followed anyway. They trailed Finn down a narrow corridor, the stone walls lined with glowing lanterns. He stopped at what appeared to be an ordinary wooden door, though the runes carved into it pulsated slightly.

"This," Finn said dramatically, "is the Room of Misplaced Objects. It's where things that are lost, or let's be honest, stolen, end up."

"What do you mean?" Clara asked, frowning at the plain-looking door.

Finn pushed it open with a bang, and Clara gasped. The room was enormous, far larger than seemed possible, packed floor to ceiling with every imaginable object: wands, quills, enchanted books, cauldrons, cloaks, even a suit of armour that appeared to be snoring.

Leo raised an eyebrow. "And do we have permission?"

Finn grinned. "Let's not dwell on minor details."

As they wandered through the maze of objects, Clara spotted a key which hovered in midair, twitching before flying off. Nearby, a stack of books shuffled themselves into order, muttering faintly about organisation.

"Does anyone ever, you know, take things from here that aren't theirs?" Clara asked.

Finn smirked. "Not unless they want to deal with Professor Mornvale. She's got a sixth sense for when something leaves this room without authorisation. Let's just say the last person who tried to sneak out something that wasn't theirs ended up with painted blue hands for a week, to deter any other prospective thieves."

"Good to know," Leo muttered, stepping away from a beautifully carved wand.

Finn led them out of the Room of Misplaced Objects and down another winding hallway, this one darker and quieter than the rest. The air felt charged, and Clara shivered despite the warmth of her robes.

"This," Finn said in a hushed voice, "is the Whispering Hall. It's where the walls … talk."

"The walls talk?" Clara repeated, narrowing her eyes.

"Sort of," Finn said, tapping one of the stone walls. "It's an echo chamber for significant events. Anytime something significant happens in Crowstone, like a big duel or a new enchantment, the whispers of it end up here. Crowstone is attuned to what goes on. What ends up here, no one has any control over. Listen closely."

Clara and Leo leaned in, pressing their ears to the cool stone. At first, all Clara heard was a faint hum, but then she caught fragments of voices: someone shouting an incantation, the clash of magic, and faint laughter.

"It's like … pieces of history," Leo said, pulling back with a look of wonder.

"Exactly," Finn said. "Some students come here to study, hoping to catch whispers of old spells. Others use it to freak out first-years with ghost stories. You never know what you'll hear."

Clara listened again, her heart quickening as she heard the faint murmur of a voice she didn't recognise: "Protect the scrolls. At all costs." She pulled back abruptly, her pulse racing.

"You all right?" Finn asked, noticing her expression.

"Yeah," Clara said quickly. "It's just … a lot to take in."

Finn gave her a curious look but didn't press further.

*

Finn stopped in front of a large mosaic embedded into one of the walls in the long hallway. It shimmered faintly, the tiles appearing to shift subtly as if alive. Clara and Leo stared, captivated by the complex design, a swirling collage of colours and shapes that seemed to tell a story just out of reach.

"These," Finn began with a dramatic pause, "are Memory Mosaics. Probably one of the coolest things in Crowstone, if you ask me."

Clara tilted her head. "Memory mosaics? What do they do?"

Finn grinned and tapped a tile with his finger. It glowed softly in response. "They're magical recordings, basically. Each tile stores a fragment of a memory, events, breakthroughs, even personal moments if someone's important enough. You can *replay* them by placing your hand on the mosaic. Watch this."

He placed his palm flat on a tile in the centre. Immediately, light erupted from the mosaic, swirling into a three-dimensional image that hovered in the air before them. It showed a scene of a battle, witches and wizards in flowing robes casting spells that lit up the sky, their magic clashing in bursts of flame and lightning. A towering figure in golden armour led the charge, his staff glowing with an intense, blinding light.

"This is from the Second Magical War," Finn explained, his tone unusually reverent. "That's Grand Wizard Eryndor, one of Crowstone's most famous graduates. He led the final battle against the Shadow Faction and sealed their leader in a magical void. Epic stuff."

Leo leaned closer, his eyes wide. "It's like … stepping into history."

"Exactly," Finn said, letting the memory fade back into the mosaic. "The public mosaics like this one hold memories of big, historical events, battles, magical discoveries, and founding moments of the academy. But there are private mosaics, too, for people who've contributed something significant to magic. You'll find those scattered around the school, usually in quieter places."

Clara reached out, her fingers brushing a smaller tile near the edge. It glowed faintly, but she hesitated. "What happens if you touch a personal one?"

Finn shrugged. "Depends on the memory. Some are just reflections, someone's thoughts while creating a new spell, for example. Others are more intense, like being right there in the moment. They're protected, though; if a memory's too personal, it won't replay unless you have permission."

"Can anyone add to them?" Leo asked.

"Not just anyone," Finn replied. "Apparently, only the headteacher can bind a memory to a mosaic. But sometimes they can just appear, as though the school itself is preserving magical history and making sure it's not forgotten."

Clara stared at the mosaic, her mind buzzing with questions. What kinds of memories were hidden throughout the school? Would she one day leave a fragment of herself in one of these tiles?

Clara touched the mosaic and froze as a faint voice

whispered, "Beware the shadows within." Her pulse quickened, but when she leaned closer, the whisper was gone.

Leo caught her expression and seemed unfazed. "If you want to leave your mark on a mosaic, you'll probably have to do something legendary first."

Clara rolled her eyes but couldn't help smiling. "Guess I'd better start planning, then."

"That's the spirit," Finn said, clapping her on the shoulder before turning to lead them to the next stop on their tour.

*

For the final stop, Finn led them to a narrow spiral staircase tucked away behind one of the academy's oldest corridors. The air grew cooler as they ascended, and Clara noticed faint runes etched into the stone walls, glowing softly as they passed. The staircase opened onto a wide, curved balcony enclosed by a sophisticated wrought-iron railing. The view it offered took Clara's breath away.

Below them, at the heart of the chamber, stood an enormous stone archway. It crackled faintly with lines of blue energy that twisted and shimmered like lightning contained within glass. Symbols etched into the arch's surface glowed faintly, their patterns shifting as though alive. The floor around the portal was carved into concentric circles marked with runes that pulsed gently, feeding into the magic of the arch.

"This," Finn said, leaning casually against the railing, "is the Portal Chamber. Or, as I like to call it, the Do-Not-Even-Think-About-It Room."

Clara leaned over the railing, mesmerised by the power emanating from the archway. "It's beautiful," she murmured, her voice barely above a whisper. "What's it for?"

"It's for portal magic," Finn explained. "Transportation, experiments, and all sorts of advanced magical studies. But don't get any ideas; this place is completely off-limits to students. You'd have better luck sneaking into Professor Mornvale's office than getting anywhere near that thing."

Clara glanced at the glowing runes encircling the portal, then at the faint shimmer in the air between the balcony and the chamber below. "Is that a … ward?"

Finn grinned. "Good eye. Yep, that's a protection ward. Stops anyone from climbing or flying down to the portal. It's keyed to the professors, so unless you've got a death wish, I wouldn't recommend testing it."

Leo raised an eyebrow. "Has anyone actually tried?"

"Oh, loads," Finn replied with a chuckle. "A seventh-year once tried using a levitation charm to bypass the ward. Didn't end well. Let's just say the ward zapped him mid-air, and he spent the next week stuck with green hair and glowing eyebrows."

Clara bit back a laugh, imagining the scene. "So how does it work? The portal, I mean."

"It's all rune magic," Finn said, pointing to the intricate carvings along the arch's frame. "Each professor has their own unique rune key. They place it on the arch, and it activates to take them wherever they need to go. Without a key, though? The portal's as useful as a broken broomstick."

Leo frowned. "What happens if someone tries to use it without a key?"

Finn leaned closer, lowering his voice conspiratorially. "Legend has it, the portal has a sense of humour. If you try to activate it without authorisation, it spits you out somewhere random. One poor kid ended up in the kitchens, locked in the larder for hours before someone found him. Another time, someone landed on the roof without their wand and with no means of getting down."

Clara's eyes widened. "And they let students near this thing?"

"It's safe with professor supervision," Finn admitted. "And unless you're a professor or you've got a key, the ward makes sure you're staying right here on the balcony."

Clara leaned against the railing, her gaze fixed on the glowing portal below. There was something about it, a strange pull, as though it were calling her. She shook the thought away, trying to focus on Finn's continued explanation, but the feeling lingered, curling in her chest like a quiet hum.

"Pretty amazing, right?" Finn said, snapping her out of her thoughts. "And totally off-limits. Which, of course, makes it all the more fascinating."

Clara laughed, her nerves finally starting to ease. Crowstone felt a less like an overwhelming maze and more like a place filled with secrets waiting to be uncovered.
*

As they left the Portal Chamber and headed back towards the main courtyard, Finn turned to them with a smug grin. "So, what do you think? Cooler than just learning about ancient runes and potion ingredients, right?"

"It's … incredible," Clara admitted, glancing back at the hallway they'd just left. "I feel like I've barely scratched the surface of this place."

"That's the best part," Finn said. "There's always something new to discover. Just stick with me, and I'll show you the ropes."

Leo rolled his eyes but smiled faintly. "I think we'll survive, even with your questionable guidance."

Finn threw an arm around each of them, steering them back towards the busy courtyard. "Survive? With me, you'll thrive. Now, let's see what they're serving for lunch. I'm betting it's roast potatoes again, with colourful vegetables and delicious gravy, my favourite."

Clara laughed, letting herself relax a little. Maybe this place wasn't so overwhelming after all, especially with Finn as their slightly chaotic guide.

*

As Finn led Clara and Leo towards the dining area, he gestured to a towering set of bronze doors that shimmered as though lit from within. "This," he said with a grand gesture, "is the Great Solstice Hall, where we eat, hold assemblies, and occasionally witness Professor Stormweaver dramatically point out to someone that they are guilty of the improper use of a fork. Welcome to the hub of chaos and culinary delight."

The dining hall doors opened, revealing an ever-shifting ceiling that mirrored constellations and cosmic phenomena, casting celestial light across the enchanted tables below. Today, it was a brilliant mixture of sunshine tones, the stars slowly coming into focus as if the room itself was falling asleep.

The walls were carved from pale woodstone veined with silver that pulsed faintly, as though alive with the collective magic of the students. Enchanted banners hung high, each representing a school house, but instead of static images, they shifted to display highlights of their achievements.

The long dining tables weren't ordinary either. They

were enchanted to resize based on the number of students, and their surfaces mirrored the constellations above, creating the illusion of dining among the stars. Plates and goblets appeared seamlessly, while the tables shimmered with magical feasts that left Clara in amazement.

At the far end of the hall, an elevated platform held a long, straight table for the professors, each seated in a chair enchanted to reflect their magical speciality. Professor Ainsley's chair flickered between earthy browns and greens, Professor Moonsong's swirled with otherworldly mist, Professor Darnel's was etched with glowing runes, Professor Hawthorne's bloomed with twisting vines and flowers, and Professor Mornvale's shimmered with silver and gold, radiating authority and wisdom.

At the centre of the hall stood the Solstice Orb, a massive floating crystal that pulsed with the time of day, glowing brighter during assemblies or dimming during evening meals. Beneath it, a large mosaic depicted the founding of Crowstone, the shimmering tiles rearranging themselves periodically to reveal different moments in the school's history.

"When announcements happen," Finn said, gesturing to the Orb. "The Orb glows, but don't worry; the professors usually save the long-winded speeches for assemblies. Meal times are for food and gossip, strictly enforced by tradition. Come and sit with the Luminaris house for now, and once your house has been chosen, you will then always sit with your house."

They all went and sat down, Clara in astonishment at it all, Leo less impressed, more like 'it will do'.

Everywhere she looked, students were proudly

wearing their house colours. Rich greens and earthy browns with the emblem of an oak tree with emerald leaves for Evergrove; red and orange robes with the emblem of fiery crimson and a roaring phoenix for Flarewood; a radiant sunburst surrounded by a protective ring for Aurora; deep purples and blacks with the emblem of a black raven clutching a bronze key for Nightspire. Finally, the blue and silver of Luminaris, their crescent moon emblem gleaming on the chests of those seated at the far-right table.

Clara felt strangely underdressed in her plain academy robes, as though she and the rest of the new students were intruding on something sacred. It wasn't just clothing; it was identity, a visual reminder of belonging. Clara felt bare, truly understanding the gravity of the house system.

"Wow," Leo muttered beside her, his eyes wide. "It's … a lot to take in."

Clara nodded silently as she sat down at the Luminaris table. Would this be her table soon? Would she find friends here? For all the excitement she'd felt earlier, the enormity of the moment pressed down on her now. Every student seemed so at ease in their house colours, laughing and chatting with their peers. Would she ever feel that comfortable?

As Clara sat there, taking in the grandeur of the hall, she felt a sense of wonder wash over her. The Great Solstice Hall, with its ever-shifting sky and glowing walls, seemed to pulse with life and magic. It was a place that held centuries of history, where generations of witches and wizards had gathered, shared meals, and forged connections. The sheer magnitude of it all was overwhelming, but Clara felt a glimmer of comfort amidst the chaos.

The sound of voices filled the hall as constellations glided across the ceiling, their light rippling across the polished floor. Clara felt the magic, vibrant and alive, weaving joy, wonder, and excitement into the room. It pressed against her senses like a gentle tide, a shared current connecting everyone.

But when her gaze shifted to Leo, the feeling changed. He stood apart, untouched by the light-hearted energy that surrounded them. Clara didn't sense joy or happiness from him, only pure, focused determination. It burned steadily beneath the surface, a quiet resolve that made her stomach tighten. It wasn't bad, exactly, but it was different, and that difference bothered her in ways she couldn't quite explain.

As Clara sat there, the atmosphere was filled with laughter and wonder, but for Clara, a lingering thread of uncertainty remained, tying her thoughts to something she didn't yet understand.

And maybe didn't want to.

Chapter 17: A Warm Welcome

The entire school was still sitting in the Great Solstice Hall catching up on summer adventures and speculating about the year ahead. Clara sat next to Finn and Leo, and across from them sat a girl with a confident, mischievous smile.

Finn introduced her with a grin. "Clara, meet Elina Sharma. She's trouble, just like me, but more organised."

Elina had a warm, deep brown complexion and rich dark hair often tied back into a braid. Her large expressive eyes seemed to hold endless curiosity and quiet determination, reflecting her sharp intellect and observant nature. She wore delicate gold bangles on her wrists, a gift from her family in India, which subtly jingled as she moved.

Elina raised an eyebrow, laughing. "Ignore him," she said with a smile. "I only get into the good kind of trouble. And it's Ellie. Only my mother calls me Elina."

Clara felt a mix of excitement and nerves, taking it all in. The noise and energy were unlike anything she'd ever experienced, but it was thrilling. At the far end of the hall, Professor Mornvale rose from her seat. The Orb glowed brighter, and the room gradually fell silent.

"Welcome to Crowstone," Professor Mornvale began, her voice clear and commanding. "To our new students in Years Seven and Eight, we extend a warm welcome. This is a journey that will test your magical abilities and shape your role within the magical world."

Clara felt a warmth in her cheeks as some students glanced her way. The weight of the words felt real, like this was more than just a new school; it was the beginning of something significant.

Professor Mornvale continued, her tone shifting slightly. "Now, as we embark on this year together, let's review a few essential expectations. Firstly, respect the halls and grounds of this school, but above all else, respect one another. Our school has seen generations of witches and wizards, and academic and personal excellence is expected of everyone."

She let the words settle before moving on. "Secondly, you are all encouraged to explore and develop your magical strengths. Each of you is unique in your talents, and our professors are here to guide you on that path. Remember, however, that magic must always be practised with responsibility. We do not tolerate reckless use of spells or magic that could endanger others."

Professor Mornvale's voice took on a more enthusiastic tone, a spark of excitement lighting her expression. "Now, onto the news of the year. I'm thrilled to announce that the annual Winter Solstice Festival will be on the same day as the Christmas dance. But before that, we shall have the Elemental Games, which is an annual competition at Crowstone Academy, where students from all houses face off in challenges that test their mastery of elemental magic. Set in the Tempest Coliseum, the games feature dynamic events like conjuring storms, navigating shifting terrains, and duelling with controlled elemental spells. Each challenge is designed to push creativity, strategy, and teamwork, while showcasing students' ability to wield fire, water, earth, and air in dramatic, high-stakes scenarios. Winning isn't just about raw power; it's about precision, adaptability, and the clever use of magic under pressure. It's open to students in Year Eight upwards. The tournament will challenge teams on a series of skills:

spellcasting precision, artefact finding, and magical strategy."

The hall erupted in whispers, students nudging each other and sharing wide-eyed glances.

Leo looked at Clara, his eyes bright with excitement. "That sounds incredible."

Professor Mornvale let the chatter settle before finishing. "I expect great things from each and every one of you. Whether honing a skill or finding where you belong, this academy is a home for all who seek to shape their magic and let magic shape them. True greatness lies in how you respond to the unexpected. The choices you make when faced with the unknown will shape not just your magic, but the person you become."

With that, she lifted her glass, and every student and professor in the hall followed. "To a year of growth, courage, and magic!" she declared.

"To growth, courage, and magic!" the students echoed, raising their glasses. Clara clinked hers with Finn's, Leo's, and Ellie's, feeling the excitement. This was her world now, a world she was still discovering but already felt deeply connected to.

"Third and final thing," the professor began. "Crowstone Academy is not just a school. It is a forge, where raw potential is hammered into brilliance. For centuries, this place has been the birthplace of the most highly regarded witches and wizards in history. Protectors, innovators, healers, and warriors: those who have dared to take the impossible and shape it into the extraordinary."

Her dark lips curved into a faint, knowing smile, though her eyes remained sharp. "Crowstone was founded by the Magical Assembly not merely to teach you how to wield magic, but to guide you into becoming the very best versions of yourselves. And that, my dear students, is a task far greater than any spell."

She took a step back, the shadows at her feet seeming to ripple as she spoke her final words. "Now, I ask you this: will you rise to the standards of those who came before you, carving your name among the stars? Or will you crumble beneath the weight of expectation, another forgotten whisper in the wind? And now, before we delve into the feast that awaits, it is tradition to honour this occasion with a gift, a gift of music."

She gestured towards a raised platform at the far end of the hall, where a group of students had silently assembled. "Allow me to introduce the Year 11 choir. Under the guidance of Professor Lyrus, they have prepared a song that speaks to the heart of our craft, our unity, and the ember that burns within each of you. Enjoy."

The hall dimmed as Professor Mornvale swept her hand through the air, commanding the lanterns to dim.

Clara turned to her new friends with wide eyes. "A magical choir?" she whispered to Finn, who had been busy straightening his robes.

He grinned back. "Just wait till they start."

And then they did. The first notes were soft, like the rustling of leaves in an enchanted forest. The choir began their song:

When ancient stars lit skies of old,
A spark was born, both fierce and bold.
Through whispered winds and shadowed halls,
The magic stirs, the magic calls.

Oh, ember bright, eternal flame,
A guiding light, a sacred name.
Through heart and hand, we cast the flow,
A magic bound, forever to grow.

Clara felt a shiver ripple down her spine. The voices melded together seamlessly, each note rising and falling like waves on an endless ocean. The magic in the air was in sync with the melody.

The forest stirs, the rivers sing,
The realms await what dreams may bring.
With courage strong and wands held high,
We shape the stars; we touch the sky.

Oh, ember bright, eternal flame,
A guiding light, a sacred name.
Through heart and hand, we cast the flow,
A magic bound, forever to grow.

"Wow," Clara breathed.

Across from her, Ellie had leaned forwards on the edge of her seat, captivated. "It's like the room itself is singing with them," she murmured.

Each path we walk, each bond we make,
The roots we grow, the steps we take.
A legacy in every flame,
One spark, one school, one timeless name.

Oh, ember bright, eternal flame,
A guiding light, a sacred name.

Through heart and hand, we cast the flow,
A magic bound, forever to grow.

Forever bright, our ember's glow,
In every soul, the magic flows.

When the final note faded, it lingered in the air like a shimmering spell, leaving the hall in stunned silence.

Then, Professor Mornvale stood once more, her hands spread wide. "A performance as brilliant as ever," she said, her deep voice filled with pride. "Let's give them a well-deserved round of applause."

The hall erupted with cheers and clapping. Clara joined in enthusiastically, her heart still alight with the magic of the song. "That was incredible," she said to Ellie, who nodded excitedly.

As the choir bowed and stepped down from the platform, Professor Mornvale smiled at the newcomers.

Professor Mornvale's voice echoed through the hall, her final words ringing with warmth and purpose. "And now," she said, a small smile playing on her lips, "let the first feast of many this year begin."

With a clap, the tables filled with shimmering platters of roasted meats, glowing fruit, and steaming soups. Enchanted goblets sparkled, and the rich aroma of magic-infused dishes filled the hall.

As the students cheered and began to fill their plates, Clara hesitated, momentarily lost in her thoughts. The sight of the feast reminded her of her first night at Nightfall Manor, when Hazel had prepared a meal so grand it had felt almost otherworldly. That memory felt both distant and strangely close, a bittersweet echo of the whirlwind journey that had brought her here.

Clara listened to the laughter and chatter around her, feeling how much her life had changed. She'd left behind everything she knew and stepped into a world she barely understood, surrounded by strangers in a school that felt impossibly vast.

She exhaled slowly, letting herself enjoy the moment. She didn't yet know where she fit in this magical world, but surrounded by warmth and possibility, she allowed herself to simply be.

Clara's gaze drifted to the enchanted ceiling, its stars shifting like a living map. She felt a pull, not just to this school, but to a purpose she couldn't yet name.

The feast began, the tables heaving with food of every variety. Clara savoured the taste of the enchanted food as laughter echoed around her.

Clara couldn't help but laugh as Leo followed suit, cautiously eyeing a bowl of soup that seemed to sparkle faintly. Despite her nerves, she found herself relaxing in the warmth and magic of the hall. Clara felt a flicker of excitement for what lay ahead.

Chapter 18: Reassurance and Choice

As dinner plates vanished, replaced by desserts and goblets of juice, the Great Solstice Hall buzzed with excitement. Clara's stomach churned with anticipation as whispers about the house selection process floated around her.

Professor Mornvale stood at the head of the hall, her robes catching the rippling light from the floating lanterns. She raised her hand, the Orb brightened, and the room gradually quietened, the students turning their attention to the imposing figure.

"I hope you all enjoyed the feast," she began, her voice commanding. "Before we move forward, however," Mornvale continued, her emerald-green eyes sweeping over the room, "there is a matter that must be addressed. Many of you may have heard whispers over the summer, rumours of unsettling events. It is my duty to confirm that those rumours are true."

The room seemed to collectively hold its breath, the warm glow of the lanterns shifting darkness across the walls.

"The Dark Wizard has escaped."

Gasps rippled through the hall, followed by a murmur of uneasy whispers. Clara's heart skipped a beat, her mind racing at the mention of him. A name that brought fear to the magical world and also symbolised a hatred towards her family.

Mornvale raised her hand, and the murmurs quickly died down. "I understand your concerns," she said firmly, her gaze steady. "The Dark Wizard is one that brings fear, but I want to assure you of this: Crowstone Academy remains a place of safety, a sanctuary built on centuries of powerful magic. The wards surrounding this school are among the strongest in existence, designed to withstand any threat."

Clara glanced at Leo, who was watching Mornvale with an unreadable expression. Beside her, Finn leaned forward, his usual grin replaced by a look of uncharacteristic seriousness.

"While vigilance is always necessary," Mornvale continued, "you must also remember that you are not alone. Your professors, your housemates, and your friends are here to support you. Together, we are stronger than any darkness."

Her words hung in the air, and for a moment, the tension in the room seemed to ease, replaced by a cautious sense of unity.

Mornvale's expression softened slightly. "This is not a call for fear, but for awareness. Focus on your studies, build your skills, and trust in the protections of this academy. Together, we will meet any challenge that arises. Now, let us move forward as one."

With a wave of her hand, the lanterns brightened, and the murmurs returned, though softer this time. Clara let out a breath she hadn't realised she'd been holding. Around her, students began talking again, some clearly reassured while others exchanged worried glances.

Finn leaned over, his grin returning as he tried to lighten the mood. "See? All fine. We've got giant magic wards. What could go wrong?"

Leo, however, didn't look quite as convinced. "Wards or not, they wouldn't tell us everything," he said quietly. "It's not just about what they're protecting us from, it's about what they don't want us to know."

Clara frowned, her nerves taut. She wanted to dismiss

Leo's words, but the unease curling in her stomach made it hard. She turned back towards the front of the hall, where Professor Mornvale was speaking quietly with the other professors.

Her mind whirled with questions. What was the Dark Wizard capable of? And why did she feel like the mention of him carried something personal, a thread tugging at the edges of her thoughts, even though she didn't know why?

For the first time since arriving at Crowstone, she felt some danger from the magical world pressing down on her. This wasn't just about learning spells or fitting in; it was about something far bigger. Something darker.

And somehow, she knew her role in it was just beginning.

Professor Mornvale began to speak again. "Now it's time to welcome the newest members of Crowstone Academy of Magic into their houses. To the Year Seven students and those new in Year Eight, tonight marks the beginning of your journey here, a journey that will challenge and inspire you in equal measure."

Clara shifted in her seat, glancing at Leo, who gave her a small, reassuring nod.

"Your house," Professor Mornvale continued, "is determined by the Celestial Mirror, which aligns you with the magic that reflects your strengths and potential."

She paused, her gaze sweeping across the hall. "However, let me make one thing clear: your house is a guide, not a definition. It does not limit who you are or what you can achieve. Most witches and wizards do choose careers aligned with their house's traits, as it often reflects where they excel naturally. But the path you walk is yours to decide.

"The houses at Crowstone serve a greater purpose than mere tradition. They are designed to nurture your magical talents and provide a foundation for your growth. Each house represents a unique aspect of magical skill, areas where you may naturally excel. What matters most is not the house you are placed in but the bonds you form, the knowledge you gain, and the person you strive to become. Your house may guide your path, but it will never define your potential."

The murmurs among the students quieted further as Professor Mornvale gestured to a figure at the side of the hall. "Professor Darnel will now escort our new students to the Chamber of Stars, where the Celestial Mirror resides."

Professor Darnel, a stern-looking man with streaks of white in his hair and a delicate rune-embroidered robe, stepped forward. His expression was strict, and the Year 7s began to shuffle nervously in their seats.

"Year Sevens and any other new students, follow me," he instructed, his voice measured and clear.

Clara's heart was racing as she stood, glancing once more at Leo as they both stood up.

Clara, Leo, and the Year 7s gathered at the side of the hall, forming a hesitant group behind Professor Darnel. As they exited the Great Solstice Hall, the whispers and encouraging cheers of older students echoed faintly behind them, leaving the air thick with anticipation.

The corridors grew darker as the group moved towards the Chamber of Stars, the glimmering lanterns creating an eerie light. Clara's nerves tightened with each step, her thoughts racing about what the Celestial Mirror would reveal.

Finally, they arrived at a set of towering wooden

doors. Professor Darnel stopped and turned to face the group.

"Beyond these doors lies the Celestial Mirror," he said. "You will each take it in turn to enter the room. The order will be in the order you are in the line at present,. Step forward and the mirror will guide you. Trust its wisdom, and know that whatever house you join, it will be the right one for you. The rest of your life at Crowstone will begin here."

The doors opened to reveal a circular room bathed in silvery light, the Celestial Mirror at its centre, rippling like liquid starlight.

Professor Darnel gestured for the first student to step forward. Clara's nerves twisted as she watched the process, the magnitude of the moment pressing down on her. What would the mirror reveal about her?

Clara watched as the students before her stepped into the Chamber of Stars, their robes shimmering as they emerged, now marked with the colours of their chosen houses. She couldn't stop her thoughts from spiralling: *What if I don't belong? What if the mirror gets it wrong?*

The fiery boldness of Flarewood felt exciting but intimidating; the grounded strength of Evergrove seemed like a distant dream. Aurora's brilliance and Nightspire's cunning were both intriguing, yet neither felt quite right. But Luminaris ... something about the quiet creativity and introspection of Luminaris resonated with her, though she wasn't entirely sure why.

The corridor now buzzed with excitement as students admired one another's transformations, their colours and symbols marking the beginning of a new chapter in their magical journeys.

Clara watched as a girl stepped out in Evergrove

colours, her face lit with a proud, serene smile. For a brief moment, she felt a sense of groundedness and warmth, as though she could feel the essence of Evergrove through the girl's presence.

Clara watched students step out of the room. For some reason, seeing everyone else find their place only heightened her anxiety.

The unknown loomed large, and each student's transformation seemed to deepen the weight of her anticipation. She couldn't help but wonder if the magic of the school truly knew her, if it could see beyond her nerves and uncertainty to place her where she truly belonged.

"Next," the professor shouted as another student came out in Luminaris colours.

Clara nodded and stepped inside, the door closing softly behind her. Standing alone before the mirror, she felt a mix of wonder and apprehension.

"Name, please," Professor Darnel said, his voice commanding.

"Clara Nightfall," Clara replied, her voice barely above a whisper.

"Ah," Professor Darnell said, surprised.

Clara was unsure what had prompted his reaction to her name but was too anxious to dwell on it.

The parchment floating beside Professor Darnel quivered slightly as a quill lifted itself and began to write. Clara watched, her heart thudding in her chest.

"Step forward, please," Professor Darnel instructed, gesturing towards the centre of the room.

Clara hesitated for the briefest moment before her feet obeyed, carrying her forward. Her palms were damp, and her breath hitched as she came to a stop before him.

Professor Darnel gave her a steady, reassuring look. "Let us see where your path lies."

As she stood in front of the mirror, it came alive.

Colours swirled: silver, green, gold, and black, each one vying for dominance. For a moment, Clara thought she saw the silhouette of an oak tree and then a burst of fiery light. The images shifted rapidly, forming a raven in flight, then finally settling into a crescent moon surrounded by twinkling stars.

The mirror pulsed once, and the crest of Luminaris House appeared, glowing softly.

The professor stepped forward, smiling. "Luminaris House. A wonderful choice, Clara."

Professor Darnell waved his wand with a practised flick, and Clara felt a gentle warmth ripple through her robes. As she glanced down, her uniform shimmered and transformed, the colours shifting into deep blue and silver. The emblem of Luminaris, a crescent moon, now rested proudly above her heart. The fabric seemed alive, reflecting the vibrant essence of her house. She traced the emblem with her fingers, a mix of admiration and newfound pride filling her.

Professor Darnell smiled faintly. "Congratulations. You're in Luminaris, Clara."

Clara's breath caught at Professor Darnell's words.

"It's the house your mother was in," Professor Darnell said with a small smile as her uniform shimmered.

"Really?" Clara said, her voice filled with curiosity. "I didn't know that. You knew my mam? Did you teach when she was here?"

Professor Darnell chuckled warmly, his barely weathered face softening. "I was a few years ahead of your mother at Crowstone. She was one of the most

206

talented witches in Luminaris. I'm eager to see if that brilliance runs in you."

Clara's heart swelled with a mix of pride and longing. "I didn't realise she was so well-known," she murmured, her voice tinged with wonder.

Professor Darnell's expression grew solemn for a moment. "I was deeply sorry to hear of her passing. She had a spark that was hard to forget. It's a sad story, her leaving it all behind." He paused, his gaze softening again. "But one good thing came from it."

"What's that?" Clara asked, leaning forwards slightly. Professor Darnell smiled, his tone warm and full of reassurance. "You, my dear girl. You're the living legacy of a remarkable witch, and I have no doubt you'll make your mark here, just as she did."

Clara's mind whirled with emotion. She had spent so much of her life feeling disconnected from her mother as she could barely remember her. Since becoming aware of magic, she had heard little about her mother's past, but now, for the first time, there was a tangible link, a shared history in the same house at Crowstone.

Her thoughts turned briefly to her grandparents. They rarely spoke of her mother's time at school, and Clara had always sensed it brought them pain. She resolved to tread carefully, but the curiosity now burned brighter in her chest. What had her mother been like as a student? What had she accomplished here?

Professor Darnell gently patted her shoulder. "You'll do just fine here, Clara. The house chose you because of what's inside you, not because of anyone else's expectations. You're here to make your own story."

Clara nodded, a mixture of nerves and excitement buzzing through her. As she turned to leave the room, her new house colours and her mother's legacy filled her with a quiet determination. This wasn't just about discovering the magical world; it was about discovering herself too.

Clara felt a sense of belonging wash over her as the professor gently guided her back towards the hallway. She gave a nod to Leo and sighed with relief as they passed in the corridor.

Clara stood, her heart still racing from the transformation of her uniform. She joined the growing line of students, and the air buzzed with their whispered excitement and the occasional glance down to admire the new badges adorning their chests. Clara couldn't help but feel a quiet sense of pride as she traced the design of the crescent moon on her own badge. She felt part of something … something her mother had once been part of too.

Leo walked into the room, and he seemed confident, but she could tell he was masking his emotions.

Clara stood in the corridor waiting for Leo, but as the minutes ticked by, her smile began to waver. She leaned against the wall, her gaze flicking towards the closed door where Leo had entered. He'd been inside for far longer than she had, or anyone else, for that matter. Most students were in and out within minutes.

A few of the remaining students murmured to each other, their whispers carrying a flicker of curiosity.

Finally, the door creaked open, and Leo stepped out. His uniform had changed, now bearing the same deep blue and silver as hers. The Luminaris crest gleamed proudly on his chest. He smiled, though it didn't quite reach his eyes.

Professor Darnell emerged right behind him, his stern

expression softening into something closer to bemusement. "And don't go asking for another try, Mr. Rutherford. One is usually all anyone gets."

Clara's eyebrows shot up. "What was that about?" she asked, her curiosity overtaking her unease.

Leo gave a quick shrug, his smile stretching wider, though it still seemed slightly off. "The mirror didn't get it right the first time, so I asked for another go. Sometimes it needs a second look."

"I thought magic was absolute, not open to interpretation. It either is or isn't," Clara expressed, her brow furrowing as she studied him.

Leo hesitated for a moment, then chuckled lightly. "You'd think so, right? But magic, especially ancient magic like the mirror, isn't always as straightforward as people assume. It's like … sometimes it needs a nudge to see the whole picture." Leo was casually tapping his thumb and finger together as he spoke.

Clara noticed the movement but dismissed it as nerves. After all, this whole process had been overwhelming for everyone. "I guess that makes sense."

"Hey, it worked out in the end," Leo said, his smile widening. "That's what matters, right?"

Clara forced a small smile back, but her thoughts lingered on his words. "Well, I'm glad you're in Luminaris," she said, her smile returning. "It's nice to have a friend in the same house."

Leo's smile became more genuine at that, his posture relaxing slightly. "Yeah, same. Looks like we're in this together."

It all felt so surreal, like a dream Clara hadn't quite woken up from. But what made her heart swell most wasn't the reputation of Luminaris or the magical traits it represented. It was the connection to her mother.

Her mother had been in Luminaris too. The revelation felt like a thread connecting Clara to a past she'd barely known. Her fragmented memories, her mother's warm laugh, the way she read bedtime stories, the way she always seemed to know what Clara needed, suddenly felt closer. Now Clara walked the same halls, wore the same colours, and stood where her mother once had.

Professor Darnell had said her mother was an exceptionally bright witch. Talented, gifted, someone who had left an impression even years after she'd left the magical world. Clara couldn't help but feel a flutter of pride at that thought, but it was quickly followed by a touch of doubt. Could she live up to that? Her mother had grown up in this world, immersed in magic, while Clara had spent fourteen years in a world of buses, biology homework, and takeaways for dinner with her dad. She was playing catch-up in a game where everyone else already knew the rules.

The connection to her mother made her feel grounded, but it also carried pressure. Would she live up to the legacy of a witch everyone seemed to remember? Or would she stumble under the weight of expectations she was only beginning to understand?

Clara decided it didn't matter if she was starting behind. She'd work harder, study longer, and carve her own path, one that honoured her mother while making her father proud.

The sound of a door creaking open pulled her from her thoughts. Another student stepped out, their uniform shimmering as it adjusted to their house colours. Clara watched them walk away with a sense of determination. She might not know everything about her mother's past, but being in Luminaris felt like a gift, a chance to learn, to connect, and to prove she belonged in this world.

*

Clara and Leo joined the returning students. The hall had transformed; students now sat grouped by house, their uniforms gleaming with their colours, while enchanted banners displayed scenes of each house's history.

Clara's eyes darted to the Luminaris banner. Its silver crescent moon gleamed softly against a deep indigo backdrop, surrounded by a constellation of stars that subtly shifted, forming shapes and symbols that seemed to tell a story. Her chest swelled with both pride and nerves as she spotted the Luminaris table.

Professor Mornvale stood and said firmly, "Make your way to your house tables. Tonight marks the beginning of your journey as a community. Lean on one another, challenge one another, and grow together."

Clara glanced at Leo, who offered her an encouraging nod. Together, they weaved through the tables until they reached Luminaris's section. Finn spotted them immediately and leapt to his feet, clapping loudly.

"Welcome!" he called, grinning ear to ear. "I knew it. Friends for life. I could feel it in my bones!"

Clara laughed, her nerves easing slightly as she slid onto the bench next to him. "You're not getting rid of us now," she teased.

Finn responded with an exaggerated groan. "Wouldn't dream of it," he said.

Leo took a seat across from them, eyeing the other students at the table. "So, this is it, huh? Luminaris."

"Best house," Finn said confidently. "I'm definitely biased."

Before Clara could respond, a figure at the head of the

table stood, drawing the attention of everyone in the Luminaris section. Professor Aurelia Nightbloom stepped forward, her silvery robes flowing like liquid moonlight. Her presence was commanding, her emerald-green eyes scanning the students with quiet intensity.

"Good evening, Luminaris," she began, her voice soft but carrying easily. "Welcome to our house, both to those returning and to those joining us for the first time." Her gaze lingered on the new Year 7s, her expression warm yet mysterious. "Professor Mornvale will have more to say before we go to the house common room."

With that, Professor Mornvale rose again with a smile on her face. "Welcome back, students!" boomed Professor Mornvale, standing at the front of the hall. Her voice carried effortlessly over the chatter. "Today marks the beginning of your journey at Crowstone, a place where magic flows as freely as breath. May your year at Crowstone be as magical as the stars above and as bright as the magic within you," she concluded, her words lingering in the air as students stirred in their seats.

Clara glanced at her Luminaris badge, the crescent moon catching the faint light from the enchanted ceiling. The anxiety of the night pressed against her thoughts, her house, the song, and the mention of the Dark Wizard, but determination steadied her nerves.

"Now, follow your house masters," Professor Mornvale instructed, her voice carrying a tone of quiet authority.

Professor Nightbloom gestured for the students to rise. "Follow me. Let me take you to your new home."

Professor Nightbloom led the Luminaris students out of the Great Solstice Hall and into one of the tower wings. The journey was filled with hushed whispers as the new students took in the sights around them: windows showing breathtaking views of the campus and softly glowing floating lanterns that lit their path.

At last they stopped before an arched doorway adorned with Luminaris's crescent moon emblem. "Welcome to the Luminaris Tower," Professor Nightbloom said. "This will be your home, a place of study, rest, and camaraderie."

She gestured to the rune panel near the archway, its swirling engravings glinting in the light. "This is the magical safeguard of Luminaris tower. Each of you carries a unique magical aura, your essence. When you place your hand on this panel, the runes will read your energy. If you are a member of Luminaris, the door will open. If you are not …" She let her words hang in the air. "Well, let's just say you won't get far."

The students murmured softly, exchanging curious glances.

Professor Nightbloom's lips curved into a faint smile. "I shall show you how it works." She pressed her hand to the cool surface, the runes glowed faintly, a soft chime sounded, and the silverstone door swung open to reveal the warm common room beyond.

As Clara stepped inside, an unexpected sense of belonging settled over her.

Professor Nightbloom waited for the last student to pass through, her gaze lingering on the group. "The tower recognises you not just as individuals, but as part of Luminaris. Treat it with respect, and it will protect you as fiercely as it guards its secrets." With that, she swept into the common room, leaving the students to marvel at their new home.

Clara's breath caught as she stepped inside. The room was vast and circular, with high arched windows that offered a perfect view of the starry night sky. The domed ceiling displayed a celestial mural, with a glowing moon surrounded by silver and gold constellations forming mythical creatures and magical moments.

Flowing rivers of stars connected the constellations, their edges blending into rich deep blues and purples that gave the illusion of a vast, endless night sky. Shooting stars arced across the scene, leaving faint trails of light in their wake, as if they were moving in real time. The mural seemed alive, a living testament to the wonder of the magical world, capturing the boundless possibilities that magic offered.

The furniture was cosy yet elegant, with deep red armchairs and sofas arranged around a fireplace that flickered with pale golden flames. Bookshelves lined the walls, filled with books on dream magic, astral navigation, and other subjects unique to Luminaris. A fountain with glowing blue water took pride of place in the centre of the room.

Professor Nightbloom moved to stand by the fireplace, her silhouette framed by the soft glow of the flames. "Welcome to the heart of Luminaris," she said. "This is more than just a common room. It is a place for reflection, creativity, and growth. A sanctuary where you can dream, explore, and connect."

She clasped her hands together, her gaze sweeping over the students. "Luminaris values creativity, insight, and the ability to see beyond the visible. Our crescent moon emblem symbolises change, intuition, and the light that guides us. Here, you'll enhance your unique gifts, but remember, with great talent comes great responsibility."

Her voice took on a more serious tone. "As members of Luminaris, you are expected to think deeply, act with purpose, and treat others with respect. Collaboration is as important as individual brilliance. While magic is a tool, kindness and understanding are what truly define us. You will be challenged here, not just academically, but personally. And that is by design."

Professor Nightbloom paused, letting her words sink in. "Being a part of Luminaris is not about being the best in any one field. It is about using your talents to illuminate the world around you, just as the moon illuminates the night."

Clara felt a warmth spreading in her chest, a mixture of pride and resolve. She looked around the room; everyone was equally captivated by Professor Nightbloom's words.

"Now," Professor Nightbloom continued, her tone softening, "the prefects will help you find your dormitories, settle in, and prepare for the journey ahead. I expect great things from each and every one of you. Together, we will make this year extraordinary."

As Clara listened, her gaze drifted to the glowing mural above. She couldn't shake the feeling that the house's values — creativity, intuition, and exploration — were a perfect reflection of her own.

With a final, mysterious smile, Professor Nightbloom stepped aside, allowing the students to explore the common room. With her new friends, Clara followed the prefects towards the dormitories, feeling a newfound sense of belonging. She didn't know what challenges lay ahead, but she felt ready to face them.

*

At the entrance of the girls' dormitories, a majestic statue of a Moondancer stood guard. It seemed to observe Clara with unblinking eyes, its magical presence reassuring yet commanding. Clara was told it was enchanted to alert prefects if any student ventured out after curfew, and she couldn't help but give it a respectful nod as she passed. Clara climbed the stairs to the Luminaris girls' dormitory, the enchanted hallway ahead of her quiet and serene. A soft plush carpet in a dusky green muffled her footsteps, and the walls glowed faintly with ever-changing light, the colours shifting as though alive.

The corridor leading to the Year 8 dormitories had an air of tranquillity, aided by the magical mirrors along the walls. Each mirror reflected not just Clara's image, but a subtle aura surrounding her, a soft blend of blue and violet. She realised they were displaying her mood, and the colours seemed to pulse gently, almost as if offering encouragement. She paused for a moment, intrigued, before continuing down the hallway.

Clara found her room at the end of the corridor. It was cosy and magical, with carved wooden bed frames etched in lunar designs. Soft lavender bedding matched the silver-glowing enchanted curtains, creating a tranquil atmosphere. A desk in the corner, charmed to glow faintly for nighttime study sessions, already had her name etched into its corner.

She was unpacking her suitcase when the door creaked open, and a tall girl walked in, carrying an armful of books.

"Hi," the girl said, her voice cheerful and easy. "You must be Clara. I'm Amelia Chen, your roommate. Welcome to Crowstone and welcome to Luminaris."

Amelia Chen had a calm, confident air about her, with deep brown eyes that were sharp with focus and curiosity. Her sleek dark hair framed her face neatly, and her posture always seemed straight-backed and composed, as though she carried her own sense of dignity wherever she went. There was a warmth to her, however, a mix of quiet kindness and determination that made her a natural leader among her friends.

Clara smiled, grateful for the friendly introduction. "Thanks. For the first day, it's a little overwhelming … but I'm glad to be here."

Amelia laughed, setting her books down on her desk. "Tell me about it. My first year was wild. Half the time I thought the school itself was testing me, with the complexities of finding your way around. I swear the corridors and classrooms move sometimes. Don't worry, though, you'll find your way. If you ever need help with anything, just ask."

Clara nodded, already feeling more at ease. She glanced out of the window, which offered a breathtaking view of the Luminaris garden terrace below. In the moonlight, the terrace glowed with soft, silvery tones, the flowers blooming as if under an unspoken spell.

"Is that our garden?" Clara asked, motioning towards it.

Amelia followed her gaze and grinned. "Yeah, it's one of the best parts of being in Luminaris. Great for studying or just escaping when the common room gets too loud. We can go later if you want."

"I'd like that," Clara said softly, her excitement was tempered by the nervous energy of starting something so new.

Amelia sat on her bed with an easy confidence. "Alright, roommate. I'll let you finish unpacking."

Clara chuckled at the thought. As she settled into her new space, she felt the lingering worries of the day slowly dissipating. The quiet magic of the room and her roommate's warm welcome made Clara feel, for the first time, like she belonged.

*

Back in the common room, they all regrouped.

Clara glanced at the glowing blue fountain in the centre of the common room, its waters swirling gently, casting flickers of light across the enchanted ceiling. She lowered her voice as she leaned toward Amelia. "What's the fountain for? It's not just ... decoration, is it?"

Amelia gave a knowing smile. "Of course not. This is Luminaris." She nodded towards the fountain. "It's called the Well of Echoes. No one's quite sure how old it is, but they say it's enchanted with centuries of spellcraft. It reacts to thought, sometimes even emotion. If your mind's clear enough, it can help you focus. Some people even claim it whispers answers if you ask the right question."

Clara blinked. "It talks?"

"Only if it wants to," Amelia said with a shrug. "But be careful. If your head's a mess, it has a tendency to splash you."

Clara smiled, allowing herself to relax. The house tower felt like a sanctuary, a place where she could study, make friends, and find her footing. As she gazed at the celestial mural above, its quiet grandeur filled her with a sense of belonging.

She imagined her mam sitting in that same common room, surrounded by the same shimmering stars and crescent moons that now watched over her. It was a fragile but profound connection, as though the magic in the room carried faint echoes of her mother's presence.

In that moment, Clara felt as though she wasn't just stepping into her own story, but into her mother's legacy.

Chapter 19: A Challenging Day

Morning sunlight filtered through the curtains of Clara's dorm room as she woke to birdsong. Her roommate, Amelia, sat cross-legged on her bed, scribbling in a notebook.

"Morning," Clara mumbled, rubbing her eyes.

Amelia glanced up and smiled. "Morning! First full day for you today, are you excited?"

"More like nervous," Clara admitted as she swung her legs over the side of the bed. "I don't even know what half the lessons are about yet."

"You'll do fine," Amelia said reassuringly. "Let's get down to breakfast before the food vanishes."

The thought of breakfast propelled Clara into action. She quickly dressed in her freshly pressed uniform, now proudly bearing the Luminaris crescent moon emblem, and joined Amelia in the corridor. The dormitory buzzed with students, some chatting excitedly while others stumbled bleary-eyed towards the stairs. Clara followed the flow, her nerves tingling with anticipation.

*

The Grand Solstice Hall was alive with morning light, its ceiling a brilliant blue sky. Laughter and chatter filled the room as students gathered beneath shimmering house banners.

Clara sat down next to Amelia with her Luminaris housemates, glancing nervously at the array of food that had appeared before them. Plates piled high with pastries, fresh fruit, and steaming dishes of eggs and sausages tempted her, but her appetite was dampened by the flurry of excitement around her. Finn, already tucking into a stack of pancakes, gave her a nod.

"Come on, Clara, eat up! You've got a big day ahead," Leo said through a mouthful of toast.

Before Clara could reply, a gentle glow of the Orb radiated through the hall, silencing the chatter. All eyes turned to Professor Mornvale, who rose to her feet. Her presence commanded attention as she surveyed the students with a warm yet authoritative gaze.

"Good morning, everyone," she began, her voice clear and calm. "To the newest members of Crowstone Academy, I hope your first night was restful. Today marks the beginning of a year filled with growth, learning, and challenges. But before we dive into our lessons, I want to explain the house points system, a tradition as old as the academy itself."

The new students leaned forward, their interest piqued.

"Throughout the year," Mornvale continued, "points will be awarded to your houses for academic achievements, acts of kindness, and displays of exceptional skill. Similarly, points can be deducted for poor behaviour, negligence, or failure to follow the academy's rules. But house points aren't just about discipline and academics."

She gestured to the shimmering banners above. "Your houses will also earn points through tournaments, sporting events, and collaborative challenges. Whether it's a game of Fenderstride, or the Mystical Maze, your participation and teamwork will contribute to your house's standing. The tournaments are not just about skill, but character," Professor Mornvale added, her gaze sweeping across the hall. "Those who rise to the challenge will find themselves tested in ways beyond magic."

"This system isn't about winning or losing," Mornvale said. "It's about teamwork, excellence, and discovering your strengths. At year's end, the house with the most points earns the Crowstone Cup."

The students exchanged excited whispers, the prospect of competition electrifying the hall. Clara felt a flutter of nerves as she glanced at the Luminaris banner. Could she really contribute to her house? The thought of her mother's legacy gave her a boost of determination.

Mornvale raised her hands, and the shimmering banners began to shift, displaying each house's current points total, zero for all. "Your journey starts today," she said. "Make it count."

*

As breakfast concluded, Finn looked at Clara. "So, how many points do you think you'll rack up before the year ends? Fifty? A hundred?"

Clara laughed nervously. "Let's see if I can manage one first."

"You'll do great," Amelia said, joining in with them.

Clara nodded, her resolve growing. She was ready to tackle the challenges ahead, not just for herself, but for her house. Clara felt excitement, pressure, and possibility. The year was just beginning, and she was determined to make her mark.

*

Professor Mornvale stood again. As the Orb glowed, the hall fell silent, her commanding presence needing no words.

"For centuries, our school has offered not only education but a journey of discovery, growth, and purpose," she began. "Each of you has talents waiting to be revealed, strengths waiting to be tested, and skills yet to be honed. To aid you in this, you will each receive an astral map, a guide that will help you unlock mysteries within these walls, and perhaps, within yourselves."

With a flick of her wand, folded parchments floated gently down, one landing before each student. Clara unfolded her map, its edges shimmering with gold lines. A tingle ran through her fingers as she touched it, hinting at the power within.

Unfolding it, Clara's eyes widened. The map was unlike anything she'd ever seen. It showed the entirety of the school grounds and its surroundings, but it pulsed, almost alive, with new paths and hidden doors appearing only when she ran her fingers across them. At the centre of the map, in delicate ink, her own name glowed, connected by a thread of light to her first task: *Find the Statue of Valmeera.*

"Your map will change as you grow," Professor Mornvale continued. "The tasks it reveals are unique to each of you. Some quests may guide you towards certain spells; others might lead you to hidden chambers or artefacts. Embrace them, learn from them, and know that they are meant to teach you not only about magic and the school but also about yourselves."

Professor Mornvale continued, "This academy is a place of great wonder, a sanctuary of knowledge, and a forge for your magical talents. Within these walls lies a wealth of discovery, but let me be clear: not all secrets are meant to be uncovered, and not all paths are meant to be trodden.

"The astral maps you possess are your guides, designed to keep you within the safe bounds of the academy. They will lead you towards growth and understanding but only if you heed their guidance. To stray from their path, to wander into places you are not yet prepared for, is to invite danger, some of which even we, your professors, cannot always protect you from.

"Crowstone is old, its magic deep and unpredictable. There are shadows here, hidden for good reason, and curiosity without caution has brought ruin to even the most gifted witches and wizards. Trust your maps, trust your instincts, but above all, trust that some mysteries are better left undisturbed until the time is right.

"This is not a warning to instil fear but to inspire respect, for the academy, for its legacy, and for the power you are learning to wield. Learn well, tread carefully, and remember: the greatest strength comes not from recklessness, but from knowing when to hold back."

As Clara studied her map, she noticed something strange. A soft whisper echoed faintly from the parchment, too quiet to make out. Leaning in, she realised the map wasn't just showing her paths; it was … going to guide her. It seemed to have a voice, though only she could hear it.

Professor Mornvale continued, her tone instructive. "Your map can also help you navigate the school, though I understand they can be a bit tricky to interpret at times, especially if they're nudging you towards a specific task. To simplify things, just tap the map with your wand and say 'Talamora Léanadh' and the name of the place you wish to go. The map will reveal the location and highlight the quickest route for you. This saves you from getting lost."

*

Clara was also given her timetable, her nerves settling slightly when she realised familiar people would be in class. She was in the same classes as Leo, Finn, Ellie and Amelia. A small wave of relief washed over her; at least she wouldn't be navigating this unfamiliar world entirely alone.

As they checked their timetables again, Finn, as usual, made light of the situation. "First class of the year. No pressure, right? Just don't blow anything up and you'll be fine," he said with a grin, nudging Clara.

"I'm more worried about not finding the classroom," Clara muttered, scanning the endless corridors ahead of them.

Amelia smiled encouragingly. "Don't worry, you'll get the hang of it soon enough. Besides, it's not like they expect us to master everything on day one. Well, most professors don't, and you should be with us mostly anyway, so for now, at least just follow us … well, me anyway. Finn can sometimes get lost. On purpose," she added with a knowing look.

Finn laughed. "*Once*, that happened!"

Leo, calm and composed as ever, led the group confidently. "It's Elemental Manipulation first," he said, pointing towards the training grounds visible through a large window. "Should be interesting."

*

As they were headed to class, Clara nearly bumped into three students blocking the hallway. The girl in the centre, tall and striking with sharp eyes that gleamed with a hint of malice, looked Clara up and down with a sneer. Clara recognised her from Hidden Row: Lucinda Vale.

"Oh, look who it is," Lucinda said with a mockingly sweet tone, her voice carrying an edge that set Clara's nerves on alert. "Clara Nightfall, isn't it? Or should I say the *Lost Witch*? Seems you finally found your way here. Did you need a map, or did someone have to fetch you like the stray you are?"

Lucinda's two friends, Verity Ashbourne and Melina Thorncroft, both sniggered, giving Clara the same disdainful look. They stood on either side of her, flanking her like guards, their expressions almost identical in their cruelty.

Finn, who had been walking with Clara, immediately stepped in, crossing his arms and giving the trio a hard look. "Why don't you go away, Lucinda," he said, his voice calm but laced with defiance. "I know it's tough, considering your family probably needs a map just to get out of the shadow of the Nightfalls. Hard to be relevant when your biggest claim to fame is being second best."

Lucinda's eyes flashed, her sneer fading for a moment before she regained her composure. She narrowed her gaze at Finn, the tension between them palpable. "Shut up, Finn. Just because your family are a bunch of nobodies," she spat, though her voice wavered slightly. She took a step back, giving Clara one last icy glare before motioning for her friends to follow her. "Come on. Let's leave the little lost witch with her *guide*."

They trailed off down the hall, their whispers carrying hints of laughter as they disappeared around the corner.

Clara let out a breath she hadn't realised she'd been holding. She turned to Finn, who shrugged casually, as if standing up to Lucinda and her entourage was an everyday occurrence. "Thanks for that," she said, managing a small smile. "But you didn't have to. I don't like bullies, and I won't tolerate them."

Finn grinned. "I had a feeling you wouldn't. But consider it an extended part of the tour, a little bonus lesson on who to watch out for. Lucinda's family and yours have a bit of … history. They're constantly trying to prove themselves as equals, which is probably why she's nasty when it comes to anyone with the Nightfall name."

Clara nodded, feeling a mixture of frustration and determination well up inside her. "Well, I'm not about to let anyone walk all over me, regardless of what they think of my family."

"Good," Finn replied, giving her a reassuring smile. "Because knowing Lucinda, this won't be the last time she tries to get under your skin. She feeds off reactions. Don't give her the satisfaction."

Clara straightened, feeling a bit more prepared for whatever Lucinda might throw at her in the future.

*

Clara clutched her books tightly as they approached their first class. Though her nerves lingered, she felt a little steadier knowing she'd have her friends by her side.

As they arrived at the Elemental Training Grounds, Clara's heart was beating faster than she'd have liked to admit. The air was crisp, and the grounds felt alive, as if they had absorbed centuries of magical spells.

Standing there waiting for everyone to arrive was a tall, stern-faced professor who was dressed all in black. Her eyes were sharp and observant, and when they fixed on Clara, she felt as though she was peering into her very thoughts. Clara took a hesitant step forward, clutching her books tightly.

"New student, I see," the professor said in a clipped tone, not taking her gaze off Clara. "What's your name?"

Clara took a breath. "Clara Cooper … I mean, Clara Nightfall."

The professor's eyebrow lifted, a faint smirk tugging at the corners of his mouth. "You don't know your own name?"

A ripple of laughter spread through the class, and Clara's cheeks flushed. She kept her chin high, refusing to look away from the professor. "I know my name. But my family insists I use 'Nightfall' here at school."

The professor's smirk grew as she studied Clara with an air of amusement, yet there was an edge to her gaze that told her she wouldn't be swayed by charm or excuses. "Ah, yes. The Nightfalls. A very powerful family." She leaned forwards slightly, her voice lowering just enough to feel like a challenge. "Let's see if you can live up to that name, shall we?"

Clara's stomach twisted at the professor's words, the weight of her name settling heavily on her. *The Nightfalls.* Always the name first, always the expectations. How was she supposed to live up to a legacy she didn't even understand?

I didn't choose this, she thought, frustration flaring. *If I'm going to carry this name, it'll be on my terms.*

She forced a small nod, masking the storm of doubt beneath a steady gaze. But the questions lingered: *What do they expect from me? And what if I can't deliver?*

"Right, let's get on with it, shall we? Welcome, students," the professor said, her voice smooth. "For those of you that do not know, I am Professor Ainsley, and welcome to Elemental Magic. It commands the forces of earth, fire, water, and air. They are not tools but untamed partners. Respect them, and they may respect you."

Clara exchanged a glance with Leo, who raised an eyebrow, clearly intrigued. Finn, ever the optimist, muttered under his breath, "Can't wait for this one."

Professor Ainsley gestured to the elemental pylons around the field. "These pillars serve as focal points for each element. They will guide you, amplify your magic, and if you're not careful, teach you the consequences of overconfidence."

With a flick of her wrist, she uttered the words 'Ventari Emera', which summoned a swirling orb of wind that hovered in her palm. "We'll start with air, perhaps the most deceptive of the elements. Gentle as a breeze, fierce as a storm. Your task today is to summon and control a current of air. Don't worry about power; focus on balance."

She stepped back, giving the students room to spread out. Clara's heart thudded as she took her place near a pillar etched with whirling lines. She raised her wand and focused, trying to recall the visualisation exercises she had practised with Fenwick.

"Feel it," Professor Ainsley called, walking among the students. "Air is everywhere, around you, within you. It's a dance, not a command."

Clara closed her eyes, feeling the wind against her skin. She murmured the incantation, "Ventari Emera," and felt a stirring of energy around her. A faint breeze swirled at her fingertips, light and tentative.

Beside her, Leo was already forming a steady current, his expression one of calm focus.

Meanwhile, Finn's attempt sent a sudden gust that nearly knocked over a nearby student. "Sorry!" he called, laughing nervously.

"Control, Mr. Adu," Professor Ainsley said, her tone firm but amused. "The wind doesn't follow chaos; it thrives on precision."

Clara focused harder, pulling the breeze into a controlled spiral. For a moment, it responded, lifting leaves, but then it unravelled, fading into nothing.

"Good attempt, Miss Nightfall," Professor Ainsley said as she passed her. "But remember, the element is not yours to own. Invite it, don't demand it."

Clara nodded, her cheeks flushing with determination. She could feel the challenge this magic posed, but she also felt a spark of exhilaration. This was different from anything she'd experienced before, a connection to something vast and untamed.

*

As the lesson progressed, the arena buzzed with the hum of attempts, successes, and occasional mishaps.

"Focus. Control is the key," Professor Ainsley called out, her fiery red hair catching the light as she paced between students. "Elemental magic is about harmony, not brute force. The elements will not bow to you if you try to command them. You must invite their cooperation."

The task was simple: summon a controlled gust of wind to move a pebble towards you. Leo had managed it on his first attempt, the pebble drifting gracefully into his hand. Even Orwell Crackshaw had managed it, and apparently, he was useless. His spells often bordered on pathetic, and even he managed.

But Clara's stone remained stubbornly still, unmoved despite her repeated attempts.

"Take a deep breath, Clara," Leo said gently from beside her, his voice calm, his own pebble in his palm. "You're overthinking it. Try to …"

"I know I'm overthinking it!" Clara snapped. She sighed, guilt flooding her. "Sorry."

"It's okay," Leo said, stepping back to give her space. Clara tried again, raising her wand and pointing it at the pebble. She whispered the incantation: "Aerion Fluctus." Nothing happened. The pebble sat there, mocking her.

As Clara stared at the motionless pebble, doubt crept into her chest. What if the Nightfalls had made a mistake? What if she wasn't who they thought she was?

But then she remembered Fenwick's words: *Magic isn't just about power, Clara. It's about intention. Spells come from the heart, then are channelled through the wand. Remember, the magic is already inside you; it's your belief in it that brings it to life.* Slowly, she raised her wand and tried again, determined not to let her fear define her

She raised her wand again, her voice steady. "Aerion Fluctus."

The faintest breeze stirred, but it wasn't enough to move the pebble. Clara's chest tightened as the familiar knot of inadequacy grew.

Clara forced a smile, but her frustration was boiling over. She felt every pair of eyes on her, every successful spell around her amplifying her failure, negative thoughts swirling around her mind like a relentless storm. *Lost witch, let's see if you can you live up to your family's name.* The self-doubt hit her in waves. She suddenly felt overwhelmed, as though the weight of the entire school was pressing down on, threatening to crush her.

But Clara wasn't listening anymore. Embarrassment, pressure, and a simmering sense of inadequacy swirled inside her like a storm. She raised her wand again, her heart pounding.

"Aerion Fluctus!" she screamed, her voice cracking with anger and desperation.

The air responded, but not as she intended. A violent gust erupted from her wand, wild and untamed. It tore through the training grounds, scattering pebbles, upending practice stands, and sending a shockwave of energy rippling across the field.

"Clara, stop!" Professor Ainsley shouted, her wand already moving to contain the chaos.

But the wind had a will of its own now, growing stronger, feeding off Clara's emotions. It whipped her hair into her face, pulling at her robes as if trying to consume her entirely. She tried to regain control, but the harder she fought, the wilder the magic became.

Professor Ainsley cast a powerful containment spell, forming a glowing barrier that encased the rogue gust. With a decisive flick of her wand, she redirected the energy into the lake. The water erupted in a dramatic spray, shimmering with magical residue, before settling back into calm ripples.

The grounds fell silent, the only sound the soft rustling of leaves in the aftermath. Clara lowered her wand, her hands trembling.

Professor Ainsley approached, her expression stern but not unkind. "And that, Clara, is why I warned you not to force it. Magic is not your servant. It reflects what's inside you. If you're chaotic, so is your magic."

"I didn't mean to," Clara began, her voice barely audible.

"I know," Professor Ainsley interrupted, her tone softening. "But you have to learn to master yourself before you can master magic. Take this as a lesson: power without control is dangerous. You must respect the magic you wield."

Clara nodded, swallowing the lump in her throat.

Leo stepped closer, placing a reassuring hand on her shoulder. "Hey, it's okay. We've all been there."

"Yeah," Finn chimed in, grinning. "Although mine usually involves more accidental explosions. Yours was just … windy."

Ellie gave a small smile. "We all mess up, Clara. It's part of learning."

Clara let out a shaky laugh, though her chest still felt tight.

"Take a break," Professor Ainsley said, her voice gentle now. "Reflect on what happened. When you're ready, come back to it with a clear mind."

Clara nodded, stepping back from the group and sitting on a nearby bench. As the class resumed around her, she stared at her wand, the events replaying in her mind. She realised it wasn't just about the spell; it was about herself, her emotions, her fears.

Magic, she thought, wasn't just a tool. It was a mirror. And if she wanted to succeed, she'd have to face what it was reflecting.

As Clara sat on the bench, her mind raced. The professor's words echoed in her head: *magic reflects what's inside you.* If that was true, what did her chaotic spell reveal about her?

*

As Clara lay in bed after her first day, her mind raced with everything that had happened. Being prejudged as a Nightfall, the burden of that name and all it stood for, pressed heavily on her. Lucinda Vale and her friends treated Clara as though she didn't belong, their sneers and whispers cutting through her already fragile confidence. Those fears had always been there, lurking in the background, but the girls' cruel words had only brought them to the forefront, making them impossible to ignore.

Then there was her loss of control on the elemental grounds. Clara had always prided herself on keeping her emotions in check, but since discovering magic, everything had shifted. The revelations about her mother, her prestigious family, and the magical world she barely understood felt overwhelming. Now, far from her dad and the life she had always known, she felt unmoored, adrift in a sea of expectations and uncertainty. Clara truly felt lost.

Clara's thoughts swirled, frustration and self-doubt pressing heavily on her. She clenched her fists, knowing she couldn't face this alone. She needed guidance, someone to help her navigate the chaos. Clara decided to speak to Professor Mornvale. She wasn't even sure if mental health was something the magical world acknowledged, but she had to try. Reaching out felt like the only way forward, and for once, she didn't want to shoulder the weight of it all on her own.

Chapter 20: A Little Support

The next day in Runes and Glyphs, Clara sat at her desk, trying to focus on Professor Darnel's lecture. But the weight of Crowstone's expectations and mysteries was weighing on her, and her quill scratched the parchment as her mind wandered. She needed help if she was going to succeed at Crowstone's.

Out of nowhere, a small, enchanted note fluttered through the air and landed gracefully on Professor Darnel's desk. Clara glanced up, curious, as the professor unfolded it, her eyes scanning the page quickly. The professor's gaze lifted, landing squarely on Clara.

"Miss Nightfall," he said, his tone calm but with an edge of importance. "You've been summoned to Room 114. Please gather your things."

Clara blinked, confused. "Room 114?" she repeated, glancing around at her classmates, who looked just as puzzled. No one had ever mentioned such a room.

The professor nodded. "Yes. Head towards the library. You'll find your way."

Clara hesitated, feeling the eyes of the entire class on her as she gathered her books and wand. With a quiet nod, she left the room, the door clicking shut behind her.

Walking the winding hallways of Crowstone, she felt an unfamiliar weight settle in her chest. She had no idea where Room 114 was or why she'd been summoned. Her steps quickened as she neared the library, but before she could push open the grand oak doors, a smaller, unmarked door creaked open just down the corridor.

A professor stepped out, one Clara hadn't seen much before. Her dark robes flowed elegantly, and her warm gaze immediately put Clara somewhat at ease.

"This way, Clara," the professor said softly, motioning for her to follow.

Clara stepped into a serene room with muted walls and golden lantern light. Plush chairs and drifting candles created a soothing, magical atmosphere.

The professor's streaked dark hair framed kind pale blue eyes. "Welcome, Clara Nightfall," the professor said, her voice carrying a gentle strength. She smiled as she sat down on a chair in the middle of the room. "Please sit." She gestured to the seat opposite. "I'm Professor Moonsong. I specialise in Divination and Prophecy, but one of my most cherished roles here at Crowstone is helping students find their balance … especially when the weight of this world feels too heavy."

The air was cool and crisp but not cold, carrying the unmistakable scent of freshly baked bread, the kind that reminded her of lazy Sunday mornings at home.

The room itself seemed to glow with pastel colours, the walls shifting between soft purple and pink, while the ceiling mimicked a sky in the early hours of dawn, just before the sun peeked over the horizon. Everything felt soothingly familiar, as if the room had reached into her thoughts and plucked out the very essence of what made her feel at ease.

Professor Moonsong's voice, gentle and melodic, broke the silence. "The Room of Reflection is designed to adapt to whoever steps inside, Clara," she explained. "It senses your emotions, your memories, and your preferences, creating an environment tailored to your inner peace. The colours, the scents, even the temperature: all of it is meant to help you let go of tension and reconnect with yourself."

Clara sank into the chair, the plush fabric enveloping

her. "It's amazing," she murmured, brushing her fingers over a warm teacup. "It feels like it knows me."

Professor Moonsong smiled. "Perhaps it does. Let it guide you. Reflection is more than just thinking; it's about finding balance in the parts of yourself you may have forgotten."

Clara shifted in her chair, unsure how to respond.

Professor Moonsong's lips curved into a soft reassuring smile. "Your grandmother spoke to me about her concerns, but it was easy enough to see for myself. Crowstone has a way of recognising when its students are feeling out of balance. It's one of the school's quiet little gifts."

Professor Moonsong continued. "In the non-magical world, they have spaces for mental health and wellbeing. This is, you could say, our equivalent."

Clara shifted in her seat, hesitating for a few seconds before speaking. "I … I guess I have been struggling," she admitted, her voice quieter than usual. "I was thinking about talking to Professor Mornvale today, especially after yesterday." She glanced down at her hands, fidgeting slightly. "Everything just feels … too much. I thought I was ready. I mean, I was nervous about coming, but after arriving and settling in, I started to believe I could belong, but that quickly unravelled yesterday."

Professor Moonsong gave a soft smile. "Adjusting to a new life, especially one as different as this, can be overwhelming. Struggles with family, unresolved grief, or simply feeling out of place are all things that weigh on even the strongest of us. You're not alone in that, Clara."

Clara shifted uncomfortably. "I don't know. I just feel lost. Like I'm stuck between two worlds, and I don't really belong in either."

"That feeling is more common than you think," the professor said gently. "But let me tell you a story. Have you heard of the Firevail Moth?"

Clara shook her head, intrigued.

"It's a magical insect, similar to a caterpillar. When it's ready to transform, it weaves a cocoon of enchanted silk. But its transformation is long and incredibly difficult. The moth struggles to free itself, and to an observer, it might seem cruel to let it suffer like that. But here's the truth: without that struggle, its wings would never grow strong enough to carry it. The fight is what makes it able to fly."

Clara thought about the story, her chest tight as she whispered, "So … struggling is part of it?"

"Exactly," the professor replied. "Your struggles, no matter how impossible they feel now, are strengthening you in ways you can't see yet. It's hard, and it's painful, but you will emerge stronger, just like the Firevail Moth." Professor Moonsong leaned back slightly, her expression growing thoughtful. "I wasn't much older than you when I lost my older brother," she began softly.

Clara's gaze snapped to her, surprised by the shift in tone.

"He was my protector, my guide, my best friend. But one day, ten older wizards attacked him. He was powerful, but even he couldn't fight those odds."

Clara's heart clenched. "That's awful …"

"It was," Professor Moonsong said, her voice touched with emotion. "Those responsible were punished, but it didn't bring him back. For the longest time, I carried that grief alone, thinking it made me weak to admit how much I was struggling. Eventually, I sought help. I learned that even as powerful witches and wizards, we are not immune to pain, fear, or doubt. Magic doesn't make us invincible."

She leaned forwards slightly, her gaze meeting Clara's. "We deal with loss and struggle in much the same way non-magical folk do. We talk, we meditate, we process our pain one step at a time. There's no spell or potion that can make it all disappear."

Clara swallowed hard, her voice trembling as she asked, "So … it's okay to feel like this?"

"It's not just okay," the professor said firmly. "It's natural. Struggling doesn't make you weak; it makes you a witch. And you're not alone, Clara. You have people who care about you, who want to help you through this."

Clara nodded slowly, feeling a little lighter.

The professor smiled. "I think you could be stronger than you know, Clara. And like the Firevail Moth, you'll emerge from this stronger, even if it doesn't feel like it now."

Clara hesitated, staring down at her hands as she struggled to put her thoughts into words. Finally, she took a deep breath and spoke, her voice quiet but steady. "I'm just not sure I belong here. Some of the kids have been calling me 'the lost witch', and the irony of it is … I actually do feel lost. I'm new to magic, I didn't grow up with any of this, and it feels like everyone's expecting me to be something I'm not ready for yet."

Her voice cracked slightly as she continued. "And it's not just the school. Coming here has brought up all these feelings I thought I'd buried about my mam. I barely remember her, but now, being in the same house she was in, hearing how talented she was, it's too much. I feel like I have to live up to her and my family's name, and I'm terrified I'll fail. And then there's my dad. He's back home, and I miss him. Everything is just … a lot to deal with all at once."

Clara paused, wiping at her eyes. "It feels like no matter what I do, I'm falling short. I just don't feel strong enough to deal with it all."

Professor Moonsong leaned forward, her pale blue eyes meeting Clara's with a quiet intensity. "Clara, strength isn't about avoiding struggles; it's about facing them. Admitting you're struggling takes bravery. Magic isn't just spells; it's resilience and growth. Your journey is your own. Take it one step at a time."

Clara nodded, a flicker of hope sparking in her. In that moment, Clara felt like she wasn't entirely alone in navigating this new world.

Professor Moonsong smiled warmly. "What if we make this a weekly thing? It will be a space for you to share how you're feeling, to reflect on your progress, or just to breathe. No judgment, no expectations, just time for you."

Clara hesitated for a moment before voicing her concern. "What do I tell my friends if they ask where I was?"

Moonsong's smile widened, a glimmer of understanding in her eyes. "You can say you're attending Reflection Sessions or tell them nothing at all if that's what you prefer. They're open to any student who wants to take time to process their journey here. It's not something to be embarrassed about. It's part of growing as a witch and as a person. But if you'd rather not explain, that's your choice. This time is yours."

Clara nodded, feeling a little lighter. "Reflection Sessions," she murmured. "That doesn't sound so bad."

As they stood outside the Room of Reflection, Professor Moonsong gestured towards a stand holding a soft green orb that had a delicate glow.

"This, Clara, is the Reflection Orb," she said, her voice melodic. "It ensures that the room remains a confidential space for those who need it. If the orb glows green, the room is free to use. When it turns amber, it means someone is already inside."

Clara tilted her head. "That's similar to traffic lights in the non-magical world."

"To maintain confidentiality, the room has a separate exit. Once you've completed your session, you'll leave through a different door, ensuring you don't cross paths with anyone entering after you," Professor Moonsong explained. "Shall we say Wednesdays at four p.m.?"

Clara gave a slight smile. "Yeah, I think I can manage that. It's already been so helpful just speaking to you today."

Professor Moonsong continued, her voice steady, like a calm current beneath stormy seas. "No one should suffer alone. Not here, not in this school, and not even beyond these walls. Today you've taken the first step in dealing with everything going on inside, and that's something to be proud of."

Clara blinked back a surge of emotion. "I feel like a huge weight has been removed."

Professor Moonsong's smile deepened, full of warmth. "That's the beauty of sharing your problems. It lightens the load, allowing the weight to be shared and easing some of the pressure, Clara. There's always someone willing to listen, willing to help. You just have to let them."

As Clara left the Room of Reflection, her negative

emotions hadn't disappeared, but she felt something shift. The struggle wasn't over, but maybe, just maybe, she could find a way through it.

Chapter 21: Shadows and a Storm Within

The common room droned with uneasy whispers. Even the rowdy Year 7s were subdued, their eyes darting nervously towards the shadowy corners lit by the wavering fire.

Clara sat at a table with Ellie, Finn, and Leo, their half-finished books and scattered notes forgotten in the tense atmosphere.

"They say they saw them," whispered a Year 7 at a nearby table. "Near the east wing, right before lights out."

"Shadows?" her friend asked, her voice barely audible.

"Not just any shadows," the Year 7 replied. "The Shadow Sentinels. The ones that move even when nothing else does. Someone said they had glowing eyes."

Clara leaned closer to Ellie. "Shadow Sentinels?" she murmured. "What are they talking about?"

Ellie frowned. "They're part of the school's security, magical entities bound to the grounds. They stay invisible unless you're somewhere you shouldn't be."

"And?" Leo asked, leaning forwards with a grin. "What's the scary part?"

Ellie gave him a flat look. "The Sentinels don't just patrol. They sense disturbances in the magical field, wards being tampered with, that sort of thing. But they're not exactly gentle about it. If they catch you, they can trap you in shadow binds until a professor arrives."

"Or worse," muttered a nearby Year 11, who had been eavesdropping. "There's a story about a student from years ago. He got caught sneaking into the library after curfew, and when the professors found him, he was babbling about whispers and cold hands grabbing at him."

Finn smirked, leaning back in his chair. "Sounds like a glorified bedtime story. A bit of drama to keep us all tucked in tight."

The Year 11 gave him a sharp look. "Oh, yeah? Tell that to the group who saw the Sentinels last night. I heard one of them swore he felt something breathe on the back of his neck."

"It's not funny, Finn," Ellie snapped.

Clara shivered, the firelight creating deeper shadows than usual. "Why now?" she asked. "If they're security that stays in the shadows, why are they suddenly everywhere?"

Ellie exchanged a glance with Leo, her brow furrowed. "The wards are linked to the school's magic. If they're detecting disturbances, it could mean the wards are weakening … or something is testing them."

The conversation lingered as more students chimed in with their own stories.

"I heard they were circling the greenhouse last week," a Year 10 said. "Professor Miron tried to send them back, but they wouldn't move."

"Someone in my charms class said they saw one by the lake," a Year 7 added nervously. "It disappeared when they got close."

Leo, who had been silent until now, spoke up. "Or they're being drawn to something," he said quietly, his gaze fixed on the trembling flames. "Something the wards can't keep out."

Clara glanced at him, his words unsettling in their simplicity. What could be strong enough to challenge Crowstone's wards? She felt a chill run down her spine and glanced towards the shadows at the edge of the room, half-expecting them to shift.

"Whatever's happening," she said, her voice steady despite her unease, "we need to be careful. If the Sentinels are on edge, it's not just random magic they're sensing. It's something bigger."

*

Later that evening, after the common room had emptied and most of the students had retreated to their dormitories, Clara couldn't shake the feeling of being watched. She was halfway up the spiral staircase to her room when she heard it, a faint rustling sound, like fabric brushing against stone.

She froze, her hand tightening on the banister. The corridor behind her was empty, the shadows long and still. But as she turned to keep walking, a flicker of movement caught her eye.

A shadow slinked along the wall, moving against the firelight. Clara's heart raced as she stepped back, her hand gripping her wand.

The shadow shifted into a humanoid form. Two cold, glowing eyes locked onto her, and a deep chill seeped into her bones.

"Clara?" Ellie's voice startled her.

As Clara and Ellie stood on the stairs, lined with lanterns quivering with a soft golden glow, footsteps echoed behind them.

Leo emerged, his usual easy stride unhurried, his expression unreadable. His eyes flicked between Clara and Ellie as he approached.

"Where have you been?" Ellie asked, arms crossed.

Leo shrugged, running a hand through his hair. "Library. Studying."

Ellie raised an eyebrow. "Where's your stuff, then?"

Leo simply tapped the side of his head, offering a lazy

grin. "I don't need it. It's all up here."

Clara studied him carefully. He looked perfectly at ease. No books or notes, not even a stray ink stain on his fingers. The library was massive, complex in its design, yet he hadn't brought a single thing?

Before she could question it, Leo turned to her, his expression softening. "Everything okay, Clara?"

"She's fine," Ellie answered quickly, steering Clara towards the dormitory. "Just getting her to bed."

Leo's gaze lingered on Clara for a second longer before he gave a small nod. "Good. Get some rest."

As they entered the dormitory, Clara cast one last glance over her shoulder. Leo stood watching them for a moment before turning away, disappearing into the shadows of the hallway.

The door clicked shut behind them, and Ellie let out a breath. "That was weird, right?"

Clara didn't answer. Her mind was still tangled in the memory of the Sentinel, and the feeling that something, or someone, had been watching her long before she'd even noticed.

*

That night, the dream came in fragments, flickering like images reflected in broken glass. Clara stood in a darkened room, the air oppressive. Shadows twisted and writhed, their whispers coiling around her ears. A voice, deep and jagged like splintering wood, cut through the haze.

"He's closer than you think," it said, its tone both mocking and dominant.

Clara turned, trying to find the source of the voice, but the shadows shifted endlessly, hiding their master. Another fragment came: a cold laugh, a flash of green light, and a sudden, suffocating silence.

She tried to scream, to push back against the darkness, but her voice caught in her throat. The air around her felt like it was crushing her chest, and then the voice returned, louder this time.

"You'll never stop me. Not while you're blind to what you are."

The darkness surged forward, consuming everything in its path, and Clara jolted awake, gasping for air.

Her chest rose and fell as she sat upright in bed, the sheets tangled around her legs. Sweat clung to her skin, and her heart pounded like a drum. She glanced around the dark room, trying to ground herself, but the whispers from the dream still echoed faintly in her mind.

"Clara?" came a soft voice from the bed next to hers. Amelia sat up, her brow furrowed with concern. "Are you okay?"

Clara nodded quickly, though her trembling hands betrayed her. "It was just a dream," she whispered, brushing damp hair from her face. "I'm fine."

But the truth was, she wasn't fine. The dream lingered, its warning gnawing at her thoughts. She knew it wasn't just a nightmare.

*

The next morning, Clara felt like a ghost of herself. Exhaustion dragged at her limbs, and her head ached as though the remnants of the dream still clawed at her. She pushed herself to join her friends for breakfast, hoping the regularity would ground her.

The Great Solstice Hall was alive with noise. Students talked loudly, their laughter bouncing off the enchanted ceiling. Plates clattered, and the smell of spiced porridge and buttered toast filled the air.

But Clara couldn't focus. As she walked towards her table, she felt a sudden surge of anger, not her own, but raw and vivid, burning through her like fire. A moment later, guilt twisted in her stomach, followed by a wave of anxiety so intense it made her knees wobble.

She clutched the edge of the table as the emotions swirled, like a hurricane battering against her chest. Faces blurred, the chatter grew louder, and she felt as though she might drown in the chaos.

"Stop it!" she shouted, her voice trembling and sharp.

The noise in the hall died instantly. Every student turned to stare, their expressions ranging from confusion to amazement.

Clara's face burned as she realised what she'd done. The emotions weren't hers. She had felt the entire hall's collective turmoil, and it had overwhelmed her.

Her friends were by her side in moments. Ellie placed a hand on her shoulder, her eyes wide with worry. "Clara, what's wrong?"

"I don't know," Clara whispered. "I … I couldn't stop it. It wasn't me, it was everyone."

Amelia exchanged a glance with Finn, and the three of them gently guided Clara towards the infirmary.

Madam Allara, the school nurse, met them with a calm, reassuring smile. "Sit her down," she said, gesturing to a cushioned chair by the window. She examined Clara carefully before pulling a vial of shimmering liquid from a shelf.

"This will help calm your mind," Madam Allara said, handing Clara the elixir. "Sip it slowly."

Clara obeyed, the cool liquid sliding down her throat. Almost instantly, the tension in her chest eased and the chaos in her mind quietened.

"You two can go. I'll take care of your friend," Madam Allara said to Finn and Amelia.

They smiled at Clara as they left.

"Take some time to rest. You seem overly stressed, dear," Madam Allara said kindly.

Clara nodded, her gratitude unspoken but clear.

*

That afternoon, Clara made her way to the Room of Reflection. Professor Moonsong was expecting her, her serene presence a comfort to Clara's frayed nerves.

"Clara," Moonsong said gently, motioning for her to sit. "I hoped you'd come today."

Clara sank into the cushions, her voice trembling as she recounted her dream and the overwhelming emotions in the Great Solstice Hall. "It's like I feel everything: everyone's anger, fear, guilt. It's not mine, but I can't stop it. It's too much."

Moonsong nodded thoughtfully, her blue eyes soft with understanding. "Ah, you're an empath, Clara. No wonder you've been struggling."

Clara blinked. "A woman at the festival said the same thing. She also told me to keep it a secret. But I don't even know how to control it. It has a mind of its own."

Moonsong leaned forward, her gaze steady and serious. "She was right, you know. Empaths, especially in someone so young and untrained, can unsettle people. Most witches and wizards are comfortable with what they choose to show the world, but the thought that you might sense what they're hiding? That can make them wary … even fearful."

Clara looked away, her hands twisting nervously in her lap. "So, I just hide it? Pretend it doesn't exist?"

"No," Moonsong said firmly, her tone both kind and firm. "You don't need to hide who you are, Clara. But until you learn to control it, it's best to keep it to yourself. People need time to trust, and you need time to understand your gift before you share it openly. This isn't about shame; it's about self-preservation."

Clara swallowed hard. "But how do I stop it? How do I make it go away?"

Moonsong smiled faintly as she stood and moved to one of the tall shelves lining the room. Her fingers brushed over a row of small, glowing crystals, selecting one that pulsed with a gentle light. Carrying it back to the table, she whispered an incantation under her breath, and the crystal began to hover in the air.

"Gaillean stria," Moonsong murmured softly. Slowly, a delicate silver thread materialised, wrapping itself around the crystal until it formed a simple, elegant bracelet. The glow of the crystal softened, steady and calming.

Moonsong fastened the bracelet gently around Clara's wrist. "This is enchanted to help reduce the intensity of what you feel. It won't block your gift completely, but it will soften the edge of it, make it more manageable."

Clara touched the charm, her fingers brushing the smooth crystal, its warmth comforting against her skin. "Thank you," she whispered, her voice thick with emotion. "But will this really help?"

"It will," Moonsong assured her. "It's not a permanent solution, but it will give you some breathing room while you learn to channel your abilities. And Clara" — she leaned forward — "your empathy is not a curse. It's a rare and powerful gift. One day, when you learn to master it, you'll see it for what it truly is: a strength, not a burden."

Clara nodded slowly, feeling a little lighter. She

glanced down at the bracelet, its soft glow pulsing in rhythm with her heartbeat. She felt a flicker of hope.

Moonsong placed a comforting hand on Clara's shoulder. "You're stronger than you think, Clara. This gift is part of who you are."

Clara nodded, the warmth of Moonsong's words soothing her. As she left the Room of Reflection, she felt lighter, the bracelet's magic a steady presence on her wrist.

She didn't fully understand her gift yet, but for the first time, she felt like she wasn't dealing with it alone.

*

Later, Clara sat in her room, her friends laughing quietly in the background. She'd excused herself from the conversation, the weight of the day's challenges pressing on her. Pulling the Silverdusk-chest from her bag, she set it on the small table in front of her, running her fingers over the etched design.

She began to write.

Hi, Dad,

I know I've only been here for a few days, but it feels like a lifetime. School is amazing and intense. I wish you could see it. There's so much magic everywhere, and sometimes I think, wow, I can't believe I'm a student here. But other times, I feel like I'm drowning in it. I miss home, Dad. I miss the normal stuff, like fish and chips Fridays and our attempts at board games.

I'm okay. Don't worry about me.

I love you.

As she placed the parchment in the chest, it gave its soft chime, and the message faded away, leaving Clara with a sense of calm she hadn't felt all day.

Chapter 22: The Map's Whisper

After avoiding it, Clara finally unrolled the astral map on her desk. Its gold lines gently pulsed, the whispers tugging at her curiosity. This time, she decided to follow.

Crowstone had been a whirlwind, with new faces, traditions, and the weight of the Nightfall name pressing down on her. She'd been too consumed by everything else, waiting for the right moment, unsure if she was ready to face whatever the map might reveal.

Now, in the quiet stillness of her room, she felt the whirlwind settle. The initial rush of fear and excitement had calmed into something steadier, something more certain. Maybe she didn't have all the answers, but she was ready to take the first step.

*

The map's whispers grew louder, pulling Clara through a maze of twisting corridors, each darker and more foreboding than the last. The torches lining the walls flickered weakly, as if reluctant to light her way. At times, the whispers faltered, leaving her standing in eerie silence, forcing her to retrace her steps or linger at intersections, unsure of where to turn.

She descended a narrow, spiralling staircase that groaned with age under her weight. The walls were damp, laced with moss and faint symbols. At the base of the staircase, a stone archway loomed, half-hidden by creeping ivy. Beyond it, a narrow passage twisted sharply, its uneven floor forcing Clara to tread carefully.

Finally, the whispers led her to a dead end, or so it seemed. She ran her fingers along the cold, crumbling stones until they brushed against an invisible seam. A faint pulse of magic rippled beneath her fingertips, and the whispers urged her to press harder. With a quiet rumble, a section of the wall slid away, revealing a hidden doorway.

The door itself was ancient, its surface etched with shifting symbols that seemed to ripple like water. A heavy iron lock sealed it shut, the mechanism rusted with time. Clara hesitated, the whispers now faint and expectant, as if waiting for her to figure out the next step.

The whispers faded into silence as Clara stood before the ancient door, its symbols gleaming faintly in the dim light. She ran her fingers lightly over the surface, tracing the lines of the crescent moon, phoenix, and open hand that seemed to emerge from the patterns. A phrase etched into the frame caught her eye, faint and almost invisible, as if it only wanted to be seen when she was truly ready.

Beyond this threshold lies knowledge untold,
For those whose purpose is steady and bold.
Unlock the path with word or deed,
Reveal your worth, and you shall proceed.

Clara frowned, murmuring the words under her breath. The symbols shimmered, but the door did not budge. She closed her eyes, letting the riddle turn over in her mind. Word or deed. Was it asking her to say something or perform a spell?

She raised her wand, murmuring a simple unlocking charm, but the runes flared angrily, the magic bouncing harmlessly back. "Not that simple," she muttered.

Her gaze fell back to the symbols, the crescent moon, the phoenix, the open hand. They pulsed faintly in sequence. Word or deed. Purpose. Her purpose.

Taking a deep breath, Clara said aloud, "I seek

knowledge, not power. I seek understanding, not control. I am here to learn."

The symbols flickered as if considering her words, but the door remained steadfastly shut. A new thought struck her. Purpose wasn't just words; it was action. She looked down at her hand, then back at the open hand symbol on the door. Slowly, she pressed her palm against the glowing outline.

The runes around the doorframe blazed to life, shifting into a new formation. The whispers returned, soft but clear: "Speak what you would sacrifice to find the truth."

Clara's chest tightened. A sacrifice? What was she willing to give? She thought of her fears, of failing, of not belonging, and then, with trembling lips, she whispered, "I will sacrifice my fear of the unknown, not because it disappears, but because I choose to face it."

The door creaked, the symbols fading into the wood as the lock clicked. Clara exhaled in relief as the door swung open, revealing the darkened chamber beyond.

At the centre of the room stood a small platform shrouded in shadow. Resting on it was *The Book of Lost Shadows*, its dark cover adorned with shimmering symbols that pulsed. Clara's breath caught. Whispers from older students flooded her mind, tales of a book so powerful it could grant immense knowledge but at a cost. Its cursed secrets were not to be taken lightly. Why had the map brought her here?

As her fingers brushed the cover, the shadows around her stirred violently, rising like a living thing. Whispers echoed in an unknown language, surrounding her with an eerie intensity. Clara froze, her instincts screaming at her to pull back, but something kept her rooted. Closing her eyes, she focused on her breathing, willing her fear to quieten. Slowly, the shadows stilled, retreating like smoke, leaving the book's pages open before her. Spells of concealment and shadow manipulation glowed faintly, their power palpable, almost calling to her.

Her hand hovered over the pages, but doubt gnawed at her. The room seemed to hold its breath, waiting for her to make a choice. Clara's mind raced. *What if this is too much? What if I don't understand the cost?*

Her heart thudded painfully as the pull of the book clashed with her own sense of caution. She thought of her mother, of her friends, of everything she didn't know about this world yet. How could she take something this powerful without knowing what it meant? What could it do to her?

Clenching her fists, Clara took a step back. "Not yet," she whispered, her voice trembling but resolute. She couldn't claim the book, not now, not when she didn't understand the risks. Her mother had hidden her from magic for a reason, and she wasn't going to let her curiosity lead her blindly.

As she turned, the shadows swirled briefly, almost as if nodding in approval. The air felt lighter, though the weight of what she had seen lingered. Clara paused at the doorway, glancing back one last time. The book seemed to pulse faintly, as though acknowledging her retreat. *It's not the right time*, she thought again, stepping out of the room and closing the door behind her.

As she made her way back to the dormitory, Clara's mind buzzed with questions. Why had the map led her to such an intense challenge so soon? She mentioned her quest to her friends that evening, expecting similar experiences, but their responses surprised her.

"Mine just led me to some secret garden," Leo said

with a shrug, though his expression flickered briefly with something unreadable. "Maybe they're testing you. Just go with it."

Finn grinned. "Or maybe they just know you're *that* special."

Clara forced a smile, but the encounter lingered in her mind. Why her? Why now? And what did it mean to be tested in this way? The answers, she knew, would have to wait. For now, she could only focus on the journey ahead.

*

As the days passed, Clara became more fixated with her map. Her friends, however, didn't seem quite as impressed. Finn had joked about it leading her to things way beyond a Year 8, and Ellie had suggested speaking to a professor about its unusual guidance.

Leo was the only one that seemed encouraging, saying, "The school wants us to learn, and each map is tailored to our need and personal journey, so clearly, it could only be good for Clara."

Their words lingered in her mind, but she brushed it aside. The map was specifically for her, and somehow, she felt certain it wouldn't lead her astray.

When Ellie invited her to join the group in the common room for some downtime, Clara hesitated. "I'd love to," she said with a faint smile, "but I've got some studying to do. Maybe later?" She ignored Finn's knowing smirk and Ellie's concerned look, clutching the map tightly as she headed for the door.

As she walked away, her heart fluttered with anticipation of where the map would take her next. She knew the map had a hold on her, but how could she resist? It was giving her purpose, guiding her through this overwhelming new world. Clara didn't have all the answers, but she trusted the map. For now, it was her mission, and it was easier to not share it with anyone.

*

The next day, the astral map began to glow as Clara unrolled it on her bed, its lines shimmering with golden light. Her heart raced as the map whispered to her again, guiding her gaze towards a new destination. A single pulsating line led to the Mystical Lake on the academy grounds, spiralling into its depths before fading out.

She traced the route with her finger, frowning. The lake, veiled in mist and pulsing with magical energy, was strictly off-limits without a professor. Why was the map leading her there?

"Clara, you coming to the common room?" Amelia called from the doorway.

She quickly rolled up the map, forcing a smile. "In a bit. I have something to sort out first."

Later, at lunch, Clara casually leaned towards Ellie, who was engrossed in a book. "Ellie, do you know any spells that could help someone swim underwater for long periods? You know, like for longer than normal?"

Ellie looked up, arching an eyebrow. "Underwater? Why, are you planning on taking a dive in the lake?"

Clara shrugged, trying to appear nonchalant. "No … just curious. It's just something I've been reading up on, and there's so much I don't know about magic."

"Well," Ellie said, pushing her glasses up her nose, "there's a mermaid transformation spell, but it's tricky. It changes your legs into a tail temporarily and lets you breathe underwater. Not everyone can manage it, though."

Clara leaned in. "Do you know the incantation?"

Ellie hesitated. "Not exactly. I think it's in the *Aquatic*

Morphology section of the library. But Clara, why would you ..."

"Thanks, Ellie! You're the best." Clara cut her off, grabbing her bag and hurrying out. She ignored Ellie's bewildered look. She couldn't risk explaining and having her friends try to talk her out of it. The map's guidance was hers alone to follow.

*

The Library of Luminaris's towering shelves loomed above Clara as she combed through the *Aquatic Morphology* section. Dusty books floated gently from their shelves, rearranging themselves as she scanned the titles.

Finally, her fingers brushed over a book titled *Transfigurations of the Deep.* She pulled it free, its weight settling heavily in her hands. Flipping through the pages, she found the spell: *Piscor Vita.*

Her lips moved silently as she read the description. The spell would grant her the form and abilities of a mermaid for exactly thirty minutes. She'd have enhanced swimming abilities, underwater breathing, and an affinity for navigating aquatic currents. But there was a warning: *The spell's effects end abruptly, and returning to the surface before time runs out is critical.*

Clara closed the book, her determination firm. She copied the incantation onto a piece of parchment and allowed the book to go back onto the shelf itself. As she exited the library, the whispers of the astral map echoed in her mind.

*

Professor Moonsong approached Clara as she was headed to class, her usual serene expression tinged with concern. The corridor was busy with students, but the professor's soft voice cut through the chatter like a calming breeze.

"Clara," she said in her gentle tone, stopping beside her. "I couldn't help but notice you missed the last session in the Room of Reflection. Is everything alright?"

Clara tensed, her fingers tightening around her bag strap. She felt a surge of frustration welling up inside her, the same frustration that had been building for days. The astral map's whispers had grown more insistent, pulling her towards more tasks and discoveries. She couldn't shake the feeling that it was guiding her somewhere important, somewhere only she could go. It was consuming her thoughts, leaving little room for anything else.

"I've been busy," Clara said curtly, avoiding Moonsong's gaze.

Moonsong's voice remained steady. "I understand. But you seemed to find the sessions helpful."

Clara turned sharply. "You said it was optional, right? I've decided not to," Clara snapped, her frustration spilling over. "I don't have time to sit in some room talking about feelings. I am trying to adjust to a new school, magic, new set of friends, being away from home and anything else this schools throws at me."

Professor Moonsong paused, her gaze steady and understanding. "I respect your decision, Clara. But I want you to know that the Room of Reflection is always there for you, no matter how much time passes. Sometimes, when we're so focused on moving forward, we forget to take a moment to understand why we're running in the first place. Taking a moment to pause and reflect doesn't mean you're falling behind; it means you're finding your balance."

Clara felt a sense of guilt but quickly buried it beneath

her growing frustration. "Thanks, Professor," she said stiffly, turning away. "But I'm fine."

As Clara walked off, her mind raced. She knew Moonsong was only trying to help, but the professor didn't understand. How could she? The map was hers, the tasks hers, and whatever lay at the end of its guidance felt bigger than anyone else could understand. She couldn't afford to stop now, not for reflection, not for anything.

The further she got away, the more she was warring with guilt. She hated how she'd spoken to Moonsong, but admitting she needed help felt like losing control, and control was the one thing she couldn't afford to lose right now.

*

Clara sat in the library, pretending to read while her thoughts drifted to the map. Finn finally broke the silence. "Clara, we need to talk."

Clara glanced up, guarded. "About what?"

Ellie crossed her arms. "You're not yourself. Skipping meals, sneaking around. You're shutting us out."

"I'm fine," Clara snapped. "I've just been busy catching up. You've all had years to learn magic; I haven't."

Amelia leaned in, her brow furrowed with concern. "Clara, you've been so distant. You barely even talk to us anymore. We're worried, that's all."

Finn stepped closer, his usual grin replaced with uncharacteristic seriousness. "This isn't just about skipping meals or blowing us off. You're acting like … like you don't care about anything or anyone."

Clara stood abruptly, her books clutched tightly to her chest. "You're all being ridiculous," she snapped, though her voice wavered at the edges. "I'm just trying to catch up. I've been busy, that's all. You don't understand how hard this is for me." The words came out sharper than she intended, and she winced as she saw Ellie's hurt expression. But she couldn't stop now. Admitting her guilt, her mistakes, felt like stepping into quicksand. Once she started, she might never stop sinking.

Leo, who had been leaning casually against a pillar, finally spoke, his tone lighter than the others. "Maybe they're just overthinking things, Clara. Everyone gets caught up in something now and then."

Finn shot Leo a glare. "Don't downplay this. We've all noticed it, Leo. You have too."

Clara's gaze darted to Leo, her expression briefly conflicted, before hardening again. "I don't need you all hovering like I'm breakable. I'm fine."

Ellie stepped forward, her voice softer now. "We're not saying you're fragile, Clara. We just care about you. Can't you see that?"

Clara slung her bag over her shoulder, her tone icy. "What I see is my so-called friends trying to control me. I'm done with this conversation."

Without waiting for a response, Clara turned and walked away, her footsteps echoing in the stillness of the library. A mix of frustration and guilt simmered beneath the surface. She knew they were only trying to help, but it was too much, too many questions she wasn't ready to answer, too many worries she couldn't articulate.

She glanced over her shoulder once, catching a glimpse of their concerned faces before going round the corner and disappearing into the corridor. Her heart sank. They didn't understand, and how could they? Clara barely understood herself. The weight of everything, the map, the growing expectations, her tangled emotions, pressed down on her like an invisible force. She felt trapped between wanting to explain and wanting to run.

Clara quickened her pace, forcing her focus ahead. She didn't have time to dwell on their worry or their unspoken words. There was too much to figure out, and she needed space to do it alone.

*

Later that day, as the sun sank lower in the sky, illuminating Crowstone's grounds with an orange glow, Clara made her way towards the lake. The stillness of the evening was broken only by rustling leaves in the gentle breeze, a quiet reminder that there was less than an hour before curfew began. Her wand was tucked securely in her pocket, and the incantation was etched firmly into her memory.

The lake was still, its surface reflecting the sky above. Clara stood at the edge, her toes curling into the damp earth as she stared at the shimmering water. The enormity of what she was about to do settled over her like a heavy cloak. Was she truly prepared for this? The map's whispers urged her on, insistent and relentless, but doubt crept into her mind. What if she failed? What if the spell didn't work, or worse, if she couldn't make it back in time? Shaking her head, Clara forced herself to focus. She had come this far. There was no turning back now.

She drew her wand, and with determination, she said clearly, "Piscor Vita."

A ripple of energy coursed through her body. Her legs tingled, then her clothes and her legs merged seamlessly into a colourful, shimmering tail. Scales glinted in the light, and her lungs expanded as she took her first breath of air that seemed to flow like water in her temporary form. She felt weightless and powerful.

With the map in one hand and her wand in the other, Clara flicked her tail, propelling herself deep into the lake. The underwater world unfolded around her in shimmering wonder. Schools of magical fish darted past, their scales glinting like tiny prisms. Strange plants pulsed with an otherworldly glow, and glowing creatures similar to jellyfish drifted lazily through the water. A heavy silence hung in the depths, broken only by the faint whispers of the enchanted map urging her onward.

As Clara descended further, the sunlight faded, replaced by the glow of the plants and creatures around her. Her heart thudded as the whispers grew louder, leading her towards a faint glow emanating from a crevice between two jagged rocks. She reached out, her fingers brushing the glow, and felt a pulse of energy ripple through her. Whatever was hidden here was powerful and dangerous.

Before Clara could investigate further, a shadow loomed over her. She froze, her eyes widening as a massive creature appeared from the gloom. Its body flowed like liquid darkness, and its glowing eyes burned with intelligence and malice. It wasn't just a creature; it was a guardian, defending whatever secrets lay within the lake.

The creature darted towards her with astonishing speed, forcing Clara to twist out of its path. She aimed her wand and cast a stunning spell, Bualadh Tuirse, but the magic fizzled harmlessly against its thick, rippling form. It turned sharply, its glowing eyes fixed on her, and Clara's chest tightened. Her spells weren't working, and she was hundreds of feet underwater, with no escape in sight.

Clara cast a shield, but the creature's shadowy tendril

shattered it. She twisted away, her tail flicking frantically. The map's whispers grew frantic as her lungs burned, panic rising with every second.

The creature lunged again, and Clara thrust her wand forward, casting a blinding flash of light with Solas Spreagadh. The spell illuminated the lake for a moment, forcing the creature to recoil. Clara seized the chance to retreat, swimming upward as fast as her tail would allow. She could feel the creature following her, its presence oppressive and relentless.

Just as she neared the surface, the transformation spell began to falter. A sharp jolt ran through her body as her tail vanished, replaced by her legs. She tumbled into the shallows, gasping for air, her clothes soaked and clinging to her skin. The creature lurked below, its glowing eyes watching her retreat, before sinking back into the shadows.

Clara collapsed on the shore, trembling. Her mind raced as she clutched the map, now silent in her hand. Whatever secrets the lake held weren't meant to be uncovered easily, and she had barely escaped with her life.

Clara clutched the map, its once-reassuring whispers now heavy with suspicion. What had seemed like guidance now felt manipulative, as if the map had been pushing her towards something darker than she'd realised.

*

The next day, the common room was quiet as Clara sat with her friends, her hands trembling slightly as she recounted her adventure at the lake. Finn, Leo, Amelia, and Ellie leaned in, their faces shifting from disbelief to concern as she described the glowing crevice, the strange creature, and the overwhelming sense of danger.

"You could've died, Clara," Finn said, his voice uncharacteristically serious. "And for what? Following some magical whispers from a map?"

Clara nodded, her cheeks flushed with embarrassment. "I know. It was stupid. I thought … I thought I could handle it. The map seemed like it was trying to guide me, helping me grow as a witch. But now I'm not so sure."

Ellie folded her arms. "Clara, I wish you'd told us what was actually going on with you. We would've dragged you to a professor."

Amelia leaned forward. "You need to take it to Professor Mornvale. She'll know what to do."

Clara hesitated. The map had felt so personal, almost alive, like it was meant just for her. But after the lake, she knew she couldn't ignore the dangers it posed. She nodded. "You're right. I'll take it to her right now."

*

After the last class of the day, Clara found herself standing outside Professor Mornvale's office, the astral map clutched tightly in her hand. Her friends stood with her, their silent presence a source of reassurance. Despite their collective support, Clara's anxiety felt overwhelming, as if the hallways outside Professor Mornvale's office might swallow her whole. She knew she had made a mistake in trusting the map, but she hadn't realised the full extent of it until now.

When the door swung open, Professor Mornvale stood waiting, her expression calm but unreadable. "Miss Nightfall, Mr Rutherford, Miss Chen, Miss Sharma, and last but not least, Mr Adu. Come in."

The group stepped inside, greeted not only by Professor Mornvale but also by Professor Thornblade, the deputy head, and Professor Darnell, both seated at the polished wooden table in the centre of the room.

Professor Mornvale said calmly, her tone even. "What brings you all here today?"

Clara hesitated before stepping forwards and placing the astral map on the table. "This map," Clara said, placing it on the table, "It's been leading me into dangerous places, intentionally."

Professor Mornvale exchanged a glance with the other professors. "Dangerous places?" she asked.

"Yes," Clara replied, swallowing hard. "And I don't think it's intended purposes were meant for me. At least, I hope not."

Professor Darnell stood and leaned over the map, his brow furrowing. With a wave of his hand, he murmured an incantation: "Folastra." The map shimmered, its gold lines glowing brighter for a moment before dimming again.

"It's as I suspected," Professor Darnell said, his voice laced with concern. "This map carries a secondary enchantment, one designed to subtly influence the holder. It's not just a guide. It's a lure, crafted with precision to earn your trust before steering you towards something dangerous."

"A lure?" Ellie echoed, glancing nervously at Clara.

Professor Thornblade leaned forwards inspecting the map, his soft voice measured. "The enchantment has been woven with incredible skill, layered to obscure its intent. It was meant to gain your trust and to compel you to seek out something specific."

"Was this a prank?" Amelia asked, her eyes darting between the professors.

Professor Darnell shook his head. "Unlikely. The level of magic involved is far beyond the capabilities of a student. This is deliberate. Whoever enchanted this map wanted Miss Nightfall to uncover something or perhaps to put herself in harm's way."

Clara gave him a concerned look. "Why would someone want me to find something or put myself in danger?"

Professor Darnell's expression darkened, his sharp features etched with unease. "That, Miss Nightfall, is precisely what we must decide. The enchantments on this map are complex, made with purpose, yet that purpose is obscured. We will need time to assess its nature and origins."

Clara's fingers tightened around the map, its parchment oddly cool against her skin. "So … you don't know why it's come to me?" she asked hesitantly, her voice quieter now.

"No," Darnell admitted, his tone grave. "Not yet. But I would recommend caution in the meantime. There are forces at play here that do not have your best interests at heart."

Leo shifted at the back of the group, his fingers tapping rhythmically against his thumb. "What happens to the map now?"

"We'll keep it for further study," Professor Darnell said firmly. "Its enchantments need to be unravelled to figure out their true purpose. I sense real danger here."

Professor Mornvale's gaze swept over the group, landing on Clara. "Why didn't you come to us sooner?"

Clara's stomach twisted. "I didn't realise how serious it was. You said the maps are tailored to each individual, so I assumed the school had set me the tasks to discover my potential."

Professor Mornvale sighed, her expression softening just slightly. "Miss Nightfall, I trust you've learned from this. In future, if something doesn't feel right, always ask a professor. Magic can be incredibly dangerous."

"Sounds like whoever's enchanting these maps could use a few refresher lessons in Professor Darnell's Charms and Enchantments class. Might help them avoid the whole *accidental sinister map* vibe next time," Finn said, trying to add a bit of humour.

Professor Mornvale's sharp gaze cut through him, silencing any further jokes. "That's enough, Mr Adu. The five of you may leave. But let this be a lesson: the next time you suspect something is wrong, come to us at once. The consequences of failing to do so could be far more severe."

The group nodded and shuffled out of the room, Clara feeling the weight of the professors' words settle heavily on her shoulders. Before the door closed behind them, she cast one last glance back at the map. Whatever its purpose, she was relieved to no longer hold it. She felt free. She felt more like herself again. Like one that needed others such as her friends. But as they walked away, a lingering unease settled over her. She couldn't shake the feeling that this was far from over.

*

The next morning, Clara woke to find a neatly folded parchment on her bedside table, accompanied by a note in elegant handwriting.

Miss Nightfall,

This map has been tailored for your use. It is protected by powerful charms to ensure it cannot be altered or enchanted further. May this map guide you on a safer path leading you to discoveries about the school, about magic, but most importantly, about yourself.

Professor Darnell

Clara unfolded the new map, its lines and symbols glowing with a warm, steady light. Unlike the old map, this one felt calm, reassuring. As she touched it, a gentle voice whispered: "Good morning, Clara. Shall we begin?"

She followed the map's guidance after classes that day, her friends walking beside her this time. The map led them to a hidden alcove in the library, where a small plaque described the history of Crowstone's founding. Behind the plaque was a secret shelf containing books written by the academy's first headmistress.

"This is more like it," Finn said, flipping through one of the books. "Safe, informative, and no death-defying underwater antics."

Clara smiled, a mix of relief and gratitude washing over her. She still felt a pull towards the mysteries the old map had uncovered, but for now, she was content with this simpler path. It was a reminder that magic didn't always have to be dangerous to be meaningful, and that she didn't have to face it alone.

*

The next day, Clara hesitated at the door to the Room of Reflection. She glanced at the orb, which was gentle green, meaning the room was free. She hadn't been back since she'd dismissed Professor Moonsong so curtly. The weight of her actions and her words weighed on her. Taking a deep breath, she pushed the door open and stepped inside.

Professor Moonsong was waiting, seated in a calm pose by the softly glowing fire. She looked up as Clara entered, her expression warm and welcoming, as though no time had passed.

Clara shifted awkwardly. "Professor, I … I wanted to say I'm sorry. For how I acted before. I wasn't myself. That map …" She paused, struggling to put her feelings into words. "It wasn't just the map," Clara admitted, her voice trembling. "It was me too. I let it change me. It made me think I didn't need anyone, that I had to prove something by myself. I ignored my friends, pushed them away, and almost got myself killed because I thought I could handle everything alone." She looked down, her fingers twisting in her lap. "I don't want to be that person, Professor. I want to do better."

Professor Moonsong's gaze softened, and she gestured for Clara to sit. "Yes, Professor Mornvale mentioned it to me. Powerful enchantments can deeply influence a witch or wizard. They feed on ambition, curiosity, even fear. Sometimes, they twist our strongest qualities into weaknesses. You were fortunate to recognise the danger when you did."

Clara nodded, her voice quieter now. "I thought it was helping me discover magic and its secrets. I didn't realise it was changing me and leading me to danger. Who would enchant a map meant for me? Was it a joke? Or a mistake? I'm just worried in case someone is trying to cause me harm. But I am so glad my friends forgave me … and that you did too! Sorry, I can be a whirlwind of worry at times."

Professor Moonsong smiled gently. "The important thing is you're okay and you're safe. That's what matters.

Professor Darnell will try to decipher its secrets, but I wouldn't worry too much at this stage, as we do not know the answers." Professor Moonsong leaned forwards slightly, her voice steady and soothing. "Everybody worries, Clara. Worry is our mind's way of trying to protect us, to prepare us for what might come. But when it takes hold, it can become its own kind of spell, one that traps us in possibilities rather than realities."

She paused, her gaze thoughtful. "Worry often lives in the future, in the what ifs and maybes. It draws your attention away from the present, where life is actually unfolding. When we let those swirling thoughts grow too loud, we lose sight of what's in front of us and forget to live. Always try to live in the present. The future is not yet written; it's just a canvas waiting for us to paint it."

Clara smiled, the warmth of the room seeping into her. She felt lighter, as if the pull of the map was finally starting to lift. "Shall we begin?"

Professor Moonsong gave an approving nod. "Let's."

As Clara settled into the familiar tranquillity of the room, she felt a renewed sense of clarity. Whatever challenges lay ahead, she knew she didn't have to face them alone.

Chapter 23: A Kind Gesture

It happened during Magical Histories. The classroom was alive with chatter, everyone in high spirits as Professor Valen collected their assignments. Clara noticed a classmate, Elyas Touchstone, shuffling to his seat, looking slightly nervous. Elyas was wiry and quiet, his frayed robes and patched satchel speaking of modest means. Despite this, his kind eyes and shy smile held a quiet resilience.

As Elyas walked past a desk, his cloak snagged on a rough edge and tore slightly, the rip making his already well-worn cloak look even worse.

A couple of mean students nearby noticed, and one of them sniggered, nudging his friend. "Nice look, Elyas," Victor Blackthorn sneered. "Really leaning into the *pitiful* vibe."

Victor, tall and impeccably groomed, exuded wealth and arrogance, his sharp green eyes constantly assessing and his tailored robes a testament to his privilege.

Darius Grimlock smirked. "Who needs a cloak when you've already got the tragic look down?"

Darius, Victor's ally, was broad-shouldered and stocky, relying on brute force and a booming voice to intimidate where wit failed. Their comments hit Elyas hard. He lowered his head, trying to brush it off, but Clara felt a surge of anger. She stood up, her voice clear and firm.

"Funny how people with everything always think they're better," Clara said, her voice steady. "Kindness isn't something you can buy. Maybe that's why you're missing it."

"He might not come from money," Finn said, his grin sharp as ever, "but he's got more personality than the two of you put together, and that's on a good day."

Victor and Darius exchanged embarrassed glances and muttered, shrinking under Clara's and Finn's gaze. Elyas's shoulders relaxed, a flicker of gratitude softening his usually guarded expression. Clara met his gaze with a small, reassuring smile.

*

A few days later, Elyas found a neatly wrapped package on his bed. Inside were new school clothes, polished shoes, and books, along with a carefully written note from Clara:

Dear Elyas,

I hope you'll accept these as a gesture of respect. I wasn't sure if I should do this, I didn't want to embarrass you, but growing up, my dad and I didn't have much, so I understand how hard it can be. If you have more than you need, why not share it? Life's hard enough without worrying about what's worn or torn.

When it comes down to it, clothes and possessions are just things. If you take all that away, what are we left with? Just people, people who are all the same underneath. Funny how easily people forget that. Some think having wealth makes them better, but in my experience, those with wealth often seem to be lacking in kindness.

You don't have to say anything in return; I haven't mentioned this to anyone and won't. Just know this comes from one person to another, with a lot of respect.

From Clara

*

The next day, Elyas walked into Charms and Enchantment class with a quiet confidence, wearing the new uniform and polished shoes. His head was held a little higher, and there was a shy but unmistakable smile on his face.

Of course, Victor and Darius took notice. One of them raised an eyebrow, sneering, "Thought you were poor. What happened, did you rob Elderstone bank?"

Elyas grinned, his voice steady as he replied, "Maybe I did. Guess that makes me more skilled than you'll ever be."

The class murmured with laughter, Victor and Darius silenced for the moment, and Elyas took his seat. Clara caught his eye from across the room, and he gave her a grateful nod. She smiled back, a quiet warmth spreading through her. In a world full of magic, small kindnesses still had the power to transform, and that was a magic she'd never take for granted.

*

As Clara left the library that evening, she couldn't help but think of Elyas's smile in Charms. For a brief moment, it reminded her of Chloe's grin when they used to talk about plans for the future, dreams of a life that now felt impossibly far away.

When she arrived back at her room, Amelia's bed curtains were drawn, leaving Clara alone with her thoughts. She fiddled with her quill, the tip smudging a small dot of ink on the page.

She sighed and began writing.

Hi, Chloe. I know it's been too long. Sorry I haven't written much. Things have been ... intense here. The new school is ... different. It's like nothing I've ever experienced before, challenging and overwhelming all at once. I barely have time to think, let alone write.

She thought of Elyas, how a few kind words and a gesture had made a difference. It was strange, really, how people could forget what it was like to struggle, how Victor and Darius could wield cruelty like a wand. Clara wondered if Chloe would have stood up for him too. She smiled faintly at the thought. Of course she would. Chloe had always been braver than her when it came to people. She couldn't tell Chloe about the truth: the magic, the castle, the lessons that had her casting shields and summoning light. But how could she capture her world without mentioning any of it?

She tried again.

The place is so old, and it feels like it holds a million secrets. I spend most of my time studying, but even that doesn't make me feel like I've caught up. It's just ... different here. I can't explain it, but it doesn't feel like home yet.

Her throat tightened. Chloe had always been her anchor, her person. Chloe knew every little thing about her, every fear, every secret, except this one. And now this secret wasn't just something Clara carried. It felt like a chasm growing between them.

She forced herself to continue.

How are things back home? How's everyone? Tell me everything about school, Chloe. I want to know what you've been up to. Is Mr. Harper still giving you grief in maths? Has Kelly tried out for netball yet? I need all the details. Even the boring ones.

Clara set the quill down, staring at the letter. It felt hollow. Wrong. She wanted to tell Chloe everything: the magic, the dangers, the sheer wonder of it all. She wanted to write about the enchanted grounds, the strange spells, and how she sometimes felt like she didn't belong in either world. But she couldn't. The weight of secrecy pressed against her chest, stealing her breath.

She folded the letter slowly, her hands trembling. For a moment, she hesitated, her thoughts tangled. What would Chloe think if she knew the truth? Would she be amazed? Hurt? Would she even believe her?

Clara shook her head. Chloe couldn't know. Not ever. That was the rule. The truth would only complicate things and drag her best friend into a world she didn't belong to, a world that wasn't safe. But keeping this distance hurt more than she expected.

She tucked the letter into an envelope and stared at it for a long moment before tucking it into her bag to send later.

Lying back on her bed, she stared at the ceiling, her heart heavy. The glow of the magical world she now inhabited couldn't dull the ache of losing the one person who'd always known her completely.

*

The next day in the library, Clara glanced at Finn as he sprawled across the armchair, his usual grin in place as he joked about their upcoming lessons. She felt a strange shift inside her, like hidden gears shifting into place inside her. She had always thought magic would be about power, spells, and grandeur. But it wasn't. Not entirely. The more time she spent at Crowstone, the more she realised magic was about people, their strength, their secrets, their struggles. And she thought, as she watched Finn laugh, it was as much about what was left unspoken as what was said.

"Finn," she said softly, cutting through his joke. "Are you okay? You don't have to pretend with me."

Finn blinked, his grin faltering for a fraction of a second before he recovered. "What? Of course I'm okay. Why wouldn't I be?" His words were light, but there was a flicker in his eyes, like a shadow passing too quickly to catch.

Clara hesitated, the feeling still lingering in her chest, but she forced a smile. "No reason. Just checking."

Chapter 24: Fun and Games

The corridors of Crowstone buzzed with the sounds of chattering students as Clara, Finn, Ellie, Leo and Amelia made their way to their next class. Sunlight streamed through tall arched windows, casting a shifting mosaic of colours on the stone floors.

"So," Finn began casually, adjusting his bag over one shoulder, "where did you grow up, then, Clara?"

"Hull," Clara replied with a smile. "Or 'ull, as we say." She shrugged. "I grew up with Hollowers my whole life."

The corridor fell silent for a moment.

"We don't really use that word," Ellie said gently.

"Yeah," Amelia added, her tone firm but kind. "It's considered offensive now."

Clara blinked, startled. "Oh, I didn't know. My grandparents always say it."

Finn sighed, running a hand through his hair. "Yeah, some families, especially the more prestigious ones, still say it. Hollowers." He shook his head. "But the word means they're hollow. Like, empty. And since you grew up with them, would you describe them as empty?"

Clara's stomach clenched. "Not at all," she said quickly. "I grew up around amazing people who just … don't have magic."

"The term most of us use now is Commonfolk," Amelia offered. "It's neutral and respectful."

Ellie nodded. "In India, we say *Sahaj*, which means ordinary. It's factual, not insulting."

Clara's cheeks burned with embarrassment. "I'm so sorry, guys. Honestly, I didn't know. I wasn't trying to …"

"It's okay, Clara," Finn interrupted with a reassuring grin. "It's not the end of the world. But maybe don't take everything your family says at face value, yeah?"

Clara managed a small, grateful smile. "I won't. Promise."

They reached their classroom door, and as Finn opened it, Ellie nudged her with a grin. "Don't worry about it. And don't forget, we have fourteen years' more experience than you."

Amelia added with a smile, "We've got your back."

Clara felt the weight of her family's expectations shift, if only slightly. It struck her that there was so much about this world, and herself, that she still needed to unlearn. And learn again. Properly.

*

The Luminaris common room buzzed with energy as Clara, Finn, Ellie, Amelia, and Leo gathered around the fireplace. The enchanted flames flickered in blues and silvers, creating playful shadows across the room. After a week of intense classes, they had finally decided to unwind, and Finn, as always, was leading the charge in finding ways to entertain.

"Right," Finn said, standing up and cracking his knuckles. "Time to show you lot a proper party trick. Prepare to be amazed!"

Finn muttered, "Criofasá Soghna!" and his face ballooned comically, his cheeks puffing and eyes disappearing into tiny slits.

The others howled with laughter as he snapped his fingers, returning his face to normal with a faint pop.

"Perfection," he declared, bowing dramatically. "Go on, admit it, that was awesome!"

"Awesome?" Ellie said, raising an eyebrow. "You looked like a poorly-drawn pumpkin!"

"Rude," Finn replied with a mock huff, but he grinned as he stepped aside.

Amelia stood next, brushing her curls over her shoulder. "Alright, let me show you something with a bit more grace." She backed up, took a running start, and leapt into the air, shouting, "Folúis Sásta!"

A shimmering bubble formed around Amelia mid-jump, lifting her into the air as it glowed with rainbow tones.

"Wow!" Clara clapped.

"Doesn't last long!" Amelia called, descending cross-legged before the bubble popped, landing her gracefully on the carpet.

"Elegant," Finn admitted, pretending to wipe a tear. "Unlike someone's pumpkin face."

"You want me to pop you next time?" Amelia shot back, though she was smiling.

Ellie stood with a smirk. "Alright, let me show you what proper magic looks like. And no bubbles or pumpkin heads involved. Athraigh Fiacha," she muttered, and in a blur, transformed into a sleek tiger. Her amber eyes gleamed as a deep roar echoed through the room.

"Ellie!" Clara laughed nervously, stepping back. "Warn us next time!"

Finn was clutching his chest dramatically. "Well, I think I may have just soiled myself. Thanks for that!"

The tiger shimmered and reformed into Ellie's usual self. She crossed her arms and grinned. "That's how it's done. Who's next?"

Leo leaned back in his chair, looking relaxed. "Alright," he said, standing up slowly. "I'll give it a try."

Everyone watched expectantly as Leo raised his wand, his movements precise and confident. "Scáil Ainmhithe."

First, a shimmering butterfly appeared, its wings glinting with golden light as it fluttered lazily around the room. "Not bad," Amelia said, nodding approvingly.

But before anyone could comment further, the butterfly burst into a cloud of shimmering particles, which then transformed into a massive eagle with outstretched wings. It flapped once, sending a gust of wind through the room. Then, with a fluid motion, the bird morphed into a small but formidable dragon, its emerald scales glinting in the firelight as it glided round the room.

The dragon exhaled a spiralling stream of fire, forming a glowing ring that encircled it in midair. For a breathless moment, the fiery arc hovered, lighting the room in golden light, before vanishing in a swirl of shimmering mist.

The room fell silent for a moment before Ellie spoke, her voice filled with awe. "You're … you're really an amazing wizard, Leo."

Even Finn, who always had a quip ready, was momentarily at a loss for words. "Okay, you win," he said finally, throwing his hands up. "No one's topping that."

Clara watched Leo, curiosity shimmering in her gaze. There was more to him than he let on.

"Well, that was fun," Leo said, smiling faintly, though his fingers absently tapped against his wand, a habit Clara had started to notice more and more.

*

The next day, the common room buzzed with energy as students gathered around tables to prepare for their next exam. Clara sat beside Ellie and Finn, who were debating the best counterspells for defensive magic. Leo sprawled across a chair nearby, tossing a quill into the air and catching it absently.

"I just can't get the hang of Scáth Díon," Ellie muttered, frustration lacing her voice. "Every time I try, it falls apart after two seconds."

"You're probably overthinking it," Clara said gently. "Try focusing on the feeling of safety. Master Fenwick told me that. He was my tutor before coming to school."

"Or maybe," Leo cut in, smirking, "you're just not cut out for shield spells. Some people are more suited for less complicated spells."

Ellie stiffened, her cheeks flushing. "That's not …"

"Leo!" Clara interrupted, her tone sharper than she intended. "That's not nice."

Leo shrugged, flicking his quill into the air again. "Just being honest. No point sugarcoating it."

Clara exchanged a glance with Ellie, unease prickling at the edges of her mind. Leo's words seemed offhand, even dismissive, but there was a meaning behind them she couldn't quite place. Was it just his blunt nature, or was there something more to it?

Chapter 25: Potionology Prodigy

The Potionology classroom was an expansive chamber with arched ceilings, its air rich with the scent of rare herbs and simmering brews. Shelves of glowing jars and vials lined the walls, while bubbling cauldrons and the rhythmic chopping of herbs created a determined, almost musical atmosphere.

At the front of the class, Professor Flint stood beside a long slate-black board etched with chalk marks of today's complex potion recipe. Her sharp blue eyes surveyed the room with the precision of a hawk. Dressed in dark emerald robes that shimmered slightly when she moved, she exuded an air of strict authority.

"Today, we'll attempt the Elixir of Serenity," Professor Flint announced, her sharp gaze scanning the room. "This advanced potion treats magical overexertion, stabilises fractured minds, and aids in memory recovery. Mastery of this elixir can save lives, but it requires precision and restraint. Few Year 8s manage it successfully."

Clara inhaled deeply, calming the flutter of nerves in her chest. Potion-making had always been a delicate balancing act for her; one moment of hesitation, and a perfectly good brew could turn into a bubbling disaster. But this time, she focused, carefully measuring the shimmering moonflower essence into her cauldron. The mixture swirled into a pale blue, its glow soft and steady. Not perfect, but not a disaster either. She allowed herself a small, hopeful smile, feeling a flicker of pride.

She glanced nervously at Finn, who muttered, "No pressure," with a smirk.

Nearby, Darius Grimlock scowled at his cauldron, his frustration already brewing. Clara caught Darius glaring at Leo, his jaw set tight, before returning to his potion with heavy, careless movements. She frowned, wondering if his anger ran deeper than a ruined brew.

Leo, stationed near Clara, was uncharacteristically quiet. His fingers drummed lightly against the edge of the table, a habit Clara had started to notice whenever he seemed deep in thought. He caught her looking and gave a small smile. "How hard can it be?" he whispered, though his thumb and forefinger now tapped together, a subtle sign of his tension, Clara thought.

As the students set to work, the room filled with the soft sounds of chopping, grinding, and careful stirring. Ingredients like moonflower essence and prism veil pollen glowed faintly as they were added with precision. The potion required exact temperatures, counter-clockwise stirring, and perfectly enunciated spells.

Clara kept her eyes locked on her cauldron, double-checking the instructions in her mind. The Elixir of Serenity was known for its fickleness: too much heat and it would burn, too little and it would remain ineffective. Carefully, she took a deep breath and whispered the final incantation, "Sámhaich Réalta."

For a moment, her potion shimmered with the soft silver-blue she had hoped for. Excitement flared in her chest. Had she actually done it? But then, without warning, the glow flickered and darkened into an odd, translucent lilac. It didn't explode, it didn't fizzle, but it wasn't quite right either.

Professor Flint swept over, her piercing gaze examining Clara's potion with a scrutinising eye.

"Hmm," she murmured, stirring the surface lightly with the tip of her wand. "Not bad, Miss Nightfall. Your balance was nearly perfect, but you hesitated just before the final ingredient. A fraction more silverdust and you would have had it."

Clara bit the inside of her cheek, frustrated at herself but relieved she hadn't completely failed.

Professor Flint straightened. "Five points to Luminaris for an admirable attempt."

Clara's lips curled into a small smile. Five points wasn't twenty, but it was better than nothing.

Beside her, Finn scowled at his cauldron, which had turned an unpromising murky green. "That's ... not right, is it?" he asked Clara, who shook her head sympathetically.

Darius's cauldron bubbled violently, plumes of orange smoke rising.

"Step back, Mr. Grimlock," Professor Flint ordered, flicking her wand to neutralise the potion. "Precision, not force," she warned.

Darius grumbled but started over, his frustration clear. Leo worked in focused silence, moving with a practised elegance. When he added the final ingredient, his potion glowed silver, its surface smooth as moonlight on water. Professor Flint approached, her sharp eyes widening.

"Great ancestors! Remarkable," she murmured, her voice barely above a whisper. "Perfect consistency. Perfect tone. Mr. Rutherford ... this is flawless."

The class collectively turned to look, their expressions ranging from astonishment to envy. Even Darius Grimlock, usually quick with a snide comment, was momentarily stunned into silence.

"No Year 8 has ever brewed this potion successfully on their first attempt," Professor Flint said, her gaze lingering on Leo with a mixture of disbelief and admiration. "Yet here it is. Extraordinary. Twenty points to Luminaris."

Cheers erupted from Luminaris students, their pride ringing through the room.

Leo gave a modest shrug, though Clara noticed the faintest flicker of a smile. "Just followed the instructions," he said, his tone casual.

"Followed them?" Finn whispered to Clara. "It's like he wrote them."

Professor Flint straightened, her sharp eyes narrowing slightly. "I imagine you've had some training from a skilled Potionology professor, Mr. Rutherford?" Her tone was casual, but there was an unmistakable undercurrent of curiosity.

Leo hesitated, his fingers stilling for just a moment. "My grandfather taught me a bit about Potionology," he said simply, before returning to clean his station. Clara noticed how carefully he avoided Professor Flint's gaze.

As the students cleaned up their stations, Clara couldn't shake her curiosity. Leo's skill seemed far beyond their age.

"That was … incredible," she said as they left the classroom.

Leo smiled again, his fingers tapping lightly against his thumb. "I guess I'm better at Potionology than I give myself credit for."

"Yeah, maybe just a bit," Finn scoffed, grinning.

As Darius stomped past, he muttered darkly, "Even you'll mess up someday."

Clara knew Leo was gifted, but this seemed to surprise everyone, even Professor Flint. The realisation that she didn't really know much about Leo's past or his amazing magical abilities was starting to set in.

*

That evening, the common room hummed with its usual energy, students laughing over magical card games, others engrossed in their books. The room had a warm glow from the firelight. Clara spotted Leo sitting alone near the hearth, a notebook open on his lap, untouched. His fingers tapped a steady rhythm on the arm of his chair, his gaze distant as he stared into the flames.

She hesitated, then made her way over. "Mind if I join you?" she asked, keeping her tone light.

Leo glanced up, startled, but gave her a small smile. "Sure."

Clara dropped into the chair beside him, glancing at the empty page in his notebook. "So," she began, teasing slightly, "are you secretly some kind of Potionology master? Because you're making the rest of us look bad."

Leo chuckled softly. "Hardly. My grandfather was … obsessed with Potionology. I spent a lot of summers helping him brew various concoctions. Guess it stuck."

Clara tilted her head. "Was he a professor or something?"

Leo's smile faltered slightly. "Not exactly. He was … unconventional. Not everyone agreed with his methods."

The flicker of hesitation in his voice didn't escape her. "What do you mean?"

Leo shrugged, his fingers resuming their steady tapping. "Let's just say he wasn't the type to follow rules. But he taught me a lot about precision, about … looking beyond the surface."

Clara nodded, sensing there was more to the story but deciding not to press. "Well, it definitely shows. You're incredible at it. In fact, you're incredible at every lesson. You're an amazing wizard, Leo."

Leo gave her a small, grateful smile. "Thanks."

They sat in comfortable silence for a moment before Clara spoke again. "You know, I don't think I've ever really gotten to know you properly. You're kind of a mystery."

He smiled faintly, glancing back at the flames. "Maybe that's for the best."

Clara hesitated, watching the shifting shadows dance across his face. "Or maybe it's not," she said quietly. "I mean, you're clearly brilliant, but … sometimes it feels like you're hiding behind all that modesty."

Leo's fingers froze mid-tap, his gaze still fixed on the fire. For a moment, Clara thought he might brush her off, but then he exhaled softly. "It's not about hiding," he murmured. "It's about … keeping things where they belong. Some parts of my life just don't fit here."

His words hung in the air, heavy with something unspoken.

Clara leaned forwards slightly, her voice gentle. "Crowstone isn't exactly a place for fitting in, you know. It's more like … finding where you're meant to be."

Leo looked at her then, his dark eyes searching hers as though weighing her words. Finally, he gave her a small, almost wistful smile. "Maybe. I guess I haven't figured that out yet."

"Maybe you don't have to figure it out alone," Clara offered, her tone light but sincere.

Leo's fingers stilled completely. "Maybe," he said again, though this time, his voice was softer, like the word was more for himself than for her.

Chapter 26: Mail Call

Students filled their house tables in the Grand Solstice Hall. It hummed with morning energy as plates clinked, chatter echoed, and enchanted lanterns bathed the room in a warm glow. Clara sat between Finn and Ellie, her plate half-filled with toast and eggs, though she was too excited to eat.

"It's mail day," Finn said, his mouth full as he gestured wildly with his fork. "Nothing like a care package to make you feel loved, right?"

"I wouldn't know," Ellie said with a smirk. "My parents usually just send a letter reminding me to study harder."

Just as the last students trickled into the hall, a soft drone echoed from the Orb, and the chatter died down. All heads turned skyward as a massive, enchanted sack floated into the Grand Solstice Hall and hovered above the centre of the room gracefully, its surface shimmering as though made of stardust, before it began to open with a flourish.

"Here we go," Finn said, leaning back and folding his arms, as if settling in for a show.

Letters and parcels floated from the sack, then streaked through the hall to their recipients, glowing faintly. Some landed gently in hands, others settled neatly beside students.

A small bundle drifted towards Clara, and she reached up to catch it. The first was a letter, sealed with the elegant Nightfall crest. She smiled as she recognised her grandmothers' handwriting. Beside her, Finn caught a bulky package wrapped in brown paper and immediately started ripping it open.

"Homemade Ghanaian snacks," he said triumphantly, holding up a tin. "Anyone want one?"

Ellie shook her head, holding up a small book that had just landed in front of her. "I've got reading material for the next term. Thanks, Mother."

Clara glanced over at Leo, who was sitting further down the table. His gaze was fixed on the enchanted sack, his expression hopeful. She watched as the last few letters zipped out, darting across the hall like birds returning to roost. But none came for him.

Leo's face didn't falter, but Clara noticed his thumb and forefinger tapping lightly against the edge of his goblet.

"My parents aren't big on writing me letters," Leo said suddenly, his voice casual as he reached for a slice of toast. "My dad's busy abroad."

Clara hesitated, her brow furrowing. "I thought you said you moved here for your dad's work?"

Leo froze, the corner of his mouth twitching slightly. He stuttered, struggling to find the words. "Oh, uh, you must've misheard me. We moved here for my mum's work. My dad's always travelling, so …"

Clara didn't press further, but something about his tone made her pause. It didn't feel right. She watched him closely, noting the tension in his shoulders and the way his tapping fingers seemed to quicken. It wasn't the first time something Leo had said didn't quite add up, and now her suspicions were harder to ignore.

Finn broke the tension by sliding his tin towards Leo. "Cheer up, mate. Nothing a bofrot from my grandma can't fix."

Leo laughed softly, taking a bofrot. "Thanks. I'll keep that in mind."

As they returned to their breakfast, Clara resolved to ensure Leo felt less alone. Sometimes, small gestures mattered most.

*

That evening, the common room was quieter than usual. Most students were buried in books or engaged in hushed conversations, the warm glow of the fire making the room feel smaller and cosier. Clara sat in an armchair, pretending to read, but her eyes kept drifting to Leo, who was sitting by the window. His notebook lay open on his lap as he stared out into the night.

She made up her mind. Setting her book aside, she crossed the room and perched on the arm of a nearby chair. "Hey," she said softly, her tone careful.

Leo glanced up, his usual smile wavering briefly before fading. "Hey."

"I just … I wanted to talk to you," Clara began, choosing her words slowly. "About earlier. At breakfast."

Leo tensed slightly, his fingers starting their familiar tapping rhythm against the chair's arm. "What about it?"

"Well," Clara said gently, "you said your parents don't write, and your dad's abroad, but … when we first met, you said your family moved here for his job. And … I don't know, it just feels like you're being dishonest."

Leo's hand stilled. He looked at her for a moment, then back out of the window. "Why are you asking, Clara?"

"I'm not trying to pry," she said quickly. "I just … I care, that's all. I want to understand."

For a long moment, Leo didn't answer. Then, with a deep breath, he turned back to her. "Okay," he said finally, his voice quieter than usual. "But promise you won't tell anyone?"

Clara nodded, leaning forwards slightly. "I promise."

"My parents are … separating," Leo admitted, his words coming out quickly now, as though he wanted to get them over with. "It's been rough. My dad's travelling all the time because he can't stand being home, and I'm just … stuck in the middle of it. I don't want people knowing because, well, some magical families don't approve of separation. They think it's … shameful or something."

Clara's chest tightened at his words. "Leo, I'm so sorry," she said softly. "That sounds really hard."

Leo gave a small shrug, though his eyes didn't meet hers. "It's fine. I just don't want everyone making a big deal about it. It's not like I can fix it, you know?"

"Yeah, but that doesn't mean you have to go through it alone," Clara said, her voice firm but kind. "Thanks for telling me. I mean it."

Leo glanced at her then, a faint smile tugging at the corner of his mouth. "Thanks for asking."

Clara smiled back, feeling a sense of relief. She didn't have all the answers, but she was glad Leo had opened up, even just a little.

Chapter 27: The Locked Passageway

Clara and her friends stood in the west wing corridor, facing an ivy-covered archway. The damp air carried a faint scent of moss as Finn clutched his astral map, looking ready to scream.

"It's here," Finn said, jabbing at the map. "I've tried everything, but nothing's happening."

Ellie frowned, crossing her arms. "Maybe the map's broken."

Finn kicked a loose stone near his foot, muttering. "It's not broken. It's enchanted. It doesn't break."

Amelia knelt by the base of the archway, her fingers brushing the ivy. "There's got to be something we're missing. Maybe a rune or a charm?"

Leo leaned against the wall, watching Finn with an amused smirk. "Maybe the map's enchanted to frustrate you and see how long until you give up. If it is, it's doing a great job."

"Very helpful, Leo," Finn muttered, turning the map over as though the answer might be written on the back. "I've tried spells, knocking, shouting at it. Nothing works. It's pointless."

"Or maybe," came a familiar raspy voice from behind them, "you're just looking in the wrong place."

The group spun around to see Thistle Grimbrook, Crowstone's eccentric caretaker, standing a few paces away. His sweeping brush trailed lazily behind him, moving of its own accord.

Thistle's robes were patched, and his wild silver hair stuck out as though he'd been fighting with a storm. Oversized glasses perched on the end of his nose, their lenses glinting as though they could zoom in and out for focus, giving him the look of a half-mad magic inventor.

He leaned on his broom, a grin tugging at his lips. "What seems to be the problem? Trying to wake the old stones?"

Finn folded his arms. "You always sneak up on people like that?"

"Only when they're making themselves look stupid," Thistle replied, ambling towards the archway. He gave it a cursory glance, then peered at Finn's map. "Hidden passage, I see? Nice map. Pity it's smarter than you."

Finn scowled. "I'm doing what it says! Nothing's happening!"

Thistle snorted. "You think a magical door opens on wishful thinking?"

Clara stepped forward, her voice hopeful. "Do you know how to open it?"

Thistle gave her a cynical look, scratching his stubbly chin. "Of course I know. But knowing and telling are two very different things."

Finn groaned. "You're really enjoying this, aren't you?"

"More than you know," Thistle replied, patting the archway with one hand. "But this isn't about me. This here's about you."

Finn blinked, confused. "What's that supposed to mean?"

Thistle crouched by the base of the archway, his fingers brushing over the ivy. "What's your map enchanted to do?" Thistle asked.

Finn hesitated. "Show me where to go?"

Thistle shook his head, a sly grin tugging at his lips. "Not exactly. It's not just about pointing the way. It's enchanted to guide you, to make you think, not to hand you answers. Big difference, lad."

Clara stepped closer, studying the map alongside Finn. "Look at how it's glowing here, around the centre. It's almost like it's pointing at something specific. Maybe the answer isn't just where to look, but how you're supposed to approach it."

Finn furrowed his brow, glancing between the map and the archway. "The map kept glowing at the ivy … but maybe it's not about the ivy." He stepped closer, running his fingers over the stone beneath it. "Maybe it's … the arch itself."

Thistle nodded approvingly but said nothing.

Finn stepped forward and raised his wand with a determined grin. "Watch and learn."

He drew a figure-eight shape in the air, his voice low and theatrical as he intoned, "Scáthaigh Dubháin!"

The tip of his wand sparked with a green light, and for a moment, the ivy shuddered as though alive. The vines began to twist and curl away from the stone, retreating like serpents, but halfway through, the magic faltered. The ivy snapped back into place, twice as thick as before.

Finn let out an exasperated groan. "What? No! It was working!"

Thistle, who had been watching with barely concealed amusement, stepped forward. "Impressive light show, lad. Pity you didn't think it through."

Finn turned to him, annoyed. "What's wrong with it? The spell's supposed to unravel enchantments!"

"You used it like a battering ram. That ivy hides if you try forcing it. Coax it, don't wrestle it." Thistle tapped his broom against the ground, causing a faint echo to ripple through the air. "Magic's like weeds, lad; pull too hard, and it digs in deeper. Coax it, and it'll come willingly.

295

This arch isn't fighting you; you're just not listening."

Thistle gestured for Finn to try again, leaning in to mutter: "Use your map, lad. Look at how it's glowing near the centre. What's it telling you?"

Finn stared at the map in his hand, its glowing lines pulsing faintly as though urging him to look closer. His frustration ebbed slightly as he traced the converging patterns near the base of the archway.

"It's showing me ... here," he muttered, kneeling to examine the stonework at the bottom of the arch. "The lines on the map, there's something here I didn't see before."

Thistle grinned, leaning on his broom. "Aye, now you're thinking. Magic likes to keep its secrets close to the ground. It's humble that way."

Ellie raised an eyebrow. "Magic? Humble? Are we talking about the same thing?"

Ignoring her, Finn held his wand steady and spoke again, this time in a calmer voice. "Foirsíolán."

This time, the spell felt softer. Finn's wand glowed, and the ivy retreated, revealing complex carvings beneath.

Thistle stepped closer, nodding approvingly. "There we go. Foirsíolán, to reveal, to clear. It's not about yanking the magic away. It's about asking it to step aside."

Finn tilted his head. "So, it's polite magic?"

"Think of it like this," Thistle said, gesturing to the now-exposed carvings. "A door's just a door until you give it a reason to open. You weren't listening to the map before; you were shouting over it. Now you've let it guide you, which is its true intent."

As the last vines of ivy retreated into the crevices of

the stone, the group leaned in to study the carvings. They depicted swirling patterns of stars, moons, and sophisticated lines that seemed to flow into one another, resembling the paths on Finn's astral map.

Amelia pointed to the centre of the archway, where a small, circular indentation sat. "That looks like it could hold something. Finn, does the map say anything about it?"

Finn checked his map, frowning as its glowing lines shifted. "It's changing," he said. "The map's pointing at … me?"

Clara tilted her head. "Maybe it's telling you to do something. What else have you got?"

Finn rifled through his satchel and pulled out a small orb he'd collected on the last task. Without hesitating, he placed the orb into the indentation.

The archway groaned, the carvings glowing brightly as the stone shifted. Slowly, the centre of the arch parted, revealing a spiralling staircase descending into darkness.

"Well done, lad," Thistle said, clapping Finn on the shoulder. "You've got good instincts, when you actually listen to them."

Finn grinned. "I wasn't doubting myself for a second."

Ellie rolled her eyes. "You were practically about to cry."

"Was not!" Finn said sheepishly.

Thistle clapped him on the back, nearly knocking him over. "Took you long enough, lad. Magic's not about shortcuts, you know. It's about using what you've got up here" — he tapped Finn's temple — "and in here." He poked Finn's chest for emphasis.

Finn rolled his eyes, but Clara could see the pride in his expression.

As the group peered down the staircase, Thistle leaned on his broom and grinned. "Go on, then. Just don't break anything, or it's cauldron cleaning duty for you."

Clara led the way down the stairs, her wand raised to light the way. Finn followed close behind, still clutching his map. As they descended, she glanced back at Thistle, who watched them with a glimmer of amusement and maybe just a hint of pride.

"Thanks, Thistle," she called.

The old caretaker waved them off. "Go on. Just remember, some doors are locked for a reason. Keep your wits about you down there."

With that, the archway sealed itself behind them, leaving Thistle alone in the corridor, humming a tune as his broom resumed its sweeping.

Chapter 28: Roots of Magic

The sunlight streamed into the tall, arched windows of Professor Miron's classroom, covering the stone walls with golden warmth. Today's lesson in Magical Histories promised to be different. The chalkboard at the front of the room displayed the day's topic in flowing, enchanted letters that shimmered as if alive.

Clara sat with her friends at their usual table, her quill poised and ready. Professor Miron, known for his commanding yet approachable presence, stood before them, his arms folded.

"Magic," he began, his voice deep and resonant, "is universal. From the frozen lands of Siberia to the vast deserts of Africa, magical practices adapt to their environment, culture, and people. Today, I want each of you to think about how magic is shaped by where it comes from. And if you're feeling brave" — he paused, his eyes gleaming — "share some examples from your own heritage."

The class exchanged excited murmurs. Finn leaned over to Clara, a mischievous grin on his face. "I think this might be the first history class that's not going to put me to sleep."

Professor Miron tapped his wand against his desk, and the air above it shimmered. A glowing map of the world appeared, dotted with floating symbols that represented different magical traditions.

"Let's begin with the basics," Miron said. "Each region of the world has its own magical specialities, shaped by the local environment and beliefs. For example, African witches and wizards are renowned for their connection to elemental spirits, while Southeast

Asian magic often involves complex rituals invoking nature's harmony. But enough from me. Who's brave enough to share first?"

Finn's hand shot up before anyone else could respond. "I'll go!" he said enthusiastically. Standing up, he cleared his throat with an exaggerated flourish. "Let me introduce you to the Spirit Guardians of Ghana."

Professor Miron gestured for him to continue. "The floor is yours, Mr. Adu."

Finn grinned. "In Ghana, magical folk believe that everyone is born with a *sunsum,* kind of like a spirit guide or guardian that's tied to your soul. Your sunsum connects you to the magical energy of the world. If you're in danger, it can warn you. If you're on the right path, it strengthens your magic."

He paused dramatically, leaning forwards as if sharing a secret. "But here's the cool part: during special ceremonies, you can actually call your sunsum to take a physical form. My grandma once summoned hers. It looked like this huge golden eagle with glowing feathers. She said it was both terrifying and beautiful."

The class listened intently, clearly impressed. Even Professor Miron gave an approving nod.

"Fascinating, Mr. Adu. A remarkable example of how cultural beliefs intertwine with magical practice. The idea of a sunsum reflects the importance of balance between self and the natural world."

Finn sat down with a mock bow, whispering to Clara, "Top that."

Ellie raised her hand next, her expression thoughtful. "In India, magic often revolves around the idea of *prana*, the life force that flows through everything," she began, her voice steady and warm. "Magical folk believe that by controlling your prana, you can manipulate the world around you."

She glanced at Professor Miron, who gestured encouragingly for her to continue.

"My family's always told stories about the mystics who lived in the mountains, practising something called *Shakti Vidya*. They used their connection to prana to create illusions so powerful they felt real. My grandmother once told me about a mystic who made it seem like an entire forest had sprung up overnight to hide a village from invaders. It wasn't real, but it worked."

Clara leaned forward, her eyes wide. "Illusions like that would've taken so much control. Could your family do something like that?"

Ellie shrugged modestly. "Not exactly on that level, but my dad did once make it look like our house had doubled in size. Freaked out some nosy neighbours so badly they didn't come back for weeks."

Finn snorted. "Please tell me he added a moat."

Ellie smirked. "No moat. But he did make it look like there were wolves in the garden."

The class chuckled, and Professor Miron's eyes gleamed with interest. "An excellent example of how magic can serve both practical and protective purposes. Thank you, Miss Sharma."

Amelia spoke up next, pushing her glasses up her nose as she began. "In China, magical creatures and their symbolism play a huge role in our magic. One of the most famous examples is the Jade River Drakes."

Professor Miron gestured for her to elaborate, clearly intrigued. "Go on, Miss Chen."

Amelia nodded. "Jade River Drakes are these magnificent serpentine creatures that live in enchanted rivers. They're said to embody wisdom and strength, and their scales shimmer like green jade. But they're not just magical creatures; they're seen as protectors of the water's magic. Families who live near the rivers often perform rituals to honour them, asking for protection and guidance."

Finn leaned in, his grin wide. "So, have you ever seen one?"

Amelia shook her head. "No, but my uncle has. He swears he saw one during a festival near the Li River. He said it rose from the water like a wave, its eyes glowing gold, and then it disappeared into the mist."

The class listened, spellbound, and Clara couldn't help but imagine the graceful creature Amelia described.

Professor Miron clasped his hands together. "Thank you, Miss Chen. The Jade River Drakes are a perfect example of how magical cultures often intertwine with the creatures of their land."

After Amelia sat down, Professor Miron gestured to Leo. "And you, Mr. Rutherford? Do you have an example to share?"

Leo hesitated for a moment before standing. "Well, there's not much to tell," he began, his voice casual. "My family's magic isn't tied to anything fancy like spirits or illusions. But my dad once told me about an ancestor who could … manipulate time."

The class sat up straighter at that, intrigued. Even Professor Miron raised an eyebrow. "Time magic is exceedingly rare," he said. "What form did this manipulation take?"

Leo gave a faint smile. "It wasn't anything dramatic. They said he could slow down a moment, make it last longer so he could react faster. But it's probably just an exaggerated family story."

Clara tilted her head, watching him carefully. He sounded sincere, but something about the way he avoided Professor Miron's gaze made her wonder. Was it really just a family story, did he just make it up, or was there more to it?

As the lesson continued, Professor Miron encouraged other students to share their cultural magic. Clara listened, enraptured, but a nagging question lingered in her mind. "Professor?" she asked tentatively, raising her hand. "Why does it seem like every culture's magic is so connected to their environment? Is it because magic comes from the world around us?"

Professor Miron smiled. "An excellent question, Miss Nightfall. Yes, magic is deeply tied to the world: its land, its people, its history. We all draw power from within and wield it through our wand. Others can also draw power from the spirits of their ancestors, the flow of water, or the pulse of the earth. Magic is as much about where you come from as it is about who you are."

Clara nodded, feeling a deeper understanding settle over her.

The thought clung to Clara's mind like an unspoken spell, weaving through her thoughts as the lesson came to an end. What about her family's magic?

Finn had the sunsum, a guiding spirit bound to his soul. Ellie's ancestors wielded prana, shaping reality itself. Amelia's heritage was entwined with magical creatures and the natural world. Even Leo, evasive as ever, hinted at something rare.

But what of the Nightfalls?

As the other students filtered out, Clara hesitated, then stepped forward. Professor Miron was erasing the shimmering chalkboard with a flick of his wand, the enchanted letters dissolving into golden wisps.

"Professor?" Clara asked, her voice quieter than she intended.

Miron glanced up, his sharp gaze settling on her. "Yes, Miss Nightfall?"

She hesitated for a moment, then gathered her courage. "Do you know anything about my family's magic? The Nightfalls?"

A peculiar silence stretched between them. Miron's expression remained unreadable, but something flickered in his eyes: recognition.

"There are … whispers," he said at last, his voice lower than before. "Stories passed through generations, but little recorded in any text. The Nightfalls are an elusive lineage, their magic bound to shadows and secrets."

A shiver traced its way down Clara's spine. "What kind of magic?"

Miron exhaled slowly, glancing around as if ensuring no one else was listening. "There are those who believe the Nightfalls were once Keepers of Ancient Magic, a lineage entrusted with knowledge far older than the Assembly itself. Magic that predates wands, woven into the very fabric of existence."

Clara's chest tightened. "Ancient magic?"

"The kind few dare to wield," Miron murmured. "And for good reason." His gaze darkened, his voice dipping and becoming graver. "It is said that for every witch or wizard who learns to control it, another is claimed by it. Ancient magic does not tolerate weakness, nor does it forgive ambition."

Clara's breath hitched. "Claimed by it?"

Miron studied her carefully, as though deciding whether to continue. "Half of those who try to wield it are corrupted by shadows, twisted by their own power. Darkness is not always born; it is shaped."

The room felt colder. Clara's thoughts spiraled back to the whispers about the Dark Wizard and his escape from Blackspire. She licked her lips, forcing herself to ask the question clawing at her mind. "The Dark Wizard … was he … was he one of them?"

Miron's silence was answer enough.

Clara's stomach twisted.

"He was not always what he is now," Miron admitted at last. "He sought to master what should never have been tamed, and in doing so, he lost himself to it."

A creeping chill unfurled in Clara's chest, curling like smoke around her ribs.

The Dark Wizard had once been like her.

Before she could ask more, Miron straightened, his tone returning to its usual measured authority. "But those are just stories. What truly matters is how you wield the magic within you, Miss Nightfall."

Clara nodded slowly, but her mind was already spinning. Ancient magic. A forgotten power. A family of Keepers.

And a warning etched into history, one she hoped she was not destined to repeat.

*

As Clara left the classroom, her friends lingered in the corridor, waiting for her.

"Your sunsum story was brilliant, Finn," Clara said. "And Ellie, I want to learn more about prana. That forest illusion sounds amazing."

"Yeah, well," Finn said with a grin, "if you ever visit

my place, I'll introduce you to Grandma. She'll tell you everything, whether you want her to or not."

Amelia laughed. "Just don't ask her too many questions. She'll make you sit through hours of family history first."

Clara smiled, feeling a sense of warmth and belonging. The magical world was vast and diverse, filled with endless possibilities, and she was just beginning to explore it.

As they walked towards their next class, Clara thought about magic being everywhere, in ways she was only starting to understand, and about her family being the Keepers of Ancient Magic. Fenwick had hinted at it, but it seemed more than likely to be true.

Chapter 29: Shadows in the Library

A few days later, the school gathered in the Great Solstice Hall for morning assembly. The enchanted ceiling mirrored the sunrise in streaks of orange and pink, while house banners swayed in an unseen breeze. Clara sat at the Luminaris table, half-listening as Finn whispered something that made Ellie laugh.

The Orb pulsed in the hall, silencing the room instantly. Professor Mornvale rose from her seat at the high table, her commanding presence drawing every pair of eyes. Her robes shimmered in the light, almost like a reminder of the authority she carried, and her voice was calm and resolute as she addressed the assembly.

"Students," Professor Mornvale began, her voice sharp. "Last night, someone breached the enchanted protections of the Library of Everglow and gained access to the Forbidden Archives."

A murmur rippled through the hall. Clara exchanged a glance with Leo, who sat across from her, looking unusually calm. Finn leaned closer to whisper, "Forbidden Archives? What could they even want from there?"

"Quiet," Clara whispered back, her eyes fixed on the headmistress.

Professor Mornvale continued, her tone sharper now. "The Forbidden Archives houses ancient and dangerous texts. Whoever entered bypassed powerful wards and disturbed safeguarded materials. This breach is a grave violation of trust."

The murmur grew louder, students speculating wildly about who the culprit might be. Professor Mornvale raised her hand, and the hall fell silent again.

"Fortunately," she said, her voice steady, "our protections ensured that no significant damage was done nor was anything taken. However, this incident serves as a warning. To the individual or individuals responsible, know this: the Forbidden Archives is far more protected than it appears, and the enchantments leave a mark to those wandering where they shouldn't."

Clara noticed Professor Darnel at the high table, his expression dark and contemplative. She remembered him as stern but fair, and the thought of someone sneaking past his enchantments seemed most unlikely.

"Any student found guilty will face severe consequences," Mornvale continued. "I would also like to remind all of you that accessing restricted areas without permission is not only against academy rules but is also a breach of magical ethics. Certain magic is forbidden, and others have age restrictions. Permission to access the Forbidden Archives must be given by a professor."

A strange unease coiled in Clara's chest, though she couldn't say why. It wasn't fear, not exactly, more like a whisper of warning threading through her thoughts. Across from her, Leo sat perfectly still, save for his fingers tapping in that steady rhythm. Clara's stomach clenched.

"Why break in?" Ellie whispered. "What's in there?"

Professor Mornvale's voice softened slightly as she concluded. "Students, I urge you to remember that this academy is not just a place of learning but a place of trust. We trust you to respect the knowledge and power contained within these walls. If you ever have questions or concerns, speak to your professors. Secrets and deception have no place here."

As the assembly was dismissed, the buzz of

conversation returned in full force. Clara found herself caught in the wave of speculation, her mind lingering on Professor Mornvale's words. Something about the breach felt unsettling, as if there were more to the story than anyone was saying.

"Wonder who it was," Finn said, half-joking. "Bet it was someone from Nightspire."

Clara didn't reply. A break-in at the Forbidden Archives. She heard Year 7s whispering, "the Dark Wizard!" Clara thought, *there's no way he could get into the school*, and yet her instincts said otherwise.

Chapter 30: Magical Creature Class

Clara stepped into the Magical Creatures classroom, an open enclosure bordered by enchanted hedges and stone walls. The air buzzed with the sounds of strange and fascinating creatures.

Her gaze swept over the pens and habitats arranged throughout the area: strange birds with metallic feathers perched in one corner, shimmering like polished silver; small, dragon-like creatures basking on heated stones; a cluster of plants that seemed to lean and hum as a group of glowing insects flitted around them.

Just as Clara was taking it all in, a small pink creature caught her eye. It was trotting near a fountain, fluffing a pair of delicate wings that sprouted from its back.

Clara couldn't help herself. "So, pigs do fly," she said, a grin breaking across her face.

Their teacher, Professor Thorn, a tall, well-built man with sharp eyes, a gentle smile, pale skin and rosy cheeks, overheard and chuckled. "Ah, yes, that's Petal. She's a porcifly. I suppose she does resemble a pig in the Commonfolk world. As far as I am aware, they cannot fly, but certain magical breeds like Petal have mastered the art, though she's better at gliding than long-distance flying," he said with a smile.

Clara's amazement only deepened as Professor Thorn gestured to a creature in a nearby pen. It was a soft, silvery shape that seemed to shift between solid and misty forms, as though it were a cloud that had decided to settle in the physical world.

"This," he explained, "is a moonshroud hare. They're rare, and as you can see, they blend with shadows beautifully, almost like living mist."

Clara stared at the creatures, feeling a mixture of wonder and disbelief. She had read about magical creatures in her textbooks, but seeing them firsthand — flying pigs, creatures that seemed made of mist — was something else entirely.

Professor Thorn clapped his hands, drawing the class's attention. "All right, everyone! Today, you'll get a chance to interact with some of our more curious creatures. I've divided you into groups. Each group will spend ten minutes with creatures before moving on. Make sure to watch closely; every creature here has its own unique habits."

Clara found herself grouped with Leo and Finn. Her heart thudded with excitement as Professor Thorn led them to a small enclosed habitat filled with soft purple moss and glowing stones that mimicked moonlight.

Nestled among the glowing stones was the medaflare fox, its silvery fur shimmering like stardust. Its orange eyes pulsed gently with light, and its six tails swayed gracefully as it observed them.

"It's … beautiful," Clara whispered, entranced.

Professor Thorn handed them a pouch filled with small silvery berries. "These are tunataberries. Medaflare foxes feed exclusively on these; they enhance their glow and give them the energy to thrive. Be gentle; medaflares can be skittish with new faces."

Leo took a handful of berries and held one out cautiously. The fox sniffed the air, its ears pricking up as it noticed the treat, but then backed away. "I guess I don't have a trustworthy face."

Finn leaned in, watching the medaflare closely. "It's like it's made of moonlight," he murmured, clearly as fascinated as Clara.

Clara took a berry herself, reaching out carefully. The medaflare's eyes flicked to her, curious but cautious. She held her breath as it moved closer, its gaze holding hers with an intelligent glimmer. Finally, it accepted the berry, and for a brief moment, its glow brightened significantly, casting a warm light around them.

"That's incredible," Clara said, smiling as the medaflare nibbled contentedly.

Finn laughed. "I guess they like you, Clara, just not Leo."

They were captivated, and as the medaflare finished eating, it settled down, curling into a little ball as its glow dimmed to a soft, silvery tone.

Professor Thorn told them to move on to another section of the habitat, this one surrounded by tall flowering plants that swayed, almost like they were moving to a soundless rhythm.

"This," Professor Thorn began, his eyes twinkling as he gestured to the small feathery creature perched on his shoulder, "is a whisperfluff, and this particular one is called Kaesia. These little wonders, once they reach maturity, become nocturnal creatures known for their ability to mimic speech, and something else far more fascinating. They can sense emotions, and in rare cases, mimic the thoughts within your head."

Clara's group murmured with intrigue, though a few students exchanged uneasy glances.

"They're often used as emotional support creatures, though their talent for reflection makes some people uneasy," the professor added.

Finn nudged Clara. "Emotional support? Sign me up."

Professor Thorn chuckled. "They're not just fluffy companions; they can be mischievous too."

Leo shook his head. "No way. My thoughts are

private, thanks."

Professor Thorn tilted his head, looking amused. "Ah, Mr. Rutherford, many feel that way at first. It's a vulnerable thing, to let someone or something sense what you're carrying inside. But whisperfluffs don't judge. They simply reflect."

Leo snorted. "No thanks. I'll pass. My thoughts and feelings are private property, and I don't need them rifling through."

Clara tilted her head, curious. "It's not really rifling, though. It's more like ... sensing, right? A whisper, not a shout."

"Well, whisper or shout, no thanks," Leo said quickly, tapping his thumb against his forefinger. "Besides, who knows what one of these things might latch onto? What if it spills something I don't want anyone to know?"

Finn leaned over with a sly grin. "Come on, Leo, what could possibly be in there? Maybe it'll reveal your secret love for Professor Mornvale."

Leo shot him a sharp look, but his lips twitched with amusement. "Mate, she's like a hundred years old. But no. I'm fine without a flying therapist, thanks."

The whisperfluff on Professor Thorn's shoulder let out a soft trill, its wide, gleaming eyes scanning the other students. "Well," Thorn said with a shrug, "like all creatures, they're not for everyone. But for those willing to trust them, they can be an extraordinary source of comfort and clarity."

Professor Thorn clasped his hands together, his eyes shining with pride. "Caring for magical creatures isn't just about study; it's about building companionship. Magic often comes from the bonds we form with those who've lived it their whole lives."

Clara felt a deep thrill as she listened and a sense that her world was expanding with each new creature she encountered. She hadn't expected to feel a connection, such warmth, from beings as varied and strange as these, but they made her feel a sense of wonder she could hardly describe.

*

As the lesson continued, a small creature with expressive ears and wide curious eyes approached Clara, sniffing the air tentatively. Clara felt a gentle pulse stirring in her chest and reached into her pocket, pulling out a small piece of dried fruit wrapped in a napkin she had saved from breakfast. She held it out cautiously.

The little creature's eyes brightened, and it inched closer, its nose twitched with interest. With an elegant movement, it took the fruit from her hand, nibbling delicately while keeping its gaze fixed on her face. Clara couldn't help but smile, captivated by its gentle nature and the soft, rhythmic cooing sound it made as it ate.

Professor Thorn, noticing the interaction, chuckled softly. "Ah, Clara, it seems you've caught the attention of this little one. They don't often take to strangers so quickly." He approached, his tone laced with affection. "This particular loddlewight is named Wisp. He's nearing full maturity, though he's still a bit timid. For him to approach you like this, that's a rare sight."

"Wisp?" Clara repeated, the name rolling off her tongue as she looked down at the creature. It seemed to suit him perfectly. "He's amazing."

Wisp had finished his piece of fruit and now gazed up at Clara with his soulful eyes. With a few more steps, he settled beside her, as though staking a quiet claim. Clara felt a wave of wonder and warmth; it was as if Wisp had chosen her.

"Loddlewights," Professor Thorn continued, addressing the class, "are creatures of loyalty and immense magical capability. As they mature, they develop extraordinary powers, especially in defensive and protective magic. A fully grown loddlewight can sense danger before it strikes and create barriers of pure magical energy, shielding themselves and others from harm."

Clara's eyes widened. "Protective magic? So, they're not just companions; they're defenders?"

"Precisely," Professor Thorn replied with a smile. "They're known for conjuring magical shields strong enough to repel curses or harmful spells. Some legends even suggest that the most powerful loddlewights can absorb hostile magic entirely, transforming it into harmless energy. Some also have the ability to cast power spells to ward off danger. They may be small, but their power is formidable."

The other students murmured in awe as Wisp nuzzled against Clara's side. She glanced down at him, feeling a deep sense of connection. She hadn't expected to form such a bond during the lesson, but it felt as though Wisp had been waiting for her all along.

Wisp chirped softly, gazing up at Clara with wide, trusting eyes. She reached out to scratch his head, feeling an unexpected but comforting bond form between them.

"Thank you, Wisp," she murmured, almost forgetting that she was in a class filled with other students. "I think we're going to be great friends."

Clara smiled, feeling a profound sense of belonging. She felt truly connected to the magical world, not just through spells or her family name, but through a bond with a creature that saw something in her worth making a connection with. As she looked down at Wisp, a sense of purpose settled within her. She wasn't alone on this journey; she had friends, and now, a little guardian too.

Chapter 31: Hidden Paths and Unseen Trespassers

The Great Solstice Hall was unusually tense as students gathered for the morning assembly. The usual morning chatter had been replaced with uneasy whispers, a strange hush falling over the room. Even the enchanted ceiling seemed subdued.

Clara slid into her seat at the Luminaris table, her gaze flicking across the hall. Finn was fidgeting, twirling his spoon like a baton, while Ellie and Amelia exchanged worried glances. Even Leo, always the picture of calm, sat unusually still, his fingers tapping a slow, rhythmic beat against the table.

At the high table, Professor Mornvale rose, her presence instantly commanding the room's attention. Her robes shimmered faintly as she surveyed the gathered students, her expression sharp.

"Good morning, students," she began, her voice carrying easily across the hall. "It has come to the attention of the staff that certain individuals have been flagrantly disregarding the rules of this academy. Let me be perfectly clear: this behaviour will not be tolerated."

A ripple of unease swept through the hall.

Clara's stomach twisted as Finn leaned in and muttered, "This is going to be bad."

Mornvale continued, her tone growing colder. "Last night, a hidden passageway within the school was accessed without authorisation. This is a restricted area, protected by wards meant to safeguard not only what lies within but all of you. These wards were deliberately tampered with, and whoever was responsible used advanced concealment spells to evade our Sentinels."

Clara's breath caught, and her gaze darted to Finn,

317

who raised his eyebrows in alarm. Across the hall, a few Aurora students exchanged sly smirks.

Mornvale's gaze swept over the students, her voice dropping into something even colder.

"At any time, breaching the wards would be dangerous. But with recent … events, we cannot afford such risks."

A murmur rippled through the students. Everyone knew what she meant.

The Dark Wizard had escaped from Blackspire. No one truly believed he would come here, not yet, but the mere thought of the wards failing while he was free was enough to make the room feel colder.

"The Assembly does not believe the school is under any immediate threat," Mornvale continued, "but let me be clear: the integrity of our wards must remain intact. It is not merely a question of school rules, but of security. If these protections fail, we leave ourselves vulnerable to forces far beyond your understanding."

The weight of her words settled over them like a heavy storm cloud.

"To ensure this does not continue," Mornvale pressed on, "we will be implementing stricter measures. Any student caught out of bed after curfew, regardless of their reason, will face detention for the remainder of the school year. Any student found tampering with wards or accessing restricted passages will face immediate expulsion."

A buzz of hushed whispers filled the hall. Clara felt Ellie stiffen beside her, and Finn exhaled sharply.

"Mornvale's not playing," he muttered.

Professor Mornvale let the murmurs linger for a moment before the Orb pulsed, as though attuned directly to her authority. The hall fell silent once more.

"To address these breaches," Mornvale continued, "the school's protective wards have been upgraded. We have implemented Memory Wards."

A ripple of unease swept through the students.

Finn leaned closer to Clara and muttered, "Sounds like they've got a magical mind-wipe machine now. Lovely."

These wards," Mornvale said sharply, her gaze narrowing as if she had heard Finn, "are not to be tested or tampered with. They are precise, designed to ensure the safety of all within these walls. The Memory Wards will not distinguish between a curious student and a true threat. You will simply … forget. The Memory Wards are not designed to harm," she stated, her voice even but carrying a significance that settled over the hall. "They are temporary. However, they last long enough for intruders to be apprehended and … dealt with accordingly."

A ripple of unease passed through the room.

Mornvale continued, her tone sharpening. "You will not lose yourselves, but you will forget why you entered restricted areas, what you sought, and how you got there. The wards will strip away intent, leaving only confusion. You will find yourself standing in an unfamiliar place, with no memory of how you arrived. And by then, it will be too late."

She let the words hang for a moment before delivering her final warning. "Test them at your own peril."

Clara's breath stilled.

A chill ran down her spine. It wasn't just unsettling; it was terrifying.

Mornvale's voice softened slightly, though the hard edge remained.

"We live in uncertain times. The wards are there for your safety and the preservation of this school's secrets. Do not test them."

With that, she sat down, signalling the end of the announcement.

For a few seconds, no one moved. The weight of her words pressed down on the room like a heavy force. Then the quiet of whispered conversations began, growing in intensity as students turned to each other in concern.

Professor Mornvale dismissed the students, her stern gaze lingering on the tables as if daring anyone to test her resolve.

As they left the hall, Finn was the first to speak.

"Well, that was worrying. Patrols, detentions, expulsions and memory wards? Someone's really stepped in it this time."

Amelia crossed her arms. "It's not just a prank. Whoever's messing with the wards knows exactly what they're doing. They're not just testing boundaries; they're looking for something."

Ellie nodded. "It feels calculated. Wards aren't easy to break, even for someone skilled. Whoever's doing this is powerful."

Clara frowned, her thoughts swirling. "If they're using invisibility spells, they know exactly what they're doing."

Leo shrugged, his tone casual. "Could just be Year Elevens trying to make their mark before they graduate. You know, a bit of chaos for their grand finale."

Finn snorted. "Or they're playing with fire. Mornvale doesn't bluff, and if she's talking about expulsion, someone's in serious trouble."

Clara barely heard them.

The Memory Wards. The invisible Sentinels.

Tampering with wards could potentially put them all in danger if the Dark Wizard ever decided to visit the school.

She couldn't shake the feeling that this wasn't just about some reckless students pushing their limits.

Someone was testing Crowstone's defences.

Her thoughts churned as they walked, but one thing settled cold and unshakable in her mind:

This wasn't over. It was only the beginning.

And whoever was behind it wasn't just looking for secrets.

They were preparing for something far worse.

Chapter 32: Hidden Paths and Vanishing Truths

The crisp morning air was filled with chatter as students filed outside to the ornate carriages waiting outside the front entrance of Crowstone. As Clara and her friends stepped out, her breath hitched at the sight before her. The carriages were sleek and black, with subtle, golden patterns etched into the wheel rims. But what truly captivated her were the creatures pulling them. Towering lion-like creatures with golden fur and translucent wings stood at the front of each carriage, their glowing tails trailing light as they moved.

"What are those?" Clara asked, her voice barely above a whisper.

Finn grinned, his eyes lighting up with delight at her reaction. "Solwings. Majestic, aren't they? Part lion, part something unexplainable. Their wings can glow brighter than the moon, but don't worry; they're as calm as they are strong."

Clara nodded slowly, unable to tear her gaze away from one of the creatures as it turned to look at her with large intelligent eyes that glimmered like molten gold. It let out a low, soothing purr, and Clara felt a wave of reassurance ripple through her.

"I keep forgetting," Finn said with a playful nudge, "you grew up with Commonfolk and you're still a total noob to magic. Adorable, really."

Clara rolled her eyes, trying to suppress her smile. "You make it sound like I lived in a cupboard under the stairs or something."

"Not a cupboard," Ellie chimed in with a smirk. "Just … 'ull."

"Hey!" Clara protested, her mock annoyance lost as

another solwing rumbled deeply, the sound resonating through the air like distant thunder. The protective warmth radiating from them was comforting, almost like being wrapped in a cosy blanket.

Amelia leaned closer, her gaze softening as she watched Clara's wonder. "They're incredible creatures. Although you should see Shuyun drakes back in China. They're a sight that could leave anyone speechless."

She paused for dramatic effect, clearly revelling in holding everyone's attention. "They live in the Yunling Enclave near the Li River, an utterly magical place. The drakes glide through the air as if they're made of the clouds themselves, with scales that shimmer like rain-soaked emeralds. When they move, it's as if the sky bends to their will, trailing streaks of silver mist wherever they go."

Her voice dropped into a softer tone, as if recalling something deeply personal. "My parents took me there last summer. I had no idea what to expect, but when I saw them for the first time ... well, it was like my heart skipped a beat. The way the sun hit their scales made them look like glowing sculptures carved straight from the heavens."

"Wow, they sound magical!" Clara said, her face filled with wonder. Then her gaze drifted back to the solwings. As the group climbed into their carriage, she ran a hand lightly along the mane of one as they passed, feeling magic emanating from its fur.

"Do you think we'll get to see the Tower of Antiquities?" Ellie asked, her cheeks pink with cold. "I read it's where the first Magical Assembly was formed."

"If we're lucky," Finn replied, grinning. "I just hope we don't get stuck listening to Professor Valen drone on about dates and treaties for three hours."

Clara laughed excitedly as she as she sat there in the carriage. Her first magical school trip: she was very excited.

As they set off towards Hidden Row, drawn by the magnificent solwings, Clara silently wondered what other incredible sights this world still had in store for her.

*

The carriages rolled to a smooth halt at the start to Hidden Row. Clara stared in awe as one of the solwings turned its intelligent, glimmering eyes towards her, offering a low, resonant purr that felt oddly comforting.

Ahead, Hidden Row stretched out in a maze of cobblestone streets, but this part felt different: older and more secluded. The towering buildings seemed to hold stories in their carved walls decorated with magical symbols. It was quiet here, the usual commotion of Hidden Row replaced with an air of quiet respect.

Clara climbed out of the carriage, her heart pounding as the solwing nearest her let out a soft rumble before turning its attention forward. She couldn't help but wonder what secrets the district and these creatures held.

Professor Valen, their Magical Histories teacher, stood at the head of the group, his black robes billowing in the wind. He held a staff etched with runes, which glowed as he raised it to get the students' attention.

"Gather around, everyone," he called with authority. "Today, we'll be exploring one of the most significant historical sites in magical history: the Hall of Maldari. It is here that some of the earliest magical treaties were forged, and it holds many relics of our shared past. I expect all of you to treat it with the respect it deserves."

Clara's heart quickened as they approached the Hall of

Maldari. The entrance was marked by two towering stone pillars, each inscribed with magical symbols. Inside, the air was cooler, carrying the faint scent of aged parchment and polished stone.

The interior of the hall was breathtaking. The ceiling soared high above, depicting magical battles across the centuries. In the centre of the room was a circular painting showing the founding of the High Assembly, with figures standing around an ancient carved table. Surrounding the painting were glass cases containing ancient artefacts, scrolls, wands, and pieces of armour that gave off a faint glow of lasting magic.

Professor Valen led the group to one of the exhibits, gesturing towards a staff encased in shimmering glass. "This is the Staff of Feldara, used to seal our magical boundaries. Only Feldara's descendants, with exceptional skill, can wield it safely, as its immense power can corrupt the unworthy."

Clara leaned in to get a better look, her eyes wide. She couldn't help but feel a strange connection to the artefacts in the hall, as though they were quietly whispering secrets she couldn't quite hear.

As the tour continued, Clara felt a pull, not quite a voice, but something tugging at the edges of her mind.

She turned towards a shadowed alcove, partially hidden between two stone pillars. It wasn't just dark; it felt empty, like a space forgotten by time.

Then, something flickered. A ripple in the air. A shift in the shadow.

Clara took a step back, her pulse quickening.

Unable to resist, Clara slipped away and peeked in. The alcove contained a small weathered plaque inscribed with symbols she didn't recognise. For a moment, she again thought she saw something move, a flicker of light or shadow. She stepped back, her pulse quickening.

"Clara, what are you doing?" Leo's voice startled her. He had appeared at her side, his expression unreadable.

"Nothing," she said quickly. "I just thought I saw something."

Leo's eyes lingered on the alcove for a moment before he shrugged. "Probably just a reflection. Come on, you don't want to get left behind."

Clara nodded, but as she rejoined the group, the uneasy feeling stayed with her.

*

By the time the tour ended, the students were buzzing with excitement. Professor Valen dismissed them to explore Hidden Row before returning to the carriages. Clara walked with her friends, her thoughts still on the strange alcove and the artefacts they'd seen.

"What do you think about all those relics?" Ellie asked as they passed a café with enchanted chairs that rearranged themselves.

"They're incredible," Clara replied, though her mind was elsewhere. "But I wonder how much we don't know about them."

Finn grinned. "Maybe one day, we'll be in a hall like that, our wands on display as the heroes who saved the magical world."

Clara smiled, but her thoughts lingered on the shifting shadow she'd seen and the unsettling sense that something, or someone, was looking for something in places just like this.

They continued to stroll through Hidden Row, and as they neared Elderstone Bank, with its imposing silver-etched facade gleaming under the sun, Clara felt a surge of excitement. "I've been meaning to check on my account," she said, turning to her friends. "It'll only take a minute."

Leo's expression flickered, just for a second, but Clara caught it. "Actually," he said, forcing a casual tone, "I need to pick something up a few blocks over. Why don't I catch up with you later?"

Clara hesitated. "Are you sure? It won't take long."

Leo's finger and thumb tapped, a habit Clara had started to notice whenever he was choosing his words carefully. "No, really. It's fine. I'll meet you at the café down the street."

Finn squinted at him. "Weird. It's only a bank, mate, nothing to be scared of."

Leo let out a short laugh. "I told you, I just have to pick something up."

With a quick wave, Leo disappeared into the crowd. Clara watched him go, unease curling through her like a breath of winter.

"Well, I suppose it's just us four. Shall we check out this bank of yours, Miss Nightfall? I could use a little taste of that high-society glamour."

Clara rolled her eyes but smiled, trying to shake off the strange feeling as they made their way up the marble steps to Elderstone's grand entrance. The imposing doors, engraved with the Elderstone crest, swung open with a soft, magical hum, inviting them into the vast echoing hall beyond.

Clara sat in the ornate waiting room of Elderstone Bank with her friends, her fingers tapping nervously against her bag. She had spent the last few days wondering how she could help her dad financially without making it obvious. The idea of giving him money directly didn't feel right; he'd likely refuse, proudly insisting he could handle things on his own. But perhaps there was a way to do it subtly, something that would keep her family's world of magic and his non-magical life separate yet supportive.

A tall, stern-looking man appeared, bowing slightly as he gestured for Clara to follow him. "Miss Nightfall, we're ready for you now."

Clara stepped forward. "Won't be long, guys." Her heart was pounding a little. She'd barely gotten used to this place, with its gilded counters, polished floors, and glowing, enchanted chandeliers that filled the room with a soft, warm light.

They reached a private meeting room, and an older, dignified banker with a grey beard and piercing blue eyes sat waiting. He introduced himself as Mr. Albrecht, the bank's senior officer in *special transactions*.

Clara sat down, clearing her throat. "Thank you for meeting with me. I … I have a request that might be a bit unusual."

Mr. Albrecht gave a small, polite nod. "First things first. Please press on the gold tablet before we proceed."

Clara pressed the tablet, and it came alive with magic.

Mr. Albrecht placed the tablet down. "Thank you, Miss Nightfall. Please go on."

"I'd like to transfer some of my funds to my father," Clara began, choosing her words carefully. "He's a non-magical person, so I realise it might be complicated. I was thinking … a thousand gold coins to start, converted into British pounds."

The banker's brow furrowed as he tapped his fingers thoughtfully against the polished surface of his desk. "That's quite a substantial amount, Miss Nightfall.

Converted to non-magical currency, the value would increase considerably." He hesitated for a moment, as though weighing his next words carefully. "It is … uncommon to transfer magical currency beyond our world. Such transactions are generally discouraged."

Clara's shoulders tensed, but she kept her gaze steady. "It's for my dad. I want to make sure he's taken care of. Is there a way to open a savings account in his name? If the funds are already set up and transferred, it will be easier to convince him to keep it when I tell him."

Mr. Albrecht studied her for a long moment, his expression unreadable. Then, with a slight nod, he adjusted his glasses and leaned forward. "A savings account … that is an interesting approach. It would allow for the wealth to remain securely placed until he chooses to access it. And, well … given your family's standing, an exception could be arranged." He cleared his throat. "Of course, certain measures would need to be taken to ensure the funds integrate smoothly into the non-magical world without raising questions."

A breath of relief loosened the tension in Clara's chest. "That would be perfect. I just want to make sure he has something to fall back on, instead of struggling all the time."

The banker made a few precise notes in a ledger, its enchanted script shifting with a faint shimmer. He inclined his head approvingly. "Then we shall begin the process immediately. You will be notified once the account is established and the transfer is made."

Clara exhaled, a quiet sense of gratitude settling over her. "Thank you, Mr. Albrecht. This really means a lot."

The banker gave a faint smile, his usually formal demeanour softening. "It is not often we see young witches ensuring the well-being of others in this way. But family is at the heart of all we safeguard here at Elderstone Bank." He rose, signalling the end of their discussion. "Consider it handled."

As Clara stepped out into the cool air beyond the bank's great doors, she felt something shift inside her: pride, relief, and an undeniable certainty that this was the right thing to do. Her life straddled two worlds, but this was a way to bring them together. Not with magic, not with grand gestures, but with something far more important. A quiet, steady kind of care.

*

Clara stepped out of Elderstone Bank, feeling content. The worry that had been weighing on her for days, not knowing if the bank could help, felt lighter now that she knew her dad would be taken care of. It wasn't a perfect solution, but it was something.

She made her way through the busy streets with her friends. Ahead, leaning against a stone pillar, was Leo. With nothing in his hands.

Finn wasted no time. "Alright, Leo. Where's the package you were collecting?"

Leo sighed dramatically, pulling his cloak tighter around himself. "Must we start with the interrogation? Can't we just enjoy the rest of the day?"

Ellie folded her arms. "Not when you're being suspicious. You ran off to collect it, refused to say what it was, and you don't have anything with you."

Leo rolled his eyes. "You lot are exhausting. It was a gift for my mum, but it's not ready yet."

Ellie and Amelia exchanged knowing looks before chiming in unison. "Aww, such a mummy's boy."

Leo groaned, shaking his head as Finn grinned and

clapped him on the back. "No shame in it, mate. But really, what kind of gift requires this level of secrecy?"

Clara, watching closely, caught something the others didn't. Leo was tapping his finger and thumb together, just barely, but enough for her to notice.

She tilted her head slightly. "Leo, what kind of gift is 'not quite ready'?"

Leo hesitated for a fraction too long before forcing a casual shrug. "It's … something that needs a bit of work before I can actually give it to her. Just a few finishing touches."

Clara narrowed her eyes. He wasn't lying, not exactly, but there was something he wasn't saying. She could feel it.

Before she could press further, Leo shifted the conversation with an exaggerated stretch. "Right, now that the great mystery has been solved, can we please eat? I'm starving."

Ellie let out an exasperated sigh but relented. "Fine. But you're paying, since you've been so shifty."

Leo groaned. "I'm not agreeing to that."

The group fell into step, making their way towards the café, but Clara couldn't shake the feeling that Leo was hiding something.

Chapter 33: Preparation and Competition

The Elemental Training Grounds were alive with crackling energy. Students stood in formation, wands raised, the scent of scorched earth lingering from the last set of drills. The Elemental Games were fast approaching, and every student knew it. No more theory, no more practice for practice's sake. Every spell cast today was preparation for the real test ahead.

Clara adjusted her stance, fingers tightening around her wand. A few months ago, she would have been at the back of the group, dreading being called forward. Now she stepped into the centre without hesitation.

Professor Ainsley's gaze swept over the students before landing on her. She nodded once. "Nightfall, step forward."

Clara moved quickly, aware of the quiet murmurs around her. It wasn't the usual low expectations she had grown used to. This was different. They were watching her.

"You will perform the elemental progression drill," Ainsley said, her voice measured. "Fire, water, air, and earth. Maintain control. No gaps. No hesitation."

Clara nodded, steadying her breath. She had struggled with the transitions before, losing momentum between elements, letting one overpower the other. But she had trained for this. She was ready.

Raising her wand, she summoned fire first. A controlled burst flared to life, bright and steady, hovering just above her palm. She held it there, feeling the warmth, the energy contained within it, before drawing the flames inward. The heat faded, shifting as water flowed from the tip of her wand, pouring into a perfect arc before forming a suspended droplet of water in the air.

Without missing a beat, she inhaled and shifted again, letting the water dissolve into mist as air took its place. A gust stirred around her, lifting the mist in delicate spirals before settling. Finally, she grounded herself, focusing on the weight beneath her feet. Fragments of soil and stone lifted gently, perfectly controlled.

Silence followed.

Professor Ainsley observed her for a moment before nodding again. "Much improvement."

Clara let out a breath she hadn't realised she had been holding.

"Your transitions are controlled. Your focus is steady," Ainsley continued. "You are no longer struggling to keep up, Nightfall. You are beginning to lead."

Something flickered in Clara's chest. She had spent so long trying to catch up, trying to prove she deserved to be here. But now, standing in the middle of the training ring with every pair of eyes on her, she felt something else.

Pride.

Finn whistled under his breath. "Took you long enough," he said with a grin.

Ellie nudged him. "She was better than you last round."

Finn scoffed. "Barely."

Professor Ainsley turned back to the group. "The Elemental Games are not a test of raw power. Strength alone will not gain you victory. It is control, adaptability, and precision that will determine your success. Those who fight without discipline will fail. Those who master their elements will lead." She paused, then added, "Five points to Luminaris for the most improved student."

A scoff cut through the quiet.

"So, she gets points for no longer being terrible at

magic? How is that fair?" Victor Blackthorn stood near the back of the group, arms crossed, a smirk curling at the edge of his mouth.

Some students exchanged glances. Others shifted uncomfortably. Clara kept her expression neutral, though she could feel the heat rising in her face.

Professor Ainsley turned to face Victor, her gaze cool and unreadable. "Would you like to prove you can do better, Blackthorn?"

Victor hesitated for a fraction of a second before shaking his head. "No, Professor," he muttered, though his expression made it clear he had plenty left to say.

Finn grinned. "Jealous, Victor?" he called. "Or just annoyed that someone else is getting the attention?"

Victor glared but didn't respond.

Clara didn't let herself react. The points were a nice bonus, but the real victory was standing in this ring, knowing she had earned her place.

She was ready.

And soon she would prove it.

*

In the days leading up to the Elemental Games, Clara found herself sitting with her friends in the Luminaris common room, a fire crackling softly in the background. Finn was sprawled on an armchair, Ellie was jotting notes in her enchanted journal, and Amelia was flipping through a book of advanced charms.

Clara leaned forward, her fingers tracing absent circles on the table in front of her. "Can I tell you something?" she asked hesitantly, her voice softer than usual.

Finn glanced up from his chair. "Of course. What's up?"

She hesitated, glancing around at the room as though

the walls might hear her. "My uncle Cassius and Grandfather Eldric both mentioned that the Nightfalls always win the Elemental Games."

Ellie raised an eyebrow. "Well, no pressure, then."

"That's just it," Clara said, a hint of frustration creeping into her voice. "I feel like they're watching me, waiting to see if I can live up to their legacy. I know I've improved, but I'm still nowhere near as good as almost everyone else in our year. But I want to prove to them I belong. But more than that … I need to prove it to myself."

Finn straightened up in his chair, his easy grin softening. "You do belong, Clara. You've got more determination than anyone I've ever met. And who cares what they think? Given where you started, by the time you finish school, I bet you'll be one of the top students."

"But I care," Clara admitted, her voice tightening. "I care because ... this world is part of me. I didn't grow up with it like you all did, but I feel it deep down, like it's been waiting for me. I just … I don't want to be a disappointment."

Amelia closed her book with a snap, fixing Clara with a determined look. "You won't be. You're a Nightfall, Clara, but you're also just … you. And that's already enough. The Games aren't about proving anything to anyone else; they're about learning what you're capable of."

Clara smiled faintly, a flicker of warmth cutting through her nerves. "Thanks. I needed to hear that."

Ellie nudged her lightly. "Besides, we're a team. Nightfall legacy or not, you're not in this alone. We're going to win because we're going to work together, and together we're unstoppable."

Finn leaned back again, smirking. "And because I'm here, obviously."

Amelia rolled her eyes, and Clara laughed despite herself, the knot in her stomach loosening slightly. She was still nervous, but now the Games felt a little less daunting.

*

The Elemental Arena buzzed with excitement, house banners waving proudly as fiery reds and oranges shimmered across the enchanted walls, signalling the start of Fire's Fury.

Professor Ainsley stood at the centre of the arena, her fiery red robes flowing like embers in the wind. She positioned her wand in front of her lips, amplifying her voice across the crowd. "Welcome, students, to the first event of the Elemental Games for Year Eights. Today we begin with the trial of fire. Your task is simple: harness the element's energy, shape it, and use it to light the six torches stationed around the arena."

Professor Ainsley gestured, and tall pyrestands appeared, spread out across the ground. Each was set at varying heights and distances, with obstacles between them. "This challenge is not just about strength," she explained. "It's about precision, control, and creativity. Points will be awarded for how quickly you light the pyrestands and how skilfully you wield the flames. Fire is as dangerous as it is beautiful. Respect it, or it will not respect you."

Clara stood with her teammates, Finn, Leo, Ellie, and Amelia, in their designated area, marked by the silver and blue banner of Luminaris. She felt her nerves flare up like the flames they were about to summon.

Finn nudged Clara. "Relax, Clara. I'm ready."

Ellie rolled her eyes. "Famous last words."

Amelia smirked. "If we all go up in flames, I'm blaming Finn."

The whistle blew, and Clara stepped forward, gripping her wand tightly. She closed her eyes for a moment, recalling Professor Ainsley's lessons on channelling fire magic. "It's not about forcing the flame," she'd said. "It's about inviting it, guiding it, letting it dance to your rhythm."

She took a breath and whispered, "Tineara Solis." A spark ignited at the tip of her wand, surging with uncertainly before blooming into a small flame. Encouraged, she directed it towards the first pyrestand. The flame darted through the air, twisting gracefully before landing in the pyrestand with a satisfying whoosh. One down.

Nearby, Finn had a different approach. With a confident grin, he twirled his wand and called out, "Braedach Fólmhar!" A fireball the size of his head burst into existence, crackling with energy. He flung it at a pyrestand, hitting his mark, but also singing a nearby banner.

Professor Ainsley raised an eyebrow. "Points for speed, minus points for recklessness."

Ellie, ever methodical, muttered, "Lasrach Snáithe." A thin, controlled stream of fire coiled from her wand like a silk thread, weaving effortlessly through the obstacle course of enchanted barriers before lighting her second pyrestand.

Leo, however, had no such struggles. With a casual flick of his wand, he whispered, "Aindreadh." A sleek, golden flame curled into existence, smooth and precise. He guided it towards his pyrestand with barely a flicker of effort, the flames settling neatly into place.

Finn groaned. "Show-off."

Amelia arched an eyebrow. "Efficiency isn't showing off. It's just superior skill."

Leo gave a dramatic bow. "Thank you, thank you. Some of us are just naturally gifted."

Ellie rolled her eyes. "Or naturally insufferable."

Clara couldn't help but smile. For all his smugness, Leo made it look easy. Maybe a little too easy.

Amelia, her expression calm and focused, lifted her wand and whispered, "Siarlas Draoi." Instead of launching a fireball, she shaped her flames into a thin, swirling ribbon, sending it spiralling through the air before coiling neatly into the pyrestand's base. It flared to life in a controlled burst of gold and orange.

As Clara moved to her second pyrestand, she encountered a challenge: a high platform surrounded by swirling wind enchantments that threatened to extinguish any approaching flame. She hesitated, thinking of a solution. Then, inspiration struck.

Clara cast Sciath Tine: Fire Shield. A shimmering barrier of heat wrapped around her flame, guiding it safely through the wind until it reached the pyrestand. The torch burst to life, and Clara allowed herself a small smile of triumph.

"Smart move," Amelia said approvingly, sending another controlled flame towards her next pyrestand. "Fire isn't just about heat; it's about adaptation."

With two pyrestands left, Clara and her teammates began working together. Finn used his raw power to clear obstacles, creating paths for Ellie's precise flames. Leo, ever the strategist, guided Amelia through a breathing technique to steady her magic, and soon she managed to conjure a small, flickering flame.

Clara stepped beside her. "Now, send it forward gently. Let it move with the air, not against it."

Amelia exhaled and followed her lead. Her flame wavered but held, reaching the pyrestand and sparking it alight. A broad smile crossed her face.

"See?" Clara said encouragingly. "You've got this."

Finally, they reached the last pyrestand, a towering torch surrounded by a moat of enchanted water. Ellie conjured a small bridge of ice, murmuring, "Droichead Reo." Amelia reinforced it with a steadying charm, Neart Fuar. Clara sent a spiralling flame upward, whispering "Drithlinn Tine," lighting the pyrestand just as the whistle blew.

Professor Ainsley stepped forward, her voice carrying across the arena. "Impressive work, Luminaris. Your teamwork and creativity have earned you high marks. However, fire is not just about power; it is about balance." She glanced pointedly at Finn. "And while some of you showed great balance, others have room to grow."

Finn rubbed the back of his neck. "Yeah, yeah, I get it. Less destruction, more control."

Amelia smirked. "Might be the first useful thing you've said all day."

As the Luminaris team walked back to their seats, Clara felt a surge of pride. The fire had tested her focus and determination, and she had risen to the challenge. But she knew this was just the first hurdle towards winning.

Professor Ainsley announced Flarewood had surged ahead, their explosive command over fire magic giving them an early advantage. Their bold approach won them points, but their recklessness cost them precision, allowing Aurora and Luminaris to close the gap. Luminaris was in first place.

Clars felt a sense of pride in her team.

The next element awaited.

*

The arena was prepared for the next trial, the fiery tones of the previous challenge dissolving into cool blues and silvers. Streams of water flowed down the arena walls, pooling into basins. The air was crisp, charged with the quiet, steady power of the element.

Professor Ainsley stepped forward, her voice carrying over the gentle rush of flowing water. "Welcome to the second trial: Water's Grace. You'll harness water's fluid nature to complete tasks requiring adaptability and precision."

With a flick of her wand, three tall transparent structures appeared at different points in the arena, each one containing an orb of light suspended in liquid. The orbs were surrounded by spinning rings of enchanted barriers. "To succeed, you must retrieve the orbs without breaking their containers or spilling any water. Be patient, be clever, and trust the element."

Clara and her teammates exchanged glances, the confidence they had felt in the fire trial wavering. Fire had been about power and control. Water was something else entirely.

"Can't we just freeze all the water, then easily retrieve the orbs?" Finn said with a smile.

Amelia gave Finn a stern look. "Professor Ainsley is much smarter than that, Finn. It will never be that easy."

"Alright," Clara said, stepping forward. "Let's split up. Finn, distract the barriers on the left orb with illusions. Ellie, can you freeze the water to slow it down?"

Ellie nodded. "I'll try. But we'll still need someone to retrieve it."

"I'll do it," Leo said quickly. "I'm better with water than the rest of you."

Clara raised an eyebrow, but Finn clapped Leo on the back. "Okay, then, go for it, water wizard. I guess we'll back you up."

Amelia crossed her arms. "I'll reinforce the water's surface tension. If we keep it stable, it'll be easier to lift the orb without breaking the basin."

The team approached the first structure. Finn twirled his wand and whispered, "Taibhse Bréige." A series of shimmering decoys flickered to life, mimicking their movements and drawing the enchanted barriers away from the orb.

Ellie extended her wand, calling softly, "Reothadh Fánach." A thin layer of frost spread over the water, slowing its turbulent movements.

Amelia, her voice calm and steady, added, "Socrú Aibhne." The water stilled beneath the orb, held in place like glass.

Leo stepped forward, his wand steady as he murmured, "Tarraingt Thonn." The water rippled and obeyed, lifting the orb gently from its container. He guided it towards the collection point marked by a glowing blue circle.

As the orb clicked into place, Leo exhaled sharply, grinning. "One down."

The second structure was more challenging, surrounded by flowing waterfalls that shifted unpredictably.

"Finn, block the falls," Clara said, her mind racing.

Finn conjured another illusion, Scáth Uisce, creating the appearance of a solid barrier to momentarily redirect the falling water.

Ellie touched her wand to the pool's surface, whispering, "Siosma Reo," freezing the water in jagged patches to slow its movement.

Clara raised her wand and hesitated. The water inside the structure churned restlessly, resisting control. It wasn't like fire, which responded to direct will; it had a rhythm of its own, something she needed to follow, not fight.

Taking a slow breath, she closed her eyes and whispered, "Éirí Tonn."

The water shifted. Instead of forcing it, she let herself move with it. The liquid curled upward, wrapping around the orb like gentle hands. She could feel it resisting at first, but as she adjusted, guiding rather than commanding, it responded.

The orb floated free, and she directed it to the collection point.

"That was amazing," Finn said as Clara wiped her brow. "How did you do that?"

"Water doesn't like to be rushed," Clara said, smiling faintly. "I just listened to it."

The third structure loomed at the far end of the arena, surrounded by jets of water that shot upward in unpredictable bursts. The orb inside glowed brighter than the others, and the barriers spun faster, their magic crackling with energy.

"We'll need all of us for this one," Clara said firmly.

Ellie nodded. "I can slow the jets, but not for long. Finn, can you distract the barriers again?"

"Already on it," Finn said, conjuring more decoys with Cealg Uisce.

Leo stepped forward, determination etched on his face.

"I'll handle the orb."

"And I'll stabilise the water," Amelia added. "I have a spell that can counter turbulence."

Clara nodded. "Let's go."

The team moved together, their spells combining in a dazzling display of cooperation.

Ellie whispered, "Sioc Ceilte," her frost creeping along the ground and slowing the water jets.

Amelia lifted her wand and murmured, "Ceangal Srutha." The swirling pool beneath the orb smoothed, locking into a gentle, controlled spiral.

Finn's illusions flickered, keeping the enchanted barriers occupied, while Leo extended his wand, whispering "Glaoch na Toinne." The water obeyed, lifting the orb with remarkable ease.

Just as it neared the collection point, a sudden burst of water surged through the air, shattering Finn's illusion. The barriers realigned, spinning faster.

"No, no, no!" Leo gritted his teeth, steadying the spell.

Clara acted without thinking, reinforcing the flow with her own magic, merging her spell with Amelia's stabilisation. The current stilled, and the orb drifted upward once more.

With one final push, Leo directed it into place.

A chime echoed through the arena, signalling their success. The crowd erupted into cheers, and Professor Ainsley stepped forward, her expression one of quiet pride.

"Well done, Luminaris," she said, addressing the team. "Water is not an easy element to master, but you showed patience, teamwork, and respect for its nature. Water is life; it flows, it adapts, and it perseveres. These are qualities you should carry with you."

As she and her teammates walked back to their seats, Clara felt a deep sense of accomplishment. The water trial had tested their ability to work together, and they had risen to the challenge.

But she knew the games were far from over. Earth's strength and air's unpredictability awaited them, and with them, new opportunities to grow.

Professor Ainsley announced the scores. "Evergrove demonstrated their deep connection to the element, weaving currents with effortless grace. Though they gained significant ground, Nightspire used cunning illusions to navigate the course with near-flawless strategy, securing their place among the frontrunners. Luminaris is still in the lead."

Clara and her teammates all erupted in cheers.

*

The arena shifted, the previous trial fading into rich browns and deep greens. Vines curled up from the edges of the stone floor, boulders rumbled into place, and towering rock pillars appeared from the ground. The air carried the scent of moss and damp earth, grounding Clara in the raw strength of the element.

Professor Ainsley stepped forward, her voice steady as it carried over the murmuring crowd. "Earth's strength lies in resilience, stability, and connection. This challenge will test not only your magical prowess but your ability to adapt and endure. Teams, your task is to build a path to the central tower and retrieve the crystal at its peak. You must use earth-based spells to navigate and construct. Be mindful, the terrain may shift."

Clara exchanged a glance with her teammates. The tower loomed in the centre of the arena, its surface rough and uneven, its peak glowing where the crystal sat.

Surrounding it was treacherous ground: deep gaps, rising ridges, and crumbling platforms. This would take precision, patience, and teamwork.

"Ellie, form the path," Clara said.

Ellie nodded, already gripping her wand.

"Finn, cover us. Leo, reinforce the boulders as we move. Amelia, keep the ground steady and make sure we don't lose our footing."

Leo raised an eyebrow. "What about you?"

Clara inhaled deeply. "I'll keep an eye on the tower and adjust our route if needed. Let's move."

Ellie took the lead, moving with careful determination as she traced her wand through the air. "Talamh Ard," she called, and the earth responded. Stones shifted, boulders rolled, and a jagged bridge stretched across a deep chasm.

Finn stayed close behind, his wand flicking as he cast Claoidh Cloch, reinforcing the less stable rock formations. A pillar groaned under its own weight, threatening to collapse, but his spell held it firm. "This place is literally falling apart," he muttered.

Leo pressed his palm to the ground. "Dún Fód," he murmured, channelling his magic. The earth pulsed beneath them as compacted soil and roots wove together, strengthening the newly formed path. "That should hold," he said, wiping sweat from his brow. "But it won't last long."

Amelia moved carefully, her magic reaching deeper into the earth. "Cosc Creathán," she whispered. The vibrations beneath their feet eased, giving them steadier footing.

As they advanced, the ground suddenly cracked beneath Clara's feet. She barely had time to react before the stone shifted, threatening to send them tumbling into the ravine below.

"Everyone, hold on!" Clara shouted, casting Fréamh Ceangail. Thick vines shot up, anchoring them just as the platform threatened to give way.

Ellie looked back, eyes wide. "Nice save, Clara!"

They pressed on, each movement deliberate. The tower loomed closer, but the final stretch was the most treacherous yet.

The crystal continued pulsating at the tower's peak, its surface surrounded by swirling energy that flickered with warning. The structure itself was unstable, its surface rough and crumbling.

"How do we get up there?" Finn asked, tilting his head.

"We climb," Clara said. "Ellie, can you create steps built with stones?"

"On it," Ellie replied, raising her wand. "Cruth Cloiche." Small ledges emerged, carving a narrow ascent up the tower.

"Leo, can you stabilise the structure?"

Leo pressed his wand to the base, calling, "Greim Fód." The earth tightened around the tower, making it sturdier. "That should keep it from toppling. Just don't take too long."

Clara placed her hands against the stone, exhaling slowly. The swirling energy crackled against her skin, pushing her back.

"Finn, can you distract the barrier?"

Finn smirked. "Thought you'd never ask." He flicked his wand. "Creathán Domhain." A controlled tremor rippled through the arena floor. The barrier flickered, unstable for just a few seconds.

Clara seized the chance. She climbed quickly, fingers gripping the rough stone, each movement precise. The energy pulsed violently, sending a sharp jolt through her arm. Her grip slipped, boots scraping against the stone. For a breathless second, she thought she might fall.

A second tremor shook the structure, Finn's work, and the energy wavered again. Clara pushed through, reaching the top. She extended her hand, and the crystal glowed in her palm. As her fingers closed around it, the barrier shattered, its energy dispersing into the air.

A chime rang through the arena. The crowd roared.

As Clara climbed back down, the crystal warm in her hand, she felt the weight of exhaustion settle over her. Her teammates gathered around, faces lit with triumph.

"You did it," Ellie said, breathless and grinning.

Clara exhaled, the tension in her shoulders melting away. "We all did."

Professor Ainsley approached, approval in her gaze. "Excellent work, Luminaris. Earth is not easily tamed, but you demonstrated resilience and teamwork."

As the earth trial unfolded, Aurora took control, their mastery of spellcraft and strategy outmatching the raw power of Flarewood. Aurora gained a lot of points, but Luminaris was still in the lead.

The final element awaited: air.

*

The arena shifted, the solid earth dissolving into floating platforms surrounded by spiralling air currents. Streams shimmered as a crisp breeze brushed Clara's face.

Professor Ainsley's voice rang out, calm and commanding.

"Air is the element of freedom, agility, and adaptability. In this challenge, you will navigate through the arena using air-based spells. Your goal is to collect as many floating orbs as possible within the time limit. But beware, this trial is about balance and precision. Power will not save you here."

Clara exchanged glances with her teammates. Finn looked positively gleeful, while Ellie's brow furrowed in concentration. Leo cracked his knuckles, giving Clara a reassuring nod. Amelia adjusted her grip on her wand, her gaze scanning the arena with cool calculation.

"Let's do this," Clara said, her heart pounding as she took in the maze of floating platforms.

The whistle blew, and the team sprang into action. Clara cast Céim Gaoithe, propelling herself onto the first platform. A cushion of air formed beneath her feet, giving her a brief moment of weightlessness before she landed.

Ellie followed close behind, using Sleamhnán Aer to create a controlled wind that carried her from one platform to the next. "There's an orb to your left, Clara!" Ellie called out, pointing to a golden sphere spinning lazily in the air.

Clara adjusted her trajectory and reached for the orb, using Gabháil Gaoth to pull it into her grasp. The moment she grabbed it, a gust of wind tried to knock her off balance. She wobbled but managed to stabilise herself by casting Teannán Aer, tethering herself to the platform.

"Nice save!" Finn shouted from above, using Preab Gaoth to propel himself higher. He snagged a blue orb, flipping mid-air to avoid a sudden wind spiral that threatened to pull him off course. "This is amazing!" he yelled, grinning like a child at a fair.

Amelia, moving with calm precision, used Stoirmeach Seasta to form small currents that kept her movements steady. She reached an orb just as it began to drift away, flicking her wand and calling, "Rópa Ghaoithe," latching onto it before it could escape.

Leo, meanwhile, took a different approach, casting Clúdach Aer to create a buffer around himself, allowing him to push through the shifting winds without losing balance. He reached for an orb, only to find himself caught in a whirlwind that trapped him mid-air.

"A little help here?" he called out, spinning helplessly.

"On it!" Finn called, using Sleasa Gaoth to disrupt the vortex. The whirlwind dissipated, and Leo managed to land on a nearby platform, muttering a breathless "Thanks."

As the challenge progressed, the winds grew stronger and the platforms became more erratic. One tilted sharply as Ellie landed, causing her to lose her footing.

"Ellie!" Clara shouted, reaching out with her wand. She cast Ardú Méith, creating a bubble of air that cushioned Ellie's fall, allowing her to regain her balance.

"Thanks!" Ellie called back, quickly hopping to another platform and grabbing a glowing green orb.

The next stretch was even trickier. Gusts of wind howled through the course, knocking them off balance. The platforms themselves began vanishing for brief moments, forcing the team to time their jumps perfectly.

"Okay, that's just rude," Finn muttered as he barely managed to land before a platform disappeared beneath him.

Amelia narrowed her eyes. "We need to predict the pattern. The platforms don't vanish at random. There's a rhythm to it."

They watched carefully, realising that every third platform flickered out of existence for a few seconds before reappearing.

Leo nodded. "Got it. We move together on the second count. Finn, give us some cover in case the winds shift."

Finn launched a wave of wind resistance with Cúl

Gaoithe, shielding them as they leapt across the unstable platforms.

They were moving seamlessly now, their movements synchronised. Then the final challenge appeared.

A massive orb hovered in the centre of the arena, surrounded by powerful gusts that formed a violent tornado. It pulsed with energy, the entire arena tilting towards it, as if pulled by unseen gravity.

"That's the big one," Clara said, shielding her face from the roaring winds. "We need that."

"Finn, disrupt the winds. Ellie, clear a path. Leo, stabilise the tornado. Amelia, reinforce the air currents around us," Clara said.

"What about you?" Leo asked, concern flashing in his eyes.

"I'll use Air Step to get through before it reforms. Trust me," Clara said, steady and certain.

Finn unleashed Géar Sceana, slicing through the outer layers of wind. Ellie used Rotha Ghaoithe to create a temporary calm in the storm's wake. Amelia cast Líon Aer, keeping the air steady so they wouldn't get thrown off course.

Leo stepped forward, eyes narrowing. He raised his wand.

But just as Clara leapt forward, a rogue gust slammed into her. She lost control mid-air, tumbling out of reach of the orb, the wind swallowing her whole.

"Clara!" Amelia shouted.

Without hesitation, Leo thrust his wand upward and bellowed, "Seoladh Ghaoithe!" The air surged around him, catching Clara just as she began to plummet. He redirected the wind, twisting it in a way no one had before, sending Clara hurtling upward instead of down, straight towards the orb.

Clara reacted instinctively, stretching out her hand. The moment her fingers closed around it, the tornado shattered. The air stilled, and for a brief moment, everything was silent.

Then, the arena erupted into cheers.

As they regrouped on the ground, panting and grinning, Professor Ainsley approached them.

"Excellent work, Luminaris. Air demands adaptability and trust, and you've shown both today. Magic isn't always about strength; it's about knowing when to let go and let the wind carry you."

Clara turned to Leo, eyes filled with gratitude. "That was incredible."

Leo gave a breathless laugh. "Guess I finally figured out how to stop fighting the wind."

As they waited for the other teams, Clara knew that the Elemental Games had pushed them all in ways they never expected. But more than that, it had prepared them for what was coming next.

Clara and her teammates watched as Aurora moved through the course with unmatched skill, each manoeuvre calculated, every spell cast with precision. When the dust settled, they knew the results would be close.

*

The arena still crackled with the remnants of magic, the air thick with energy as the teams stood together, waiting. The shimmering echoes of the Elemental Games lingered like embers refusing to fade. Clara could still feel the rush of wind against her skin and the exhilaration of the final trial right down to her bones.

Professor Ainsley stepped forward, a scroll in hand, her expression composed and unreadable. The hush that fell over the crowd was near absolute.

"You have all faced the elements with skill, perseverance, and imagination," she began. "Every trial tested not only your magical ability but your ability to work as a team, to think beyond yourselves, and to trust in forces beyond your control. And now the final results."

Clara glanced at her teammates. Finn rocked on his heels, restless. Ellie stood with her arms crossed, her brow furrowed in thought. Leo's usual smirk was subdued, his hands clasped behind his back. Amelia remained still, watching the professor intently.

Professor Ainsley unfurled the scroll.

"In fifth place, with a total of 121, is Evergrove."

A round of applause spread through the students in deep green and bronze. The Evergrove team took the results with quiet dignity. Some nodded in acceptance, while others already seemed deep in discussion over what they could improve next time. Their strengths lay in strategy, patience, and their deep connection with nature, but the fast-paced, chaotic nature of the Elemental Games had tested them in ways they had not expected.

"In fourth place, with 128, is Nightspire."

The students from the sleek, dark tower accepted their placement with composed smiles, though there was a glint of calculation in their eyes. Nightspire played the long game. They might not have won today, but they would undoubtedly be plotting their path to victory next time.

Clara swallowed. Three houses remained.

"In third place, with 143 points, is Flarewood."

A mix of cheers and groans came from the house of fire and passion. The Flarewood team had fought fiercely, pushing the limits of their elemental magic, but their bold approach had also cost them points in precision-based tasks. Despite the loss, they took the news with their usual energy, clapping each other on the back and already discussing next year's competition.

Clara's stomach twisted. Only two houses remained.

Professor Ainsley paused, letting the weight of the moment settle over the arena. "And now the final two. It was an exceptionally close competition. Only one point separates first and second place."

Clara felt her breath catch as the arena seemed to shrink around her.

Her mind raced through the trials. Had they done enough? They had worked together seamlessly, adapted to every challenge, and fought for every point. But had it been enough?

"The winners of this year's Elemental Games, with a total score of 152, are Aurora."

A thunderous cheer erupted from the students in deep purple and gold as Lucinda Vale stepped forward, head held high, a victorious smile on her face. The scholars and strategists of Aurora had outmanoeuvred everyone, their mastery of spellwork and tactics securing their victory.

"Luminaris finishes with 151. A single point difference. An incredible effort and a performance worthy of the highest respect."

Clara exhaled slowly. They had come so close.

Finn ran a hand through his hair. "One point. That is cruel."

Ellie shook her head, but there was no bitterness in her expression. "We did everything we could. We should be proud."

Leo chuckled. "At least we made them work for it."

Amelia glanced at Clara, her eyes sharp with determination. "That was the best we have worked together. If we lost by one point, then next time, we will win by ten."

Clara met her gaze and smiled.

As Professor Ainsley handed the winning trophy to Lucinda and her team, the crowd erupted once more. Clara watched the way the Aurora students stood together, confident and proud. They had earned their victory, but so had Luminaris.

As the teams walked out of the arena, Clara felt a quiet and unwavering determination.

They had come second this time.

Next time, they would not settle for anything less than first.

Chapter 34: Festival and Dance

The morning of the Winter Solstice Festival dawned with a magical stillness that touched every corner of Crowstone Academy. Clara awoke to frost-laced windows glistening in the morning light, while snow blanketed the grounds like a sea of diamonds. Even the forest seemed more alive, its trees swaying gently as if honouring the day.

As Clara stepped out into the courtyard with Leo and Finn, she was momentarily stunned by the transformation before her. The school grounds had become a sparkling winter wonderland. Rows of stalls stretched across the open space, their canopies wrapped in chains of holly and glowing lights. Snowflakes fell lazily from the sky, disappearing just before they touched the students, who moved between the stalls with wide eyes and excited chatter.

"This," Finn declared, throwing his arms wide, "is Crowstone at its best. Forget the lessons; this is what matters."

Clara couldn't help but smile at his enthusiasm. She turned to Leo, who looked just as impressed, though more controlled in his reaction. "It's incredible," she admitted, her breath visible in the crisp air. "I've never seen anything like it."

"You wouldn't have, growing up in 'ull," Finn said with a wink. "The Winter Solstice Festival at Crowstone is as unique as each falling snowflake. Rumour has it, the festival is older than the school itself."

The trio began wandering through the rows of stalls, each offering something more extraordinary than the last. One vendor displayed enchanted snow globes, each capturing a scene that moved and shifted as if alive. In one, fairies danced around a frozen lake, and there was even a miniature version of Crowstone itself, where tiny figures moved within the glass. Another stall sold steaming mugs of spiced apple juice that warmed you from the inside out, no matter how cold it was.

Clara stopped at a booth of glowing ornaments.

"Solstice Charms," the stall trader explained. "Good fortune for the new year."

Finn squinted at one. "Do these include a *clean your room* spell?"

The stall trader laughed. "Only if someone buys it for you."

Finn laughed as he walked off.

They continued exploring, passing stalls offering enchanted scarves that changed colours with the wearer's mood, books filled with winter-themed spells, and even a stall selling 'frost blooms', flowers that glowed faintly in the dark and thrived in icy conditions. Clara couldn't resist buying one, tucking it carefully into her pocket for safekeeping.

At the centre of the festival stood its main attraction: an enormous ice sculpture of the Winter High Wizard, a legendary figure associated with the festival. The sculpture depicted the High Wizard holding a staff, its tip radiating a soft, golden light. Surrounding the sculpture were dozens of candles, each lit by a different student's spell, creating a soft, multicoloured glow that reflected off the ice.

"Every year, students light candles to honour the solstice," Finn explained, watching as a Year 7 struggled to cast the spell for her candle. A professor stepped in to guide her, and soon the tiny flame flared to life, joining the others in a rainbow of surging light.

Clara picked up a candle, watching how the coloured flames from the others flickered. For Clara, this day had meant nothing: just another day, cold, dull grey skies, and the quiet routine of home. No enchanted ice sculptures. No floating snowflakes that never touched the ground. No crowds of students laughing and casting spells like it was the most natural thing in the world.

Was this her world now?

Her fingers tightened around her wand. She wasn't sure what to wish for as she lit the candle. But she wanted to belong.

She whispered the spell. A sapphire-blue flame flickered into life, steady and strong.

Something in her settled.

*

As Leo browsed a stall of rare potion ingredients, Clara noticed him pause, his sleeve slipping back to reveal an angry, blotchy rash trailing along his wrist.

"What happened to your arm?" Clara asked.

Leo tugged his sleeve down casually. "Potion spill. It's fine."

Clara frowned. "That doesn't look fine. You should see the nurse."

Leo waved her off, but his fingers tapped together absently, as they so often did when he was thinking too hard or when something was bothering him.

A stall nearby caught his eye, a table filled with shimmering potion vials. His whole body tensed before he turned sharply away, stuffing his hands into his pockets.

Clara opened her mouth to say something, but he was already moving.

Finn called out, "Are you two coming or starting a potions lab?"

Leo raised his hands. "I'm fine. Let's go."

Reluctantly, Clara followed, but her suspicion lingered. Leo's rash and his quick dismissal of it did not sit right with her.

As the festival continued, Clara, Finn, and Leo met up with Ellie and Amelia, joining in the celebrations together. They tested their skills at charm-weaving contests, attempted to conjure the most intricate frost patterns, and even took turns on the enchanted ice rink, where the ice shifted beneath their feet in swirling patterns of olive-green and sun-kissed yellow.

Laughter and warmth carried them through the day, the scent of spiced apple juice lingering in the air as they wandered between the glowing stalls. By the time the final lanterns floated into the sky to mark the end of the festival, Clara felt quietly contented.

The Winter Solstice would be more than just another day from now on. It would feel like belonging.

*

Students began dispersing from the festival grounds, making their way to their rooms to get ready for the grand finale of the evening, the Winter Solstice Dance in the Hall of Echoes

A tradition woven into the very fabric of Crowstone, the dance marked the turning of the season, a night where magic, unity, and renewal were celebrated in equal measure. It was said that centuries ago, the first solstice dance had been held beneath the open sky, with students casting spells to paint constellations in the air. It was an evening where past, present, and future intertwined beneath the spell-lit glow of enchanted lanterns.

Excitement rippled through the students as they left the festival behind, eager to prepare for the night ahead. Clara and her friends exchanged glances, a shared anticipation buzzing between them.

"We should go and get ready," Amelia said, already tugging Ellie's arm.

"Agreed," Finn added, clapping Leo on the shoulder. "No offence, mate, but you could do with a bit of polish."

Leo rolled his eyes, but even he smirked.

With that, they all parted ways, retreating to their dormitories to change.

By the time they met up outside the Hall of Echoes, the transformation was complete.

Ellie's gown was a deep emerald green, the fabric embroidered with golden paisley patterns that shimmered with subtle enchantments. Tiny charms shaped like peacock feathers hung from her earrings, glowing faintly as they swayed. She grinned at Clara, adjusting the gold bangles on her wrists.

Amelia's dress was a masterpiece of deep sapphire and silver, inspired by flowing Hanfu robes, its wide sleeves lined with faint constellations that flickered as she moved. A delicate silver hairpin shaped like a dragon rested in her neatly coiled bun, and as she tilted her head, the dragon's eyes sparked with hidden enchantment. The intricate patterns on her dress told a silent story, magic woven into every thread.

Finn stood tall, his Luminaris colours woven into his tailored jacket, though his suit carried something distinctly his own. His blue and silver attire was lined with rich Kente patterns, the traditional Ghanaian designs subtly enchanted, catching the light with every movement. Silver threads curled along the cuffs, shifting like water whenever he gestured. Around his neck, he wore a beaded necklace that had belonged to his grandmother, a quiet reminder of home.

Leo had opted for sleek black and silver, his suit sharp yet understated, with subtle magical patterns shifting across the fabric like shadows.

And Clara, dressed in a deep crimson gown, felt both nervous and exhilarated. The dress was simple but elegant, its fabric catching the light like embers beneath the moon. It was different from anything she had ever worn before, but as her friends turned to her with approving smiles, she felt a spark of confidence settle within her.

"You look amazing," Amelia said.

"You all do," Clara replied, glancing around at her friends. For a moment, the weight of the past term faded away, replaced by something lighter, something closer to belonging.

Finn gave a dramatic bow. "Shall we?"

They stepped forward, the grand doors of the Hall of Echoes swinging open, welcoming them into a night of magic, music, and the whispers of the past.

Tonight they would be part of it.

The Hall of Echoes was alive with magic. The ceiling rippled with moving murals that depicted the academy's history. Tonight the scenes glowed softly, shifting to match the rhythm of the music. Beneath Clara's feet, the starlit surface shimmered with every step, as though the floor itself was responding to the energy of the room.

Multi-coloured banners hung high in the vast space, rippling gently despite the still air. Floating lanterns shaped like miniature moons drifted lazily above the crowd, their light creating a glow of tranquillity. Clara stood near the entrance, her breath catching as she took in the sight. It felt as though the hall had been designed to hold not just dances, but memories.

Her gaze lingered on the Everflame Torch, which stood tall at the far end of the room. The flame shifted from gold and red to a rippling blue, the same colour as the candle she had lit earlier.

A strange sensation crept over her skin, as though she were standing at the edge of a vast unseen current, something just beyond reach.

She took a step closer.

"Clara?" Ellie nudged her shoulder, snapping her out of her daze.

The flame had returned to normal.

Clara exhaled. Maybe she was imagining things.

Before she could dwell on it, movement caught her eye. A flash of red darted beneath a table, disappearing behind the curtains.

A small creature popped out into the open, its spiky red hair bobbing as it crept towards an unsuspecting boy on the dance floor. With a swift tug, it yanked on his robe, making him stumble. The creature let out a raspy cackle before vanishing under a nearby table.

"You are looking at a dorrig," a girl beside her said, adjusting the ribbon in her hair. "Mischievous little fae. Harmless, but they live for chaos."

Another dorrig scurried past, snatching a pastry. Clara hesitated before offering a piece of cake to one near her. It snatched it with a dramatic bow.

"Thank you kindly," it said in a deep voice.

Clara blinked. "You can talk?"

"Talk, laugh, and cause a bit of harmless trouble," it replied. "It is what we do best."

With a gleeful cackle, the dorrig pounded on the enchanted drums, turning the waltz into a lively jig. Students stumbled, laughter rippling through the hall.

Professor Thorn appeared near the stage, his sharp gaze sweeping the hall. With a clap of his hands, he addressed the creatures. "Off with you before you cause the floor to start spinning."

With playful bows and grins, the dorrigs retreated. Clara exhaled, watching the Everflame Torch. For all its grandeur, Crowstone still held surprises.

But it was starting to truly feel like home.

The students danced and laughed, the music weaving through the hall like a spell of its own. Magic shimmered in the air, dresses and suits catching the light in ever-changing colour, while enchanted lanterns floated above with their golden glow. The Hall of Echoes teemed with life, the energy of the night carrying them forwards in a perfect balance of elegance and chaos.

As the final song played, Clara glanced around at her friends, Ellie laughing as Finn tried an overly dramatic twirl, Amelia gracefully weaving through the crowd, Leo leaning against a pillar with a rare contented smile. The warmth of the moment wrapped around her like a cloak.

It had been an incredible night, the perfect end to an unforgettable term. Whatever challenges lay ahead, for now, she was exactly where she was meant to be.

Chapter 35: Parting Gifts and Gratitude

The next day, before they were all due to leave, Clara sat with Finn, Ellie, Amelia, and Leo in their usual corner of the Luminaris common room. The air was filled with anticipation for the holidays.

"Before we leave," Clara began nervously, "I have something for you all."

Finn perked up immediately. "Presents? Clara, you shouldn't have!"

"Don't make a big deal out of it," she said, laughing as she pulled small wrapped packages from her bag. "I just wanted to say thank you for being amazing friends."

She handed each of them their gift, encouraging them to open them right away.

Ellie's eyes widened as she unwrapped the charm bracelet. "It's beautiful, Clara. Thank you." She clipped it on, watching the glowing charms sparkle.

Amelia unwrapped her notebook, her eyes lighting up as she ran her fingers over the shimmering cover. "An enchanted notebook? Infinite pages? This is perfect! I can't wait to use it for studying."

Finn received enchanted dice and laughed as a miniature dragon roared and vanished in smoke. "Clara, they're brilliant. Thank you."

Leo studied his gift, a compass, its needle settling before he smiled softly. "This means a lot. Thanks."

She smiled back, feeling warmth spread through her. "You all mean so much to me. I just wanted to show it."

Ellie and Amelia exchanged glances before reaching into their bags.

"We got you something too," Amelia said, handing Clara a neatly wrapped package.

Clara unwrapped a beautiful quill set from Ellie, its feather shining in colourful tones. From Amelia, she received a sleek case of ink pots that adjusted to any parchment.

"These are perfect," Clara said, her voice thick with emotion. "Thank you."

After a final laugh, they hugged goodbye, promising to write over the break.

"Don't have too much fun without me," Finn called, earning Clara's grin. "And don't cause trouble without me!"

*

Clara made her way to Professor Moonsong's office, knocking on the door.

"Clara, I thought you would've left by now," Professor Moonsong said, setting aside a scroll.

"I wanted to give you this," Clara said, offering the small wrapped package.

Professor Moonsong unwrapped it, revealing a crystal globe that shimmered with starbursts inside. She turned it in her hands, watching the swirling patterns of constellations shift beneath the glass.

"It's beautiful, Clara. Thank you."

Clara blushed, fidgeting with her hands. "I mean it, Professor. I don't think I would've made it through this term without you. You helped me deal with ... everything."

Setting the globe down, Professor Moonsong placed a hand on Clara's shoulder. "You have faced your fears and grown so much. That takes real courage. I am proud of you."

Clara smiled, feeling a swell of gratitude and pride. "Thank you, Professor. I'll see you next term. Have a wonderful time with your family."

The corridors were quiet as Clara made her way back to her room, her fingers brushing against the enchanted quill set in her pocket. A week ago, she had been counting the days until the holidays. Now, as she passed the flickering lanterns that lined the hall, she found herself wishing she had just a little more time.

Pushing open her door, she stepped inside and froze.

A small figure sat curled up on her pillow, its wispy form shifting with soft violet-blue light. Its round eyes blinked at her, wide and watchful.

Clara inhaled sharply. "You again!"

The loddlewight, Wisp, tilted its head, then launched itself at her in a flurry of glowing limbs. Before she could react, it wrapped itself around her, pressing its tiny body into her chest.

Clara stood completely still as Wisp hugged her.

Tentatively, she brought her arms around it, feeling nothing but the faintest hum of warmth, like catching the edge of a spell. "Where did you come from?" she whispered.

Wisp burrowed into her arms, trembling slightly. It felt … relieved. Like it had been waiting for her.

She glanced towards the door, half expecting someone to explain why a loddlewight had taken up residence in her room. No one came.

Wisp shifted, looking up at her with an expression far too knowing for something so small. Then, just as suddenly as it had clung to her, it darted away, vanishing into the shadows beneath her bed.

Clara blinked. "Wait …" She knelt, peering under, but there was nothing. Just the quiet crackle of the enchanted lantern on her desk.

Her heartbeat slowed, though the warmth of the embrace lingered.

Something told her she had not seen the last of the loddlewight.

As she left her room, she smiled faintly. Crowstone still had its mysteries.

And, for once, she was in no rush to solve them.

Chapter 36: A Magical Christmas

Snow fell softly over the huge grounds of Nightfall Manor, blanketing the towering trees and winding pathways in a thick untouched white. The lanterns along the manor's entrance glowed against the ancient stone walls.

Clara peered out of the carriage window as the Moondancer glided smoothly over the snowy landscape. The creatures, silver coats shimmering, pulled them effortlessly through the winter air. She could barely feel the carriage move beneath her, the ride as smooth as drifting through a dream.

Across from her, her dad sat bundled in a thick coat, his arms crossed tightly. He had been silent for most of the journey, his expression unreadable.

"You alright?" Clara asked, tilting her head.

Her dad let out a slow breath, his gaze flickering towards Nightfall Manor looming ahead. "I'm still wrapping my head around the fact that I'm actually doing this."

Clara bit her lip. She knew this wasn't easy for him. He knew very little about the magical world, and now he was about to step through the doors of a world he would never belong in.

"I promise, if they act like snobs, I'll spell them," Clara said lightly.

Her dad huffed a quiet laugh. "You get that adorable temper from your mother."

The carriage slowed, and before Clara could respond, the doors swung open on their own. A rush of cool air met her as she stepped out onto the snowy path leading to the manor. The towering doors opened, revealing the grand, candlelit entrance hall, where her grandparents stood waiting.

Her grandmother was the first to greet them, her deep emerald robes flowing as she stepped forward. She surprised Clara by pulling her dad into a brief hug. "Jeff," she said softly, "thank you for coming."

Jeff looked utterly thrown. "Uh, yeah. Thanks for inviting me."

Her grandfather, though more reserved, gave her dad a nod of acknowledgment. "We appreciate the effort," he said, though his tone remained measured.

Clara, not wanting to break the moment of politeness, quickly changed the subject. "I almost forgot how beautiful the manor is."

And it was. Garlands of enchanted holly lined the walls, while flickering snow-lit chandeliers hung from the ceiling, their glow shifting between purple and gold. The scent of warm spiced ale and roasted chestnuts filled the air, and soft music played from instruments playing independently near the staircase.

"It should be," Selene said with a hint of pride. "The winter feast is a tradition, and this year, it is in your honour."

Clara blinked. "My honour?"

Eldric nodded. "It is your first winter feast being part of the magical world and at the manor. It is ... significant."

Clara's dad gave her a look but said nothing.

Before the conversation could drift into tense territory, her grandmother smiled and gestured towards the grand staircase. "Come, we should get ready. Dinner will begin soon."

*

As they took their seats in the Grand Dining Hall, Clara noticed a mix of unfamiliar faces: extended relatives, members of old magical houses, people who had likely once known her mother. They all watched her with keen interest, though no one dared to say anything outright.

Eldric sat at the head of the table, his presence commanding but not overbearing. "Tonight," he began, lifting his goblet, "we celebrate family, old and new. We honour those who came before us and those who will carry our legacy forward." His piercing gaze met Clara's. "To Clara, may she find her path within this world."

A murmur of agreement rippled along the table as the guests raised their glasses. Clara hesitated, then lifted hers as well.

The meal was nothing short of magical, with succulent meats roasted with enchanted herbs, bread that remained warm no matter how long it sat, and desserts that sparkled with frost-kissed sugar. Clara caught her dad sneaking extra portions of honeyed pastries, clearly won over despite his earlier reservations.

To her surprise, the conversation flowed with relative ease. Her grandmother kept her dad engaged with light-hearted questions, while her grandfather, though still somewhat formal, made an effort to acknowledge his presence. The tension Clara had braced for never fully arrived.

As the meal wound down, gifts were exchanged.

Clara's grandmother clasped a silver bracelet with volcanic charms onto Clara's wrist. "For protection," she murmured, her expression unreadable.

Clara's dad handed her a small neatly wrapped box. Inside was a brand-new iPhone.

Clara grinned, ignoring the slight look of disapproval from her grandparents. "Thank you, Dad!" she said, hugging him tightly.

"I know it's not magical," her dad said with a chuckle, "but I figured you could use a little bit of home."

Clara then presented her own gifts.

For her dad, she handed over a gold pocket watch. When he opened the front, a shimmering hologram of Clara appeared, switching between different moments in their life: her as a child, them laughing at old board games, a memory of them watching fireworks together. "A little reminder of me, but it also doubles as a watch. It has a button which locks it as a watch, just in case anyone else opens it."

Her dad's throat bobbed as he stared at it. "You're amazing, love," he said, pulling her into a tight hug.

To her grandmother, Clara gifted a pair of elegant earrings that glowed in the candlelight.

For her grandfather, she presented an ornate monocle infused with a spell that revealed hidden texts.

Her grandfather turned the monocle in his hands, inspecting it carefully before nodding. "Thoughtful," he murmured, slipping it into his pocket. "Very thoughtful."

As the night wound down, Clara sat beside the roaring fireplace, sipping a mug of Metatayan hot chocolate while her dad marvelled over everything he had seen.

"Thanks for bringing me, Clara," her dad said, his voice quieter now. "I see why you love it."

Clara smiled. "It's even better with you here."

*

Later, as she lay in bed in her old room, listening to the distant hum of the manor's magic, she let herself sink into the warmth of the evening.

Clara felt she could belong in both worlds.

*

The next morning, long after the last embers in the fireplace had burned, Clara found herself drawn to the Hall of Mirrors.

Whilst she was back at the Manor, she could seek answers about her mother, answers she had somehow forgotten she desired while she had been at Crowstone.

The oak door stood before her. She reached for the handle, then stepped inside, where the mirrors stretched endlessly around her, their ornate frames glowing in the faint light.

Clara had only been here once before, but even then, she had felt the Hall's watchful presence, its quiet demand for truth. Her boots echoed as she stepped further inside.

The largest mirror stood before her, its surface shifting like water disturbed by an unseen force. Clara's pulse quickened as she stepped closer, her chest tightening with a feeling she couldn't name. She had already seen glimpses of her mam's past within it, but this time, she wasn't waiting for answers to come to her.

She stopped before the mirror, looking at her own reflection. Her breath curled in the cold air.

"I need to know," she whispered.

As Clara's reflection disappeared in the mirror, a voice stirred, wrapping around her like an unseen thread of magic.

Clara exhaled slowly, letting the words settle in the quiet air of the Hall of Mirrors.

A name once whispered, now feared by all,
A shadow that lingers, though chains may fall.
He does not seek, yet always finds,
The lost, the broken, the chained binds.

The rhyme twisted through her mind like a puzzle half-formed, its meaning just out of reach.

"A name once whispered, now feared by all," she murmured, rolling the phrase over in her thoughts. "Someone who wasn't always feared. Someone who … changed."

A creeping unease curled through her. Whoever this was, their name had once been spoken in trust, in respect, until something happened.

Her fingers curled into fists as she worked through the next line.

"A shadow that lingers, though chains may fall …"

Chains. The word sent a chill through her.

"That means he was locked up," she muttered. "Imprisoned. But he's free now."

Her breath quickened. The mirror wasn't warning her about someone from history; it was speaking of now.

"He does not seek, yet always finds …"

That made no sense. If someone wasn't searching, how could they keep finding?

Unless.

Clara's breath caught.

"He doesn't need to seek," she muttered, "because what he wants always comes to him."

A sickening thought settled in her chest.

"What does that even mean? That people, power, whatever he's after, it just … finds its way back to him?" She shivered, stepping away from the mirror.

Her mind turned to the final line.

"The lost, the broken, the chained binds."

Lost. Broken. Chained.

"He's not just powerful," she whispered. "He's bound to something. Or someone."

The thought made her stomach lurch.

A shadow that lingers. A name once whispered. A man who didn't need to search because his past, his power, his claim on the world, whatever it was, always found its way back to him.

Her heart pounded as realisation clicked into place, piece by piece.

This wasn't just some dark figure in history.

This was someone still out there.

Her breath came faster, her fingers trembling at her sides. She didn't know his name yet, but she knew this:

The Dark Wizard wasn't a forgotten relic of the past.

He had never truly left. "The Dark Wizard." Clara whispered.

The mirror shuddered, its surface twisting. Her reflection blurred, reforming into an image she had seen before: her mother, younger, her hands resting gently on Clara's small shoulders, a soft smile on her face.

The image cracked.

Shards of light scattered across the mirror's surface like a shattered window, dissolving into the shadows beneath. A voice, soft and low, echoed through the chamber.

You seek the truth
though it brings no peace
Ask your question
but beware its release.

Clara swallowed against the tightness in her throat. "I want to know about my mam. Why did she leave the magical world? And ..." She hesitated, the weight of her next words pressing against her chest. "Who is Therin, and what did he do to my mother?"

The mirror recoiled violently, its surface rippling in waves. The air around her turned icy, pressing in like unseen hands. Her breath came sharp and shallow as the mirror began to clear once more.

A forest appeared from the swirling light, dense and shrouded in mist. Clara's mother stood at its centre, her hair loose over her shoulders, her face tight with worry. She clutched something small and faintly glowing in her hands, her grip firm despite the fear in her eyes.

Clara moved closer. "Mam …"

The scene shifted. Her mother was running now, breath coming in ragged bursts. Shadows twisted and surged behind her, moving unnaturally, like vines of ink spilling through the air. At the centre of them stood a man.

His face was obscured, but his eyes burned violet, twin flames cutting through the darkness.

The scene dissolved, replaced by another: a nursery, dimly lit, her mother kneeling beside a crib. Clara's tiny form lay inside, bundled in soft blankets. Her mother's hands trembled as she clasped a small silver necklace around her neck.

"This will keep her safe," she whispered, her voice breaking. Tears streaked her face as she pressed a desperate kiss to her baby's forehead. "Please let her be safe."

Clara's fingers instinctively reached for her neck, grasping at the empty space where her necklace had once rested.

A shield from whoever was chasing her.

The mirror flickered again, showing her mother standing before an older man with sharp features and silver-streaked hair. Clara recognised him from the portraits in the manor.

Her great-grandfather.

His mouth moved in urgent words she could not hear, his expression grave. Her mother stood frozen, her face pale, hands clenched at her sides.

The image shifted once more.

The shadows returned, unfurling like storm clouds as Therin Shadowthorn stood at their centre. His hands stretched towards the sky, dark power coiling around him like living smoke. Though the image was silent, Clara could almost hear it: magic humming in the air, the whispers of something ancient, powerful, and wrong.

Then came the final image.

Her great-grandfather lay motionless, his robes darkened with blood. Her mother stood nearby, staring in horror, her body trembling as though she were barely holding herself together. And Therin, he stood above them both, watching with unreadable eyes, his violet gaze glowing through the shadows.

Realisation crashed into Clara.

Her mother had once loved him, Therin Shadowthorn, and he was the Dark Wizard.

That was why her grandmother never wanted to speak of it. That was why this secret had been buried.

Therin Shadowthorn had not only been part of their family's past; he had once been close to her mother, someone she had trusted. Someone who had become corrupted by darkness and shadows.

And he had killed Clara's great-grandfather.

The mirror went still, and her own reflection returned, staring back at her with wide haunted eyes.

The silence pressed against her ears.

She backed away, her thoughts spinning, her breath

coming in shallow bursts. The Dark Wizard wasn't just a distant threat; he was entwined with her family, a shadow that had never truly left.

And if the mirror's warning was true, he would come for her.

Not as an enemy.

As something far more dangerous.

A flicker in the glass caught her eye. She turned just in time to see his violet-eyed reflection standing in place of her own, his lips curved into the faintest of smiles.

And then he was gone.

*

Clara lay in bed, staring at the ceiling, her mind too restless to settle. Outside, the snowfall had slowed to a quiet drift, the world beyond the manor still and untouched. But inside her head, the storm had only just begun.

The riddle echoed in her mind, threading itself through every thought.

The Dark Wizard was a real threat. He had been imprisoned. And now he was free.

And her mother had feared him.

That was what unsettled her the most. Helena Nightfall, the woman Clara barely remembered, had once shared a love with this man until darkness consumed him. Her mam had run. She had chosen to leave magic behind, to build a life in the non-magical world rather than be anywhere near this danger. Was her family in danger? Was she?

She sat up, shoving the blankets aside and swinging her legs over the edge of the bed. The cold air nipped at her skin, but she barely noticed.

If her family refused to talk, she'd find the answers elsewhere.

She could talk to her friends, Finn, Leo, Ellie, and Amelia. They had solved problems before. But this wasn't just another hidden puzzle in Crowstone's corridors. This was something bigger.

A professor, then. Someone who had been at Crowstone long enough to remember the truth. Someone who wouldn't dismiss her or fob her off with half-answers.

Professor Moonsong.

Clara's heartbeat steadied. If anyone could be trusted, it was her.

She lay back down, staring into the darkness. Her mind still raced, but now it had direction. She wasn't going to let this fade into silence. She wouldn't let this become another secret swallowed by time.

Chapter 37: Shadows of the Passed

The Luminaris common room offered a welcome refuge from January's chill. Snow clung to the arched windows, and the fire crackled cheerfully. Students returned from winter break, swapping stories and laughter as the room filled with familiar energy.

Clara sat with her friends near the fire, their usual corner alive with laughter. Finn sprawled across the comfiest armchair, Ellie adjusted her charm bracelet, Amelia scribbled notes in her enchanted notebook, and Leo toyed with his compass in quiet thought.

"I missed you all," Clara said warmly. "Christmas was nice with my family, but I definitely missed you."

Finn tossed a cushion her way with a grin. "Don't get too emotional, Clara. You'll ruin my image as the strong, silent type."

Ellie rolled her eyes. "Strong, silent type? They're the last words I'd use to describe you."

Everyone laughed, the sound filling the common room with an ease that Clara hadn't realised she'd missed so much.

The group spent the rest of the evening catching up, sharing stories of their holidays. Finn recounted a disastrous attempt at baking with his siblings, which had ended with half the kitchen coated in flour. Ellie had visited her grandparents and brought back a tin of enchanted chocolates that changed flavour with each bite. Amelia proudly showed off her notebook, already half-filled with plans for study sessions and research projects.

Leo, however, remained unusually quiet, his attention repeatedly drifting back to Clara. She noticed but decided not to say anything.

As the fire crackled and the evening wore on, Clara felt a renewed sense of purpose. She had survived her first term at Crowstone and was ready to tackle whatever challenges the new year would bring.

Clara had considered talking to her friends about what she learned, but something stopped her. She wasn't sure what it was, but she decided to listen to it, for now at least.

*

The first day of lessons flew by, Clara in a daze from the information she had learned about her mam. She tried to suppress it to concentrate in class, but it kept niggling at her as though it needed her attention. As the final class of the day, Runes and Glyphs, finished, the classroom emptied, leaving only the rustle of parchment and the distant sound of voices from the corridor. Clara lingered at her desk, her fingers tracing the edge of her book, though she barely noticed. There was something in the air, something expectant.

Professor Ashwood remained seated behind her desk, her glasses resting beside a stack of old scrolls. She exhaled slowly before speaking, as if she had carried the weight of this conversation for years.

"Clara," she said at last, her voice quieter than usual. "There's something I need to tell you. I am not sure how much you know already, but I felt it was right you had all the information, given the potential dangers ahead."

Clara hesitated. The shift in the professor's tone sent a strange, uneasy flutter through her stomach.

Ashwood studied her for a moment, then leaned forwards slightly. "I knew your mother."

Clara stiffened.

"Helena Nightfall was one of my brightest students,"

Ashwood continued. "Brilliant, kind, fiercely loyal. She had a way of seeing the best in people … even if they didn't deserve it. We stayed in touch long after she left school. Right up until she left the magical world behind." A small sad smile crossed her face. "When she left *him*."

Clara already knew who she meant, but she asked anyway, as if saying his name aloud would make it easier to believe. "Therin Shadowthorn?"

The professor nodded. "They were happy once. For a time, at least. She believed in him, even when others doubted. She thought she could help him, guide him. And for a while, I think she did."

Clara swallowed, her stomach twisting. She had imagined her mother as distant, unknowable, someone forever out of reach. But to hear she had once loved the man who had become the most feared wizard of their time, it made the past feel too close.

"He was ambitious," Ashwood continued, her gaze darkening. "But that ambition was never just for power. He wanted knowledge. Ancient magic. The kind that was lost for a reason."

Clara's fingers curled against the edge of her desk. "Did my mam know the dangers of ancient magic?"

"She did, and she warned him not to meddle with things he could never truly understand," Ashwood said softly, "and the potential dangers of doing so."

Clara exhaled, already dreading the next words. "So, he ignored my mam's warnings and put himself … and everyone else in danger?"

Ashwood nodded. "He had been searching for years until he eventually found an old cave, lost to time. There were wards, protections; perhaps he figured out a way to bypass them, or perhaps they had withered with time."

She hesitated, choosing her words carefully. "When Therin used the ancient magic written on the scroll … it changed him."

A chill crept up Clara's spine. "How did it change him?"

"The magic didn't just grant him ancient power. It fed on him. His worst thoughts, his deepest fears, his darkest impulses: it turned them into something greater, something monstrous. Half the witches and wizards that wield ancient magic are consumed by darkness, by shadows. That magic was never meant for our kind. Therin reached a point of no return. The man your mother loved was gone forever."

The quiet that followed was thick with unspoken things.

Ashwood rose from her chair and moved towards the window. Outside, the last light of day stretched thin against the horizon. "As the darkness corrupted and consumed all that was good, it gave him the thirst for power. He began looking for more ancient magic," she said. "The magic he learned was never enough. One victory was never enough. He then learned the truth about your family."

Clara felt her pulse quicken. "What truth?"

"The Nightfalls are the Keepers of Ancient Magic," Ashwood said, turning back to face her. "Your family doesn't just protect knowledge; they guard it. When Therin realised that Alaric Nightfall, your great-grandfather, was the last protector, he confronted Alaric. He demanded the truth. Demanded to know where it had all been hidden." She paused, her gaze dark. "Alaric refused."

A cold weight settled over Clara.

"He stood his ground," Ashwood said. "He told Therin that some knowledge was never meant to be wielded and that the cost was too great, and he refused to tell him where it was hidden." Her expression turned solemn. "So Therin killed him."

Clara's breath left her in a sharp, disbelieving gasp. She had learned some of this from Fenwick and from the Hall of Mirrors, but to hear it all pieced together like a complex jigsaw stunned her.

"What he didn't realise at the time was that most of the ancient magic contained in scrolls and relics was protected by blood," Ashwood said. "Without the Nightfalls, he struggled to gain what his dark heart desired."

Clara barely heard the next words.

"But your mother," Ashwood's expression darkened. "She went after him."

Clara's fingers tightened against the desk. She had already seen it, her mother standing against Therin.

"She wasn't just trying to stop him," Ashwood said. "She wanted revenge."

"Your mother tracked him down," Ashwood said. "She fought him. But by then, he was too powerful. The ancient magic had already warped him, made him something far beyond what she could face alone. She barely escaped with her life."

Clara's hands curled into fists.

"She knew then that she would never be safe," Ashwood continued. "Not while he was still out there. So, she did the only thing she could: she disappeared."

A lump formed in Clara's throat.

"She left the magical world behind," Ashwood said. "She had always been gifted with concealment charms. This time, she made sure no one, especially Therin, would ever find her."

Silence stretched between them.

Finally, Ashwood spoke again, her voice quieter now. "So, you see, Clara … if Therin Shadowthorn has returned, you could be in danger."

Clara's heart pounded. "Why me?"

"Because you're a Nightfall," Ashwood said simply.

Clara shook her head. "But I don't know anything about ancient magic. Even if my family guards it, I know nothing about it."

"He may think otherwise," Ashwood interrupted. "Or … maybe you do know. On some level." Her voice dropped lower, carrying something heavier than a warning. "The magic is tied to your blood, Clara. It may respond to you whether you understand it or not."

A slow, creeping unease settled over Clara.

"So, if he can't access the ancient magic," she whispered, "he may come after me instead."

Ashwood didn't answer.

She didn't need to.

Clara already knew the truth.

Chapter 38: The Locked Tower and Whispers in the Shadows

Clara, Finn, and a small group of Luminaris students were making their way back to the tower after a long day of lessons when they spotted Leo standing outside the shimmering silverstone archway, his expression dark and frustrated.

"You're not going in, then?" Finn asked, raising an eyebrow as they approached.

"I would, but it's not working," Leo muttered, tapping his thumb and finger together in that fidgety way he had. "Apparently, it's a little temperamental at times."

Finn tilted his head, his eyes narrowing. "Temperamental? That's a new one. We've never heard of that happening before. Are you sure ..." He paused dramatically, grinning. "Are you sure you belong in Luminaris?"

Leo stepped back, his face drained of colour, and for a brief moment, he looked genuinely terrified. His hand dropped from the rune panel as he glanced quickly between Clara and Finn, his mouth opening as if to say something.

"Only joking!" Finn added quickly, his grin softening. "We know you belong here, really. Here, move out of the way, I'll get us all in."

Leo's shoulders visibly relaxed, and a faint smile played at the corners of his lips. "Thanks," he muttered, stepping aside.

Finn pressed his palm to the rune panel. The glowing runes responded immediately, flaring with silvery light before the door swung open. "See? No issues," Finn said, glancing at Leo. "But maybe have a word with Professor Nightbloom about this. I'm sure no one else wants to get stuck out here."

"Yeah, I'll do that," Leo said, but he didn't sound entirely convincing.

Clara watched him as they filed into the tower, a flicker of curiosity sparking in her mind. She didn't know why, but something about the way Leo had reacted unsettled her. He did belong. He had been in Luminaris since the start of school. Perhaps he was just embarrassed about getting stuck.

*

The next day, a strange tension settled over Crowstone Academy, a quiet unease creeping through its ancient halls. Clara first noticed it during breakfast in the Great Solstice Hall when she overheard hushed conversations between students from other houses. The usual chatter about classes and house points had been replaced with murmurs of something far more unsettling.

"Did you hear what happened in the Archive Hall?" one student whispered, glancing around nervously.

Another nodded, lowering their voice. "The glass casings were shattered. Some of the relics were disturbed, like someone was searching for something specific."

Clara turned to Finn and Leo, her brow wrinkled. "The Archive Hall?"

Finn exhaled sharply, pushing his plate aside. "That's not just some section of Crowstone. It's where they keep historical magical texts, stuff they don't trust students to handle without supervision."

Leo, sitting across from them, tapped his thumb and finger together absently. "I overheard a prefect saying someone was spotted near the Archive Hall after hours. They think it might have been one of us sneaking out."

Clara's stomach churned at the implication. The

Archive Hall was restricted, reserved only for the most trusted students under staff supervision. Whoever had broken in hadn't just been careless; they had been desperate.

*

Later that day, Clara and Ellie found themselves outside the Archive Hall, their curiosity outweighing their hesitation. The grand double doors, usually warded with layers of protective enchantments, stood ajar, an unsettling sight, with Professor Mornvale pacing the hall.

Clara and Ellie stood behind a large pillar, peering into the long chamber, which was lined with glass display cases, each holding ancient scrolls and relics of magical history. Normally, the protective charms over the cases shimmered faintly, a constant reminder of their security.

Now, several of them lay shattered.

Fragments of glass glinted on the polished floor, and a few scrolls were partially unrolled, their edges torn as if someone had rifled through them in haste.

Professor Darnell stood near the largest damaged display, his wand drawn, examining the destruction with a sharp, calculating gaze. His expression was a mix of frustration and concern.

"Who would do this?" Clara murmured, stepping closer to Ellie.

Ellie shook her head. "It's like they weren't just causing damage. They were looking for something."

Professor Ainsley appeared from nowhere. "Miss Nightfall, Miss Sharma … back to class, please.

They both looked at the floor as they walked off, feeling the shame of snooping and being caught.

*

By the time dinner rolled around, the tension in the Great Solstice Hall was thick, bearing down on the students. At the head of the room, Professor Mornvale stood, her usual composed demeanour overshadowed by sternness.

The Orb brightened as Professor Mornvale spoke. "Students," she began, her voice cutting through the murmur of conversation, "There has been a breach of the Archive Hall. It occurred last night. Historical texts and relics were disturbed, and protective enchantments were forcibly broken."

A ripple of unease spread through the room. Clara caught a few students exchanging wary glances, some whispering behind their hands.

"Accessing restricted areas, destruction of property, and theft will not only mean expulsion for those responsible, but also punishment by the Magical Assembly," Mornvale continued, her gaze sweeping over the hall. "Those responsible for this reckless act have not only violated academy rules but have shown blatant disregard for the preservation of magical history. Some of those relics were thousands of years old."

Her eyes flickered, just for a moment, towards the Luminaris table. Clara tensed, her stomach twisting uncomfortably. The accusation was unspoken but clear.

"I remind you all that the rules of Crowstone exist to ensure the safety of every student," Mornvale went on. "Anyone caught breaking curfew or tampering with protected relics will face serious consequences."

As she finished speaking, the banners overhead flickered slightly, as if reflecting the sombre mood of the hall.

*

Back in the Luminaris common room, Clara, Finn, and Leo sat by the fire, the tension from the day still hanging over them.

"It's not fair," Clara said, breaking the silence. "Just because someone was spotted near the Archive Hall doesn't mean it was one of us."

Finn leaned back in his chair, his usual humour absent. "Doesn't matter what people think. I just hope it wasn't one of us."

Leo, who had been uncharacteristically quiet, finally spoke. "Maybe it's not about who's sneaking out, but why. What are they looking for?"

Clara considered this. The broken cases, the missing relics, the strange sense of magic still clinging to the air: it all pointed to someone searching for something important. But what could be so valuable, so urgent, that they would risk expulsion and punishment from the Magical Assembly?

"We'll just have to keep our eyes open," Clara said firmly. "Whoever it is, even if they belong to our House, they need stopping."

As the fire crackled, they sat in silence, each lost in thought. The shadows in Crowstone seemed darker than usual, and Clara couldn't shake the feeling that something serious was about to happen

Chapter 39: The Crow's Gaze

It began with a fleeting shadow, a whisper of black wings in Clara's peripheral vision as she crossed the courtyard of Crowstone Academy. She paused, glancing over her shoulder, but saw nothing unusual. Shrugging it off as a trick of the light, she continued towards the Great Solstice Hall, her thoughts drifting towards the strange disturbances at the Archive Hall as well as her conversation with Professor Ashwood. She had decided not to tell her friends, not yet anyway. Everyone keeps secrets about their family, she thought. And this was a huge secret, her mam's connection to the Dark Wizard. But just as she reached the stone archway, she saw it again: a black crow perched on top of one the carved statues overlooking the courtyard, watching her with an unnervingly intense gaze.

A faint chill prickled over Clara's skin. It wasn't just the way the crow stared; it was the sense that it somehow seemed to *know* her, in a way no ordinary bird should.

It was larger than the usual birds that circled Crowstone's spires, its feathers sleek and dark, appearing almost blue in the late afternoon light. Its sharp black eyes followed her every movement, unblinking. She hesitated for a moment before giving it a small nod, as if acknowledging its presence might ease the tension. But as she walked through the archway, the feeling of being watched stayed with her, heavy and unsettling.

*

The next day, she saw it again, perched on the stone railing outside the Luminaris Tower. This time, it was even closer. Clara paused mid-step, gripping the strap of her bag, and the crow moved its head slightly, as though it were waiting for something.

"Alright, that's odd," she muttered under her breath.

The crow didn't flinch at the sound of her voice. Instead, it continued to observe her with its eerie, unwavering gaze.

At lunch, she brought it up with her friends, hoping they'd laugh it off.

"A crow?" Leo asked, his expression sharpening. "And it's been watching you?"

Clara nodded. "Yeah, and not just once. I keep seeing it everywhere. It's like it's … following me."

Finn raised an eyebrow. "That's weird. I'm sure crows don't usually attach themselves to people, and they're not exactly the friendliest birds either. Are you sure it's the same one? I mean, they all look pretty much exactly the same."

Ellie frowned slightly. "Crows are clever, but they don't tend to fixate on people. If it keeps watching you, perhaps there's a connection, magical or otherwise."

Leo leaned back. "Maybe it just thinks you're fascinating, Nightfall. Birds have good taste, and Nightfalls are interesting," he said, but there was something guarded in his tone.

"There's something about its eyes," Clara said. "It's like it's looking *through* me."

Amelia and Finn exchanged a glance. Amelia leaned in slightly, lowering her voice. "Crows are tied to the Morrigan, an ancient goddess of war and fate," she said. "In magical lore, they're omens, sometimes of danger. If it's her crow, it's not just a bird. It's watching you for a reason."

Clara felt a prickling at the back of her neck. "An omen? What does that mean for me? Am I in danger or what?"

"Yeah, I remember reading something about this. It depends," Finn said, his usual grin subdued. "Some believe a crow watching you is a warning, especially before something dangerous happens. Others think they're guides, protecting you through uncertain times. But it's never without purpose. If the Morrigan's crow has chosen you, there's definitely a reason."

"Did anyone hear what Finn just said? He's been reading? Now we know that can't be true," Ellie said with a huge grin.

Clara forced a laugh, though she didn't feel much like laughing. "Great. So now I have a supernatural stalking bird." But as soon as the words left her mouth, she couldn't shake the feeling that this was not a joke. The crow's gaze lingered in her mind, its presence that she couldn't quite explain.

Leo's voice was quiet. "I would just ignore it, Clara. Superstitions are usually just nonsense."

The group drifted to their own thoughts, Clara wondering why things kept happening to her.

*

Over the next few days, the crow's presence became impossible to ignore. No matter where she went, it was there, perched outside the dining hall, waiting near the greenhouse when she passed by, watching her from the ledge of the Grand Staircase. Even during lessons, she spotted it outside the window, perched atop a tower, its gaze locked onto her through the glass.

By the fourth day, she had had enough.

At dusk, just as the sun began to set, she spotted it again, this time on the outskirts of the academy, perched on a gnarled branch beyond the Botanical Gardens.

Clara made her way towards it, her steps steady

despite the knot forming in her stomach.

The crow watched her approach, unblinking. It did not move or caw. It simply waited.

She stopped a few feet away, crossing her arms. "Alright," she said quietly, "why are you following me?"

For a moment, the world seemed to still. The distant sounds of the academy, the rustling of leaves, even the faint murmur of students in the halls: they all faded into silence.

Then, to her surprise, the crow tilted its head, as if acknowledging her question. It spread its wings and lifted into the air, gliding in a slow, deliberate circle before landing a few feet away, closer to the entrance of the restricted Archive Hall.

Clara frowned. "You want me to follow you?"

The crow cawed softly.

Against her better judgment, she did.

The sky darkened as Clara approached the Archive Hall, the last remnants of daylight sinking behind Crowstone's towering spires. The grand doors loomed before her, their brass decorations shimmering as the warding spells wove a web of protection across the entrance. Ever since the break-in, the enchantments had been reinforced, their magic thrumming through the air like an unseen barrier.

The crow landed on the railing beside her, its talons clicking against the ancient stone. It watched her with that same unreadable intensity, its dark eyes reflecting the fading light.

Clara hesitated, then took a deep breath. "Do you know who broke in?"

The crow let out a low, deliberate caw, its voice rasping through the silence.

A strange sensation crawled over Clara's skin, a whisper of unease that set her pulse quickening. The air around her felt heavier, charged with something unseen, something watching.

She turned back to the bird, her voice barely above a whisper. "You know who it was, don't you?"

The crow didn't respond. It simply held her gaze, its black feathers ruffling slightly as if stirred by an unseen wind.

Then, without warning, it snapped its head towards the far end of the courtyard. A sharp, urgent cry tore from its throat, its wings flaring wide.

Clara stiffened.

A shadow moved.

Just beyond the trembling lanterns that lined the pathway, something shifted between the trees. A figure, half-shrouded in the increasing dusk, lingering at the very edge.

Her breath caught in her throat. Someone was watching her.

The crow cawed again, more insistent this time, flapping its wings as if urging her to move.

Clara didn't hesitate. She stepped back from the Archive Hall, forcing herself to walk at a steady pace even as her instincts screamed at her to run. The presence in the darkness remained, like a silent warning.

She took one last glance at the crow. It was still watching her, still waiting.

And somehow, Clara knew, it had just saved her from something she wasn't ready to face.

*

Clara made her way to the Luminaris common room, her thoughts tangled as though caught in a spider's web. Her friends were gathered around the table, a half-finished game of Spellbinding Tiles in front of them. Finn would usually be loudly celebrating his victory, Leo would be pretending not to care, Ellie concentrating, determined to win, and Amelia would be commenting on their strategy, but tonight, the atmosphere was suppressed.

Clara hesitated, running her fingers along the edge of her sleeve. She wasn't sure how to start. It all felt too strange, too heavy to just blurt out.

"I need to tell you something," she finally said, her voice quieter than she intended.

The group stilled. Leo, who had been flipping one of the game pieces between his fingers, set it down. "What is it?"

Clara exhaled slowly. "The crow that's been following me. Watching me. Tonight … it led me to the Archive Hall."

Ellie frowned. "Led you?"

Clara nodded, feeling the intensity of their gazes. "I followed it to the entrance. The wards have been reinforced since the break-in, but … the crow was acting differently. Almost restless. Then it turned its head, like it was warning me. And that's when I saw someone. Watching me. Just standing there in the dark."

Amelia leaned forward, her expression sharp. "Who was it?"

"I have no idea," Clara admitted. "They were too far away, but they didn't move. They were just … standing there … staring. I realise you won't understand the reference, not growing up around Commonfolk, but it was like something out of a horror film, something sinister."

Finn let out a slow breath. "Yeah, I don't know what

that is, but it sounds creepy."

Leo's jaw tightened. "So, the crow was trying to protect you."

Ellie glanced between them. "But from what? Or who?"

"That's it, I don't know," Clara said, frustration creeping into her voice. "And that's why I'm telling you all. If the crow is tied to the Morrigan like Amelia said, then it's not just an ordinary bird. It's watching me for a reason. And whoever was outside the Archive Hall tonight … they were watching me too."

A heavy silence settled over them.

Amelia was the first to break it. "It's too much to ignore. The break-in, the crow, the shadow figure … they're connected. Someone is searching for something, and I don't think they want anyone else finding out what it is."

Finn tapped his fingers against his knee, deep in thought. "Which means if you're being watched, perhaps it's because you're getting too close to something."

Clara swallowed. She hadn't thought of it like that, but too close to what? She had no idea who had broken into the Archive Hall. The crow had been following her for days. What if it had been keeping something away?

Leo shifted, his usual guarded expression giving way to something darker. "You need to be careful. If this is a warning, I wouldn't go looking for trouble."

Clara looked at each of them, the seriousness in their faces mirroring her own. "But I think we need to figure it out," she said firmly. "Together."

Ellie nodded. "Agreed."

Amelia folded her arms. "We need to start with the Archive Hall. If someone's looking for something there, we should at least try to find out what it is."

Finn smirked, though the usual playfulness in his expression didn't quite reach his eyes. "Well, I was getting bored anyway."

Leo leaned back, rubbing his fingers together in thought. "I am just not sure it's a good idea to seek out creepy people hiding in the shadows. Maybe listen to the creepy bird trying to warn you. If the professors can't figure it out, how are we supposed to?"

Clara felt her tension ease slightly. She had no idea what she was caught up in, but at least she had her friends by her side.

But deep down, she knew something bad was going to happen.

Chapter 40: Pushing the Limits

Clara sat stiffly at her desk in Magical Defences, her wand clutched tightly in her hand. The air buzzed with energy as Professor Thornblade announced the day's exercise: paired duelling practice. The task was straightforward. One student would cast an offensive spell while the other defended themselves.

Straightforward, except Clara's stomach was twisting itself into knots.

"You'll be paired with Pippa Blackwood," Professor Thornblade announced to Clara as he stood there, tall, exuding strength. He was six feet six inches, with huge shoulders and hands like shovels. Fortunately for the students, he was soft as a kitten, the complete opposite of his stature.

Clara's heart sank. Pippa was fast, sharp, and ruthless, everything Clara wasn't when it came to defensive and offensive spells. Clara viewed it as a form of fighting, something she hated. Yes, this was in a controlled setting and was meant to teach them to protect themselves, but Clara could never respond quickly enough. The tall girl grinned as they stepped into position.

"Try not to embarrass yourself, Nightfall," Pippa sneered, raising her wand.

Clara forced herself to take a steadying breath. *Magic isn't just about power. It's about intention and control*, she remembered from her many lessons with Fenwick.

"Begin," Professor Thornblade commanded.

"Luas Tine!" Pippa shouted, sending a jet of fire barrelling towards Clara.

Clara's hand shot up. "Scáth Díon!" A faint shimmer of light flickered before her but collapsed instantly. The flames struck her square in the chest, knocking her backward. A sharp gasp escaped her lips as she hit the stone floor, her wand skittering from her grasp. Laughter rippled through the watching students.

"Oops. Did I go too hard?" Pippa said, feigning concern.

Clara scrambled to her feet, her cheeks burning with humiliation. She barely heard Professor Thornblade's reprimand over the rushing in her ears. Before she could stop herself, she grabbed her wand and ran out of the room.

*

Clara slumped against the cool stone wall of an empty corridor, her breath uneven. She felt useless. Pathetic. How was she supposed to survive at Crowstone if she couldn't even hold up a simple shield?

"Hey, Clara."

She jumped at the voice.

Leo stood a few feet away, hands in his pockets, his usual smirk softened with something that almost looked like concern. "Are you okay?" he asked.

She quickly wiped at her eyes. "I'm fine."

"Doesn't look like it," Leo said, crouching beside her. "You know, everyone struggles with certain spells. Even me."

Clara scoffed. "Right. Like you've ever messed up a spell."

"Plenty of times," Leo said with a grin. "But you don't get better by running away. You get better by pushing through. How about we train at the end of each day for half an hour just to hone those amazing skills you have hidden away?"

"You would train me?" Clara asked.

"Of course," Leo replied.

She glanced at Leo. "Alright. But don't go easy on me."

Leo grinned. "Wouldn't dream of it."

*

The next afternoon, Clara met Leo in the duelling grounds. The crisp air carried the scent of damp stone and fallen leaves. He stood with his arms crossed, his wand twirling between his fingers.

"You sure you're not signing up to a lost cause?" Clara asked.

"I'm sure. And honestly? You're stronger than you think. You just need to harness it properly."

She hesitated, glancing at him. "Harness it?"

Leo pulled something small from his pocket and opened his palm. Resting inside was a delicate silver bracelet, its surface engraved with runes.

"This will help you focus," he said, holding it out to her. "It'll make it easier to channel your magic, help you tap into your true potential."

Clara eyed the bracelet warily. "Are you sure?"

Leo nodded. "It helped me when I was learning control. It will help you channel that energy."

A part of her hesitated, but the sting of her failure in class still burned in her chest. She reached out and took the bracelet, the cool metal tingling against her skin. As soon as she fastened it around her wrist, a warmth spread through her arm, her magic settling in a way that felt … smoother.

"Right, let's get to it, shall we? Let's start with Scáth Díon," Leo said. "A shield isn't just a spell; it's something to help you stand your ground."

Clara raised her wand, trying to summon the

confidence she lacked. "Scáth Díon," she whispered, and a faint shimmer appeared. It was stronger than before; she could feel the warmth from the bracelet.

Leo stepped back, aiming his wand. "Don't flinch."

"Wait …" She barely had time to react before a spark of light shot towards her. She yelped, bracing for impact, but the shield held.

"That's more like it!" Leo said, clapping. "Let's do it again. Stronger this time."

They continued training, repeating the spell until Clara's arms ached. Each success brought a flicker of pride, but there was something else. Something beneath her skin, something in her magic that hadn't been there before.

*

Only days had passed, and Clara's progress had grown exponentially. Her spells were sharper, her reflexes quicker. The bracelet made it much easier; everything felt more precise, more natural.

But something about it nagged at her.

When she took it off, her magic felt sluggish, harder to control. And when she wore it, she felt … different. More focused, but also more restless. More determined, but also more impatient.

One afternoon, Finn saw her practising alone in the duelling grounds. His gaze flickered to the bracelet.

"What's that?"

Clara hesitated. "Leo gave it to me. It helps me focus."

Finn frowned. "Helps or does the work for you?"

She bristled. "It's not like that."

Finn crossed his arms. "Just be careful, Clara. Magic isn't just about strength. That thing on your wrist looks like it's ramping up your spells significantly. These things come at a cost."

She turned away, pretending not to hear him. But later that night, as she lay in bed staring at the faintly glowing runes, unease gnawed at her.

Leo had told her the bracelet helped her *harness* her potential.

So why did it feel like it was changing her instead?

*

A few days later, the duelling grounds were alive with energy from students in every year. There were clusters of students watching and taking part in friendly challenges. Spells sparked in the air, flashes of light illuminating the platform where Lucinda Vale stood, smirking triumphantly over her latest opponent. Her robes were pristine, her golden hair tied back neatly, not a single strand out of place.

"Unbeaten again," Lucinda declared loudly, her voice carrying over the crowd. She held her wand in her hand and had a smug glance at her friends, who clapped and cheered. "Is there anyone here brave enough to take me on?"

Clara stood off to the side with Finn, Leo, Ellie, and Amelia, watching the scene unfold.

"She's insufferable," Finn muttered, arms crossed. "I wouldn't duel with her. She's the best in the year."

Lucinda's sharp gaze swept the crowd, and when she spotted Clara, her smirk widened.

"Oh, look who it is, the Lost Witch," she said, loud enough for the students watching to hear. "Tell me, Clara Nightfall, do you have the courage to face me? Or are you afraid you might tarnish your family's reputation?"

Laughter rippled through Lucinda's entourage.

Clara clenched her fists. She could feel Finn shift

beside her, ready to whisper a warning, but Leo was faster.

"Why not?" Leo said, his voice casual yet edged with challenge. "You can take her, Clara. She's not as good as she thinks she is."

Clara hesitated. A duel was exactly the kind of situation where she'd struggled before, but this time was different. This time, she had trained. This time, she had the bracelet.

She lifted her head and stepped forward.

The crowd quietened down briefly before excitement erupted in the air. Lucinda's eyes gleamed as Clara climbed onto the platform.

"Oh, this will be fun," Lucinda said with a smirk.

Lucinda struck first. "Tine Lasrach!" she shouted, sending a bolt of fire racing towards Clara.

Clara reacted instantly. Her wand flicked up. "Sciath Uisce!" A shimmering wall of water rose before her, dousing the flames in midair. The heat never even reached her skin.

Lucinda's smile faltered, but she recovered quickly, following up with a blinding light charm, Solas Chaoch.

Clara narrowed her eyes, already moving. She flicked her wand, summoning a mirrorlike shield, Gaoth Guthmhar. Lucinda's spell rebounded off it, forcing her to duck as her own light flared back towards her.

A murmur went through the crowd.

Lucinda exhaled sharply, annoyance flashing in her eyes. She flicked her wrist, sending a gust of wind barrelling towards Clara.

Clara countered. "Aer Gaoth!" The wind met hers and merged, then surged back towards Lucinda. The force knocked her off balance. She staggered once, then tumbled off the platform entirely.

Gasps rippled through the crowd, followed by hesitant claps.

Clara's heart pounded. It had been too easy. Her movements had been quicker than expected, her magic more precise. The bracelet pressed warmly against her wrist, a silent reassurance.

She stepped forward, offering a hand. "Are you alright?"

Lucinda slapped her hand away, her face burning with embarrassment. "Again."

She didn't wait for the signal.

Her spells came sharp and fast, her frustration bleeding into every strike. Clara gritted her teeth, her wand moving in instinctive, fluid motions, blocking, countering, deflecting using a shadow shield, Sciath Scáthaí.

Then something inside her clicked. Lucinda was attacking wildly. She wasn't thinking. Clara could use that. She stepped forwards instead of back. "Enough!" With a decisive flick of her wand, Clara summoned a wave of water, fast and forceful, "Tonn Rabharta!"

Lucinda raised her wand too late. The wave crashed into her, sending her sprawling across the platform, soaking her from head to toe. The water poured over the edge, drenching her friends as well.

Screams of shock filled the air. The rest of the crowd erupted into laughter.

Lucinda pushed herself up, hair dripping, her once-perfect robes plastered to her skin. Her friends looked no better, their smug expressions replaced with sheer disbelief.

Clara's breath came fast. That had been too much,

hadn't it? She hadn't meant to hit all of them. Had the spell been stronger than she'd intended? Did she really have control?

Lucinda stared at her, and for the first time, there was no arrogance in her gaze, just cold, simmering anger.

Clara stepped forwards again, but Lucinda was already pushing past her. "You'll regret that," she muttered, storming off the platform. Her entourage followed, still wringing water from their sleeves.

The cheers picked up again, louder now.

Amelia vaulted over to Clara, clapping her on the back. "That was brilliant!"

"You were amazing," Ellie said, grinning.

Leo smirked, arms crossed. "Told you she's not as good as she thinks she is."

Clara smiled back, but something inside her still felt … off.

Her victory should have felt exhilarating, but instead, there was a strange, unsettled feeling coiling in her chest. Her magic had been strong, too strong: the way she had known when to counter, the ease with which she had cast that final spell.

She glanced down at the bracelet, its runes glimmering. Clara wondered whether she was controlling her magic … or whether the bracelet was controlling her.

*

Later that evening, Clara found herself in the Luminaris common room, replaying the moment over and over in her mind. The effortless way she had moved, the instinctive knowledge of how to counter Lucinda's every attack: it had felt incredible. Like she had unlocked something inside her that had been waiting all along.

Finn sat across from her, arms folded, watching her

closely. "You haven't stopped staring at that thing since we got back," he said, nodding towards the bracelet.

Clara's fingers unconsciously brushed over the cool metal. "It's just … helping," she said, shrugging. "It makes everything clearer, like I know exactly what I need to do."

Finn frowned. "Yeah. That's what worries me."

She exhaled, rolling her eyes. "Finn, it's fine. Leo gave it to me. He said it helps with focus and skill."

Finn leaned forward. "I'm not saying it's dangerous; I'm saying you've been acting differently since you put it on. You weren't just good out there, Clara, you were too good. Your spells were faster, sharper. And that wave you sent at Lucinda? It wasn't just a bit of water, it was enough to knock her flat and drench half the duelling grounds."

Clara tensed. "So what? She deserved it … The bracelet is helping me."

Finn studied her, something faltering in his expression. "That's exactly what you said about the astral map."

Clara's breath stopped. She remembered how she had become obsessed with solving the map, with unlocking its secrets. How she had refused to listen, convinced she was right. How Finn had stood in front of her, just like this, telling her she was changing, and she had ignored him.

She looked down at the bracelet again, at the soft glow of the runes. She felt the warmth it carried, the way it made her feel unstoppable. "I don't need it," she said suddenly, though the words felt hollow.

Finn's expression softened. "Then prove it."

Clara left without saying bye and went to her room.

Clara lay awake that night, staring at the ceiling. She had taken the bracelet off before bed, placing it on her bedside table, but without it, she felt … incomplete. Like a part of her had been stripped away. She squeezed her hands into fists. That wasn't normal.

Finn was right. She had felt this before, this creeping obsession, this unwillingness to let something go because it made her feel powerful.

She turned her head towards the bracelet. The runes still pulsed faintly, like it was waiting.

With a deep breath, she reached out, then hesitated. Instead of putting it back on, she curled her fingers around it, held it for a moment, then closed her eyes.

She had done this on her own before. She could do it again.

She let go of the bracelet and rolled onto her side, forcing herself to sleep.

*

The next morning, Clara found Leo outside, leaning casually against one of the stone pillars near the training grounds. He gave her a lazy grin when he saw her.

"Morning, Nightfall," he greeted. "Feeling good after yesterday?"

Clara pulled the bracelet from her pocket and held it out.

Leo's smirk faded slightly. "What's this?"

"I'm giving it back," Clara said, keeping her voice steady. "I don't need it."

Leo's gaze flickered from the bracelet to her face, his expression unreadable. "You sure about that? You saw how much stronger you were with it."

Finn stood near her, arms crossed, watching the

exchange.

Clara hesitated, just for a second. She had been stronger. Faster. She had won. But at what cost? "I'm sure," she said, pressing the bracelet into Leo's hand. "I have to do this my way."

Leo rolled the bracelet between his fingers, studying her. He didn't argue, but there was something calculating in his expression, something unreadable.

"Alright," he said easily, slipping the bracelet back into his pocket. "Your choice."

Finn exhaled, giving her a small approving nod.

As they walked back towards the academy, Clara felt lighter. The unease had gone. She had been sucked into using something she thought was helping her, but it was actually dangerous.

She did wonder why Leo would have such a thing but argued against herself, thinking Leo was an amazing wizard and perhaps it wouldn't have affected him in the same way.

Clara knew one thing: in future, she would be more careful about accepting magical items that could lead her astray.

*

Later that night, Clara couldn't sleep. Her thoughts refused to settle, tumbling one over the other until the sheets felt too tight and the room too small.

She slipped from bed and padded softly down into the Luminaris common room. The air was cool and still. The fountain's glow cast ripples across the stone floor, soft and silent. But something about it felt … wrong. Or maybe not wrong. Just different.

She stepped closer.

The water, usually calm, was stirring in tight,

deliberate circles. There was no breeze, no footsteps. Just the water's motion.

Clara hesitated, then crouched beside the basin. She didn't speak. She didn't dare.

And then the water lifted, only a little, a thin thread rising into the air like a strand of silk. It twisted once, twice, then coiled around itself like a loop... and vanished.

The surface fell still.

Clara blinked as she reached forward slowly, trailing her fingertips just above the glow, but nothing happened.

The moment had passed.

But something had shifted. She didn't know what it meant, only that the fountain had moved for her. Chosen to show her something. Or perhaps warn her.

She looked once over her shoulder, then stood. There was no one there. Clara sensed something was off, as though something bad was about to happen, but she had no idea what.

Even the fountain could sense it. Clara knew she had to be on her guard for whatever was coming.

Chapter 41: The Descent into Shadows

The Luminaris common room was dimly lit, the enchanted lamps giving off a calm glow and the dying embers in the fireplace crackling softly, filling the space with a faint, smoky warmth. Clara sat curled in an armchair, a book open in her lap, though she hadn't turned a page in several minutes.

Across from her, Leo was pacing, his fingers tracing absent patterns in the air, his thumb tapping rhythmically against his forefinger. Clara recognised his tell, the habit he had when he was thinking.

"I'm stuck," Leo announced suddenly, breaking the quiet in the room.

Finn looked up from where he was slouched on the sofa, one eyebrow raised. "Stuck?"

Leo stopped pacing and pulled out the astral map. "It's my final challenge," he said, unfolding it on the table. "It's leading me somewhere beneath the school. The paths keep shifting. This is by far the most challenging one yet. I feel like the school's testing me, making sure I live up to my potential."

There was something in his voice that made Clara pause. He said it lightly, almost playfully, but there was an intensity in his eyes that she couldn't quite interpret.

Clara leaned forward, studying the map. The lines pulsed and realigned in shifting patterns, forming corridors and stairwells that disappeared and reappeared in an ever-changing maze. "The school is testing you?" she repeated, glancing up at him.

Leo nodded. "It makes sense, doesn't it? Crowstone is full of enchantments, and Luminaris is all about intelligence, proving yourself. I think it wants to see if I can figure it out." He exhaled sharply. "But I can't do it alone."

Ellie, who had been listening quietly, frowned. "Beneath the school? What exactly does that mean? The lower archives? The crypts?"

"Probably somewhere between the two," Leo said. "I don't think it's dangerous. The map wouldn't lead me somewhere I wasn't meant to go."

Finn let out a dry chuckle. "Right, because ancient magical schools have such a great track record for not leading students into life-threatening situations."

Leo shot him an unimpressed look. "Come on, you lot. What's the worst that could happen?"

"Er, we could all die! That's probably the worst thing," Finn replied, only half-joking.

Clara hesitated, her fingers tightening on the arm of her chair. "We don't even know what's down there."

"That's the point," Leo said, stepping closer. "It's a magical academy; we're not going to find trolls or giants down there."

Finn sighed dramatically. "I mean … it's not like we've ever followed bad ideas before."

Ellie rolled her eyes. "We seem to have a knack for it, actually, Finn."

Amelia, who had been silent up until now, leaned forward. "I say we do it," she said, her voice thoughtful. "We'll be careful. And if anything feels wrong, we turn back."

Clara looked around at her friends. She didn't like this. Something about it pulled at her, an unease she couldn't quite shake. But at the same time, her curiosity was undeniable. Maybe this was just another challenge, just another test like Leo said. Maybe for once, they could live a little. She exhaled, nodding. "Alright. Let's do it."

Leo grinned, rolling up the map. "Knew you'd come round."

And despite her best instincts, Clara wasn't sure what was giving her pause.

*

The next day after class, Leo leaned forwards in his chair, his voice low and urgent, as Clara, Finn, Amelia, and Ellie huddled around him. His astral map lay open on the table, its glowing lines pulsating as if summoning them forward.

"Tonight's the night," Leo said, his thumb and finger tapping as he leaned closer to the group. "The map's been guiding me to this spot for weeks. This isn't just any quest; it's the final one, and I heard no one ever completes their maps. I wonder what Mornvale will award me for being the best wizard at the school."

Finn raised an eyebrow, scepticism clear in his tone. "I don't think you get a prize for completing the map. Its completion is its own reward."

*

They all made her way to the East Wing stairwell. The halls, usually busy with students and the chatter of the day, were now eerily quiet, the only sound the faint flicker of enchanted torches lining the walls.

"This is it," Leo whispered, unrolling the astral map. Its glowing lines pulsed, guiding them forward. "The entrance is just ahead."

Clara inhaled deeply, nerves twisting in her stomach. "One last chance to change our minds."

Finn grinned. "And miss out on sneaking beneath the school? Not a chance."

Ellie adjusted her glasses, looking less thrilled. "I'd like to point out that this is highly irresponsible."

Amelia exhaled, her fingers brushing her wand. "But we're doing it anyway."

Leo smirked. "Exactly."

With that, he led them to an alcove at the end of the corridor, where the astral map's markings aligned perfectly with the carved stone wall before them.

"There's got to be a mechanism," Amelia murmured, running her hands over the stone. "A switch, a rune … something."

Before she could finish, Leo pressed his palm against a faint engraving of a four-pointed star, and the stone shifted beneath his touch.

A deep, muted rumbling filled the air as the wall slid inward, revealing a narrow, spiralling staircase that led down into the unknown. A gust of cool, stale air rushed past them, carrying the scent of damp stone and something else, something older.

Finn peered down into the darkness. "Well, that's ominous."

Leo didn't hesitate. "Let's go." He descended first, the glow from an orb illuminating the worn steps as he cast Solas Ceo. Clara followed, her grip tightening around her own wand. The further they went, the colder it became, the warmth of the castle above left behind entirely.

The staircase eventually opened into a vast underground corridor, its high, arched ceiling disappearing into shadow. The walls were lined with ancient symbols, their meaning lost to time. Faint blue flames flickered in iron light fittings, giving just enough light to reveal multiple paths stretching ahead of them.

Leo studied the map, his brow furrowing. "It's still

changing. It's … leading us somewhere."

Ellie shivered. "And what if it leads us somewhere we don't want to be?"

Before Leo could respond, a sharp caw echoed through the corridor.

Clara stiffened. She turned her head just in time to see the black crow perched on a broken archway ahead, watching them with eerie stillness.

Another caw.

Then another.

Clara's stomach clenched. "It's warning us."

Leo scoffed. "Or it's just a bird."

Clara wasn't so sure. The crow had followed her before, appearing to warn her.

A soft rumbling echoed through the chamber. The ground beneath them trembled ever so slightly.

Ellie's eyes widened. "Did anyone else feel that?"

Leo's fingers tightened around the map. "We keep going."

But Clara wasn't so sure anymore. The deeper they went, the more she was certain this wasn't just a challenge. It wasn't just a test of skill.

As they continued their descent, the air became heavier with an oppressive silence that seemed to muffle their footsteps. Each footstep echoed ominously. Clara took a few deep breaths to control what she was feeling. It wasn't just her emotions, it was everyone else's too. Since Professor Moonsong had given her the bracelet, it had curbed her empath abilities, but down here, for whatever reason, the bracelet no longer worked. She could feel their emotions swirling around her: Finn's fear, despite his brave face, Ellie's apprehension, Amelia's excitement, and Leo's sharp, focused resolve. They buzzed in her mind like static, each one pulling at her own nerves.

"Are you okay?" Finn whispered, his hand brushing her shoulder.

"I'm fine," Clara lied, though her voice trembled. She clenched her fists, trying to shut out the noise and the pull of everyone else's feelings crowding her thoughts. But one emotion stood out: Leo's confidence. It was too smooth, too controlled, and Clara wondered if it was entirely real.

The shadows stretched along the corridors, their wavering movements giving the impression of something lurking just out of sight. The astral map glowed faintly in Leo's hand, its light pulsating with an almost living rhythm. They stopped in front of an ornate door, which Leo pointed to on the map.

"This is it," Leo whispered.

Finn raised an eyebrow. "You're sure? It doesn't look like it's been touched in centuries."

Leo didn't respond. He reached for the handle and tugged, but the door didn't budge. Muttering under his breath, he flicked his wand, casting a series of unlocking spells. Nothing happened. "It's … stubborn," he said, frustration creeping into his voice.

"Great," Ellie muttered, crossing her arms. "So much for your plan."

Clara frowned, stepping closer to the door. Her fingers brushed against the wood, searching for any clue. Her eyes caught a faint indentation near the edge of the frame, a small, almost invisible button. Without hesitation, she pressed it.

A low rumble echoed through the hallway as the door creaked open, revealing a pitch-black void beyond. The group exchanged uneasy glances.

"Well, that's not sinister at all," Finn quipped, though his usual bravado wavered.

Suddenly, a heavy thud echoed from the darkness, followed by the flicker of a distant light. The glow revealed a narrow wooden bridge suspended over a vast chasm of impenetrable darkness. The air felt heavier, charged with an unnatural energy.

"This ... doesn't feel right," Ellie said, her voice barely above a whisper.

Leo stepped forward, his expression resolute. "We've come this far. We can't turn back now. This could be monumental, for me, for Luminaris."

Clara hesitated. "Leo, are you sure about this? We don't even know what's down there."

"I have to finish this," he said firmly, his finger and thumb tapping together. "Trust me."

Reluctantly, the others followed as Leo took the first step onto the bridge. The moment their feet touched the planks, a golden sphere appeared, hovering in mid-air. It emitted a warm glow, illuminating the path ahead. Then, a deep, resonant voice filled the air, echoing from the void around them:

The way ahead is dark and steep,
For those who dare, no time to weep.
The bridge will hold your weight and fear,
But tread with care, your end is near.

Beyond the dark lies wisdom's door,
A test of hearts and minds in store.
To reach the truth, one rule to learn,
To light the path, you must discern.

The voice faded, and the sphere pulsed once before floating away, disappearing into the darkness ahead.

As the words echoed into silence, the bridge trembled beneath their feet, sending a shiver through the group. A faint mist began to rise from the chasm on either side, curling like ghostly fingers.

Clara stepped back instinctively, her grip tightening on her wand. "It's like this place is alive," she whispered.

Finn shivered. "Well, that's encouraging."

"What do you think it means?" Amelia asked, frowning at the cryptic lines.

Clara's mind raced as she replayed the riddle. "The part about *to light the path*, maybe it's a spell? Something to guide us forward."

Leo's jaw tightened. "Everyone think. We need to solve the riddle."

The group stood there, the oppressive darkness pressing in on all sides, as the bridge stretched endlessly into the void. The only way forwards was to decipher the riddle and face whatever challenge awaited them in the shadows beyond. The riddle's forbidding words hung heavily in the air, and Clara felt a chill run down her spine.

"This feels wrong," Ellie murmured, her voice barely above a whisper. "What if this isn't a test? What if it's a trap?"

Leo stepped forward, his jaw tight. "It's a challenge," he said firmly. "The kind Luminaris students should embrace. Do you think the school would send me into a trap?"

"Probably not," Finn shot back, his hand gripping his wand tightly. "But you're not the one with sweaty palms just thinking about falling into … whatever's down there."

"We're not going anywhere unless we figure this out," Clara said, her voice more confident than she felt. "The riddle said we need to *light the path*. Let's focus on that first."

Leo nodded, his expression unreadable, though Clara noticed his hand twitch, his thumb tapping his forefinger briefly before he stopped himself. "Good idea. Let's move."

Clara raised her wand, remembering the lessons from Charms and Enchantments. "Solais Beag," she said, casting a spell to create a giant, floating orb of bright light. The orb hovered beside her, illuminating the bridge in sections.

The group gasped as glowing runes appeared along the surface of the bridge, lighting up with each step forward. The symbols shimmered like liquid gold, forming a faint path through the shifting darkness.

"I knew it!" Leo said, a triumphant gleam in his eyes. "The riddle was guiding us to reveal this."

But the light revealed more than just runes. Small gaps lined the bridge, and the wisps of dark mist seemed to rise from the chasm below. The mist curled and reached towards the group, dissolving when the light touched it.

"Watch your step," Ellie warned. "That mist doesn't look friendly."

They began walking in single file, the bridge creaking faintly beneath their weight. Each step brought them closer to the light at the far end of the bridge, but the oppressive silence and the endless void on either side made every movement feel like a gamble.

Halfway across, the glowing sphere reappeared ahead of them, pulsing brightly. A deep, resonant voice echoed from it, startling the group.

To light the path is not enough,
When trials ahead are sharp and rough.
To face the truth, you must combine,
Your hearts and minds to form a line.

"What does that mean?" Ellie asked, her voice trembling.

Clara scanned the bridge, her eyes catching on the glowing runes beneath their feet. "The symbols," she said quickly. "They've changed."

The group looked down. The golden symbols now formed scattered patterns along the bridge, almost like puzzle pieces. Clara crouched, her mind racing. "We have to connect them," she realised. "It's a sequence."

"How?" Finn asked, looking around nervously. "Do we just … guess?"

"No," Clara said, tracing the symbols with her finger. "Each rune is part of a constellation. Look." She pointed to one symbol, a star, and another shaped like a crescent moon. "We need to find the order and step on them in sequence."

Finn hesitated. "What happens if we get it wrong?"

"Let's not find out," Leo muttered.

Working together, they began identifying the symbols, stepping carefully from one to the next. Finn almost slipped once, stepping on an incorrect rune, but Leo yanked him back just in time. When the last symbol lit up, the sphere pulsed again and the mist began to dissipate.

"Well done," the voice intoned. "But the way forward demands more than clever minds. Step boldly or turn back."

As they approached the end of the bridge, the light

revealed a large stone door etched with ancient carvings. It loomed before them, radiating a faint magical energy. But as they stepped closer, the door did not open. Instead, the sphere hovered above them, speaking again.

Strength is shown not by spells or might,
But those who face the endless night.
A single step, a boundless fall,
To reach your goal, you risk it all.

Finn looked around, alarmed. "I don't like the sound of that."

"What does it mean by *boundless fall*?" Ellie asked, gripping her wand tightly.

Clara's eyes narrowed. "It's a leap of faith," she said slowly. "It's testing us. We're supposed to step into the darkness."

"Are you insane?" Finn blurted. "That's not bravery, that's stupidity!"

Leo stepped forward, his expression unreadable. "She's right. The map led us here for a reason. If we don't trust it, we fail."

"Or we fall to our deaths," Finn muttered.

Clara hesitated, her instincts warring with her logic. She glanced at Leo, who stood at the edge, his thumb tapping his forefinger again. "If you're so sure, why don't you go first?" she asked.

Leo looked at her, his expression softening for a moment before hardening again. "Because this isn't about me. It's about all of us." Without waiting for another word, he stepped forwards and disappeared into the void.

Clara's heart leapt into her throat. "Leo!" she cried, rushing to the edge. But before she could do anything, the light shifted, revealing Leo standing on an invisible platform just a few feet below.

"It's safe!" he called, his voice echoing. "Come on!"

Reluctantly, one by one, the group stepped into the void, landing on the hidden platform. As they did, the stone door creaked open, revealing the next chamber beyond.

Clara's breath caught in her throat as she peered inside, but Leo was already moving forward, his determination unshaken. Whatever lay ahead, Clara knew they were about to face something far greater than they'd imagined.

*

The next chamber was vast and foreboding, its arched ceiling disappearing into shadows. The walls were covered with ancient carvings depicting witches and wizards who battled against colossal stone guardians. At the centre of the chamber stood a towering statue, a knight carved from gleaming black rock, its massive double-edged axe resting on the ground.

Clara stepped forwards cautiously, her wand drawn. "Is this … it?" she whispered, her voice echoing.

Finn, who was still catching his breath from the leap of faith, glanced at the statue warily. "I don't like how it's just standing there. Too convenient."

Leo, ever confident, was already moving towards the next door at the far end of the chamber. As he approached, a low rumble echoed through the room, causing the floor to tremble. The statue's head turned, its glowing red eyes locking onto the group.

"I knew it!" Finn yelled, stepping back.

With a deafening roar, the statue came to life, its joints grinding as it lifted its massive axe. The group scattered as the axe came crashing down, splitting the stone floor where they had been standing moments before.

"Get back!" Clara shouted, her voice cracking with panic as she cast Sciath Dìon, a shimmering barrier of magic forming just in time to deflect the knight's axe. The impact sent shards of stone flying, the force rattling through her bones.

Ellie pointed her wand, her voice steady despite the tension. "Fiathán Fásra!" Thick vines erupted from the ground, twisting around the statue's legs, their vines tightening with each passing second. For a moment, the knight's movements slowed, stone cracking beneath the strain.

But then, with an unnatural jerk, it pulled free, shattering the vines with a single mighty step.

"It's too strong!" Ellie cried.

Finn darted to the side, raising his wand. "Solas Chaoch!" Blinding flashes burst from his wand, flaring around the knight's carved helmet. The glowing red eyes flickered, the light momentarily disorienting the creature.

"Nice one!" Clara called, seizing the opportunity to aim for the knight's weapon. "Tairgne Scealp!" A jagged bolt of magic shot from her wand, striking the axe. The spell sent a fine web of cracks splintering along the surface, but it held firm.

The knight roared, raising its now-damaged weapon high. It swung in a downward arc, the sheer force making the ground tremble. Finn barely threw himself aside in time, landing hard against the stone floor. The knight lifted its axe again, preparing for a fatal strike.

Before anyone could react, Leo stepped forward, his wand raised, its glow not just bright but alive, pulsing unnaturally against the shadows.

"Ceangal Fóthalach!" he bellowed, slamming his wand towards the ground.

The earth beneath them convulsed as jagged spikes of stone erupted from the floor, driving into the knight's legs. The creature faltered, its stone splintering beneath the force.

Clara staggered, her gaze snapping to Leo. That spell … it wasn't like anything she'd ever seen before. Too powerful, too raw. It left the air buzzing, the magic lingering like a static charge against her skin.

"Where did you learn that?" she asked, her voice barely above a whisper.

Leo didn't answer. His eyes remained fixed on the knight as he lifted his wand again, murmuring another spell. "Gaoth Guthmhar!" A twisting vortex of wind howled through the chamber, slamming into the knight's chest, pushing it back just enough for Finn to scramble out of reach.

"Focus on the weak points!" Leo commanded, his voice sharp. "The joints! They're the least reinforced."

Clara, Ellie, and Finn exchanged uncertain glances but obeyed.

Ellie thrust her wand forward. "Saighead Reo!" Spear-like shards of ice shot towards the knight's knees and elbows, the cold biting deep into the cracks in its stone joints.

Amelia followed up, aiming her wand at the fractures forming in the stone. "Dílleachtán Biorach!" A piercing spell shot forward, chipping away at the structure.

Finn added his own spell. "Sciath Briste!" A shattering force slammed into the knight's arm, widening the cracks.

For a moment, it seemed like they were winning.

The knight let out another deep, unnatural roar and

ripped free from their combined assault. It swung wildly, its axe carving through the air like a blade through water. Ellie barely had time to roll aside, while Clara stumbled, her legs nearly giving out beneath her.

Finn, still catching his breath, tried to raise a barrier. "Sciath Dìon!"

But the knight was faster.

The stone fingers closed around him, lifting him into the air as he kicked and struggled. His wand clattered to the floor.

"Finn!" Clara screamed.

Leo's eyes flashed with something fierce. He didn't hesitate.

His wand lifted. He murmured an incantation, one too quiet for Clara to hear. A chain of glowing blue light lashed out from his wand, snapping around the knight's arm and yanking it backward with force. The knight staggered.

Finn tumbled free, gasping as he landed on the cold stone.

"Stay back!" Leo barked, stepping forward, his voice laced with an authority Clara had never heard before. He raised his wand high, eyes locked onto the creature. "Stróic Aethera!"

The air itself fractured.

A wave of raw, violent energy surged through the chamber, slamming into the knight with enough force to shake the ground beneath them.

The knight froze. Its glowing eyes flickered once.

Then, with a final, deafening crack, its body shattered, jagged pieces of stone raining down onto the chamber floor.

Silence fell.

Clara's breath came fast, her heart still racing. She turned to Leo, staring at him, at his too-calm expression. "What was that?" she asked.

Leo only lowered his wand, dusting off his robes. "A spell," he said lightly. "And it worked."

But as the last echoes of magic faded from the air, Clara couldn't shake the feeling that it had been more than that. It didn't seem like any spell a teenager would know.

The group stood in stunned silence, their breathing heavy as the dust settled. Finn got to his feet, brushing off debris. "Thanks for the save," he said, looking at Leo with wide eyes. "But what was that? Those spells, where did you learn them?"

Leo shrugged, avoiding eye contact. "Books, practice, you know. Let's just focus on getting out of here."

Clara stared at him, her chest tight with unease. His magic had been too advanced, too calculated for someone their age, and yet he acted as though it were nothing.

"I think we may be lost. I'm pretty sure that you weren't meant to come down here, Leo, even if you did save us all," Clara said, her voice shaky.

"Or maybe the professors knew I could handle it," Leo said, his tone firm.

As they all stood in silence, the door at the far end of the chamber creaked open, revealing another dark passage. The group exchanged wary glances before stepping forward, their wands lit, knowing that the true challenge still lay ahead.

The passageway led to a grand circular chamber bathed in an eerie white light. At the centre stood a raised platform, surrounded by symbols on the ground. Encased in a glass-like barrier atop the platform was a scroll, ancient and ornate, its edges lined with gold. The air around it pulsed as though the magic guarding it breathed softly, alive and watchful.

Clara, Finn, Ellie, Amelia, and Leo stopped in their tracks, their eyes fixed on the scroll. The atmosphere was heavy, electric with latent magic.

"This has to be it," Leo said, his voice filled with an uncharacteristic respect.

As they stepped closer, a glowing golden sphere materialised above the scroll, its light warm and inviting. A voice echoed through the chamber, deep and calm, speaking in riddles:

> *Not all who seek can retrieve this prize,*
> *For only the worthy claim what lies.*
> *Power you'll need, but alone you must stand,*
> *Lest this treasure slip through your hand.*
> *Speak the spell and find your might,*
> *But beware, this test isn't for the light.*

The sphere faded, leaving them in silence. Finn was the first to break it.

"That doesn't sound gloomy," he muttered, nervously glancing at the others.

"What does it mean by alone?" Ellie asked.

Leo stepped forward, his wand already in his hand. "It's clear one of us has to do this. The spell, the power, it's all on one person. I'll go first."

Leo climbed onto the platform, the air thickening as he approached. He glanced at the symbols on the floor, his expression was unreadable. Pointing his wand at the glass case, he muttered, "Fulminis Excoria!" under his breath, too low for the others to hear.

Lightning erupted from the tip of his wand, crackling as it struck the barrier. The entire chamber lit up, the sound deafening. For a moment, it seemed as though the case might break, but the lightning fizzled out harmlessly, leaving the case untouched.

Leo cursed under his breath. "It didn't work," he said, stepping back. His face was taut, his jaw clenched. "Clara, you should try. Maybe it needs a different kind of magic."

Clara hesitated. "Me? Why me?"

Leo's voice softened, his usual confidence replaced by something almost pleading. "You're a powerful witch, Clara. I've seen it. Just try."

Clara stepped forward, her heart pounding as she climbed onto the platform. The closer she got to the glass case, the more the air seemed to press against her, heavy with expectation. She raised her wand, her hands trembling slightly.

"What's the spell?" she asked, glancing back at Leo.

"Fulminis Excoria," he said smoothly. "Focus all your energy into it."

Taking a deep breath, Clara steadied herself. "Fulminis Excoria!" she shouted, and a bolt of lightning shot from her wand, slamming into the glass.

Nothing happened.

"Try again!" Leo urged, his eyes narrowing.

Clara gritted her teeth. Summoning every ounce of magic she could muster, she cast the spell again, this time pouring her emotions into it, her frustrations, her doubts, her fears. The lightning struck the barrier, and for a moment, the glass seemed to ripple.

As Clara cast the spell again, she felt an unexpected warmth radiating from her wand, pulsing in time with her heartbeat. A voice, soft, almost like a whisper, seemed to echo in her mind: *You are more than you know*. The sensation fuelled her determination, and she poured every ounce of magic into the spell, ignoring the growing strain on her body.

"It's working!" Leo said, his voice filled with excitement. "Keep going!"

Clara pushed harder, her energy waning as she poured everything she had into the spell. The glass began to crack, tiny fractures spidering out across its surface. Finally, with a roaring shatter, the barrier exploded, sending shards of light scattering into the air.

Clara stumbled, her legs buckling beneath her. Finn rushed forwards to steady her, but Leo was already at her side.

"You did it," he said, his voice low and urgent. "Now grab it!"

Still dazed, Clara reached for the scroll. Her fingers closed around the ancient parchment, and a surge of energy coursed through her. She unrolled it slightly, catching glimpses of spells she didn't recognise, their complexities beyond anything she had studied.

As Clara's fingers brushed the scroll, a surge of magic rippled through her, raw and unfiltered. Images flashed in her mind, of ancient battles, swirling storms, her ancestors standing tall against a shadowy figure. The scroll pulsed once, and she pulled her hand away, her heart pounding. "It's … alive," she whispered, looking at the others. "This isn't just a scroll. It's something far more dangerous."

"Let me see," Leo said, stepping closer.

As soon as Leo took the scroll, his entire demeanour shifted. He straightened, his smile turning cold and calculating. "Thank you, Clara," he said, his voice dripping with mock gratitude. "I literally couldn't have done it without you."

"What are you talking about?" Clara asked, her stomach knotting.

Leo held up the scroll, studying it with a delighted astonishment that sent chills down her spine. "It needed a Nightfall to retrieve it. Your stupid ancestors saw to that, thinking only they were worthy of this power. The arrogance."

Clara's mind raced. "I don't understand."

"Of course you don't," Leo snapped, his tone turning harsh. "You're just a silly little girl. The lost witch. How fitting."

His expression darkened, and suddenly his features began to shift. His face aged, his jawline sharpening, his eyes growing colder. His posture straightened as if he were shedding a disguise, and when he spoke again, his voice was deeper, more menacing.

"Let me introduce myself properly," he said, his lips curling into a cruel smile. "I am Therin Shadowthorn."

The words hit Clara like a physical blow. She stumbled backward, her wand trembling in her hand. Behind her, Finn, Ellie, and Amelia froze, their faces pale with shock.

The air in the chamber seemed to thicken, and Clara's mind raced. Therin Shadowthorn. The name she'd only heard in whispered warnings, the villain of her family's history, and now he stood before her, his presence suffocating. "You've been lying to us all this time," she spat, her voice trembling with anger and fear.

"Oh, Clara," Therin said, his tone mocking. "You've been so wonderfully naïve. It was almost too easy." He took a step closer, the scroll glowing faintly in his hand. "You're more like your mother than you realise. Always trusting, always hopeful, and always in the way."

"You've all been such delightful pawns," Therin continued, "You see, Clara, you're so full of promise, yet so blind to the truth. You're an empath, aren't you? Such a rare and beautiful gift. If only you'd truly listened to it, if only you'd trusted those little whispers of doubt in the back of your mind, you might have worked out who I was before it was too late."

He chuckled darkly, taking a slow step closer. "But no, you silenced that precious intuition of yours, didn't you? That charm your dear Professor Moonsong gave you, it dulled your senses, your instincts. It gave you peace, yes, but it also gave me the perfect cover. You couldn't feel the shadows lurking right in front of you."

Therin leaned closer, his voice dropping to a chilling whisper. "Your greatest strength, Clara, was your empathy. And thanks to that charm, it became your greatest weakness. How poetic."

He straightened, his smirk deepening. "Still, I must thank you. You made this far easier than I could have hoped. But don't worry, Clara, you'll feel it all soon enough. Every scream, every tear, every drop of despair. And when you do, you'll finally understand the true cost of your gift."

The room seemed to close in on her as his words sank in. Clara's thoughts spiralled, dragging her back to the first time she had met him, when he was just Leo. She remembered the handshake, the way a ripple of unease had passed through her, faint but insistent. The feeling that he was bracing himself, wearing a mask. She'd brushed it aside then, convinced it was nothing more than nerves.

Clara's breath came fast, her pulse roaring in her ears. The pieces clicked together, forming a picture she should have seen long before now.

She swallowed hard, her voice unsteady. "I should've known." The words felt heavy, thick with disbelief and anger. Her mind raced through every moment, every small crack she had ignored, the unease that had curled in her stomach whenever he was near, the way her instincts had whispered warnings she had brushed aside. How many times had she second-guessed herself? How many times had she dismissed the feeling that something was *off*?

Her gaze locked onto him, her fingers curling into fists. "It was you all along. You enchanted my map. You broke the wards, stirred chaos through the nights, made sure we were always looking in the wrong places. My dreams were warning me about you. And the crow too. And the rash …" Her voice wavered as the realisation cut deeper. "That was from the prolonged use of an appearance charm."

She took a shaky breath, anger rising to fill the void left by shock. "You were never supposed to be in Luminaris. You struggled to get in because you didn't belong." Her stomach twisted. The signs had been there, woven into every interaction, every moment that had left her unsettled. And she had ignored them. She had let him in.

Her voice dropped, quieter now, but sharp enough to cut through the air. "Why do you tap? You were always tapping. I bet it's something to do with disguising yourself."

Therin's eyes lit with cruel amusement. "Clever girl. If

only you'd listened to yourself."

He stepped forward, just enough to cast his shadow a little farther.

"The tapping helped me focus. A rhythm to steady the glamour. Appearances like mine begin to fray without attention. Magic likes to be known for what it is, and I was forcing it to lie. The tapping was a thread. Something to anchor it. So simple. So human. That's the thing about people, Clara. They trust habits more than truth."

Clara flinched. She hadn't even realised she'd moved until her shoulder brushed the edge of the wall. It was barely a step, but it felt like retreat.

Therin chuckled darkly. "Don't be too hard on yourself, my dear Clara. Empathy is a gift, yes, but it's also a burden, isn't it? You didn't want to see the truth because that would mean trusting yourself, even when it hurt. And you're not quite ready for that yet, are you? I almost called it all off upon realising you were an empath, but then that stupid professor gave you that silly bracelet. Without it, you would've figured it out months ago."

Clara's jaw clenched, but she said nothing.

Not yet.

Not until the shaking stopped.

She pressed her palm to the bracelet on her wrist. It was warm. Not just surface heat, but a living pulse beneath the silver thread, as though it recognised what was standing in front of her.

The trembling in her hands faded. Her thoughts stopped scattering.

The bracelet had been made to steady her magic. But maybe it did more than that. Maybe it reminded her who she was when everything else tried to shake it loose.

Clara's hands clenched into fists, her nails biting into her palms. His words stung because they were true. She hadn't trusted herself. She'd doubted her instincts, silenced the nagging feelings that had tried to protect her.

But no more.

She straightened, her jaw tightening as she met Therin's gaze. She ripped off the bracelet, dropping it on the floor. "You're right," she said, her voice steady despite the storm inside her. "I didn't trust myself before. But I do now. And you're going to regret underestimating me."

Therin's smirk faltered for a fraction of a second, but it was enough. Clara felt a spark of resolve ignite within her, stronger than the doubt that had plagued her before. She had ignored her instincts once, but she wouldn't make that mistake again.

Clara's wand trembled in her grip as she aimed it at Therin, anger and fear coursing through her veins. "You're not getting away with that scroll!" she yelled, firing a stunning spell directly at him.

Therin deflected it with a lazy flick of his wand, and the spell bounced off harmlessly into the shadows. "Is that really the best you can do?" he sneered, his tone dripping with disdain.

"Everyone together!" Clara shouted, glancing back at her friends. "If he gets away with the scroll, who knows what he'll do?"

Her words spurred the others into action. Finn, Ellie, and Amelia raised their wands, firing a barrage of spells at Therin. Blinding lights, binding chains, and freezing gusts streaked towards him in a dazzling display of magic, but Therin moved with inhuman speed and precision. Every spell was deflected effortlessly, his movements fluid and calculated.

"You're wasting your energy," Therin taunted. "You've only scratched the surface of what magic can truly do."

With a sudden sweep of his wand, he conjured a massive flaming dragon that roared to life, its molten scales glowing like embers. The beast loomed over them, its fiery breath igniting the air. Clara and her friends barely had time to react as the dragon unleashed a stream of flames.

"Shield up!" Clara cried.

"Scáth Díon" was uttered in unison, raising a defensive barrier just in time. The others followed suit, their shields shimmering as the fire licked at their edges. The heat was unbearable, and their barriers strained under the force of the attack.

"Keep holding it!" Amelia shouted, her voice tight with effort. "We can't let it break through!"

Just as it seemed their shields might collapse, a sudden ripple of energy filled the room. A loddlewight appeared, its form shimmering in the light. The creature strode forward, its feet clicking softly against the stone floor, exuding an aura of otherworldly calm.

The loddlewight raised its head, its glowing eyes locking onto the flaming dragon. With a single flick of its paw, a massive wave of water materialised out of nowhere, crashing into the dragon and extinguishing it instantly. Steam hissed and swirled in the air, leaving behind only the faint scent of smoke.

Therin's eyes narrowed as he turned his attention to the loddlewight. "You again," he growled. "Always meddling."

It was Wisp. Somehow, he had sensed Clara was in

danger. Wisp stepped between Therin and the group, raising a paw as Therin launched a volley of spells. Each spell dissipated harmlessly against an invisible barrier the loddlewight conjured with a simple gesture.

"Run, Clara!" Finn urged, his voice strained. "We can't beat him!"

"No!" Clara shouted, her resolve hardening. "If he leaves with the scroll, he'll only grow stronger. We have to stop him!"

Wisp extended its tiny paw, and a stream of white mist shot towards Therin. The mist crackled with energy, forcing Therin to conjure a defensive shield. The force of the mist pressed against him, his shield shimmering under the strain. For a moment, it looked as though Wisp might overpower him, but Therin's expression shifted to a dark smile.

"Impressive for such a little creature," he said, his voice laced with mock admiration. "But not enough."

As the mist subsided, Therin raised his wand and slashed it through the air, summoning a swirling portal of shadow. "This isn't over," he declared, his voice echoing through the chamber. "Not by a long shot."

"NOOOOO!" screamed Clara.

With a final smirk, Therin stepped into the portal, the scroll still clutched in his hand. The portal closed behind him, leaving the chamber silent except for the sound of their ragged breaths.

As the last echoes of Therin's laughter faded, Clara sank to the ground, her wand clattering beside her. The air still buzzed with residual magic, oppressive and heavy. Finn placed a hand on her shoulder, but she barely noticed.

"He's too powerful for us," Ellie said firmly, though

her voice shook.

Clara stared at the spot where Therin had disappeared, her jaw tightening. "He's not just after power," she murmured. "He will destroy the magical world. And we just handed him the key."

The loddlewight turned to Clara, its gaze steady and inscrutable. Then, with a flicker of light, it vanished, leaving Clara and her friends to process what had just happened.

As they stood in the aftermath, Clara's knees buckled, and she leaned against Finn for support. "What just happened?" she whispered, her voice shaking.

"He tricked us all," Finn said bitterly. "And now he's got the scroll."

Clara clenched her fists, anger and guilt boiling inside her. "This is my fault," she said. "I should have realised."

"No," Ellie interrupted firmly. "We'll figure this out. Together."

"We need to tell Professor Mornvale immediately," Amelia said calmly.

But Clara couldn't shake the feeling that Therin's escape was only the beginning of something far darker.

Chapter 42: The Truth Unveiled

The tension in Professor Mornvale's office was palpable. Clara, Finn, Ellie, and Amelia sat stiffly before the headmistress's imposing desk, their pale faces reflecting the gravity of the moment. Around them stood Professor Darnell, Professor Moonsong, and Professor Thorn. A fire crackled in the corner, its warmth doing little to dismiss the cold weight of realisation that hung over the room.

"It was Leo all along," Clara whispered, her voice heavy with guilt. "I should have seen it sooner. The maps, the disturbances, everything. And he wasn't actually Leo. He's … Therin Shadowthorn."

Her friends exchanged uneasy glances, their silence heavy with unspoken agreement.

Finn broke it first. "He tricked us all. I mean, there were signs, sure, but hindsight's great. How were we to know?"

Professor Darnell rubbed his temples, his usual calm giving way to visible frustration. "Therin Shadowthorn," he muttered, his voice filled with dread. "The Assembly has been trying to locate him, but no one would've thought he'd dare infiltrate Crowstone."

Professor Moonsong nodded solemnly. "It explains why the wards failed and how he was able to manipulate so much without detection. The Assembly must be informed immediately."

Professor Thorn stepped forward, his jaw tight. "I'll send word to the Assembly. They'll need to convene and decide how to proceed."

"Clara," Professor Mornvale said, her tone softer than usual, "can you recount everything for us? From when you first met Leo … Therin?"

Clara nodded, her voice steady despite the turmoil within her. She detailed everything, ending with their journey through the secret chambers, the riddles, the challenges, and finally, the moment Therin had revealed his true identity. Every word seemed to weigh heavier on the room.

When she had finished, Professor Mornvale stood, her eyes sharp with determination. "Thank you, Clara. You've shown great courage tonight, all of you. Now I must ask you to leave this matter to us. This is a threat far beyond what students should face."

As Finn, Ellie, and Amelia were escorted out, Clara lingered behind at Professor Mornvale's request. The headmistress motioned for her to take a seat, her expression unreadable.

"Clara," Professor Mornvale began, sitting opposite her, "you've been through a great deal in such a short time. I want you to know that none of this is your fault."

Clara stared at her hands, her fingers curling around the edges of her chair. "But he used me," she whispered. "If I hadn't opened the case, he wouldn't have the scroll."

Professor Mornvale leaned forward, her voice gentle but firm. "Therin Shadowthorn is a master manipulator. He preys on the kind-hearted and the unsuspecting. You were brave, Clara. And you acted with the information you had at the time. The fault lies entirely with him."

Clara's throat tightened as Mornvale's words hit home. She'd trusted Leo, no, Therin, not just because he was a friend but because he'd seemed so earnest, so human. How could someone so ruthless mask themselves so well? She clenched her fists, her nails biting into her palms as shame and anger churned within her.

"But what if he comes back?" Clara asked, her voice barely above a whisper.

Professor Mornvale's gaze softened. "He won't return. Not now, at least. He has what he wanted, and his focus will be on wielding it. This is a matter for the Assembly and your family to handle. Your role now is to continue learning, growing, and preparing for whatever may come."

Clara looked up, meeting the headmistress's eyes. "Preparing for what?"

"For the future, Clara," Professor Mornvale said, her voice resolute. "Therin Shadowthorn may have slipped through our grasp, but the Magical Assembly will deal with him. You need to concentrate on your education."

As Clara left the office, the sound of students in the corridors reminded her that life at Crowstone would go on. But she knew deep down that nothing would ever quite be the same.

Clara felt more lost now than ever.

*

The Luminaris common room was unusually quiet. A few students sat in clusters, talking in hushed tones, but the usual hum of chatter and laughter was absent. Clara sat in her favourite chair by the fireplace, staring blankly at the flames as they danced and crackled. Her thoughts were heavy, looping endlessly over the events with Therin. She had been used. Manipulated. And now the weight of it bore down on her like an unrelenting storm.

Finn plopped into the chair opposite her, his usual cheeky grin subdued. He studied her for a moment, as though deciding how best to break through the walls she'd put up.

"You don't have to keep everything bottled up, you

know," he said, his tone unusually soft.

Clara blinked, startled out of her thoughts. "I'm fine."

Finn gave her a knowing look. "You've been staring at that fire for the last hour like it's going to tell you all of life's answers. You're not fine, and that's okay."

Clara frowned, crossing her arms. "It's just ... a lot. I don't even know where to start."

"Then don't start alone," Finn said simply. "What happened was horrific. Therin fooled all of us, but especially you. And yeah, it's going to take time to get over it, but that's what we'll do, together."

She didn't reply, her eyes dropping to her lap.

"You should make sure you talk through it all with Professor Moonsong," Finn added. "She's great with this kind of thing."

Clara's head snapped up. "How do you know I see her?"

Finn leaned back in his chair, surprised. "I just assumed you would be."

Her confusion deepened. "Why would you assume that?"

Finn shrugged, his tone light but sincere. "Clara, come on. You found out you're a witch, got thrown into this whole magical world, discovered you have this massive, prestigious family, and, well, there's your mum. You're incredible for keeping it together as much as you have. Most people would've crumbled under all that."

Her throat tightened, and she couldn't bring herself to reply.

"I mean," Finn continued, his voice softening, "Professor Moonsong helped me when I was struggling. First year was rough. I'd just lost my dad. He was an adventurer, fearless and larger-than-life. But one day, his team never returned from an expedition. They told us it was an accident, but it felt like the whole world shifted overnight."

Clara stared at him, shocked. Finn rarely spoke about his family, and she'd never known this.

"Anyway," Finn said, glancing at the fire, "I didn't handle it well. Thought being the class clown would distract everyone from what was going on with me. Professor Moonsong saw right through it. Without her ..." He paused, smiling faintly. "Let's just say I would've been far more mischievous than I already am."

Clara let out a soft laugh despite herself. "I can't imagine that."

Finn grinned. "Exactly. She's brilliant, Clara. Talk to her. You don't have to go through this alone."

Clara nodded slowly, the weight in her chest lifting just a little. "Thanks, Finn."

"Anytime," he said, standing up and ruffling her hair. "And hey, don't forget, you've got us. Whatever happens, we'll deal with it together."

Ellie walked over, her expression softer than usual. "Finn's right, Clara. You've been carrying so much, and it's okay to lean on us. That's what friends are for."

Amelia nodded, her usual practicality giving way to warmth. "We're not just a team in class. We're a team in life. And we've got your back."

As Finn walked away, Clara sat in silence, her mind calmer than it had been in hours. Maybe he was right, and she didn't have to face this alone.

One thing was sure, though: her journey as a witch was only just beginning, and if she could help stop Therin Shadowthorn, she was going do it.

About The Author

I am a new author who, despite facing the challenges of dyslexia and ADHD, has found the determination and inspiration to finally complete a story.

My children are my greatest inspiration and the driving force behind my work. I am a single father of two incredible children who mean the world to me. Their curiosity, imagination, and enthusiasm have encouraged me to craft stories that not only entertain but also instil important values.

By day, I work for an autism and ADHD support service, a role I am deeply passionate about.

Ever since I was a young child, I've been captivated by books and stories, particularly those set in the realm of fantasy. Despite the challenges dyslexia posed, my love for reading and storytelling only grew stronger. I persisted, finding joy in the magic that stories could bring to life. Now, as an author, I have the incredible privilege of creating my own worlds, ones filled with enchantment, adventure, and a touch of wonder.

My greatest wish is for my stories to be out in the world, offering readers a glimpse of magic and wonder, just as books did for me when I was young.

www.blossomspringpublishing.com

Printed in Dunstable, United Kingdom

64159876R00255